Praise for *A Matter of Trust*

"Warren captures both the beauty and danger of the life of a competitive snowboarder, transporting readers through vividly detailed descriptions to a treacherous world of snow-covered mountains and daring displays."

Booklist

"Everything about this story sparkles: snappy dialogue, high-flying action, and mountain scenery that beckons the reader to take up snowboarding."

Publishers Weekly

"Warren excels at creating flawed characters the reader cares about, as well as building a suspenseful adventure. She draws vivid word pictures in her stories, with a faith element that is present but not preachy. Readers will be engaged from the first page until the last."

Christian Library Journal

Praise for *Rescue Me*

"Multilayered, complex characters with real-life flaws and faith struggles provide a large amount of depth and food for thought throughout the book."

RT Book Reviews

"A fast-moving, high-stakes romantic adventure set against the backdrop of Glacier National Park, which will leave longtime fans and new readers alike anticipating the next book in the series."

Publishers Weekly

"With action, adventure, romance, and a large, nuanced cast, *Rescue Me* is classic Susan May Warren. Pitting characters against nature—and themselves—in a rugged mountain setting, Warren pulls readers in on page one and never lets go."

Irene Hannon, bestselling author
and three-time RITA Award winner

"*Rescue Me* is the second book in the Montana Rescue series, and Susan May Warren has once again created characters that dig into your heart and latch on. Characters so real I missed them after the end."

Patricia Bradley, author of *Justice Betrayed*

"Action, drama, adventure, flawed individuals, and emotional and spiritual challenges are hallmarks of Warren's books."

Christian Library Journal

STORM FRONT

Also by Susan May Warren

MONTANA RESCUE

Wild Montana Skies

Rescue Me

A Matter of Trust

Troubled Waters

+5+

STORM FRONT

SUSAN MAY WARREN

a division of Baker Publishing Group
Grand Rapids, Michigan

Published by Revell
a division of Baker Publishing Group
PO Box 6287, Grand Rapids, MI 49516-6287
www.revellbooks.com

Printed in the United States of America

Library of Congress Cataloging-in-Publication Data
Names: Warren, Susan May, 1966– author.
Title: Storm front / Susan May Warren.
Description: Grand Rapids, MI : Baker Publishing Group, [2018] | Series: Big sky rescue ; 5
Identifiers: LCCN 2017053946| ISBN 9780800727475 (pbk. : alk. paper) | ISBN 9780800735135 (print on demand : alk. paper)
Subjects: LCSH: Rescue work—Montana—Fiction. | GSAFD: Christian fiction.
Classification: LCC PS3623.A865 S76 2018 | DDC 813/.6—dc23
LC record available at https://lccn.loc.gov/2017053946

This book is a work of fiction. Names, characters, places, and incidents are the product of the author's imagination or are used fictitiously.

Published in association with The Steve Laube Agency, 5025 N. Central Ave., #635, Phoenix, AZ 85012

18 19 20 21 22 23 24 7 6 5 4 3 2 1

Soli Deo Gloria

1

TY REMINGTON BLAMED the homemade orange marmalade cake for why he found himself huddled under an overhang off some faraway path in Glacier National Park, shivering, praying he might live through the night.

Rain bulleted the enclave, a shallow divot in the granite at the lip of a now-rising flowing mountain creek. Wind tore at his thin rain jacket—he'd given his fleece to the couple huddled behind him, eking warmth from the scant fire he'd built. The blaze gave off a meager trickle of smoke and heat, but hopefully enough to keep them from hypothermia.

If it hadn't been for the growl in his stomach when the fragrance of Karen Reycraft's signature cake tugged at him, arresting his escape from the Fourth of July celebration at Mercy Falls Community Church, he'd be sitting on his leather sofa, watching through his window for fireworks to light over the river bridge in town.

Or he might have said yes to Gage Watson's invitation to join him and his girlfriend Ella for a movie.

Instead, he'd grabbed a plate and fallen into the potluck line ahead of Renee Jordan, proprietor of the local Free Fall B & B. Who happened to be worried about a couple of guests who hadn't shown up for breakfast this morning. "They left for a hike in the park yesterday and never came back."

Yes, she'd knocked on their door, just in case.

Ty reined in the urge to remind Renee that she ran a vacation rental. That maybe Mr. and Mrs. Berkley wanted to be left alone.

She added, "I just know how scary it is to be out there alone in the park with a storm coming. I was hoping, since you're on that rescue team . . ."

There went his appetite, because unwittingly Renee had landed a lethal blow with the trifecta of arguments: in a storm, alone, and they might be in real trouble.

Most of all, maybe he could help.

Ty's gut had begun to roil with the weight of *what if*. He pulled out his map of the park and found the moderately strenuous and remote trail Renee had suggested to them. "The Dawson Pass hike has the best huckleberries," she said in defense.

Yes. It also passed through prime grizzly territory.

Not to mention the 2,935-foot climb.

Although, with its sweeping views of Dawson Pass, the seven-mile trek to No Name Lake could be the most dramatic day hike in the park.

"Maybe I'm overreacting," she said.

Ty had finally left his cake behind and headed over to PEAK HQ.

"You sure they're out there?" This question had come from Chet King, co-founder of the team.

After a thorough study of the map, as well as a call to local park rangers, Ty's best answer had been, "Not in the least. But my gut thinks yes."

His gut. He'd actually looked at Chet and delivered that statement. And yes, okay, he'd added a wince, a little *what-to-do* shrug, but still, he'd stood there like his gut might be the homing beacon they needed to activate a callout.

Chet had pursed his lips. Added a deep breath.

So maybe Ty shouldn't be listening to his gut. But it had told him the truth more than once.

Like when it warned him that journalist Brette Arnold would only cause trouble. He just hadn't quite realized it meant she'd break his heart.

Clearly, his gut needed to be more specific.

With Renee's words, however, it had grabbed ahold of him, an uncanny, bone-deep feeling that someone was hurt. *"Since you're on that rescue team . . ."*

A placeholder, really, the guy who helped carry things. Once upon a time, he'd been the chopper pilot, but he'd screwed that up, and royally, so now he simply showed up for callouts and hoped not to ride the bench.

Maybe he could really help, for once.

"It's a holiday, no need to call in the team. I'll just ride out there and take a look," Ty had said.

"It won't be nice for long, so put a hup into your step," Chet said. "Take a radio with you."

Ty parked his truck at the Two Medicine Lake campground and knocked off the first four miles by taking the ferry across the lake.

A mile in, as he turned toward the Dawson Pass trail, the faintest rumble of thunder sounded beyond Flinsch Peak to the north.

Spotting a couple hikers headed down the trail from No Name Lake, he asked them about Jan and Richard Berkley, but they hadn't seen them.

He stopped for a moment at No Name, sweat trickling down his spine. He'd shoved a first aid kit, an overnight survival kit, and an extra blanket into his pack. The weight of it burned into his shoulders.

Maybe his gut was just reacting to the wannabe inside him. The fact that he hated standing on the sidelines, that without

EMT training or rescue climber certification, he usually drove the truck or hauled up the stretchers, muscle that filled a gap in the team's roster.

He'd thought about upgrading his certifications, but getting EMT training felt like admitting that his days as a pilot were behind him. So what if he hadn't flown anyone but himself . . . and recently, Chet, for his biennial exam. He would get back in the cockpit when he was ready.

Eventually.

Really.

Shoot, maybe it was time to face the truth. Without something to add to the team, he could be replaced with any number of the volunteers that showed up every year for callout training.

Ty had no doubt that only Chet's affection for him kept him on the payroll.

Ty had glanced at the storm gathering to the northwest—a rolling black thunderhead still forming on the horizon, bisected by jagged mountain peaks and rimmed on all sides by the midafternoon sun.

A couple miles later, he emerged through the tree line to the spit of a light rain. No Name and Two Medicine lakes were tucked into the valley below. The wind bit at him as he turned and ascended the south slope of Flinsch Peak. Bighorn sheep scuttled off the shale-littered trail.

When Ty's foot slipped on the slick rock, he stopped, breathing hard.

This was silly. The Berkleys had probably risen early and headed to Bigfork for breakfast at the Echo Lake Café.

Ty was leaning over, cupping his hands over his knees, when he heard it. A scream, and it echoed through the canyon, up the slope, and niggled the weight in his gut.

Maybe a hawk, but he stood up, listened.

It sounded again, and this time he recognized it as the shrill rasp of a whistle.

He reached for his own whistle and let out a long blow.

Three short bursts answered, the universal signal for help, and the hum in his gut roared to life. After returning the signal, he dug out his binoculars and cast his gaze over the trail that jogged up toward the pass. Then he swept his vision down, across the forest of lodgepole pine and huckleberry that dropped into a steep tumble from the trail.

The whistle continued to blast.

He stepped off the trail to angle his search and nearly slipped on the now-icy layer of snow that crusted a fissure in the rock. As he looked down, his heart stopped, lodged in his ribs at the footprints that bled down the snowfield.

Not a steep pitch at first, but the crust had broken off, and as he dragged his glasses over the field, he spotted the debris of where falling bodies had churned up snow, probably fighting for purchase before plunging down a scree slope into the trees.

A fall of nearly a hundred feet, although not straight down. He couldn't make out anyone at the bottom but followed his hunch anyway and backtracked down the trail. Finding a crossing place, he hiked down the base of the scree, shot out three blasts from his whistle, along with a shout, and received an answering report and headed into the trees.

Jan and Richard Berkley had huddled up for the night under the wings of a towering lodgepole, both nursing significant ambulatory injuries.

When she spied Ty hiking down through the bramble of forest and shaggy fir, Jan had dropped the whistle from her mouth, pressed her hands over her face, and wept.

"Hey, hey. It's going to be okay." Ty swung his pack off his shoulder and assessed the couple. Jan, who looked to be in her midfifties, suffered from a seriously sprained, if not fractured, ankle.

"It's my fault. I was taking a picture, and I just . . . it was stupid." This from husband Richard, who spoke through pain-gritted teeth. Medium build and athletic, with graying hair at the temples, Richard reminded him a little of Mark Harmon. He held his arm possessively to his body, but it was his leg that had Ty worried. Broken for sure, the foot hanging at a grotesque angle.

"I tried to stop him, but he just went over—" Jan started.

"And I took her with me." Richard's voice tightened. "Stupid. We tried to hike out, but . . ."

Yes, okay, Ty would sign up for that EMT course at the local college because he'd really love to know whether it was shock, pain, or just the cold of the storm turning Richard pale. He worked off Richard's shoe and checked for a pedal pulse.

"He has blood flow," Jan said. "I've been checking. And I think we're past the danger of shock, although I know he's in a lot of pain."

Lean and tall, with her brown hair pulled back in a ponytail, Jan wore a rain jacket, Gore-Tex pants, and hiking boots. She wiped her eyes. "Sorry. I'm just tired. And cold."

Cold, yes. Because with the storm spitting down at them, hypothermia, even in July, could be their worst enemy. "Let's find protection, and then I'll go for help."

"What?" Jan grabbed his arm. "No—please. You can't leave us."

"I have a radio, but the mountains will block the signal. I need to hike out if I hope to contact my team."

"There's a storm coming. Please, don't leave."

Please, don't leave.

Like a punch to the sternum, the words, the earnestness of her voice unseated him. He drew in a shaky breath, the memory of his mother's voice just as swift and brutal. *"Please, Ty, don't leave."*

"Let's find shelter," he'd said, hating the promises he was already making.

He'd twisted his bad knee carrying Richard down the mountain, but he gritted his teeth until he found the overhang, and by the time he gathered kindling and made a fire, the night was falling in a hard slash around him, the sky igniting with slivers of lightning, the rain icy on his skin.

Not a hope of the PEAK team hearing from—or finding him—on a night like this.

Ty slid back inside the cave, made sure that the fleece stayed tucked up to Richard's neck, then coaxed the fire back to life with one of the few still-dry branches he'd found on a low-hanging nearby pine tree.

"How did you find us?" Jan pressed her fingers to her husband's neck, checked her watch.

"Renee Jordan corralled me at church. Said you were missing."

Jan settled by the fire, put her swollen ankle up on her backpack. "And that's it—you just decided to look for us?"

Huh. When she put it like that . . . But he could hardly add, *My gut told me you were out here.* "I dunno. I guess the thought of you out here, alone, hurt . . ." He lifted a shoulder. "Besides, I'm on a rescue team."

"Oh, so you're a natural hero." Jan smiled at him from across the flames, and for some reason, it spilled warmth through him.

Still, he shook his head. "No. Trust me, I'm not the hero on the team. I just . . . I know what it feels like to be alone and hurt and . . ." He couldn't say much more, the memory lurking.

So he shut his mouth, his throat burning. He didn't look at Jan.

The silence that fell between them turned lethal to his resolve to keep the story to himself. He blew out a breath. "I was in a car accident when I was ten, in the middle of a blizzard, and I . . . I wanted to go for help, but . . . anyway, I watched my mom die right in front of me. So . . ."

He clenched his teeth against the rise of a forbidden and ancient grief. Strange timing, but he decided to blame Jan and her uncanny resemblance to Elyse Remington.

"I'm sorry," Jan said.

He looked out at the storm. "I should have hiked out—"

"And get lost in the storm? You were ten."

He blinked at her for a second, then caught up. He was actually talking about the storm raging here, on the mountain. Nevertheless, Jan's words still sunk in. But it didn't matter how often he heard that truth. It still felt like he should have done *something* to save her.

He stopped shivering and held his hand to the warmth of the flames. "I'll leave at first light. We'll get you out."

"Richard's injuries aren't life-threatening." Jan grabbed his hand, squeezed. "I'm a doctor, trust me. We'll be okay. It's enough to know we're not alone."

Not alone.

And for some reason—maybe the fatigue, the storm, maybe even the ache in his knee—right then, Brette Arnold tiptoed into his brain.

Even after eighteen months, or nearly, still she had the power to run an ache through his bones, right to his heart. With it rose a desire to hit something, to let out a shout.

In his less sane moments, it even caused him to resume his search for her.

Because, deep in his gut, he knew that she was in trouble. And regardless of the fact that she didn't have the courage to stick around, didn't have the courage to reach out, didn't have the courage to admit she needed him . . . she did.

And if Ty knew one thing, his gut was rarely, if ever, wrong.

+

How Brette had hitched herself to three daredevil storm chasers who followed clouds for a living, she didn't quite know. One day she'd snapped a picture of a funnel churning up a Colorado prairie, the next she'd hitched a ride with the team from Vortex .com as their blogger-slash-photographer.

No, wait, in between there she'd posted the legendary picture on Facebook and sold it to *Nat Geo* for enough money to pay her cell phone bill and the monthly rent on her long-term POD container in Boston. A container she might never see again, the way Geena drove.

"We're going to hydroplane! For cryin' out loud, slow down!" A rare shout from their fearless captain, Jonas Marshall, as he slammed his hand on the front dash. Dressed in a black T-shirt, the orange Vortex.com emblem on the breast, and a red cap with his short brown hair curling out the back, he looked every inch the storm warrior who regularly reported on-the-scene updates to the Weather Channel.

His other hand steadied his computer on the front seat mount. On the screen, Doppler radar spit out, every two seconds, what looked like a child's coloring of an amoeba twisting and curling across a gridded map of Kansas.

Hopefully Jonas had an idea where to send them to intercept the forecasted tornado, because to her eye, they'd driven right into a line of squalls. And everyone knew that a squall line was a series of thunderstorms all in a row, and while impressive, it fought for the warm air necessary to fuel tornadic conditions.

In short, on the other side of this torrential rain might be nothing but blue sky. No swell of winds, no mesocyclones, no storm hook inside which the tornadic winds would organize, form a funnel, and drop to earth.

A wild-goose chase that netted them nothing but another day of endless driving and fatigue, and frankly, she couldn't remember the last time she'd eaten.

"Listen, you wanna get out of this mess or are we actually going to catch a tornado on this little cross-country trip?" Geena snapped as she gripped the wheel of their extended Suburban. Petite and tough, with a tribal tattoo up her arm and her jet-black hair twisted into an Oklahoma Sooners ball cap, Geena drove with the tenacity of a NASCAR champion. "Is this the gust front or not, Mr. Weather?"

Beside Brette in the backseat, Nixon smirked at Geena's name for Jonas, even as he angled the camera out the window to the northwest where the eerie green horizon turned black. He'd freshly shaved his head and face, and with his mocha skin and eyes, he looked fierce and very capable of standing up to and capturing on video whatever nature dished out.

Jonas blew out a breath and examined the amoeba on the screen. Encased in an outer edge of green that marked the precipitation, the layers comprised a fiery mix of yellows, oranges, and reds all the way to the supercell core.

"We're on the southern edge of the storm. Just keep going west. We'll break free of this and hopefully be right in the path of the mesocyclone. But please stay on the road."

"That's why you hired her, Big J, to bring you up close and personal," Nixon said.

"I hired her because you wanted your girlfriend on this summer's excursion," Jonas snapped. "Look out—there's *trees*! Sheesh, Geena!"

Brette tightened her grip on her seat belt as Geena maneuvered around a downed branch scooting across the road.

Geena glanced at him, smacked her gum. "Take a breath there, boss. I'm only going thirty."

Brette held up her camera, searching through her viewfinder for the right shot. Strange thing, storms. Unpredictable and chaotic, they possessed an ethereal beauty that held her captive, enthralled. Like watching an accident in slow motion, the dread curling up like a fist inside, tighter, arresting every breath until the release came in a gust of horror. Or perhaps awe.

She could never truly get a handle on her emotions, just the painful fact that she couldn't look away.

The sky to the north had turned an eerie sea green, bubbling with black frothy clouds. Like a turgid wave along the front edge, a dark gray wall of rain and thunder rolled, churning and hungry as it devoured the blue sky to the south. Under it all, the deep green prairie grasses of rural Kansas undulated, whipped to a frenzy by the 60 mph winds.

Lightning flashed, a skeletal hand reaching from the heavens, and illuminated a farmhouse in the distance, its white silo a grim sentry to the oncoming assault. She waited and focused on the mushroom clouds forming to the far southwest, found her payoff in another brilliant surge of light caught in the cumulonimbus cloud.

"I think it's starting to organize, Jonas," Brette said. As he'd explained it once to her, back when she first joined, a tornado was a combination of warm, wet air rising into the atmosphere, colliding with the cool air to create a cycle of falling and rising air until it collected into a uniform, circular current. The current then spun faster and faster, not unlike the Tilt-A-Whirl she'd ridden as a child. When the air began to rotate on a horizontal axis, it turned into something called a mesocyclone.

AKA, tornado.

The rain turned to bullets pinging off the roof.

"Hail!"

"Stop the car!" Nixon shouted and reached for a motorcycle helmet behind the seat.

"Not now, Nix!" Jonas said. "We're nearly through, and we need to get in front of this wall to lay down the probe."

When the season ended, Brette would miss the ongoing squabble between Nixon's on-the-side hail research and Jonas's commitment to field testing equipment for the SPC—Storm Prediction Center out of Norman, Oklahoma.

The wipers could barely keep up as the deluge turned deafening. Brette found herself ducking even as Geena fought to keep the car on the road.

Then, suddenly, just like that, they broke free. The hail dissipated, the rain turned into a spring shower, the gusts died.

They drove into what remained of the sunlight.

"Crazy," Jonas said and turned his hat on backwards. "But I love it when I'm right."

"Oh please," Nixon said.

"I told you those were just gustnados. And, for the record, when I say get through the gusts, I never mean punch the core," Jonas said.

"You're no fun," Geena said.

"But I am alive, and I'd like to stay that way. Still, good driving." He lifted his fist, and she met it with a bump. "And good eye, Brette. The hook on that Cb to the south is starting to organize."

Cb—shorthand for cumulonimbus, aka thundercloud—just another of Jonas's crazy words she'd had to learn. Words like *gunge*, the haze that blocked their vision, or *bear's cage*, which described the weather they'd just escaped.

And the easiest, Cu, or the general term for cumulus. All words she used now with alarming regularity.

They'd passed the farmhouse, and Brette took a shot of it—the silo, the tiny white house, a truck in the dirt driveway. Sheets whipped to a frenzy on the line, like ghosts in the wind. She hoped the inhabitants had found shelter.

"I still say there's tornadic activity in this mess to our north."

Nixon trained his video camera on the green haze on the opposite side of the road. Indeed, even from here, Brette recognized debris—roof shingles, hay, dirt caught in the wind.

"Nixon's right—this is a multicell storm. We could have a slew of mesocyclones!" Jonas shot a grin at the backseat.

And right then, Brette had her answer as to how she'd ended up here, as a member of this crazy group of storm enthusiasts. Jonas Marshall had called her on Skype and his charismatic personality had practically reached through the computer and grabbed her by the heart. Made her feel again, at least a rush of adrenaline. And yes, it might be dangerous, but in this moment, her heart thundered, the excitement of seeing something bigger than herself enough to make her forget the last year. She desperately needed to be a part of something that she didn't have to think about, something that would catch her up and drag her along for the ride, something she could lose herself inside, if ever so briefly.

And if she could capture it with her camera, tame it for a brilliant nanosecond, perhaps she could also find the beauty in the storm.

"C'mon, drop. You know you want to," Jonas said, coaxing the sky.

She trained her lens on the cloud. Almost on cue, nearly a half mile away, a thin funnel dropped from the clouds, white and skinny, dancing across the open field.

"Oh, she's so pretty," Nixon said, turning his camera on the sidewinder.

"Let's get up in front of her, drop the probe, and then we'll back up for a ringside view."

Geena punched it up the road as the dancing funnel thickened, veed-out in a nice Hollywood twister, one even Dorothy would have appreciated.

Three months ago, when Brette had joined the team, the danger would've stopped her heartbeat, caused her to scream, hold her breath, beg them to find shelter. But she'd learned that they could tiptoe right up to the beast, take their shots, and edge away without being swept up into the destruction.

In theory. Yes, the storm-chasing community told tales of renegades, chasers who edged too close to disaster and found themselves injured, their vehicles torn apart, and even a few giving their lives for the chase.

But Jonas was smart. He'd been chasing tornadoes since high school, knew how to read them, and most of all, pledged to keep them all alive.

"Stop here," he said. "She's moving northeast. This should put us right in the path." Jonas and Nixon jumped out to dump the probe, a flat box with recording equipment under a domed glass. They carried it ahead of the car and settled it into the grass on the side of the road.

Brette lowered her window and snapped the funnel. From this angle, the sun lit up half of it a bold, cottony white. At the base, the fury tore up the earth, and a cloud of dark Kansas prairie dust webbed the cone. A massive magenta thunderhead mushroomed above and behind it like smoke. And, to add mystery to the awe, clear blue sky backdropped it all to the west.

She needed a better angle, so she got out of the vehicle. She took a few bursts, Nixon shouting behind her. "Let's go!"

But, as she turned to get in, the eerie green sky to the northwest caught her up.

A second vortex had formed, this one a thick black wedge emerging out of the web of rain and hail heading southeast.

"Nixon! You're right!" She ran up the road for a better view.

Two tornadoes in one sky, telling two different stories. One white, one black—she loved the dichotomy of it. And the rarity. *Nat Geo* would lose their minds for this exclusive shot.

Brette stood in the road, the wind a locomotive in her ears, and sorted out the shot. She could get them both in her viewfinder. She just needed to wait until they converged.

"Brette!" Jonas stood on the runner of the car, his door open. "What are you doing?"

"There's two of them! And by the looks of it, they might even collide!"

"Come back to the truck!"

"Just wait!"

"We'll pull back, you can get the shot—"

The roar throttled his words, and she stilled as the dark funnel exploded through a barn a half mile away. The roof shattered, boards ripped into shreds like toothpicks. Debris darkened the sky.

She set the camera on burst again and took her shots.

"Brette!"

A moment later, she turned to the white tornado, now graying as it fell under the hood of the cloud, into the grasp of the larger supercell. The cone at the earth had turned black, and it slowed as it plowed through a copse of trees, ripping them from the earth.

She caught it all, ignoring the roar. Maybe she could sell to the Weather Channel too—shots this close, this clear—

"Brette!"

Her name in the wind gave one second of warning before arms slammed around her. In a second she went airborne. She screamed, clutching the camera to her body even as she tumbled into the soggy ditch, barely cushioned by the hard planes of Jonas's body.

For a moment, she lay dazed, staring at the frothing sky.

"What are you doing?" She pushed off him, but Jonas had already found his feet and was pulling her up by her elbows.

"*That* is what I'm doing!" He pointed to a sheet of metal that lay where she'd stood. "Get in the car. Now!"

Right. She ducked her head against the debris now raining down and fled to the car.

Geena slammed the gearshift into reverse.

"Go, go!" Jonas shouted even as Geena looked over her shoulder.

"Hold on!"

In a second, she popped the truck into neutral, spun the wheel hard, then shifted into drive and gunned it, in a classic car-chase U-ey.

"Seriously?" Jonas shot Geena a look.

"Told you she could drive!" Nixon shouted.

But Jonas was looking past him, toward the back window. "Faster! It's hooking toward us."

Brette couldn't help but turn. Behind them, the black locomotive churned toward the road.

"It's sucking us in. We can't outrun it!" Geena said.

Why had she ever thought this was a good idea?

"What about the overpass?" Nixon pointed to the highway overpass a half mile away. "We could climb up under it."

"And be impaled or decapitated," Jonas said. "That's the worst place we could go—it turns into a wind tunnel. We'd be cut to pieces."

"How about the farm?" Brette pointed to the farm they'd passed earlier, now coming into view. "I'll bet they have a storm shelter—"

"Maybe, but we don't have time. Get off the road, Geena!"

Geena hit the brakes.

"Drive into the ditch!"

She plowed into the drainage ditch, and the Suburban bumped hard along the rutted ground.

"Everybody out!"

What? The tornado had hit the road and now carved a path toward them, a bulldozer that churned up the gravel, along with flying debris. "We need to stay in the car!"

Jonas had already gotten out. Nixon too. Now Jonas yanked open her door. "Get out!" The look on his face turned her cold.

"Run down the ditch!"

She stared at him, and he grabbed her arm and pulled her behind him.

"This is crazy!" The roar drowned out her words. *My camera!* She'd dropped it in the truck. She yanked out of his grip, turned. The twister had jumped the road, out toward the field, headed toward the farm.

An arm clamped around her waist, and Jonas threw her down. His body landed on top of hers, his voice in her ear. "Stay down!"

She couldn't get up if she wanted to, not with him pinning her in the mud, not with his arms tenting over their heads, his legs clamped over hers.

The wind howled over them.

Oh . . . oh . . . She pushed her head down into the cocoon of her arms and just tried to breathe. To concentrate on her heartbeat inside of the ravenous wind, the squeal of metal, the way Geena—or maybe Nixon—screamed near them.

The wind swept over them, and as he held her, Jonas began to shake.

She closed her eyes and tried not to cry.

Then, just like when they'd broken free of the hailstorm, the wind died. Just moved away from them, taking the earth-shaking thunder, the roar, the flying debris, and the scent of upturned soil with it.

The chaos fell to a blood-curdling quiet. Her heart banged, loud and clear, in its effort to leave her body.

Jonas didn't move, and for a second she feared he'd been wounded. "Jonas?"

"Just give me a second here."

He breathed out hard, and she didn't blame him. She waited in silence until he eased off her, climbing onto his hands and knees, backing away from her.

She pressed herself off the ground and sat up.

The twister had missed them and—thank God—veered away from the farmhouse, leaving a swath of knotted, uprooted field nearly fifty feet wide through the cornfield.

She sat back and only then realized that she, too, was trembling.

"What were you thinking?"

She stared at Jonas, his dark expression.

"You nearly got killed—twice," he said.

"You nearly got *us* killed!" Nixon stood not far away, his arms wrapped around Geena. "For a picture?"

Brette drew in a shaky breath. Swallowed. Bile filled her mouth. "Sorry?"

Nixon closed his eyes, looked away from her. Geena raised an eyebrow, her mouth tight.

Brette got up and walked away from the crew, watching as the white twin curled up into the clouds, swallowed by the darker twister.

Jonas finally walked over. Settled his hands on her shoulders. "Maybe we need a little break."

She turned. "What, are you firing me?"

He paused, maybe too long, but finally shook his head. "No, but . . . you did put us all in jeopardy."

"It's my job to get the great shots—"

He held up his hand. "I'm the first to say that I can get overzealous, but you were just . . . you nearly got decapitated."

Oh. "Sorry. And, uh, thank you."

He nodded, his expression softening. And for a second, she thought . . .

Oh no.

She backed away. "I need to check my camera."

"I'm serious about taking a break, Brette." Jonas followed her as she opened the door to the SUV. "We need to stop in Norman, and then maybe we call it quits. The season is nearly over, and we—"

"Need more footage. More epic photos. C'mon, Jonas, don't do this to me." She didn't know where all the pleading came from, but . . . "I'm not ready for the summer to be over."

And there came that look again, something so tender in his blue eyes that she looked away. She studied her camera, scrolled through the shots.

"Come home with me to Minnesota."

She froze.

"Nixon is from my hometown, and maybe we just take a rest. You can meet my family, and . . ."

She swallowed and looked up at him, hoping her face didn't betray the sheer panic at the idea of stepping into his personal life.

The last time she'd gotten involved with a guy, walked into his world, and let him into hers . . . well, she still went to sleep at night thinking of the way Ty Remington broke open the guarded places, made her long for something she'd never had.

In a way, she could never forgive him for that. It made the wounds that much deeper.

"Geez, Brette, take a breath," Jonas said. "I'm just suggesting that we take a couple days off. Regroup. There will be more tornadoes, I promise."

"Right." She sighed. "Okay."

He shook his head. "And I thought I was the zealous one."

She gave a high-pitched laugh. Because no, she wasn't zealous. He simply had no idea that she had nothing left but the storm.

2

Ten thousand cheering souls in front of him, and none of them the person country music star Benjamin King really wanted to see. Or rather, persons, because he'd gladly endure being center stage at the Duck Lake Country Music Festival, under a scorcher of a summer evening, sweat dripping down his spine, if his beautiful sixteen-year-old daughter Audrey, and the woman he longed to marry, Kacey Fairing, were standing in the wings. Or even in the front row, grinning up at him, singing along to his latest hit.

Turn down the lights
Turn up the songs
Come dance with me, baby
Right where you belong

The crowd raised frothy beers, cold lemonades, and even a few hot dogs, singing along. The concert grounds occupied nearly twenty acres of field and parking lot, now jammed with tents, RVs, pop-ups, and people bedded down in pickup beds for three days of nonstop concerts. The Woodstock of country music in the Midwest, and Benjamin King headlined day one of the event.

One more gig in his never-ending tour schedule. He'd spent

a total of a month, tops, at his ranch house in Mercy Falls since he'd inked the deal on the property nine months ago.

Well, Ian Shaw's ranch house. Ben still felt like an interloper in the expansive log-sided home. More, he might have gotten in over his head with that purchase. The debt forced him back on the road, to depend on ticket sales to keep his fledgling studio, Mountain Song Records, afloat. But that seemed the cost of going independent—endless touring, interviews, social media events, and gigs like this one where he poured everything out for his fans.

His muscles ached, and with everything inside him, he'd wanted to lock himself in his RV and hide today.

I see you standing there, alone in the light
C'mere, baby, I'm the one that will treat you right

Ben leaned into the mic, needing the music to roust him, to thread through his lonely, frustrated soul, to give him a reason to keep smiling, to add a little flirt and swagger to his performance.

The music had always filled most of the hollow places and for a long time masked his hunger for family and the woman he'd walked away from.

In a way, the music had saved him, at least long enough for him to find his way back home. Back to Kacey.

I know you're scared, that you think I'll hurt you
But baby, I'm nothing without your love . . .

Wow, he missed her. And he tried not to let her absence stir up worry. Or irritation.

Kacey—and Audrey—should have been here by now.

He spotted a woman with long blonde hair and pale blue eyes, wearing a shirt with his image decaled on the front, swaying to his music. She smiled, waved.

He met her smile and directed the next lyrics her way. Shae Johnson, aka Esme Shaw, the missing niece of billionaire Ian Shaw. She'd shown up backstage, and he'd spent a few minutes meeting the girl he'd spent a summer searching for nearly five years ago. He'd thought she was dead, but she'd surfaced almost a year ago in Mercy Falls, long enough to help search for her uncle, who had been thrown overboard in the Caribbean.

Of course, Ben had been on the road during all that excitement.

He'd been on the road for the better part of a year and a half. Too much. He'd even had to postpone his wedding, twice.

He wasn't doing it a third time.

Which was why he'd arranged this little surprise trip for Kacey. The reason he'd kept secrets, conspired with Audrey, and even involved his father in the plan. And why he'd asked his father to go back to the B & B he'd reserved on a nearby lake to make sure that, while the owners had kept a lid on his plans, they'd also followed his instructions.

No more waiting. As soon as this gig ended, he was taking five sorely deserved days off to elope, starting with a preacher at the Duck Lake B & B and ending with someplace quiet and unfrenzied with the woman he loved.

His gaze fanned out over the crowd.

So let's get out of here, let me take you home
I promise you, you'll never again be alone . . .

He launched into the chorus again and glanced at the sky behind them. No rain, but an ominous dark wall of angry cumulus hovered in the distance, and the wind had begun to kick up, rippling the orange-striped awnings of the autograph areas and the merch tents. The carnival lure of cotton candy, fried cheese curds, and popcorn melded with the acrid smell of the hot rubber hoses, beer, and the heat of too many bodies jammed together on a muggy summer evening.

He ended the song and raised his hands to the audience. "Thanks for being here today. I know it's hot, but it's a beautiful evening in Minnesota!"

Cheers cascaded through the crowd.

"A few of you might recognize this one. It's one of my oldies, but sometimes you just have to go back to your roots, right?"

He glanced at his bandleader and nodded his head as the drummer tapped out three beats before they launched into the intro. Ben leaned into the mic.

Early riser, gonna catch the sun
Gotta start 'er early, gonna get her done
Rounding up the herd, putting on the brand
Then I'll kick off my spurs and head out with the band

This song belonged most of all to Kacey, and he imagined her in the crowd, her long red hair piled up, those beautiful green eyes shining. And beside her, beautiful Audrey, long auburn hair in a thick braid, her eyes so big they could hold him captive.

I've got a Mountain Song
I'm cowboy strong
Working all day
It's where I belong
But after the work's done
I'm gonna sing my song

And there it was, the easy beat he needed, the stir of the old zing.

Waiting on a break, hoping on a star
Believin' that the dreamin's gonna get me far
I've got a Mountain Song

He ripped out the mic from the stand, about to walk into the audience, when the lightning crackled through the twilight. As if God might be reaching down with a fiery splinter of divine power, the bolt touched the earth, just outside the festival grounds, near the municipal airport. An explosion, and the entire world shook.

The sound system died as thunder cracked, so close the hairs of Ben's arms rose.

The crowd shifted from cheers to screaming.

The first drops of rain pinged on the shell overhead. He turned to the band. "Can we get sound back?" He glanced toward the wings, saw his sound guy shaking his head.

Nice. Perfect.

The rain pelleted the front of the stage, and he turned to the crowd, not sure what to do.

Like a blanket of doom, the wall of clouds closed in, turned the sky an eerie green, and eclipsed the sun.

"Take cover! Everyone!" Ben moved to the front of the stage. He blamed instinct, perhaps, but he'd been in on the search the summer Shae went missing, and reaching for her seemed the only thing that made sense.

Shae opened her mouth in surprise, then grabbed his hand.

Meanwhile, the crowd ran for cover.

"It's just a rainstorm," Shae said as she climbed on stage.

"Maybe, but we had a couple tornadoes when I lived in Tennessee, and I don't like that sky. We need to get inside, or at least under something solid."

His brain went blank.

Cover. Where, in the middle of all these RVs, tents, and pickups?

He turned to his band, Joey and Duke, Buckley and Moose. "Get to the storage lockers!" Behind the stage, the festival grounds hosted permanent buildings that stored the tents, mechanicals, and stage equipment. "Run!"

He grabbed Shae's hand and his custom Fender and nearly jumped off the stage. The crowd massed near the back exits, but terrified fans had pushed over the flimsy metal blockades and headed away from the festival grounds, running for who knew where.

"Stay with me!" He hoped his bandmates heard him as he pushed through the crowd, his hand clamped on Shae's. By the time he cleared the row of musician RVs, a warning siren whined through the air.

Funnel on the ground. He should have listened to his instincts to cancel.

"C'mon!" He crossed the now-muddy lot, his boots slipping against the deluge, and ducked as the rain pinged his neck.

"Hail!" Shae screamed, curling her arm over her head.

"Keep running!" They cut around a row of tractor-trailers lined up like dominoes, through a parking lot now jammed with escapees in their cars, and toward the warehouse in the center. A row of trucks blocked the five garage doors.

Ben squeezed between the barricade to reach the first garage door. It was locked at the bottom. So was the next, and every one down the row. Even the entrance at the front stayed secured, shut. He fought with the handle of the door for too long.

A roar tore through the pea-green sky, like the sound of jet engines passing overhead. Wind shook the semis.

"We need to get inside that office now!" He glanced at Moose, his drummer. A handful of fans had followed him—more than he'd realized—all looking at him for salvation.

Without a second thought, he turned and slammed his custom Fender guitar, the one given to him by Garth Brooks, into the glass of the door.

The pane shattered, and he reached in, felt for the handle, and turned the lock. Didn't even realize he'd cut himself along the inside of his arm until he'd gotten them all inside and down the hallway in the center of the building. "Find an inner wall!"

He hunkered down along a cement wall and pulled Shae down beside him. "We'll be okay."

She nodded, swallowed, her eyes huge.

"Really," he said.

"You're bleeding."

He lifted his arm and grimaced. Blood muddied his arm, puddled on the floor.

"Here." Across from him, a guy probably no older than Shae, with nearly black hair, brown eyes, and the build of an athlete, whipped off his shirt and crawled over. He wrapped it around Ben's arm, holding it tight.

"Ned Marshall," he said just as windows shattered in the front lobby.

Shae stiffened. But she gamely applied pressure to Ben's arm, her hands next to Ned's. She met Ben's eyes. "We're going to be fine."

He leaned his head back against the cement, listened to the fury of the storm, and prayed with everything inside him that the women he loved had decided to stay home.

A storm could save her life. One more epic shot, that's all she needed.

Brette stared out the window of the Tulsa Cancer Center, looking at the cumulonimbus clouds. She'd plugged in her extra camera battery last night at the hotel, as the sunset bled red across the horizon, and set her camera on a tripod to capture the halo moon.

Her shots of a molten, melting moon landed on thirty syndicated blogs this morning. Enough residuals to pay for this stupid appointment.

She'd have to scour up more than just a pretty moon, however, to dig herself out from under her pile of debt. She wanted to wince at her pitiful voice, still resounding in her head. *"C'mon, Jonas, don't do this to me."* But in truth, an epic F-5 storm, complete with pictures, could launch her into a new life.

Even if, deep inside, she was still shaking, the sound of the storm passing overhead playing mayhem in her head.

"All done," said the phlebotomist, a young man barely sprouting a beard, as he pressed cotton to the needle wound on the inside of her arm. At least this time, they hadn't had to go hunting. How she hated the pokes in the top of her hand, the inside of her wrist, next to the bone, or even once in her thumb.

"Good job," she said and pushed her sleeve down. No hospital gown for her today. In fact, she'd debated not coming in.

She glanced again at the sky. A slight wall gathered above, gray and ominous, the leading edge of trouble. This better not take long. She'd only stopped in because Jonas and Nixon's meeting with the SPC gave her the time to sneak away for her six-month checkup. At least Dr. Daniels's office would stop leaving her voicemails now.

Not that the doctor would tell her anything she didn't already know.

God had put a timer on her life, and she wasn't dodging it, no matter how much chemo and radiation she had or how many parts they removed. And sure, she might be in remission, but she shouldn't hold her breath.

She read the name of the phlebotomist. Nurse Bellamy.

"I'll bet you're pretty tired of being stuck, huh?" he said as he packed up.

He had no idea.

"That's a lot of blood." She counted six vials as he gathered them into his tray.

"Dr. Daniels will be in soon," Bellamy said and offered her a smile. Patted her knee.

And didn't that make her feel like a victim. She managed to return the smile but turned back to the window.

She just might suffocate if she didn't get out of here soon. The hospital smells, a pungent mix of cleaning solution and medicines, had turned her stomach long before she became a regular patient. Gripping the sides of the table, she closed her eyes, ran a map of Tulsa inside her brain.

They'd have to get on 64 going south, connect with 364, and hook around the city. With the storm running from the northwest, they could shoot north on 75, maybe hit 412, or perhaps they could cut it off on 44, although—

A knock, and her head shot up just as the door opened.

"Hey, Brette, great to see you."

She liked Dr. Daniels, despite herself. He reminded her of the British actor who played the current James Bond—sparingly handsome, thinning gray hair, serious demeanor, the body of a man who worked out, even at sixty. It made her think that maybe she had an action hero fighting the cancer with her.

Except they weren't exactly a dynamic duo. Doctor 007 stayed on the sidelines, giving directions and writing orders while she went to war with her invasive lobular carcinoma. Daniels hadn't suffered from the months of pain and bloody discharge from a double mastectomy, hadn't stared into the mirror at her deformed body, and hadn't helped her gather the handfuls of her hair, long golden strands that puddled on her pillow at night. Hadn't held her hand as she shaved her head, rubbed her back while she huddled in the bathroom, her body dry heaving from the nausea. Hadn't wiped her tears as she'd wept from the ache of her mouth sores or watched her body waste away. Hadn't forced her to get up, to muscle forward when everything inside her wanted to crumble into a ball and vanish.

No, there was no *we*—just Brette, chin up, teeth clenched, whittling out courage to accept whatever mission Doctor 007 decided to assign her.

She forced a smile. "Hey, Doc."

He put down a folder on the table next to her and reached up to touch her lymph glands at her neck, prodding. He had gentle hands, but the feel of them on her skin made her bristle at the memories.

Please, let the cancer be gone.

She shook away the thought—maybe the prayer—before it rooted.

She would accept the storm and ride it out without a whimper.

Even if—probably—it took her life.

He stepped back and pulled his stethoscope from around his neck. "Deep breath."

She obeyed, and he pressed the cold chestpiece to her décolletage. She stifled a shiver.

"Okay," he said. "Just breathe normally."

Right. She hadn't breathed normally since, well, since that day in Montana when the doc came in, palpated a suspicious lump in her armpit he'd seen during her emergency appendectomy, and asked to run a few tests.

A few expensive tests.

Tests she didn't have insurance to pay for.

Tests that would only cause Ty Remington to foot the bill, again, for her hospital stay. And she couldn't do that to him.

Nor could she bear the look of pity in his eyes as the surgeons carved her apart. She knew the drill—had endured every moment of the process with her mother.

The last thing she needed was to crumple into a man's arms, afraid, alone, and hurt. Thanks, she'd been there, done that, and still had the scars to prove it. And sure, Ty wasn't pretty-boy-turned-thug Eason Drake, but he had enough of the markers.

Rich boy saves poor girl and thinks he's entitled to payment.

Nope.

"Okay," 007 said as he stepped away from her. "We won't have the CBC back for a few days, but we should think about scheduling you for reconstructive surgery."

Oh. She refrained from looking down at the pitiful prosthetic she wore. Not out of vanity—at this point, she'd gotten used to seeing the damage done to her body. The fake size Bs just deflected obvious questions. And with her hair almost two inches long, she'd actually started to not flinch when she looked in the mirror. A little curly, with wisps of auburn at the roots, her hair could someday look cute.

She even had eyebrows again.

In truth, the external ravage of her body didn't destroy her as much as the reminder that she'd lost so much of the person she'd been inside. The old Brette would have looked beyond the storm to the sunshine, found the hope between the thunderheads.

Now, she belonged to the storm. To the chaos and destruction and howling winds. It would only destroy her to embrace some kind of fragile hope, or lean into a future that might never be.

"I don't think so, Doc. I'm . . ." She sighed. "I don't know that I've licked this thing, and . . . it's . . ." *Expensive.*

And, really, needless. It wasn't like she planned on getting married. Or dating.

Or ever letting someone far enough into her life that it might matter. *"Come home with me to Minnesota."* Oh, she dearly hoped Jonas didn't look at her and see anything more than his backseat blogger. She didn't have the strength to let anyone else inside. Especially since Ty wouldn't leave.

Daniels folded his arms over his white jacket, frowning. "It's painful, I know. It takes some recovery time, but you have to think positively. You're young—"

"I'm thirty."

"That's young. And your last CBC showed no abnormal cells. It's early, but we treated this thing aggressively."

Yeah, she remembered exactly how aggressively.

"You're strong, and while I can't make any guarantees, I think you should look forward, Brette."

"I am. I have a job, I'm traveling—"

"I know." He offered her a smile. "I saw the picture you took of the F-5 that hit in Colorado last summer. That was when you went to visit your friend?"

"It was only an F-3, but yes, it was . . . I was in the right place at the right time."

The right place because her best friend, Ella, had finally tracked her down and insisted on helping her recuperate.

So maybe she hadn't been completely alone.

But Ella had only dragged in memories of Ty and the fact that for one smidgen of a moment, Brette had found a hero. In her weak moments, she could still taste his lips on hers, still remember the smell of him—clean and cottony—as he'd swept her into his arms, carried her to his truck, and raced her to the hospital before her appendix burst.

She probably owed him her life.

"Cool how your picture made the national news," Daniels was saying, referring to her epic shot. "I didn't know you were into photography."

"The hazards of being sick . . . you get restless. Start new hobbies."

"And if you're Brette Arnold, you start a blog about weather and become a national sensation."

Her mouth opened.

"Your email signature had a link to it in our last correspondence. I couldn't help but click on it. Great blog, although you should update your bio photo." He raised an eyebrow. "People need to see what a fighter you are. It's a great metaphor—you faced your own storm and won."

Her throat thickened. So yes, she'd uploaded the *before* cancer photo, the one where she still possessed her curves, her long blonde hair. A strong and invincible version of herself.

"No one knew I had—or still have—cancer," Brette said quietly. "I'd like to keep it that way."

Daniels held up a hand. "No worries. But if only others could see the woman I see. A woman who chases storms and predicts disasters and chronicles survivors. You're an inspiration."

She shot him a sharp look and couldn't stop herself. "No. I'm not. Every morning when the alarm rings, my body screams at me. I have to pry myself out of bed, force myself to eat breakfast. And when I get coffee into my veins, I'm fine for a whole ten minutes until I look in the mirror. Then it all comes back, and I see who I've become, a ghost of the person I knew. It's horrifying." She wanted to clamp her hand over her mouth. She looked away, blinking fast. "I just want myself back. Or at least some version I can live with."

And yes, she'd only made it worse, because now he wore pity in his 007 eyes. "Brette. This is why you should go ahead and have the surgery. You can rebuild your life, show the world what a hero looks like—"

"Stop." She looked at him, and didn't care that a tear escaped. "Listen, there's nothing heroic about what I do. I chase storms because a group of weather zealots pays me to take pictures and blog about our adventures. It pays the bills. And if I get really lucky, I might plant myself in the path of an F-5 and land a photo in *Nat Geo*."

His eyes widened, as if visualizing that moment.

"I have a lot of bills to pay. I don't have insurance, I don't have a home, I don't even own a car. I have this gig, a backpack, and today. And that's all I need. All I can expect."

"There are grants for people like—"

"Me? Oh, you mean charity cases? No thanks, Doc. I'm going to pay back every cent of my treatment, even if it takes the rest of my life. Which might not be long, so sorry for that."

He frowned and she wanted to wince. He didn't deserve that.

"What you do is dangerous, Brette. Especially for someone in your state of recovery. You could get hurt."

And now he was almost being fatherly. She schooled her voice and fended him off with sincerity. "Listen, I'm grateful. I really am. You took my case, and maybe we really *did* lick this. But let's be honest. My mother died of breast cancer. My odds of long-term survival are so low, what's the point of caution?"

He stared at her.

"Can we be done here?" She slid off the table.

"I'd really like you to think about the reconstruction." But he stepped away, as if rattled.

"Why?" She reached for her satchel. "This is who I am. If you need a metaphor, here I am, the debris after a storm." She reached for the door, turned back. "There's no fixing this mess, no starting over, and no reconstruction that will give me back what I lost. It's just this wreckage of my life." She paused. "And don't bother calling if the cancer is back. I'm just . . . I'm done, Doc. I mean it. I don't have any more fight in me. Thanks for everything."

The door closed behind her as she practically ran down the hall.

She stopped, however, in the bathroom before she hit the lobby. No good having her team thinking she might drop dead on them before the season ended.

Okay, she might be a little overly dramatic, but one look in the mirror at her gaunt face rimmed with shadows, the spiked blonde hair, the gaps in her clothing as it hung on her . . . her lifeless chest.

Yeah, if she were to compare before and after pictures from eighteen months ago, she looked ravaged.

And if she ever wondered if she'd done the right thing AMA-ing herself out of the hospital in Kalispell and practically running from Ty Remington, her visage in the mirror confirmed that she'd saved them both a collision with disaster and heartache.

Better to go it alone, all the way to the bitter end.

Washing water on her face—what was the use of makeup?—she hid the marks of any tears, emerged, at least more intact, and strode through the lobby.

Geena sat outside, leaning against a cement planter, texting. She looked up at Brette as she exited, then pocketed the phone. "The guys are on their way. There's a storm heading for their hometown. And it looks bad."

+

Ty needed a shower, a nap, and a pizza. Not necessarily in that order.

So, he couldn't say why he was driving up the road to PEAK headquarters, a former two-story ranch house and towering white barn that hosted all their SAR equipment, not to mention their shiny new Bell 412EP chopper.

Maybe he just needed to feel a part of a rescue mission. Sure, he'd found the Berkleys, helped feed the fire that kept everyone warm and alive, had hiked out to call in the team. But from there, Kacey had been the one to fly in the chopper, Gage, the EMT who ferried down the line to the creek bed, twice, to retrieve first Richard, then Jan. It had been Miles, their incident commander, who made sure they got onto the deck safely and whisked off to Kalispell Regional Medical Center.

Leaving Ty alone on the soggy creek bed, waving as they flew away. He'd wanted to pick up his truck, and they didn't have time to drop him.

It had taken him nearly six hours to hike back to his pickup. Another two to drive out of the park, and he'd gone straight to the hospital.

His team had been there and gone, but he stopped in to see Jan as she waited for Richard to get out of surgery. She'd only suffered a severely sprained ankle.

"We would still be out there if it weren't for you." Jan had pressed her hands to either side of his grimy, whiskered face, and he turned seven years old at the warmth in her eyes.

"Aw, you're pretty tough, Jan. I have no doubt you would've saved Richard." He winked and pressed a kiss to her forehead, not sure why he did it. It just felt right.

"If you ever need anything . . ." She whisked away tears.

He'd called himself just a little bit of a hero by the time he left.

The summer sun hung just above the granite peaks, the rain clearing the sky to a brilliant indigo. He should probably head home to the ranch sometime soon, see if his brother needed a hand with anything, although Ty couldn't remember the last time Powers needed his help.

Fact was, he was about as useful on the ranch as on the PEAK team.

He wished Ben King were in town, maybe playing a gig at the Gray Pony Saloon, but Ben had a full schedule this summer at festivals and state fairs. With Pete working for the Red Cross around the globe and Jess Tagg jetting back and forth from New York, the PEAK team had been stripped down to just himself, Gage, Kacey, Miles, Sam, and Sierra, their administrator. And Chet, of course, but he'd gone AWOL this weekend.

Ty sort of wondered if the old guy might be proposing to Maren,

Sam and Pete's mother. Ty had seen a brochure of some bed and breakfast on his desk.

He turned into the parking lot and spotted Ian's black pickup, along with Gage's Mustang and Sam's truck. He guessed he might be walking into some kind of legal powwow.

Ever since Esme Shaw, now Shae Johnson, had walked back into Ian's life, armed with a crazy story about Sheriff Randy Blackburn killing a woman, Sofia d'Cruze, five years ago, Ian, Sam, and Gage's girlfriend, attorney Ella Blair, had been working overtime to build a case they might bring to the county prosecutor. Ella especially, because the victim had been a former roommate.

But they needed evidence, a case that didn't sound fabricated and built on what-ifs.

Ty got out of his truck and climbed up the porch steps, hearing their voices through the screen even before he went in.

Yep, Gage, with his long hair tied back in a man bun, wearing a pair of cargo shorts and a T-shirt, leaned over the table in the center of the room, papers spread over the top. "And you can't track down this number, honey?"

Ella, her curly auburn hair tied back, stood with her arms folded, brows raised. "Believe me, I've tried." She glanced at Ty. "Hey you." She frowned at his appearance. "Somebody had a hard day."

He slid onto a stool at the counter, and Sierra, a woman who could read a man's mind, handed him the entire jar of cookies. "You did good today."

"Thanks."

He held the jar on his lap and glanced at her husband, Ian, who was leaning against the wall, his arms folded, looking grim.

The running theory, based on Shae's story, was that Sofia, an exchange student from Spain, had met Blackburn while on a skiing trip. An affair had sparked between them that eventually ended in a fatal argument off a hiking trail in Glacier National Park.

"We just need more than a list of phone calls to Montana between Blackburn and Sofia to convince Shae to testify," Ian said. "She's afraid that if we don't have evidence to back up her testimony, Blackburn will walk, and then . . . well, Shae will disappear again. And I wouldn't blame her, after what she's been through."

He let the silence fill in the rest—the fact that Shae and her boyfriend, Dante, had watched Blackburn push Sofia off a cliff, and when he discovered the eyewitnesses to his crime, Blackburn had tracked them down and beaten Dante to death before Shae's eyes. By some remote miracle, Shae had gotten away, only to keep running all the way to Minneapolis.

It took four years, but Sierra had tracked Shae down and convinced her to return home.

"What about the necklace Blackburn said proved the body was Shae's?" Sam said. Ty hadn't even seen him sitting at the kitchen table in the nook. Their deputy-slash-SAR-liaison had a get-'er-done attitude that accounted for why they never gave up a search. "I talked to the coroner, and she doesn't have Shae's necklace on her list of items discovered with Sofia's body. So how did Blackburn get ahold of it?"

Ty well remembered the dark months after they'd found Sofia, whose body had decomposed after three years in the Mercy River. Months when Ian feared the body could be Shae's.

"When Blackburn showed me a picture on his phone of the necklace, he told me the coroner found it," Ian said, pushing off the wall.

"Are you sure it's Shae's?" Ty said.

"Yes. I gave it to her on her eighteenth birthday."

"She said Blackburn ripped it off her during their fight," Sierra said, setting a glass of milk in front of Ty. "He must have kept it, just in case the body was ever found."

"Then he used it to make me think Shae was dead. But still, it's not evidence. It's my word against his," Ian said. "He could have easily deleted the picture."

"And there's no other evidence of his so-called relationship with Sofia?" Ty asked, picking up his milk.

"Trust me," Ella said. "They were involved. Sofia was crazy about this guy named Randy. Would text him, write letters."

"And you never saw them together," Gage said.

"Nope. My guess is he wanted it to stay secret," Ella said. "Considering he's married."

Sam walked over to the list of numbers. Looked through them. "So, you're saying that all these calls to Montana from Sofia's phone are to a burner?"

"Would you give out your home number if you were cheating on your wife?" Ian said.

"I wouldn't cheat on my wife," Sam said, something sparking in his eyes.

Probably that something had to do with the fact that, well, he had kissed his current girlfriend while dating another woman. But he had reasons, and a good story to go with it.

And frankly, the other woman hadn't loved him, and everybody knew it.

Some people were just destined to be together, and Ian himself had run around that truth for years before surrendering last fall and proposing to Sierra. They'd tied the knot in a small ceremony right before Christmas. In the house he'd once owned.

In fact, everyone in the room—Gage, Sam, and Ian—had found the woman they belonged with.

Which left, of course, Ty, the man who'd let a woman steal his heart and run away.

Sam put the list down. "You have no idea how it feels to work with Blackburn every day, knowing what he's put us all, but especially Shae, through. The fact that he killed Ella's friend and poor Dante."

"That he allegedly killed," Ella said.

Everyone, even Gage, looked at her.

Ella held up her hands. "Listen, I believe every word Shae said. But I've also learned my lesson about jumping to conclusions. I just want to make sure we nail this guy with evidence. That we can *prove* he's guilty."

"He's guilty," Ian said, his voice low. "I know it in my gut. I just need five minutes—"

"Take a breath, Ian," Sam said. "We'll figure this out. But if the guy invites me over to watch one more baseball game on his new flat screen, I might have to level him."

"From my research, he's up to his ears in debt," Ella said. "My guess is that he's a sports gambler."

"Which probably accounts for the stack of sports magazines he's constantly bringing to the station or leaving at the gym," Sam said. "But it doesn't help us nail him for Sofia's murder."

Ian shook his head. "I'm so tired of the people I love feeling alone. Helpless. It's time for Shae to come home, if she wants."

And with Ian's words, there went Ty's gut again, that feeling that something was deeply, terribly wrong with Brette. No, he couldn't put a finger on why, or what, but he couldn't shake it.

He could be, of course, clinging too hard to something that clearly was never meant to be.

He finished off the milk. Set his glass on the counter. "I need a shower."

"Yeah, dude, you do," Gage said as Sierra pulled a tray of pigs in a blanket from the oven.

Maybe he'd stay a little longer.

The door opened, and Kacey walked in carrying a duffel over her shoulder. She dropped it onto the floor, sighed. She wore a pair of yoga pants and a T-shirt and looked like she'd wasted a few hours in the airport chairs. Behind her, her daughter Audrey looked just as wrung out and annoyed. "Our flight out was canceled."

Kacey came over, grabbed the cookie jar from the counter, and clutched it to her chest.

"Oh, c'mon, it's not that bad," Sierra said.

"We haven't seen Ben in six weeks," Kacey said and held out the jar to Audrey, who pulled out two cookies.

"Dad was really looking forward to seeing us," Audrey said and slid onto one of the stools. She glanced at her mom. "Are you sure we can't just drive?"

"To Minnesota? It would take us two days, in good weather, and with the storm front going through . . . no, honey. We only have five days off, and it would eat up two days each way, if not more."

"Storm front?" Sam said, reaching for one of the pigs in a blanket that Sierra piled onto a tray.

"Apparently there's one ahead of us, between here and Minnesota, that the forecasters were hoping would die down, but . . . no. And there's another one coming in behind us from the west coast. So, we're grounded." She put her arm around her daughter. "We'll see your dad when he comes home after Labor Day."

"But that's almost two months away!"

"It's the tour, honey. It's the price of being a country music star. It's not all red carpet events and parties."

"I'd like to go to just *one* red carpet event, please."

Kacey laughed, but Ty agreed with Audrey. What was the use of having a superstar father if she never got to ride in a limousine, attend the Country Music Awards, or even hang out at a sold-out concert? In their efforts to keep Audrey out of the limelight, the poor girl barely got to bask in the outer glow.

But Kacey didn't seem to want that life either, preferring her privacy over Ben's alter-ego life. Ty had started to wonder just who might be behind the delay of their wedding. Twice, already, postponed. Not that Ty had a stake in it, but he felt for Audrey. And Kacey.

No one should be separated from someone they loved. Especially because of weather.

A phone rang, and Ty glanced at the cell phone lying on the counter.

Brette's picture popped up on the screen, and for a second, he just stilled. Well, well. And yes, he knew that Ella had tracked down her wayward friend. But . . . he couldn't ignore how Brette sat at the top of his thoughts and . . .

Ella picked up the phone, glancing at Ty. He gave her a smile. "Don't worry about it." If Brette didn't want him in her life, there was nothing he could do about it.

Ella took the call over in the corner, but an "Oh, you're kidding!" made everyone turn.

When she added, "Was anyone hurt?" it had all of Ty's instincts firing.

Ella's hand touched her mouth. "Wow."

What was wow? But he didn't want to pry. He snagged one of the pigs in a blanket and took a bite.

Ella had glanced toward the group, nodding. "Yeah, that sounds pretty epic. But I'm sure there will be more . . . oh." She sighed. "You could always come . . . yeah, right. Have you heard from—"

She turned away then, one hand clasped around her waist, her voice low.

"She didn't want to keep it from you," Gage said, glancing at Ty. "She knows how much you care about Brette. But Brette—"

"Doesn't care about me. It's fine."

Gage's mouth tightened in a line. "That's not quite it, but . . ."

Ella walked over, sliding her phone onto the counter. "Brette's in Oklahoma," she said, glancing at Ty, then at Gage. "She caught twin tornadoes near Dodge City—but just missed an F-4 going through Minnesota."

"Where in Minnesota?" Kacey asked.

"I don't know."

"Ben's playing a music festival in southwestern Minnesota."

"Hopefully it wasn't up near Minneapolis," Ian said. "Shae is living off campus with some friends in a house that could blow over in a gentle breeze."

As if on cue, Ian's phone vibrated. He dug it out of his pocket. "Shae?"

He walked away, but Ty's gaze stayed on him, even while trying to sort out Ella's words. Brette caught two tornadoes?

"Okay, calm down. Are you hurt?" Ian said, his voice carrying across the room.

Everyone went silent.

"Oh good. Yes. Oh, I'm so glad."

Kacey turned to Ty. "Must have hit near Minneapolis." When her phone rang in her jacket, she pulled it out, stared at the screen. Frowned. "It's Ben. But . . ." She put the phone to her ear. "Hey."

The entire thing had Ty's gut clenching, because as he watched, Kacey's face whitened. She swallowed and looked up, first at Ty, then Ian, who had strangely turned to meet her gaze.

"Okay, yes. Of course," Kacey said. "And you're not hurt?" She nodded, listening. "Okay, we're on our way. Somehow, we'll get there. I love you."

She hung up. Ian had already walked over, his mouth tight. They looked at each other, then Kacey turned to the team. Took a breath.

But before she could speak, her breath hiccupped, and her eyes filled. Ian pressed his hand to her shoulder.

"A tornado hit the music festival. Shae was there, with Ben—he got her to safety. They're both okay."

Ian swallowed then, looked at Kacey, sighed. "But Chet was there. And now he's gone missing. We need to get to Minnesota, pronto, and help Ben find his father."

So yes, that nap could wait too.

3

THE WRECKAGE OF THE TOWN of Duck Lake, Minnesota, made Brette want to turn and run. Her stomach rolled, and she had to press her hand against it, take a few deep breaths.

She'd seen plenty of destruction this summer—mostly in fields, a few barns, livestock, and yes, an occasional farmhouse—but nothing prepared her for the damage a twister could do when it ripped through a neighborhood.

She'd actually called Ella last night, bemoaning the fact that she'd missed capturing the twister on film. Brette gritted her teeth, wondering for a moment at the person she'd become. But Jonas's enthusiasm for tornadoes was infectious, and she'd focused on the power and mystery that created the cyclone and how she could capture it.

Now, a question burrowed into Brette as they drove through the remains of the tiny town at the break of dawn.

How did anyone put their life back together after such complete devastation?

According to the Doppler radar and some videos and online reports, the F-4 touched down just north of Duck Lake, tore through the north side of town, across Highway 7, through the festival fairgrounds, past the county high school, and finally died just outside the next town of Chester, some ten miles away, where Jonas and Nixon lived.

Brette had listened as Jonas and Nixon called their families last night. The Swans lived in Chester, and they'd been untouched. The Marshall family farm, located between the two small hamlets, also survived. Still, Jonas had taken the wheel at the border and driven tight-lipped for the past hour. The sun was just rising, and the sound of cicadas already buzzed in the summer heat, tempered just slightly by last night's soaking.

They'd slowed as they motored along Main Street, which was littered with ravaged vegetation, shingles, splintered wood, insulation, and glass. The air reeked of upturned dirt and sheared foliage, not unlike freshly mowed grass. The only stoplight in town blinked yellow. Water flooded the gutters, dragging leaves and sticks into the grates. Glass from a coffee shop window littered the sidewalk. A man up early had begun to shovel up the debris, having already pulled the destructive branches onto the street.

A few community trash cans rolled on their sides, and posters and other papers pancaked onto the asphalt. Surface destruction, but as they passed through town, closer to the tornado's wrathful edge, the ruin became more dire.

A bungalow's front porch lay ripped from its moorings. The windows of the house were shattered, and an American flag was in strips, soggy and lilting in the scant breeze. Shingles cluttered the yard. An oak tree, broken and half-rended from the ground, spread its branches across the road.

A dog ran alongside them, barking as if in warning.

Farther down the street, an entire garage had collapsed onto the cars inside.

Brette snapped pictures, feeling like a voyeur. They finally stopped just outside town and got out.

"Was that a bowling alley?"

Geena's question barely registered as Brette turned and got a wide-angle view of the mess.

"Yes, that's the Dine and Bowl," Jonas said. "Or it was."

Brette zoomed in on a set of vinyl chairs lined up for bowlers and orange and pink marbled bowling balls parked on top of a grimy mattress. The machinery was entangled with two-foot-long pieces of wood, insulation, broken furniture, countertops, dishware, glass, wire—a tumble of nondescript chaos that snarled her brain.

She finally let her camera fall around her neck.

Jonas came up behind her, reading his phone. "According to reports, there's only about twenty people injured, no casualties. The sirens went off early enough."

Nixon had his camera out, was taping the destruction as Geena tiptoed through the mess.

"I forget about this side of it," Brette said. "How people's lives are ruined."

"I was ten years old when a tornado hit St. Peter, a nearby town," Jonas said. "My dad packed up the entire family for two days and we went to help with cleanup. I was already enamored with storms, but for the first time I realized that I could help." He glanced at her. "I don't just chase tornadoes for the thrill of capturing it on camera and maybe selling footage to local media outlets. I'm a weather geek, sure, but I'm also the guy out there calling in the data to the weather stations, helping warn of the danger. And the more data we can get on how a tornado behaves, the more time we'll have to get out of its way."

Geena came back, shaking her head. "According to the latest update, the twister hit the school."

"Oh no," Nixon said.

"It's summer, so hopefully no one was there," Jonas said. "Still . . ."

They piled back into the SUV and drove in silence. Brette took more shots as they followed the tornado's route. When they came up to the county school—a U-shaped connected high school, middle school, and elementary—they stopped.

The roof of the high school had blown off and landed on the elementary wing on the other side, pancaking the structure. The damage to the middle section seemed mostly cosmetic.

The great winds had stacked two busses together on one side of the parking lot along with a handful of cars twisted and piled up along the elementary wing.

Jonas idled in the parking lot. "Wow."

He pulled out and headed down the road toward Chester, following evidence of the tornado's dying strength—fences ripped up, a half-scalped tree, more crop havoc—but by the time Jonas pointed out the highway that led to his farmhouse, the twister had run its course.

The sun cleared the horizon, turning the day bright and bold as they pulled into Chester, a matchbox town only five streets wide, with seven churches, two banks, one grocery store, and a sleepy suburban neighborhood at the outskirts. The main street hosted a country bar, an ancient courthouse, and a library circa the early 1900s.

Jonas dropped off Nixon and Geena at Nixon's parents' place, a small ranch house across the street from his father's church, Grace Chapel. Nixon's father came out in his bathrobe and grabbed him up in a hold that had Brette looking away, tears in her eyes.

Brette climbed into the front seat that Geena had vacated and waved as they pulled away.

"I was the one that talked Nixon into chasing storms, way back in high school. Scared his poor parents to death," Jonas said quietly. "I think they blame me for his fascination with storms, but really, he's a film major, so all this footage only helps build his future."

They stopped at a light, and Jonas waved to a passing driver.

"You know a lot of people in this town?"

"There are only 1,700 people, so yeah. Everybody." He turned at the light.

"Are you sure you don't want me to stay at a hotel or something? Your parents just lived through a terrible—"

"There are no hotels in Chester, and the nearest B & B is on Duck Lake. It's probably in rubble."

Oh.

"Besides, my mother would murder me if I didn't bring you home." He looked over at her and flashed her a smile that had her stomach tightening. Oh, Jonas was cute, no doubt. Possessed a charm about him that could cajole a girl's heart from her, make her doodle his name in her spare time. But she had no room for anyone else in the tragedy of her life.

"Thanks," she said and looked away.

Besides, she'd already broken one man's heart, according to Ella, who'd spent too much breath trying to convince her to call Ty this spring. She shuddered to think of what he might say or what he might think of her if he saw her now. Probably wouldn't even recognize her.

And she wasn't unaware of the fact that every time she called Ella, her boyfriend's best friend might be within earshot. Like last night—Brette could have sworn she heard his voice in the background. Or maybe she simply wished it.

She probably should remember that she'd been the one to walk away. No, rather she'd run, full tilt.

And kept running.

Besides, their forty-eight-hour friendship could hardly be called a relationship, even if they had shared a kiss. Ty had probably long forgotten her.

The Marshall family farm sat four miles out of town on a swath of rolling countryside attached to the Crow River. She noticed the signage as Jonas turned into the driveway.

"Your family runs a vineyard? In Minnesota?"

"Yeah. We raise cold-climate grapes—Marquette and Frontenac as well as La Crescent white grapes. They make fantastic wines. We also have cranberry and strawberry fields for our fruit wines."

"When you said *farm* I thought . . . well, pigs. Or cows."

"My great-grandfather used to run a dairy herd, and we still have horses, a few chickens, and I'm sure there's a goat around here somewhere. Mom likes her cheese."

She had no words for the world that opened before her. A classic red barn with a giant wooden sign with the words *Marshall Family Winery* sat to the left of the open circle drive, a gravel surface edged by hostas. A cobblestone walk led up to a porch that wrapped around a massive two-story colonial-style home, with black shutters and a red double door. Another structure jutted out from the end, a two-story traditional square farmhouse that must have been the original house, now updated. A rooster weather vane circled at the apex of the roof.

Geraniums overflowed from containers at the entrance of the walk, and white rocking chairs invited family to sit down for a while and chat.

She'd never seen a more Rockwellian picture of a homestead in her life. And couldn't deny the conflicting urge to both run for the hills and hold on to one of the pillars along the porch with everything inside her.

"Brace yourself. It's bound to be loud in there. I don't see my brother Creed's car, but I see Ned's, and it looks like we have company. My sister, Iris, is still overseas, and Fraser—well, who knows where he is—but Mom always manages to fill up the house anyway. She loves to feed people."

He pulled up behind a Suburban. "We'll stay a couple days, just long enough to decide what we want to do next and if we have the footage we need for Nixon's master's project—he's hoping to put together a sort of documentary of the tornado season."

"I'll upload the photos and update the blog."

"Jonas!"

The voice made them look up. A man with dark hair emerged from the front door. He looked a year or two younger than Jonas.

"That's Ned." Jonas reached for the door handle.

More Marshalls emptied from the house. A woman with dark blonde hair tied back in a handkerchief—Brette pegged her as his mother. And right behind her, his father, an older version of Jonas with dark hair, salty around the edges, and a piercing focus on his son as he came down the walk.

Jonas met his brother in a hug.

Brette walked around the front of the truck, watching the greeting.

"Man, are we glad to see you," Ned said. He wore a grizzle of dark whiskers, and he appeared a little rattled.

"I got here as fast I could," Jonas said.

"Jonas." His father embraced him. "So glad you're safe."

"You too." Jonas then went to his mother. She wrapped her arms around her son's shoulders, hung on. Closed her eyes.

Brette should have insisted on a hotel room, even if she had to bunk in Minneapolis.

As if reading her mind, Jonas looked at her. "Brette—these are my parents, Garrett and Jenny Marshall."

Jenny Marshall made a move to hug her, but Brette stuck out her hand.

"Thank you for letting me stay with you, Mrs. Marshall."

"Jenny. And, of course." She enclosed Brette's hand with hers, as if just restraining herself from yanking her into a hug. "We have lots of room, but we have a bit of a full house. There were quite a few festival-goers who lost their RVs and tents. Thankfully, the festival didn't suffer a direct hit, but the gusts dismantled most of the flimsy housing."

She seemed tired, and Brette had the distinct feeling that something wasn't quite right here.

Maybe Jonas felt it too, because he said, "Is everybody okay?" He frowned at Ned. "You seem upset."

Ned's mouth made a tight line. "Creed's missing."

Jonas's sharp intake of breath stabbed at her.

"He texted Mom from the Duck Lake trail, where he'd gone for a run with the cross-country team. He said he'd finished practice and was going to spend the night with Andy, one of his cross-country buddies. But when he didn't come home this morning, we started to get worried. The phone lines are down, but Dad and I just got back from Andy's house." Ned shook his head. "He's not there. Andy didn't even go to practice."

Jonas stared at his brother, as if not comprehending. "What do you mean, practice? School is out."

"His team was having informal practice. No formal coaching, although the coach sometimes shows up to just work out. Creed is one of the captains, and he's been running with his team every day at the Duck Lake trail outside town," Ned said.

"I tried calling him, but the lines were down. I should have double-checked he was at Andy's instead of just assuming he got there safely . . ." Jenny said softly. "Now, no one knows where he is."

Oh. Brette pressed her hand to her gut. Took a breath as Jonas just stared at Ned, then his mother.

"Please tell me he didn't go to the school," Jonas said.

"You're scaring me, Jonas," Jenny said.

"Sorry, Mom. I just . . ." He looked at his father, at Ned, then back to his mother. "We drove by the school. It was hit, and . . . well, there's not much left."

"We know, son," Garrett said. "We helped pull out a janitor and a first-grade teacher working on her classroom, but otherwise, the school was empty."

"Are you *sure* he wasn't there?"

"We didn't see his car at the school," Garrett said. "He may have driven it to practice."

"But there's a lot of destruction, so it's hard to know. When the coach is there, they often drive the coach's van," Jenny said.

"He texted us ten minutes before the warning siren sounded, and our guess is that he couldn't have made it back to the school by then," Ned said. "We thought he went right to Andy's. He lives out of town, close to the lake."

Brette looked at Jenny and read the unspoken question.

Then where is he?

"And you haven't heard anything?" Jonas looked over to the porch, where more people had assembled. A blonde came out onto the porch, folded her arms, and watched from a distance. She wore a T-shirt with a face on the front. Behind her, another man had emerged and was talking on his phone, pacing away from them to the edge of the porch. He was wearing a baseball hat and his left arm was bandaged.

"No," Garrett said. "We keep trying to call him, but . . ."

Jenny pressed a hand to her mouth, and Brette ached for her.

Sweet Jonas pulled his mom into his arms. "Shh, Mom. Creed is smart. I'll bet he found a place to hunker down. We just can't get in touch with him, what with all the cell towers in town down. We'll find him, I promise."

"He's not the only one who's missing."

The voice came from the man on the phone, who now came off the porch. "I can't find my father either."

It took a second for the recognition to click into place, almost like a hand closing around Brette's throat.

Benjamin King. Country music star and friend of Ty Remington. He worked on the same search and rescue team that Ty did back in Montana. What was he doing—

"This is Ben," Ned said, neatly omitting his last name, like they might be old friends. "And his friend Shae Johnson." He indicated the woman on the porch. "They're the reason I'm alive. I was at the festival and—"

"We hid out in a storage building," Shae said, coming down the stairs. "But Ned is the reason Ben didn't bleed out. He cut his arm pretty good, and Ned helped stop the bleeding."

She looked at Ned then, and something akin to admiration flickered in her eyes.

It brought Brette right back to last winter, when Ty Remington had nursed her through an inflamed appendix. She might have even called him her hero.

Oh boy.

And then, just as she began to put the puzzle pieces together, Ben said, "I just got off the phone with my fiancée. She and the PEAK team just landed in the Chester ball field. Any chance I could catch a ride from someone?"

And with those words, Brette's entire body went cold.

Oh no.

The PEAK team. Ty Remington's team.

Which meant . . . Ty was *here.*

"I told them they could stay with us," Jenny said quietly, glancing at Jonas.

"Let's go," Garrett said and headed off the porch to a Suburban lined up in the drive.

"I have some hot pancakes and homemade syrup inside," Jenny said. "Then, maybe—"

"Yeah, we'll head out and see if we can trace the route Creed might have taken," Jonas said. He and Ned fetched their gear and carried it inside.

Brette just stood there, not sure what to do, where to go, still frozen. Until Jenny took her hand. "You look hungry. When was the last time you ate?"

No, she always looked hungry these days. But she had no appetite.

And, as Jenny led her into the house, apparently nowhere else to run.

+

Kacey was here to do a job, not break anyone's heart. She drew in a breath as she hung up with Ben, his voice like honey to her raw and fatigued body.

Lethal honey because she had a terrible, heartbreaking suspicion she knew exactly why he'd wanted her to fly out to Minnesota, although why he'd asked Audrey to join them seemed a little odd. Still, Ben loved Audrey with everything inside of him and probably wanted to assure her of that when they finally admitted the truth.

They just couldn't make this crazy idea of marriage work.

It wasn't just postponing the wedding two times. Or the time away. It was time to admit that their romance couldn't survive Ben's superstar career. Truth was, Kacey wasn't cut out to be the glittery wife of a country music icon.

Some things weren't meant to be, no matter how much you wanted them.

Ben had suggested that they needed to have a serious conversation about their future in their last phone call, that things needed to change. He wanted her to be with him on the road, or at awards events, and frankly, he wasn't happy. Neither was she, and since then the words had sunk in, and she had shored herself up for this weekend of honesty.

She would be strong. And with Ben traveling so much, of course he wanted to look Audrey in the eyes and tell her he loved her. Kacey would stand beside him and help her daughter see that her daddy still—would always—be her daddy. Even if their happily ever after might be in pieces.

"Is Dad okay?" Audrey stood in the outfield of the Chester sports complex. Now sixteen she looked every inch the daughter of handsome Benjamin King, with her beautiful blue eyes and dark hair the color of rich mahogany. She wore a Mountain Song Records T-shirt and cutoff shorts, her eyes bright as if she'd actually slept over the past twelve hours as they'd hopped their way from Montana to Minnesota in their tired but champion chopper. Sam had allowed them to requisition the chopper from the county, and Ty had stepped in with the funds to get them in the air. With five refueling stops, Kacey dodged the weather fronts and landed just as the sun tipped the dewy grass.

If she let herself, Kacey could curl up in a ball right here in the soft grass, sleep for a week. Except for the fact that Ben had sounded so tightly strung, so weary on the phone. He needed her, and even if they might never be husband and wife, they would always be friends.

"He's worried about Grandpa," Kacey said as she walked back to the chopper. She hadn't been sure where to put the bird down, but Ben suggested the athletic field after consulting with one of the locals, so . . .

Ty pulled out his duffel bag, looking a little less worn than last night. He'd grabbed a quick shower before they took off while Ian had swapped the seats back in, securing the two stretchers in the cargo area and turning the rescue chopper into a transport for all of them—Ian, Ty, Gage, Audrey, and Kacey.

Now, Ty placed a ball cap on his head, donned a pair of aviator sunglasses, and nodded at her.

He'd agreed to ride copilot for the entire trip and had taken over as navigator even if he hadn't exactly offered to relieve her. But she'd flown longer sorties than this trip, with less sleep, and under the fatigue, her body buzzed with a layer of adrenaline. Especially since they hadn't yet located Chet.

Please, God, let him be alive. Stay with him.

"Should we bring the medical gear?" This from Gage, who stood next to the belly of the chopper, indicating the large duffel of supplies. She hadn't known what to expect, and since they were in the business of rescue . . .

"Leave it for now."

Gage nodded and shut the door. Ian had come around from the other side, shouldering a backpack. Kacey grabbed her own rucksack and tossed it over her shoulder just as a Suburban pulled up in the parking lot.

Audrey took off in a run toward Ben, who got out of the Suburban, rounded the gate, and ran toward her.

He caught his daughter up in a hold that thickened Kacey's throat. The man did love his daughter—that much would never change.

She swallowed back a burr of pain. Clearly now wasn't the time for her and Ben to confront the truth about their relationship.

Ben set Audrey down and walked over to Kacey. He'd replaced his cowboy hat with a gimme cap, one that had the Mountain Song Records logo on the crown, and his blue eyes bore into hers with a hunger that reached in and grabbed her heart. He hadn't shaved, and he needed a haircut. He wore a pair of faded jeans, cowboy boots, and a faded light blue T-shirt that read "Kick Off Your Spurs." That was when she noticed the bandage on his left arm.

Before she could examine it, however, he caught her in a hold, pulling her to his chest, his entire body shaking.

"Babe." Ben King had never been the guy to let his emotions too far off his leash, but now she sensed he might be close to unraveling. "I can't tell you how glad I am to see you."

She wrapped her arms around his lean torso, and with everything inside her, she longed to hang on, to bury her nose into his tanned skin, smell the soap on him, the hard work. Just being around him made her want to sing along to his song.

She missed him already, and the thought of their imminent breakup burned her eyes, made her push away from him before she began to weep.

"What happened?" She backed away and went right for the arm, neatly deflecting the kiss he aimed at her. No need to make it harder.

His kiss landed on her cheek, but he made no comment. See, he was trying to make it easier too.

"I had to break into a building to get away from the storm. I cut my arm on the glass."

"Did you get stitches?"

"Yep. Fifteen. I'll be fine."

Ian, Gage, and Ty had joined them now, and Ben gave them bro hugs, gratefulness in his eyes. Audrey wrapped her arms around his waist and leaned into him. He hung his arm around her and continued. "The twister hit the far edge of the festival, but it still did enough damage to the grounds and trailers to leave ten thousand people without a place to stay. Quite a few were able to get on busses back to Minneapolis—some went to a high school about thirty minutes from here. My trailer is a wreck, but we might be able to salvage it. In the meantime, we're staying with the Marshall family."

He turned and glanced at a bigger man, maybe midfifties, standing in the parking lot. "That's Garrett Marshall. His son, Ned, worked as a smokejumper in Montana last summer. He apparently knows Pete."

Pete Brooks, their former EMT and mountaineering specialist.

"Small world," Gage said.

"Even smaller. Shae Johnson was at the festival. She told one of the security guards that she knew me, and when I found out, I let her backstage before the show." Ben looked at Ian. "She's okay. She followed me into the storage area."

"Thank you for rescuing her, Ben," Ian said.

"Oh, she kept up, and she helped me get the bleeding under control. She's a real trouper. I can see how she survived on her own so many years."

Ian's mouth tightened, but he nodded.

"It wasn't until about an hour later, when I heard that the tornado had touched down in Duck Lake, that I called my dad. He didn't pick up—his phone went right to voicemail."

They started walking toward the Suburban, Ben holding Audrey's hand. He reached out for Kacey's, but she tried to pretend she didn't see it and held on to her rucksack.

Don't, Ben. Please.

"We drove out to the . . . um . . ." He looked at Audrey then, and made a face, and Kacey caught it out of the corner of her eye. "I was hoping to take a few days off, and I rented a B & B near Duck Lake for us."

Oh. Yes. Well, a private time away from prying eyes for them to explain things to Audrey. To remind her that they could still be a family, even if they lived separate lives.

But that was Ben. Thoughtful, not wanting his public life to interfere with his private life.

"The B & B was completely destroyed."

Audrey gasped.

"Grandpa wasn't there, honey. He hadn't shown up. Or at least by the time the owners got into their storm shelter—they all survived, by the way."

Now Kacey longed to grab his hand, give it a squeeze.

"We drove along the highway, trying to find his rental car, but it's . . ." He swallowed, then blew out a breath. "He's vanished. We can't find any sign of him. And then it got dark and . . ."

Okay, that was just enough. Kacey reached out and took his hand. "We're going to find him, Ben. I promise."

His eyes glistened then, and he nodded.

She reached up and brushed her thumb across his cheek, wiping the wetness there. Old habits, grabbing her up, winding through her. The gesture made her ache.

He pressed his hand over hers, leaning into her touch. "Thank you for coming."

"Of course we came. That's what PEAK does."

Something flickered in his eyes, but he recovered fast, nodding. "Yeah," he said. "Right."

Then he turned and followed Audrey to the parking lot. He climbed into the backseat with Audrey, and Kacey slid in beside them, aware of Ben's body pressed next to hers.

"That's what PEAK does."

She was here to do a job. She just had to remember that.

And when it was over, she'd figure out how to break up with the only man she'd ever loved.

+

Ty should have spelled Kacey, not let her take the helm for the entire trip. The guilt built in his gut after the third stop for gas at the Miles City municipal airport around midnight.

But the words "Chet's missing" had surfaced every buried memory of two years ago when he'd nearly killed the man who'd taught him to fly and convinced him that life might be worth more than a bottle of whiskey.

Ty had no business flying a chopper. Not when the last time he'd taken the helm for a rescue mission, he'd dismantled all their lives.

The bigger truth was that Chet had given him a thousand second chances until it nearly cost both their lives one snowy spring night, and if the man was still out there, Ty planned on finding him.

So, even if he couldn't—or rather, didn't—fly a chopper anymore, he could still listen to his instincts. And those instincts told him that if anyone could survive a tornado, it was a former Vietnam chopper pilot who'd seen more destruction in his life than a man deserved.

They pulled up to the Marshall home—a sprawling two-story farmhouse already jammed with cars in the circle lot. He noticed the winery sign on the barn, along with the rows and rows of vines that stretched out as far as his eye could see into the horizon.

He squeezed out of the middle bucket seat and was opening the back end when he saw a woman run out of the house. "Uncle Ian."

Shae Johnson, formerly Esme Shaw, with her blonde hair and mysterious eyes, had grown into a beautiful young woman despite the horrors she'd endured. Ian grabbed her up, held her tight, his eyes closed.

"You scared me. I had no idea you were at the country fest."

She backed away, put her hands on his arms. "I'm okay. It's because of Ben." She glanced toward the Suburban where Ben was climbing out with Audrey and Kacey.

Ty handed Gage's backpack to him and followed Garrett Marshall into the house.

Inside, the old farmhouse had apparently gotten an up-to-date overhaul. The dark oak floors were shiny and the ceilings beamed, and he could look right through to the backyard. In the kitchen, an island topped with black granite seated eight, and a woman with blonde hair tied back in a headband made pancakes at an enormous range. More people gathered around a long farmhouse table on the other side of the room. As Ben and Audrey came in, he heard Audrey greet them.

Oh, Ben's band members.

To the right of the entryway, in a breakfast nook, a round kitchen table held the accoutrements of breakfast—juice, syrup, plates, sausages, and a massive pile of pancakes. He set his duffel down near the door, walked over to the long dining table, and stared at the massive map unrolled over the top.

"Hey, I'm Jonas," said one of the guys, not a band member by the looks of his shirt with the Vortex.com emblem on the breast. Good-looking guy who looked like he could handle himself. He reached out his hand.

Ty shook it. "Ty Remington. I'm with PEAK."

"Thanks for coming out."

"Of course. Chet's a good friend."

Jonas nodded, then glanced at Ben. Back to Ty. "We're also missing my brother, Creed. And, well, the newest update is that there are more kids and a coach missing."

"Kids?" Gage said, dropping his backpack onto a chair.

"High school and middle school runners," said a dark-haired version of Jonas. "Ned Marshall." He offered his hand to Ty, then Gage and Ian, who had joined them. "I was with Ben and Shae at the festival."

"It's Creed's cross-country team," Garrett said as he walked over. "Coffee anyone?"

Ty took the proffered cup, sipped the liquid black and hot, and the heat found his bones. He still vibrated from the chopper.

"Creed's a captain, and he called summer practice. Since our county school is combined, the high school team often practices with the middle school too. We think yesterday was one of those days."

Jenny Marshall came over, wiping her hand on a towel. "Ten kids are missing." Her reddened eyes betrayed a woman trying not to unravel. No wonder she was cooking enough pancakes to feed the entire defensive line for the Minnesota Vikings. "In total, there's thirteen people reported missing."

"I've mapped the path of the tornado," Jonas said, putting his finger down at the starting point of his line. "It touched down just north of the lake to the west of town, travelled along the shoreline, then headed south toward town. It dragged itself along the north side of the town, then jumped the highway and moved south following Garden Avenue, until it died out about two miles north of here."

"It looks like it was on the ground for about fifteen miles," Ty said.

"Twenty-five minutes. It started as an F-3, progressed to an F-4, and finished, well, they're still doing the math." Jonas wrapped a hand around the back of his neck. "The worst of it was north of the town. Right where Creed . . . and maybe Chet King were." He leaned on the map, picked up the salt shaker. "They were practicing outside town on a trail around the lake, so let's say this is Creed. He texted Mom at 5:05 when he finished practice, but he didn't mention the tornado."

Jonas reached for the butter dish and put it down on the northern shore of Duck Lake. "The twister hit the ground at 4:57 p.m. here and traveled about a half mile a minute. The trailhead is six miles away, so we can guess it hit their location about twelve minutes later, around 5:09. Hopefully Creed would have been gone by then, but he only had a four-minute lead."

He picked up the pepper shaker, then cast a look at Ben. "You said your dad left for the Duck Lake B & B right before you took the stage?"

"I took the stage around 5:00, and he left before that. Maybe 4:50?"

"The festival grounds are only three miles east of town." Jonas moved the pepper shaker along that route. "Considering he drove the speed limit, which is 40 through there, he would have been through the town of Duck Lake around 4:55, maybe already headed south around the actual lake by 5:00, although, given the traffic at that time of day, it's more likely he was here." He set the pepper shaker on the west side of the town limits.

"Of course, if he went south around the lake, he would have missed the funnel completely."

Ben drew in a long breath. "So, let's say he went north around the lake," Jonas continued. "That would have put him ahead of the tornado, but he could have spotted it."

"That's an awfully tight time frame," Ben said. "Anything—stoplights, traffic, even my dad's propensity to fiddle with the radio could have slowed him down as he went through town."

"Putting him right in the path of the tornado at 5:09," Jonas said.

"And maybe even passing Creed and the van of kids going to the high school," Ben concluded.

Ty ran the route in his head. "So, you're saying that Chet could have driven right into this thing?"

"Maybe," Jonas said.

Silence, a beat as the facts settled in.

"I'm sorry," Jonas said. "I'm just trying to create scenarios based on the weather."

"Chet is smarter than that," Ty said. "He's a pilot, for Pete's sake. He flew sorties in 'Nam. He had to learn to read weather, and I guarantee that he wouldn't have driven right into a wall of cumulonimbus clouds."

Jonas raised an eyebrow.

"I'm a pilot too," Ty said quietly.

Ben crossed his arms, his chest rising and falling. "He would have driven away from the twister, if he'd seen it, or driven someplace safe."

"So let's say you see a twister headed your direction. Where do you go?" This from Gage, who studied the map beside Ty. "Not west, into the storm, but south, then east, back through town?" He followed the path of the highway with his finger. "But the way the tornado ran, diagonally, this would have brought him right back into the path."

"He wouldn't have known that," Kacey said. "He would have just followed the road to get away."

"The sirens started going off in the town at 5:15," Jonas said. "If he turned around, that would put him right back in the center of town around then. Would he have taken shelter somewhere? Maybe he's still trapped in town."

"So, he might be somewhere in the destruction of the town of Duck Lake," Ben said quietly.

"Seems unlikely," Garrett said. "The EMS has been scouring the town for survivors."

"There's still three people, besides the cross-country team, unaccounted for," said Ned. "Chet is just one of them."

Right.

"And what about Creed?" Jenny asked. "Where would he have gone?"

"Back to the high school is my guess." Jonas ran his finger along the same route to town. "It's possible the twister intercepted them here, where it crossed the road, about a mile past the festival."

"And a couple miles before the school," Ned said. "That's where we should start looking."

"Is there a shelter they're taking everyone to?" Ian asked from where he stood behind Shae, his hands on her shoulders. "Maybe they're both there and just haven't been able to contact anyone."

"They're taking everyone to the community center in Winthrop," Garrett said. "Someone can take one of the winery trucks and check it out."

Ty glanced at him, nodded. "Good idea. Ian, you head to Winthrop."

"I'll take the chopper up, see if I can spot a white van, and . . . what was Chet driving?" Kacey asked.

"A rental. A gray Ford Taurus."

"Oh, that'll be easy to find," Gage said.

Ty shot him a frown but then put his gaze on Kacey. "I'll go with you. You're tired. You need a copilot."

No one said anything, but really, she needed a *pilot*.

She just nodded.

Jonas leaned forward. "I'll go to Duck Lake to talk to the police. We drove through there on our way here, and Brette got a number of pictures. Maybe she captured something we missed."

And just like that, Ty's world screeched to a halt, the name ringing in his ears, every muscle jerking. *Brette?*

His gaze followed Jonas, the casual way he walked over to the stairs. Leaned on the railing and shouted up. "Hey, Brette, you out of the shower yet? We need your camera!"

Ty's heart stopped. A sharp, brutal jolt that also cut off his breathing as a woman came down the stairs, toweling off her hair.

Her short, *very* short hair. She hung the towel around her neck. "It's in my pack, why?"

Gage's hand landed on Ty's shoulder, as if he was holding him back, or down, or maybe just trying to keep him from shaking as the woman he'd tried to forget walked over to her backpack and pulled out a rather nice Nikon. She turned to Jonas.

Her gaze fell on the congregation around the table. She blinked, and in that space of time, Ty's gut roared to life with such fury he nearly gasped.

Something devastating had happened to Brette Arnold. Her bones protruded from her face, her collarbone ridged out from the T-shirt that hung on her. Even her arms appeared thinner. And her hair—oh, that golden long hair had been shorn so short it now stuck up, as if she might be a cancer patient.

Still, despite the changes, she possessed a beauty that took a hold of him, riveted his gaze to her. Her blue-green eyes seemed bigger, albeit haunted.

He managed to close his mouth, swallow.

She'd been hurt, or maybe attacked, or something *terrible*—and she hadn't called him. That wounded him even more than the way her gaze bounced off him, the way she took a long breath, as if in resignation, and offered a grim smile to the group.

"Hi."

"Hey, Brette," Gage said from behind him. "Good to see you."

She simply nodded, turned to Jonas. "What are you looking for?"

"A gray Taurus. Or maybe a white van. Chet's car, and the cross-country coach's van."

"Okay. I'll take a look." She sat down at the bench near the door and flipped through her digital shots, not looking up.

Ty just stared at her. She wore a pair of baggy, faded jeans, her bare toes peeking out the cuffs.

He noticed a scar at her neck, something thick and dark red and it stirred a darkness through him. He'd find out what happened, and if anyone had hurt her . . .

"Everyone grab something to eat before you leave," Jenny Marshall was saying, but he barely heard her. His feet moved on their own.

"Ty—"

He ignored Gage. What was she doing here, with Jonas . . .

And then the thought had him around the throat.

Was she *with* Jonas? Dating him?

Jonas had helped himself to a plate of pancakes and a couple sausages and headed over to the coffeepot.

Ty couldn't stop moving, couldn't stop looking. Couldn't ignore the gut-twisting sense of regret that burned through him.

It didn't matter.

He should have searched harder for her. Should have never left well enough alone. And okay, yes, if she needed him, she would have called him—those words shouted somewhere in the back of his brain—but he couldn't get past the fact that he'd been *right*.

Something was desperately, horribly wrong with Brette Arnold.

His mouth, apparently, had stopped listening to his brain, right along with his feet, because he edged up to her and fell to his knees before her. She raised her eyes to him, frowning, gathering her breath, maybe to tell him to leave.

But he couldn't stop the words, the emotion, the shock from bubbling out of him as he reached out, so wanting to touch her. "Oh my gosh, Brette, what *happened* to you?"

4

WHEN HAD TY TURNED into such a jerk? *"Oh my gosh, Brette, what happened to you?"* Even as the words left his mouth, Ty wanted to yank them back. Or maybe reach out and clamp his hands over Brette's ears. No, *no*—

Appropriately, her eyes widened, her mouth opened. He cringed. "Oh, Brette, I'm so sorry. I . . . I don't know why I said that."

She took a breath. Then her eyes started to glaze, and she looked away. "No, it's fine. No big deal. I know I look . . . different."

Around him, the searchers were loading up their breakfast plates and shoveling food down as they outlined their search grid.

Ty had lost his appetite. "It's not fine. I can't believe I said that—I'm so sorry." He longed to take her hands, no, to pull her into his arms.

Tell her that she was safe, that whatever had happened to her would never happen again—

"I forgive you. Now, please just leave me alone." She ran her hand across her cheek, intensely focused on her camera.

He deserved that, he knew it. But he couldn't move, permanently affixed on his knees right in front of her.

Until Gage's hand on his arm dragged him to his feet. Gage,

who wore such a fierce, protective expression it made Ty wonder just how much Gage knew.

And then he found out. Because Gage hauled him out onto the front porch, closing the door behind him.

"Seriously?" Gage said. He had his long hair tied back in a low man bun, wore a bandanna around the whole mess, looking less SAR and more hitchhiker. Except for the seriousness in his eyes. "Dude, she had cancer."

Ty stared at Gage. *Cancer.*

"Yeah." Gage pitched his voice low. "She took off because she had breast cancer. She's been in and out of the hospital for the past year and a half. Had some pretty major surgery, if you know what I mean."

Oh. *Oh.* Then, wait one doggone moment . . . "She had cancer and you didn't tell me?"

He realized his voice held an edge, but he couldn't stop his emotions from running roughshod over his common sense.

"She asked Ella to keep her condition private. She didn't want anyone feeling sorry for her."

"She did this *alone*?" His voice had turned into a growl. He shook his head, darkness like a fist inside him. "I don't care what she said, she shouldn't have been alone."

Gage didn't move. "You better step back, pal, because I don't like the way you're looking at me."

Ty took a breath, his jaw tight. Yeah, maybe, because he had a visual right then of slamming his fist into his best friend's face.

He turned and walked away from Gage, down the porch. *Cancer.*

"It wasn't my idea not to tell you. And let's remember that she walked away from you."

Ty glanced at him, not sure he *shouldn't* act on his first impulse. Still, maybe this was his fault, at least partly. "She took off because she didn't want me paying her bills."

Gage had caught up to him. "Huh?"

"You and Ella weren't there—you were on the mountain searching for her brother—when Brette got really sick."

"I remember, she had appendicitis."

"Yeah. And I know it was only forty-eight hours, but we . . . we got close."

Gage raised an eyebrow, and Ty didn't contradict him. He relished the memory of their late-night conversation and the way she had let him kiss her when she woke from surgery. "So close, I thought we had a future." He turned away. "She didn't have any insurance. And when I found that out, I paid her hospital bill."

"Whoa, that's—"

Ty rounded on him. "C'mon. Besides, my family has a foundation for these kinds of things. But she was . . . furious."

"You barely knew each other, Ty. That's a pretty big step. What is it with this girl?"

Ty's voice dropped. "I knew her enough. And I'll tell you what's with this girl . . ." He stepped back, blew out a breath, and dredged up the raw, frustrating truth. "I can't shake her, Gage. Yeah, I only knew her for two days, but there was more than that between us. And I can't get her off my mind. Maybe it's because she has nobody else—"

"She has Ella."

Ty's mouth tightened.

"I'm just saying, she wasn't completely alone. But . . ." Gage nodded. "Okay, I do get it. I couldn't forget Ella either, regardless of how much I tried to kick her out of my system. But clearly Brette's not the person she was eighteen months ago, and maybe it's time to let her go."

Ty folded his arms. "By the looks of her, maybe it's time I step in." He glanced over his shoulder. "What's she doing with this Jonas Marshall guy, anyway?"

"She took a picture of a tornado last summer, in Colorado, and it ended up being sort of an internet sensation. Jonas runs a storm-chasing team, and she's hitched on with them this summer to be their reporter-slash-photographer."

And now Ella's words yesterday made horrifying sense. "You mean, she's been chasing tornadoes all summer? Risking her life?"

"She needed a job."

Ty closed his eyes.

"You can't fix everything, Ty."

He didn't want to fix everything. Just the things he could do something about. Like find Chet. And be a friend to Brette.

He wanted to weep at the haunted look in her eyes. "When I met her, Brette was . . . she was full of life. She searched for the good in people, wanted to write about heroes, and change the world just a little by her inspirational stories." He met Gage's eyes. "The woman I see sitting in there is dark and shadowed and hurting. And . . . it's killing me."

Despite himself, his emotions bled into his words. "I've been praying for her for nearly a year, bro, and for some reason, God brought her back on my radar today."

"Because Chet's missing," Gage said. "That's why we're here."

"We're here because someone needs help. It's not just Chet. Or Creed."

"Or me."

Brette stood on the porch, barefoot and holding a glass of juice. She set it on the railing. "Talk a little louder, I don't think the people in Missouri heard you."

"Sorry," Ty said, but frankly, he didn't care who heard him.

He cared about her, and it wasn't a secret to anyone who knew him.

Maybe, however, she hadn't gotten the message. He advanced toward her, ignoring Gage's warning look. "Brette, I'm sorry for what I said in there. But you should have told me that you were sick. I . . . I could have helped."

She drew in a breath. "See, that's the problem. Yeah, you would have helped. You would have dropped everything to take care of me, and I would have been helpless to stop you. I could barely crawl to the bathroom to throw up. Sometimes I just slept in there because I was too weak to go back to bed."

"Brette—"

"I would have started depending on you. Needing you. And yeah, you would have paid my massive bills, and then suddenly I would have looked up and you would be so far in my life I wouldn't be able to breathe without you."

"How is that bad?"

"Because I don't want to be dependent on anyone, Ty. I don't . . ." She closed her eyes, pinched the bridge of her nose. "It's never wise to depend on someone . . . they'll always let you down."

"That's not fair—"

Her eyes flashed. "My parents trusted Damien Taggert to invest their money, and he destroyed them."

Right. The author of the biggest Ponzi scheme in history, and the man to whom her parents had given their life savings. The savings they might have used to fight her mother's cancer. When all else had failed, her father had taken his life, trying to make it look like an accident in hopes of giving her the life insurance policy.

"I'm not seeing how I'm like Damien Taggert," Ty said quietly.

Her mouth tightened. "When I met you, you swept me off my feet. For the first time, I'd found a real hero. And then I found out you lied to me."

Ty opened his mouth to defend himself, but she held up her hand. "And it's not because you're a thief, like Damien, but because you care. Too much. You care *too much*, Ty."

She could have punched him with less effect.

"Listen, I get it. You were protecting your friend Jess, aka Selene Taggert, when you said you didn't know her. But you didn't think twice about paying my bill."

"I was trying to help."

"You're always trying to help. And all of that is gallant, but . . . that's my point. You're the kind of guy who wants to fix everything, but you can't fix this." She fanned her hands over her body.

"I don't have to fix it. I just wanted to . . . I wanted to help."

"I don't want your help."

He stared at her, the words digging in, finding root. "Okay, Brette. Fine. You're right, you don't owe me an explanation. Or even a footstep into your life. But I'm here if you need me."

She shook her head. "You just don't give up, do you?"

Kacey pushed out the door, onto the porch. "You ready to go, Ty?"

Not hardly. "Yeah."

Brette glanced at Kacey. "I'll go with you. We need aerial shots so we can blow them up and see if we missed anything."

"Good idea," Kacey said and stepped aside as Jonas, Ned, and Garrett, along with a few of Ben's bandmates, walked past them and headed to parked cars.

Ben came out, put his arm around Kacey, and drew her aside. Ty heard the conversation as he headed inside. "You're so tired, honey. Are you okay to fly?"

Brette hadn't said she didn't have feelings for him—in fact, it sounded like the opposite. *"I would have started depending on you. Needing you."*

Maybe he did care too much. Except, was there such a thing? And sorry, but the last thing he would do is let Brette down.

As long as he had strength in his body, he planned on being the guy who showed up, stayed the course. Rescued.

She didn't know him, not at all. And he barely knew her. But he knew one thing. God had brought her back into his life. And Ty planned on showing her exactly who he was.

The guy who cared so much he brought the people he loved home.

Really, she didn't know who she was anymore.

Brette put the earphones on and heard Kacey's voice over the coms, checking in with her passengers.

"All set," Brette said, her gaze on Ty, who sat in the other pilot seat, helping Kacey run through her checklist.

Yep, she simply hadn't believed her own words when she'd stood on that porch and neatly taken poor Ty apart. Ripped to shreds all his good intentions, deliberately wounding him.

He hadn't deserved it.

Because Ty was a good man. Kind and sweet and sacrificial, and when he'd been on his knees before her, his pale green eyes had looked at her with such longing, she nearly forgot her common sense and threw herself at him.

Nearly told him how it had broken her heart to leave him.

Sometimes she let herself imagine what it might have been like to stay, to cling to him. To let him be the hero she'd seen he could be.

But that what-if included her hair falling out in clumps in his hands, him scraping her off the bathroom floor, holding her as her body was racked with the dry heaves.

Cancer was embarrassing, heart-wrenching, and thoroughly exhausting, for the caregiver as much as for the patient. And Ty would spend himself for her, just like she had for her mother.

She'd seen that truth in his eyes when she'd woken after surgery to see him sitting by her bed. He wasn't walking out of her life. And she couldn't take him into the darkness with her.

They finished their preflight check and Kacey fired up the chopper. Brette had only ridden in a chopper once—with Eason. Unfortunately, the memory dragged up all the good reasons she needed to shut the door on Ty.

Despite how good he looked, with that dark hair tousled and nicking the collar of his shirt. He wore a T-shirt, a pair of jeans, and hiking boots and looked every inch the guy who could save the day.

Keep the storms from destroying her world.

Worse, the man had an addicting kind of smile, and she probably needed to avert her eyes around him.

Ty handed back a map, a search grid of the area to the south of Highway 7, the first possible escape point.

Ben, Jonas, and the rest of the searchers would take the highways and side roads around Duck Lake.

The power of the bird hummed through her as they took off. They rose above the baseball field, then higher, until they soared over houses, the main street. Not high enough for the cars to turn to Matchbox, but it afforded her an ample view to snap a wide shot of the destruction.

"I'll fly along the highway, first one side, then the other. If you see something and you want me to come in closer, let me know," Kacey said.

They lifted over the tiny town of Chester, then headed west. She snapped a shot of the Marshall vineyard, and then Kacey angled them along Garden Avenue.

The sun had turned the fields a rich emerald, still glistening with the dew. From this angle, Brette got a view of the totality of the tornado's power—trees torn from the roots now strewn on metal buildings, machinery upended, fencing wadded and tangled. Like a spoon, the twister had dragged through the road, carving out a trough now filled with water and debris.

Brette took a picture of the destructive trail through the fields. The crops were squashed and ripped as if trampled by the legendary blue ox.

The carcasses of cows and a horse bloated in the morning sun.

They flew past a family digging through the splinters of what had once been a garage. A damaged silo spilled a half-year's harvest of sorghum onto the earth.

She took a shot of a car trapped in a copse of trees and even pointed it out to Ty. He nodded, and Kacey flew in for a closer look.

A pickup, rusted, its back end filled with water.

They flew on and finally hit the highway. In the ditch, a giant power line stanchion was mangled like a twisty tie. She imagined herself being chased by a tornado—where would she go?

Definitely not toward the dilapidated gray barn, its slats strewn across a barren yard. Or toward the steel feed bins, now gutted.

It gave her a moment of pause. Where did someone go for shelter when they were facing death?

She glanced at Ty, those wide shoulders. He navigated for Kacey as they worked the search grid.

"I used to be a pilot." She didn't know why, but the words he'd spoken to her eighteen months ago shifted through her. That, and the fact that although he hadn't told her everything, he'd been *willing* to tell her the story of his accident, the one that had destroyed his knee and nearly gotten Chet King killed.

She hadn't thought about how this search might dredge up memories, even a desperation to find the man he'd nearly killed, to save his life, again.

"We were caught in a tornado this summer and we had to get out and hide in a ditch," she said into her mic.

Ty turned in his seat, his eyes hard in hers.

So maybe she shouldn't have said that, but . . . "What if Chet did that? Maybe his car got swept up, and he's just wandering around in a field."

Ty paused. "Good thinking."

She focused on the ditches but saw nothing that looked like a gray Taurus.

They repeated the search along the next stretch of highway, this one farther west and untouched by the tornado.

"Where to now?" Kacey said, glancing at Ty.

He ran his finger along the highway. "Let's follow the tornado's path north."

Kacey took them along the highway, where the funnel had jumped the asphalt, and then north toward the school.

Brette spied Jonas talking with a cop in the parking lot of the school. A small group of what she assumed might be worried parents wandered around the debris. Jonas looked up, tenting his hand over his eyes.

They followed the highway toward town, taking the trail through the festival grounds. She took shots of the upturned RVs, the tents strewn across the mud, the remains of the snack shacks. She spied the building where Ben and Shae had hidden out, a warehouse in the middle of the parking lot. Toppled semis lay like carcasses glinting in the sunlight.

They flew farther north, toward Duck Lake, and the destruction lessened, with only a house or two in the path. A suburban pocket of new construction, however, lay in splinters, an entire neighborhood of uninhabited, newly developed houses down to two-foot boards.

The road to the housing development dead-ended in a depressed culvert jammed with construction debris. An excavator had fallen on its side, the treads like feet against a drainage culvert.

"At least the neighborhood was still uninhabited," Ty said in his mic, voicing her thoughts.

Duck Lake glistened in the distance, on the other side of a two-lane paved road. Off the side of the road, an abandoned farmhouse had lost its roof. Giant elms, probably once planted by an industrious owner, littered the drive like sticks after a storm, the branches turning to gnarled hands reaching heavenward in supplication. A windmill miraculously missing only a few of its blades blew in the breeze.

As they drew nearer, she spied a glint of metal hidden under the great branches and focused on it. Snapped a shot, then looked at it.

"Get in closer to that car." She leaned up, pointing to the tree off to their right.

Kacey angled the chopper toward the tree, hovered above, and Brette took another shot. The tree had fallen smack on top of the car, crushing the roof. She handed her camera up to Ty. "That look like a Taurus to you?"

"I don't know. But it's gray. Kacey, can you put her down?"

Kacey angled the chopper away, to a nearby field.

Ty was out nearly before the rotors stopped spinning, Brette on his heels. The air still smelled of fresh-cut grass, so much torn foliage and dirt in the wind. The car's hood was pancaked beneath the broken trunk of the elms, encased in its scruffy arms. Ty scrambled over to the car. Peered in the window. "There's someone in here!"

Oh no, *no* . . .

She remembered Chet from her time in Montana. Kind, wise, in his early seventies. Salt-and-pepper hair, blue eyes like his son, Ben—and with his wry smile, he sort of reminded her of Harrison Ford, the recent version. *Please, please, let him be alive.*

Ty was pulling at the door.

She peered in the other side.

Crushed along the front seat, a man lay unconscious. "Hey there!" She pounded on the hood, trying to wake him, but he didn't move. Cracks webbed the front glass.

"I can't get the door open." Ty climbed onto the hood and peered into the glass. "It doesn't look like Chet, but . . . this is definitely a gray Taurus."

"Maybe it's the owner." She glanced at the farmhouse. From here, she could see that another elm had crashed through the roof in the back, tearing through the house. Glass littered the lawn, and curtains were blowing through the windows. But otherwise, the place looked deserted—the grass was jungle high, vines were snaking through the siding, and the paint was peeling off the porch.

"I don't think he belongs here. He might have been trying to get away from the storm."

And only managed to trap himself in his car. Her thoughts ran back to the near miss in Dodge, the way she'd fought Jonas's help.

"I'll call the team," Kacey said and ran back to the chopper.

"Do you think he's dead?" Brette said.

"I don't know, but we need to get in there and assess him. I think I can go in through the back window."

"Ty, be serious. That tree is heavy, and any shift of weight could make it fall farther."

He slid off the hood. "I am serious. He needs help, and I'm not just going to stand here and wait for the team to show up." He jogged toward the chopper and returned with a large duffel bag.

He set it down, opened the bag, and dragged out a blanket, gloves, and what looked like a long, curved wrench. "Aw, I love ya, Gage."

"What is that?"

"It's a rescue tool—sort of a wrench and pry bar." He picked up the blanket and headed to the back of the car. "Okay, listen, you watch the tree. Tell me how much it moves."

How much, not if. Oh, she didn't like this.

Kacey was running back to him. "Ty, what are you doing?"

He stepped up to the back window, put on the gloves, and shoved the pry bar into the frame. "Getting inside."

The window broke, shattering in one solid, webbed piece as he worked the bar into the frame, but the safety glass kept it from exploding out. After managing to tear it free from the frame, he grabbed the glass and peeled it out in nearly one piece. It fell onto the lawn.

"I'm going in."

"Oh, Ty, please be careful." Brette couldn't help it, nor the tone of her voice as he stretched his lanky self over the trunk, then slid into the hole made by the back window. The tree had crushed the roof onto the front bucket seats, but Ty was able to scoot into the back and crouch into the well of the backseats.

Kacey pointed the flashlight into the depths of the car, which was shadowed and creaking with the adjustment of Ty's weight.

"He's wedged over the console," Ty said. "I think I can reach his carotid artery."

He pressed his arm through the opening between the seats.

If she'd doubted it before, watching Ty maneuver his way into the tiny compartment told Brette one thing. Yes, he cared, too much, but didn't people need rescuers in their lives, people who wouldn't give up on them?

"I got a pulse! He's alive!" Ty backed out just as she heard a siren mourning into the midafternoon air. A police cruiser, followed by Jonas's Suburban, kicked up mud as the vehicles turned into the farm drive.

"We have a fire truck on the way," the patrolman said as he got out.

Ty had turned back to the victim and was speaking in low tones.

"We need chainsaws, chains, and muscle," Kacey said as Jonas ran over.

"I have a toolbox in the bed of my truck," Garrett said and headed for his truck.

Moments later, they had assembled and gripped one end of the tree as Garrett Marshall attacked it with the chainsaw.

One section of the massive elm separated from the roots, guided to the ground by the team.

Jonas climbed onto the hood and took the chainsaw and safety glasses from his father and attacked the massive trunk from the other side. The other side fell, leaving only the trunk that dented the car.

"Let's get this tree off the roof!"

Ty was still inside.

"I'm not leaving him," he said, looking out the back window at Brette. "He's awake, I think. He's got ahold of my hand." He glanced out at his team. "Try not to kill me!"

Not funny.

A truck pulled in, and in a second, Gage and Ben piled out.

"Get him out!" Ben said.

"It's not Chet," Kacey said, intercepting him, her hands on his shoulders.

"But this is his rental vehicle," Ben said. "I recognize the plates."

Indiana plates. Yes, maybe a rental. Brette took a picture of the team fighting with the tree.

"Let's see if we can roll it off the front," Garrett said.

The team, including Kacey and the cop, braced themselves on one side, Jonas, Ned, and Garrett on the other, and on the count of three they picked it up and rolled it over the hood. It smashed onto the ground with a lethal thud.

Gage went to work on the driver's door. "No good—we gotta go through the back."

In a moment, he'd wedged the back driver's side door open. "Let me in, Ty."

"No. I got an idea—can you rip off the back of the driver's seat?

Or maybe put it down all the way? We could maneuver him out through the back."

Gage was already reaching inside for the drop handle. The seat fell back. Ty did the same with his side.

"Let's get a collar on him before we move him," Gage said and handed a pressure cuff to Ty.

Ty took his pressure.

"His pulse is weak, and he's lost a lot of blood," Ty said through the broken window. "Slide in a backboard."

He worked on the collar while Kacey procured a backboard from the chopper. Gage and Ben moved the victim's legs onto the board as Ty held his head steady, then in one motion they rolled him onto the board.

"Slide him out—I'm stuck in here," Ty said.

The man came out of the car, Ty balancing his head. He bumped his own on the car getting out, and Brette winced.

They put him on the ground, and Gage dropped down beside him to check his vitals. Brette put down her camera, a little woozy at the man's injuries. A dislocated and severely lacerated shoulder, a head trauma from the ugly hematoma over his eyes, and internal bleeding, given the bruise that turned his skin a deep red along his stomach.

"Who is he?"

The patrolman walked over. "Oh, wow. That's Craig Nelson. He's one of the assistant coaches for the cross-country team."

"What's he doing in my dad's car?" Ben asked.

"His BP is low—we need to get him to a hospital," Gage said, removing the cuff. He flickered his phone light over the man's eyes. "His pupils are unequal but reactive. He's got a serious head trauma."

He stood up. Looked at the patrolman.

"There's a clinic in Winthrop, but the closest trauma hospital with a helipad is the Ridgecrest Medical Center in Waconia."

"Call them," Ty said. He walked over to the chopper, and as Brette watched, he began taking out her seat, along with the one next to it. He dumped them on the grass.

Ben picked up one end of the stretcher, Gage the other.

And just like that, they'd loaded Craig into the chopper, secured him to the floor. Gage got into the back, and Kacey strode toward the chopper.

"I'm going," Ben said. "I need to know if he knows anything about my dad."

Ty had caught up to him. "Ben—listen, I'll go. Kacey needs a copilot—"

"Give it up, Ty. We all know you're not flying this chopper anytime soon. I need to be there, find out what happened. Gage will come with us. You take the truck and keep looking."

Brette wanted to flinch at the look on Ty's face, the intake of his breath, the way his mouth tightened. She searched for fight in his eyes, but he blew out a breath, nodded. "We'll keep you posted."

Huh.

Ty stepped away from the chopper as Kacey fired it up.

By the time the fire engine had arrived, the bird had lifted off and was soaring into the blue.

Ty cupped his hand over his eyes, watching it go. Jonas pulled a map out of the glove compartment of his vehicle and spread it over the hood, ready for a new search grid.

But Ty kept watching the chopper, so much raw worry, even a hint of regret on his face, that Brette couldn't help but wonder if that was the expression he'd worn when she walked out of his life.

And heaven forgive her, a weak, pitiful side of her desperately hoped so.

Ben wasn't sure how, but he'd managed to make everything worse. Instead of spending the weekend, right now, married to his beautiful fiancée, enjoying the first night of a very overdue honeymoon, he was pacing the waiting area of Ridgecrest Medical Center. Alternated staring down the hallway toward the ICU and turning to look out the window at the manicured lawns and the parking lot.

Occasionally his gaze landed on Kacey, who'd curled up on the waiting area love seat, her head on her hands, collapsed into slumber.

He sat down on the chair next to her, wanting to run his fingers through her curly hair, trace the way it ribboned down her neck. She slept hard, falling completely away within seconds of putting her head down, a practice probably honed from her years in the military sleeping on cots, dirt, or wherever she could find shut-eye.

They'd lived such different lives. The regret could consume him if he let it, the way events had played out sixteen years ago when their daughter Audrey was born. He'd managed to rebuild their life into something close to what they'd dreamed of during their teenage romance.

Almost.

He leaned forward, scrubbed his hands down his face. If he hadn't been so intent on rebuilding his music career too, if he hadn't decided to start a record label in the nowheresville of western Montana, their lives might be perfect right now. Okay, maybe he would be shuttling back and forth to Nashville to resurrect his career, probably going out on tour for a few months at a time. But the choice to start his own label also meant he had to manage the album production and releases of the fledgling artists he'd signed. It meant investment, which meant capital, which meant him practically living on the road to scrub up enough cash with his own talents to float the launch of the rookies he'd signed.

And yes, when those rookies sold albums, the money eventually made it back to Mountain Song Records, only to be recycled for more advertising, more production costs.

He leaned back, exhausted with the numbers.

With his life.

With the longing to leap off the hamster wheel and just be a husband. A dad to the most amazing daughter on the planet.

And a son to a dad who'd already had one brush with death.

He couldn't go through this again.

Lord, please, please let my dad be okay.

Ben pulled out his phone and texted Ty. *Have you found him?* He'd been a little rough on the guy back when Ty suggested getting into the chopper, but Ben offered desperation as his excuse.

Ty texted back in moments. *No, sorry. Still looking.*

Maybe his incoming text had awakened Kacey, because she sat up, blinked. She pulled the ponytail holder from her hair and finger combed it. "Is Craig out of surgery?"

"Yeah. They said they'll let me know when he wakes up."

"Has his family been notified?"

"I don't know. I left that to the police. But it's been nearly four hours since we got here . . ." He sighed and she looked over at him.

"My dad's been missing for nearly twenty-four hours." He shook his head. "He's so resourceful. The fact that he hasn't gotten to help . . ."

To his horror, his throat tightened, his eyes burned. He looked away from her, blinking.

"Babe." She came around in front of him, kneeling before him. "It's going to be okay. We'll find him."

"It's all my fault." Shoot, his voice emerged just a little wrecked. But, there it was. "I screwed everything up."

She frowned.

He met her beautiful eyes. "I thought I could juggle our lives and figure it out, but . . . I'm in over my head, Kace. I never see you, and Audrey's growing up without me. And my dad . . ." His voice broke, and he closed his eyes. "He's out here because of me. And I can't live this way anymore."

Kacey put her arms around him. "We don't have to talk about this right now, Ben." She tucked his head on her shoulder. "It's okay, I get it. I've been . . . I agree. It's . . . hard. Too hard."

He closed his eyes, his hand over his mouth to keep himself from completely unraveling. Took a shaky breath.

"Shh," she said, and he leaned into her embrace. He wanted to stay like this forever, no more goodbyes, no more long-distance phone calls and Skype sessions. He wanted to go out on the searches with her and maybe someday have more children, and finally move into the home he'd purchased for them, let her fill it with all the things that made Kacey exactly the woman he loved. Always loved, from the first day he'd met her.

He lifted his face and caught hers in his hands, the emotions thick in his chest. Her eyes widened only a moment before he leaned down and kissed her. Something sweet and lingering, reacquainting himself with the taste of her. Salty skin from the long hours she'd already put in, but beneath that, he savored the deeper, familiar fragrance that belonged to the woman who would be his wife. His hand went to her hair, his fingers tangled through it. He backed away, touched his forehead to hers, still trying not to cry. "Wow, I love you."

Tears glistened in her eyes as she nodded. "I love you too. I always will, no matter what happens." She took a breath, and he noticed how it shuddered out, as if she might miss him just as much.

The need, the hunger for her rose through him, made him lean toward her. But she stopped him, taking his hands in hers. "I just think, though, we shouldn't make it any harder than it is."

Oh. Right. Because seventeen years ago they'd walked down that road, went too far, and well, he would never call Audrey a mistake, but they were trying to walk a different path this time around.

He nodded, but really, what did she think would happen here in the waiting room?

Still, maybe the last thing they needed was him stirring up temptation. "Okay."

"Okay," she said, her mouth a tight line.

A nurse emerged from the double doors. She wore a lavender uniform, her blonde hair in a ponytail. "Hey. I'm Jen. You wanted to see your brother?"

Ben startled just for a second before he realized his lie had circled back around. "Yeah."

"He's awake but a little groggy, but I'm sure he'll be glad to see family."

Kacey gave him a sidelong glance.

They followed Jen down a hallway, through double doors, and found Craig in a bed in the recovery room, attached to an IV, a heart monitor, and oxygen.

The chill in the room raised gooseflesh on Ben's arm, seeped into his bones. Kacey slipped her hand into his.

"Can I talk to him?" Ben asked.

"Yeah, go ahead. I'll be at the desk if you need me." Jen headed across the room to a counter flanked by monitors.

Ben stepped up to the bed rail. "Uh . . ." He leaned close. "Craig. Can you wake up, buddy?"

Eyelids flickered and the man rolled his eyes toward Ben. "Who are you?"

Ben glanced at the nurse, but the mumble wouldn't reach the desk, so . . . "I'm one of the guys who found you. You were in a car, under a tree."

"Mmmhmm."

"But the car—it belongs to a guy named Chet King. He's . . . my dad. And I'm looking for him. How did you get the car, and . . . where's my dad?"

Craig looked at him, blinking heavily. "Um . . . he . . ."

His eyes closed.

"Aw, c'mon, stay with me."

Craig's eyes opened again. "Who are you?"

"We found you," Kacey said, her voice a little rougher than Ben's. "What were you doing in that car?"

He looked at her. "I was trying to get away."

"From the tornado?"

"Mmmhmm."

"But where did you get the car?"

"From the ole guy . . . I wen' to the house. I wanted to fin' a shelter, but he pulled up. Tol' me to keep driving . . ."

"It's like talking to a drunk man," Kacey muttered.

Craig, however, ignored her. "I didn't wanna go. He said we had no time . . . and then, it was *there.* Ri' there. So loud. An . . . He leff me there."

Ben stared at him. "He *left* you there?"

"He leff me. Just leff me. So I hid, but . . . storm was too big. I got in the car . . ." His eyes closed. "So loud. So . . ."

"Where is the van? And what happened to the old guy?"

"Dunno," he said, his eyes still closed. "They *leff* me." He took a long breath, sighed. "The kids . . . they leff me!" He closed his eyes, emitted a snore.

Ben took Kacey's hand. "C'mon."

He nodded to the nurse as they left the recovery area and headed out past the waiting room, all the way up the stairs to the roof. He dialed Ty.

"Anything?" Ty said, without greeting.

"Yeah. I think I know what happened. I'll bet my dad saw the clouds on his way to the B & B. Maybe he even turned around, but somehow he met the van of kids. Sounds like Craig had pulled up to the farm, hoping to find a storm shelter. Maybe my dad saw him and realized they didn't have time, that their best bet was to keep driving, outrun the storm, but the driver didn't want to. It sounds like my dad made the hard decision to leave him there and take off with the kids."

"He took the van?"

"Apparently."

"And where did he go?"

"I don't know. Craig said the twister was on top of them, so my guess is, as far away as he could get."

"Okay, we'll map it out, come up with a new search grid. Are you coming back?"

Ben looked at Kacey still holding his hand. "Yeah. We'll meet you back at the Marshalls'."

He hung up and shoved the phone into his pocket. Kacey glanced at the chopper. "I need to do my preflight check."

"I know. But first . . ." He pulled her to himself, his arms around her, holding her tight, just needing to hang on for a moment, to feel something solid and real and permanent. Something that wouldn't disappear when life swept in and knocked him over.

"Babe," he said, putting her away from him, meeting her eyes. "Thank you for being here, for staying with me, for flying out through the night from Montana. I don't know what I would do without you."

She touched her hand to his cheek. Sighed. "I'll always be here for you, Ben."

Then she kissed his cheek in the soft place right below his eye, and he sighed, a long release of the regret and fear wadded up in his chest.

Then she turned and headed to her chopper.

The first thing he planned on doing after he found his father was to marry the woman he couldn't live without one day longer.

5

THEY WERE RUNNING OUT of daylight. Right now, Chet could be injured. Dying. And Ty couldn't do a thing about it.

Ty leaned up from the kitchen table where Jonas and his family, as well as Ben's bandmates and the PEAK team, had reunited to enact a new game plan.

Gage had gone upstairs to grab a shower, probably to wake himself up. A stack of chocolate chip cookies piled next to where Jonas drew their search routes on the map.

The Marshall family kitchen stirred together the scents of fresh-baked cookies and the sloppy joe meat simmering in the slow cooker, ready to feed the army of searchers.

"I don't know what else to do," Jenny Marshall had said to Ty as she handed him a couple cookies wrapped in a napkin. "I keep thinking, if I feed you all, you'll have the energy to keep looking and bring my boy home."

They were all grasping at anything, any ideas, at a fragile hope. But the fruitless search had started to turn them all brittle. Worse, Ty's gut had stopped talking to him. He hadn't a clue where to look for Chet.

Ben's words burned inside him. *"Give it up, Ty. We all know you're not flying this chopper anytime soon."*

The words had dug in, sharp-edged, bruising him all day.

Now, the barbs flared to life as Ben and Kacey walked into the farmhouse, as Kacey slid onto a stool at the long counter, burying her head in her folded arms.

At the end of the table, Brette worked on her computer. She wore a baseball cap with the Vortex.com logo on the crown, a T-shirt, and yoga pants, and bit the corner of her lip as she downloaded and blew up each aerial picture she'd shot.

A glass of milk and a cookie sat untouched beside her.

She'd said nothing to him, except for a "good job" as they climbed into the truck Ben and Gage had vacated and resumed the search. Funny that she chose him to search with, since there was plenty of room in Jonas's car. But he chalked it up to the fact that they'd started the search together.

Ben came over to the map, appearing fierce and exhausted. He bent over the map. "Craig said that my dad intercepted him at the farmhouse." He took a cookie and used it as a marker, drawing it south, along the path of the tornado. "Apparently, my dad ended up taking the van, with the kids, hoping to outrun the funnel."

"But in what direction?" Ned asked. He'd grabbed a sloppy joe sandwich and spoke with a full mouth. Shae came up behind him, eating a handful of potato chips.

"At this point, driving north would have put him into the mouth of the twister, so, my guess is south," Jonas said. He took a drink of his milk. "But we already drove that road, a couple times. No sign of the van."

And there it was. They'd run out of places to look. Silence fell as they scoured the map.

Brette leaned back, took off her hat, and ran her hands through her short hair. About two inches long, it curled into unruly waves around her head. It had grown back in variegated shades of blonde, darker at the roots, lighter as it grew longer. The shorter look highlighted her cheekbones, made her eyes wider, more luminous.

He liked it.

Too much.

Ty blew out a breath, took his milk, and walked out onto the stone patio. It overlooked the vineyards, with a grape trellis thick with foliage that folded along the top of the beamed portico roof. Teak Adirondack chairs circled a fire pit, and he imagined the Marshall family during happier days, roasting marshmallows.

Ty sat in one of the chairs, set his milk on the edge of the stone pit, and leaned back, closing his eyes. *Lord, we could use a little help here.*

The protest of the screen door made him open his eyes. Brette came outside, carrying her laptop, and walked over to where he sat.

"Do you mind?"

He raised an eyebrow. "No."

She sat down, balancing her laptop on one of the chair arms. Stared out at the vineyard. "I remember when Gage and Ella were looking for her brother. The waiting was the hardest part."

"Yeah. Except we're not waiting. We're grasping at anything to give us a clue where they might be." He leaned forward and reached for his milk. "I don't know what's harder—to be the rescuer or to be the desperate one waiting for rescue."

He took a drink of his milk. Wiped his thumb across his upper lip. "After Chet and I crashed the chopper, he was in bad shape and we did nothing for about eight hours, waiting for rescue. It didn't look good. We'd been blown off course, lost in the mountains in the middle of the night. The next morning, we woke to a sky that had turned to soup. A late-season blizzard. I had to make the hard choice whether to hike out or stay with Chet."

He stared at his half-full glass of milk. "I decided that we couldn't wait, and I started hiking out."

"Didn't you have a broken knee?"

He glanced at her. "Good memory. Yeah. It was . . . brutal. I fashioned crutches and a splint, but there were times I just wanted to collapse, just stay there and die."

She looked out, beyond him. "Yeah, I get that. I wanted to curl into a ball and die for most of last year."

He fought the urge to suggest that she hadn't needed to do that alone.

"There was this little chapel off my ward that was always empty. It had a view of a lake, and sometimes I'd just go down there, camp out on the floor, and try not to wish I could die."

He tightened his jaw.

"I'm sorry for what I said to you earlier, Ty."

He glanced at her, frowning.

She had lifted her gaze, caught his. "The truth is, it hurts for you to give me so much when I can't . . ."

"You think I want something from you, Brette?"

Her mouth tightened, and her eyes glistened. She looked away, out toward the late-afternoon sky, the line of innocuous clouds tufted against the deep blue. "I . . ." She sighed. "After my mother died, I was alone. Really alone. I started attending Middlebury, and I was a little overwhelmed. I had no money, I had a full course load, was working as a journalist for the local paper, and I met this fraternity guy."

He should walk away, right now, before she told him more than he could bear.

"Eason had money and a car, and he offered to help. He'd drive me to work and school, and once he paid my rent without me asking . . ."

Ty winced.

"Then came the day when . . . well, it might have been partly my fault, but we were at his frat house and it was late and he'd had too much to drink and—"

"Oh, Brette, please tell me he didn't . . ."

She drew in a breath, looked at her hands. "Maybe he thought he was entitled, I don't know. But I didn't go down without a fight, and afterward I ran out of the frat house without even one of the guys acknowledging that they'd heard anything."

He leaned forward, his head in his hands, his stomach knotted.

"Ella took me to the hospital, and they did a rape kit, but . . . he had money, and I was in his room, had been drinking . . ."

Ty got up, walked away from her, took a deep breath. Grabbed on to a pole as he stared out into the vineyard.

She'd gone silent.

"So, he got away with it," Ty said quietly.

More silence, and he turned, almost expecting her to be in tears.

She sat staring at him, her face stoic. "I dropped the charges. But I made a vow—"

"That you wouldn't depend on anyone."

She lifted a shoulder, gave him a wry smile. It vanished fast, however, leaving behind just the raw, stripped truth.

He was wealthy. And he'd paid for her hospital bill. And then he'd gotten angry with her for not being allowed into her life. Almost as if he might be forcing himself on her.

"Oh Brette, I'm so sorry. I never . . ." He came over to the fire pit and sat on the edge. "You have to know that I never would think, never—" He blew out a breath, shook his head, not able to put any of it in words.

"I know," she said softly, the toughness dropping from her expression. "I do know that. Now. But I was scared and I thought it would be better if I was alone." She swallowed. "I still do."

He frowned, passion building in his retort, but the sudden wash of fear in her eyes stepped it back. His voice softened. "Listen, Brette. I'm not asking for anything but to be your friend, okay? I know we started something, and yeah, I haven't stopped thinking about you for over a year. But more than anything, I hate the thought of you being alone." No, he wouldn't reach out, take her hand. He fisted his hand closed on his knee. "No one should go through what you have by yourself. You deserved to have someone with you who cares about you."

Now she did blink hard, as if fighting tears.

"For the record, I regret not chasing after you, although I did try to find you."

"I know. I got every one of your voicemails and text messages."

He tried not to let that dig a hole through him.

"I meant what I said last year. You are a hero, Ty. I couldn't believe it when you climbed into that car today. You could have been injured or killed—"

"It's the least I could do."

She stared at him. "Wait, does this have something to do with what Ben said? That you aren't ever going to fly again?"

He stilled. Swallowed past the fist that suddenly grabbed his throat. Looked away. "I nearly killed Chet . . ."

"It was an *accident*."

"An accident that could have been averted," he said softly. "I did the preflight check and . . . well, we were low on oil pressure and I missed it." He couldn't bear to tell her the rest.

"Still, an accident."

Then, before he could elaborate, she pressed her hand to his closed fist. "You didn't make it through that storm on a broken knee only to never fly again. You need to forgive yourself and get back to flying."

"Maybe I don't deserve to fly again."

"Like I don't deserve to . . . to have someone care about me? Take care of me?" She managed a tiny smile.

But the smile reached in, and in a moment, the light and beauty and all the crazy, unrequited feelings he'd been trying to douse for more than a year exploded inside of him.

The woman he'd known was still in there. The one who believed in hope, who looked for the good in people and wanted to inspire with her stories.

He saw her in his mind's eye, laughing, a smile lighting her face, those green-blue eyes shining as she looked at him. He could almost feel her arms around his neck, her body pressed to his. The hunger thickened inside him. How he longed to be everything she needed.

Maybe the desire shone on his face because she was just staring at him. "You okay?"

"You have so much to give, Brette, even if you don't know it."

Her smile dimmed. But he didn't care. "And yeah, you do deserve to have someone care about you. Someone who wants nothing from you. Okay?"

She gave him a dubious look but lifted a shoulder anyway.

But it was enough. Because she chased it with another smile.

"Good. Now, let's find Chet King, okay?"

Kacey could sleep for a week, even if it might be on a gravelly, bug-infested bed under a blazing sun.

For now, however, the granite counter would do. She nested her head into her arms, listening to the conversations around her, a quiet hum in the large room. She had taken two freshly baked cookies from Audrey, who wore an apron and helped Jenny feed the rescuers. But the sweets churned in her gut.

If she hoped to climb back into the cockpit, she needed protein, an energy drink, and . . . well, a quiet place to cry. *"I can't live this way anymore."*

How had she managed to hold herself together as Ben delivered those words, his sweet blue eyes filling with the same agony that burned through her veins, all the way to her heart. Yeah, she'd been thinking the same thing, but for him to admit it . . .

Oh, if she were honest with herself, she'd wanted to be wrong. She'd wanted to tell him that she couldn't live without him. That she wanted him to come home, be a family and finish what they'd started seventeen years ago. At least that was what her heart screamed as he kissed her so sweetly.

But her brain, her common sense, the former soldier in her had done the speaking for her. *"It's okay, I get it. I've been . . . I agree. It's . . . hard. Too hard."*

Her breath shuddered out, and she gulped it back before she dissolved into tears.

The last thing Audrey needed was her mother turning into a brokenhearted puddle with her grandfather still missing.

No, Kacey had to hold herself together, right now, and possibly for a good long while. *"I'll always be here for you, Ben."*

Yes, she meant it, but how much harder it would be now. *Please let Chet be okay.* Then she could get home and start building a world without the love of her life.

She heard Ben's voice from across the room, discussing with Jonas the possible escape route Chet might have taken. Without effort, his latest single hummed inside her.

Turn down the lights
Turn up the songs
Come dance with me, baby
Right where you belong

She bit back a whimper, hating that Ben had the ability to tear her asunder with a song. She might as well give in and find a place to unravel, at least to get it out of her system.

The back door squealed, and she lifted her head to see Brette and Ty walk in. Brette carried her open computer and now set it on the table, right on the map. "I found something."

Kacey slid off the stool and gathered with the rest around Brette's computer.

She'd downloaded a picture of what looked like a construction site. "I took this as we headed northwest, toward the lake. It's a cul-de-sac neighborhood in development, completely destroyed, but . . . look at this." She blew up the picture to 300 percent and moved her cursor to the center of the screen over what looked like a tumble of plywood and two-by-fours. "Look right here."

Even Kacey leaned forward. "Is that a white car?"

"A white van, maybe. It's on its side, so my guess is that it was blown into the house, and with all the debris, we couldn't see it from the air. And I don't think anyone even went up this road. It's not even finished."

"You think they're in the van?" Ben said.

"It's a good place to start," Ty said.

Ben nodded, and Jonas blew out a breath, backed away, folded his hands behind his neck.

"We've only got a couple hours of daylight left. Let's get going," Garrett said.

Kacey turned, but Ben grabbed her arm. "Babe." The other searchers headed toward the door.

She frowned at him.

"You're staying here." His voice settled inside her. "You're dead on your feet. Get some shut-eye, and if we find my dad and need your help, I'll call you, I promise."

She blinked at him, her mouth opening, but he touched her cheek, shook his head. "I need you fresh and on your game in case this is bad." His mouth tightened into a grim line.

Right. To hold him together. He made a point of glancing at Audrey too.

"Please," he added softly.

She nodded.

"That's my girl," he said and kissed her forehead before heading out.

Oh. Would she ever get over not hearing those words anymore?

"I put your bag upstairs in the bedroom at the end of the hall," Jenny said, glancing up from where she was loading the dishwasher. Audrey removed her apron and came over to Kacey.

"I'll show you, Mom."

She led her mother up the stairs and down a hall balanced on either side with bedrooms. Most of the rooms were jammed with duffel bags and sleeping bags on the floor. Audrey led her to a room with two twin beds. A patchwork quilt lay on each bed, adorned with fluffy white pillows. Her duffel sat on a bench at the foot of one of the beds. A sleeping bag was spread out on the other side of the bed, Audrey's backpack situated at the end.

Clearly, they'd be bunking with some other female guest.

"I like this house," Audrey said. "I was thinking maybe my new bedroom in Dad's house could have a fireplace." She gestured to a vintage fireplace that held a scattering of white candles.

Kacey just reached for her. "I'm sure it can, honey." She kissed the top of her head before she let her go and sank onto the twin bed. She curled her legs up, put her head on the pillow. Closed her gritty eyes.

"Do you think they'll find Grandpa?"

"Yes, honey. I know we will."

Audrey sank on the bed opposite her. "Good. 'Cause Dad looks so upset, and so do you."

"Everything is going to be fine. I promise."

"Really? Because Dad's been working so hard and he's been away so much . . . He was really looking forward to this weekend, you know?"

Kacey stilled. "What do you mean?"

"Just . . ." Audrey swallowed, fear rippling across her face that made Kacey sit up. "He was already worried how you'd react, and now with Grandpa missing—"

"He talked to you?" Kacey blamed her fatigue for her tone. Still, she fought the rise of something ugly. Was Ben talking to Audrey about their breakup without talking to her first?

"Yeah, of course. He's been thinking about this for a while."

The words, all of them, stung.

"How long of a while?"

Audrey lifted her shoulder. "I don't know. A few months. Right after the Christmas wedding was canceled, I think."

Oh. Kacey couldn't figure out what question to tackle first. Why wasn't Audrey more upset? When did Ben come to this conclusion? Clearly before she did, but how long before?

Maybe she didn't want to know.

Now wasn't the time to dive into either her anger or her broken heart. She took Audrey's hand. "Listen. The most important thing is that we find your grandpa. We don't have to talk about the future right now, okay?"

Audrey nodded, a smile tipping her lips. "It'll be okay, right, Mom?"

Kacey managed a shaky breath, but nodded. "Yeah. I promise. We'll be fine, honey. We always are." And they had been long before Ben walked back into their lives.

Still, as Audrey gave her a hug, then left the room, closing the door behind her, the words turned to claws. Kacey curled onto the bed, drew her legs up, pulled the pillow over her head, and finally let her heart break.

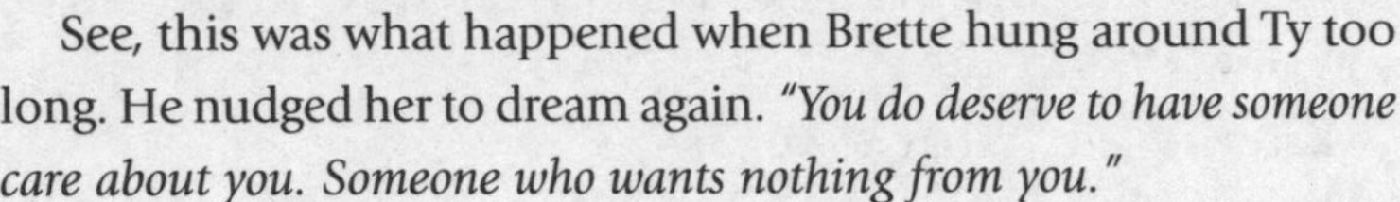

See, this was what happened when Brette hung around Ty too long. He nudged her to dream again. *"You do deserve to have someone care about you. Someone who wants nothing from you."*

She wanted to believe him, but really, life didn't work that way. Eventually he'd ask more of her than she could give. Maybe not the way Eason had, but still, relationships always cost something.

The longer she hung around, the harder it would be to leave him. Again.

She just had to make sure that she didn't give away her heart to him before they found Chet and she could escape the way-too-homey world of the Marshall family.

Garrett had taken his truck to the construction site, loaded with Ian, Ned, and Shae. She could have climbed in with them, but somehow she found herself in the Suburban, Jonas at the wheel, with Ty and Ben and Gage, his hair still wet from his shower. He radiated clean, and with his hair tied back, the grizzle of brown whiskers across his chin, those chocolate eyes, yeah, she could see why Ella had never forgotten him.

Some guys just found their way to a girl's heart and never left.

"Ella says hi, by the way," Gage said quietly as Jonas drove through the streets of Duck Lake, talking with Ty in the front seat. "She wishes she could be here."

"Sorry I made you two keep my secret for so long." She glanced at Ty in the front seat and cut her voice low. "I think I might have misjudged him."

"He's a good guy, Brette. But we understood. You barely knew him, and like you said, what you went through . . . well, not every guy can handle that."

Oh.

"But Ty could have," Gage added. "He's loyal to the bone, the kind of friend who shows up without a word of complaint."

"He would have put his life on hold to help me."

"And been glad to do it."

"Now I feel like a jerk."

"Don't. I just want you to know that you have options."

No, she didn't. "I'm only here until Jonas says we're on the road again. I can't . . . there's nothing between Ty and me, Gage, and there won't be."

His mouth made a thin line of disapproval. But then he shrugged, and his mouth quirked up to one side. "That's what I said about Ella."

She gave him a look, then turned back to the road and raised her voice. "I think it's just up ahead. I mapped it, and the new construction is on the end of Jade Road."

Jonas met her gaze through the rearview mirror. "Good job, Brette."

She noticed as Ty glanced at him, then back to the road.

"You two—" Gage started.

"No. I work for him."

They passed a number of houses with their shingles pancaking the yard, a few stripped trees, and one playset turned over on its side. Then the road turned to mud and they slowed, driving around construction debris—pink insulation, ribbons of Tyvek, rebar, and so much splintered wood that Garrett had to stop his truck. Ian got out, and he and Ned cleared a path. The remains of a construction trailer were scattered through the nearby field, and the excavator she'd seen from the air sprawled on its side in a nearby ditch, wounded.

"It's the last house," Brette said, motioning to the wreck that she thought imprisoned the van.

They pulled up, and she got a good look at what she'd seen from the air. The tornado must have dragged its tail right through the cul-de-sac because every house lay in ruin, every stick torn from the walls, every shingle ripped from the roof, the windows shattered, the chimneys poking up like the rubble in London after the Blitz.

The wheels of a large vehicle stuck out from what remained of a three-car garage. Jonas parked in the center of the cul-de-sac, and Brette scrambled out behind Ty.

Ben had already reached the van, started working his way into the chaos. "Dad?"

Brette's heart went out to him at the quaver in his voice.

"Dad, are you here?"

"Careful, Ben," Ty said as they examined a way to pry the boards away. The mess seemed almost unmovable, a giant game of Jenga. She guessed the twister had picked up the van and tossed it into the garage, taking out the outer wall, which had collapsed inward. The roof then fell in on top of the wall.

"I can't believe you saw this thing," Ty said as he climbed up onto the roof. "Garrett, you still have that chainsaw in your truck?"

Garrett headed for the truck, but Ben had wiggled his way around the back and gotten ahold of the back door. "It's stuck!"

Gage ducked in beside him and pulled out the wrench-slash-pry-bar they'd used to free Craig. He wedged the door open, and Ben pushed his body inside. "Dad?"

Brette held her breath, looking up to catch eyes with Ty. He seemed to have the power to calm her heart, hold her together as the seconds ticked by.

"It's empty!" Gage yelled.

Gage emerged first, then Ben. She noticed blood along the bandage of Ben's arm but didn't say anything. Ty scrambled off the roof, and for a long moment they stood there, in silence, defeat thick in the air.

"But it's their van, right?" Ty said.

Gage shrugged. "There's a couple backpacks in there. One had running shoes in it."

Ben cupped his hand over his eyes, turned away.

Jonas blew out a breath.

Garrett returned with the chainsaw, set it on the ground.

Shae slipped her hand into Ned's.

"Okay, let's think," Ty said. He put his hands on his hips, turned to survey the mess. "Chet's smart. And yeah, we don't have many tornadoes in Montana, but he certainly knows how to find cover. He would have found something concrete, or . . . wait." He ran over to the edge of the cul-de-sac. "There's a drainage ditch, with a metal culvert over here."

He slid into the ditch. Ben followed him down, Jonas behind him.

Brette ran over, stood at the top of the ditch. Debris from the field—dirt, crops, fencing—mounded against a corrugated metal tube, completely blocking the entrance. Ty scrambled up the ditch, over the road, and picked his way down the other side. He straddled the massive treads of the excavator.

She followed him and watched as he climbed between the treads and pushed his head into the dark space that blocked the tube. "Chet! Are you in there?"

Her body shuddered when a muffled yell came from the depths of the culvert, as if buried deep in the bowels of the earth.

Ty popped up, and despite being covered in grime and dirt, he smiled. "It's them," he said quietly, as if in disbelief. Then, louder, "It's them! They're in the culvert!"

He bent down again. "Do you have some teenagers with you?"

A smile. A nod, and she heard Garrett behind her thank God.

Jonas grabbed Ned around the neck.

Ben ran over and Ty climbed out, making room for Ben as he wiggled himself beside the excavator. "Dad, it's me. Are you okay?"

She couldn't make out his reply but saw it in the way Ben closed his eyes, bowed his head.

Ty walked over to her, and without stopping, pulled her against his grimy, tall, muscled self.

Oh. She sank into him, wrapping her arms around his waist, and held on. Because yeah, right now they were on the same team. Even friends.

Too soon Ty let her go, put his hands on her shoulders, and leaned down to meet her eyes. "Good job, Brette." Then he winked.

Her entire body reacted as if he'd done something crazy like kiss her. Her pulse jumped to attention, her breath caught . . .

Probably, they'd found Chet none too soon.

The sooner she hit the road with Jonas, the better.

The team moved down to the debris-filled entrance to start excavation. She returned to the truck and grabbed her camera, not sure why, drawn by the monumental, combined effort of everyone working to free Chet and the track team.

Garrett produced a shovel and a tire iron, which Ben used to dig at the dirt while the others pulled away the tangled fencing, rebar, wood, bricks, a tire, and too many cement blocks. Garrett dug away the dirt until the top of the corrugated metal surfaced.

The debris had pushed nearly three feet into the ten-foot tube, but by the time they cleared it, sirens whined in the distance.

Shae ran over. "Jenny is on the way, with Kacey and Audrey."

And that would be oh-so-devastating if Chet or any of the kids were seriously injured, but Brette kept her mouth shut.

They'd cleared out two feet of the tunnel by the time the fire engine arrived. Volunteers in turnout coats hustled over with more shovels, but Jonas and Gage simply threw down the two-by-fours they'd been using and grabbed the shovels out of their grips.

A hand appeared in the dirt from the other side, and Ty reached for it. "You're okay. We're going to get you out."

He kept ahold of the hand as the others unearthed the rest of the dirt, enough for another hand, then shoulders, and finally the very grimy face of what looked like a thirteen-year-old girl. She let Ty pull her free of the enclave.

She clung to him, then, crying.

Brette watched Ty hold her, and the sight took ahold of her heart and squeezed. She snapped a picture.

Another hand appeared, this time a young man, maybe fourteen. After prying himself free, he stumbled down the debris pile, caught by Gage, who led him over to the grass. Gage knelt in front of him, checking his pulse, his breathing.

They widened the hole, and another student climbed out, a girl who broke into tears as she ran to one of the firefighters. A young man, he grabbed her up, weeping, and Brette guessed him to be a big brother.

Two more students, both grimy but uninjured, climbed out.

Jenny Marshall had driven up by the time the guys widened the hole enough for Chet to escape. He groaned as he came out, his body caked with mud, an ugly scrape across his forehead. Ben and Ty grabbed either arm and helped him stagger free. He collapsed on the pile.

"Get him some water," Gage said, and one of the firefighters produced a water bottle. Chet guzzled the liquid down, letting it dribble onto his shirt.

Gage pressed his fingers to Chet's carotid artery and glanced at his watch. "It's a little fast, but that's to be expected."

Chet's voice emerged rusty, and he wiped his mouth. "I don't know what I was thinking, trying to outrun it, then climbing into that culvert. We were lucky that the excavator landed on the far end or it would have created a wind tunnel that cut us to ribbons." He took another drink, his hand shaking. Ben sat down beside him, put his arm around him, and took the bottle from his hand.

"How's their coach? We left him behind."

"He's alive. We found him in your car," Ben said. "What happened?"

Chet leaned onto his knees. "The twister was on my tail, and suddenly I see this guy pull into this abandoned farm. He gets out and starts running around, and I spot all these kids in the van. The guy is losing it. So I follow him, hear him shouting something about a storm shelter. But there's no storm shelter, and there's no time, so I got into the van and told him to get in."

"He refused," Ben said quietly.

"I had to take off. I put the pedal down, and we got ahead of it. The funnel looked like it was going to head right into the town of Duck Lake, so I thought I'd drive us out of its path. I headed north—"

"But it changed directions," Jonas said. "It mowed through a copse of trees, and the debris turned it eastward."

"Yeah. And I ran out of road. I saw it coming and thought, what had I done? But by then, we'd run out of time, so . . . I just reacted. Pure impulse. Told the kids to run to the culvert." His gaze scanned them. "Brave bunch, every one of them."

"Let's get the rest of them out," Garrett said, reaching to help Chet up, but Chet just stared at him.

"What? That's all of us."

For a beat, no one moved. The cicadas buzzed in the fields, the wind whipped against some loose Tyvek.

"What do you mean?" Jenny said from behind Brette. "What about Creed and the high school team? These are the middle schoolers."

"They weren't with us," said the girl who stood near her firefighter brother. "They didn't practice with us today. They went somewhere else."

"Somewhere between the school, the trail, and who-knows-where, we've lost five more kids," Garrett said quietly.

Jenny crouched to the ground, and Garrett came over, landed next to her, pulled her into his arms.

Ty wore an expression of such defeat that Brette's heart broke for him. But it wasn't his brother lost, so she walked over to Jonas, reached out, and took his hand. "We'll find him," she said softly.

And sweet, broken Jonas put his arms around her. "Thanks, Brette. I don't know what I'd do without you."

6

JUST LIKE THAT, *BAM!* Ty figured it out. Not why Brette had run—he got that loud and clear, thanks to the story about Eason, which had done a neat job of tearing through his insides—but why, when Ty walked back into her life, she didn't exactly greet him with open arms.

Because they were probably already occupied by Jonas.

Ty tried not to let that thought and the memory of her comforting Jonas distract him from the most important thing . . .

Creed Marshall and four other high school runners were still lost somewhere in the wreckage of the tornado.

Ty stood outside on the porch of the farmhouse, staring out at the darkening twilight as it fell over the broken landscape of the Marshall Vineyards. The storm had ripped leaves and vines off their wires, and the backyard still glistened with puddles under a now-rising moon.

Inside, the murmur of conversation included scenarios and information from the other parents who had joined them, trying to nail down and organize the search for Creed and the team.

Chet, accompanied by Ben, Kacey, and Audrey, was at the local hospital, getting evaluated. Other than suffering from dehydration, Chet seemed his usual stalwart self.

A hero for all times.

Ty blew out a breath.

"You okay, pal?"

Gage had come out on the porch, letting the screen door close behind him. "They're getting ready to huddle up in there and put together a new search plan. Maybe you want to come in and—"

"Yeah, sure." Ty turned, but Gage blocked his path.

"What's eating you?"

"We still have missing kids," Ty snapped.

Gage held up his hand. "Ho-*kay*. Don't shoot the messenger."

So maybe Gage hadn't deserved that. "It's nothing. Just . . ." He turned away, his jaw tight. "Just be straight with me. Is Brette dating Jonas?"

A pause, then . . . "No."

"Are you sure? Because maybe you missed the hug she gave Jonas, right there in front of everyone?"

"Because his brother is still missing? They're friends. Nothing more."

Ty shook his head. "I know I shouldn't even be thinking about this. It's stupid, especially when we have people still missing. But I can't shake it." He gritted his jaw but let the question escape anyway. "What if she doesn't need me because she has Jonas?" He let his voice drop, low enough to be a mutter. "I never thought about the fact that she might have someone else in her life."

"Really, I think you're making a leap here."

"I think the leap is thinking that I made an impact at all on her life. We barely knew each other, and I should probably get that through my head. I told her I'll always be her friend, and maybe that's all I'll ever be."

He started to move past Gage, but his friend wouldn't budge. "So, you don't want to get in the way of her and Jonas? If I'm . . . uh, wrong?"

"Oh no, I very much want to get in the way." Ty turned, stared out at the darkness. "But maybe that's not the right thing for Brette. I bowled her over the first time, so maybe the right thing is to just . . . step back. Just friends. Period."

Gage went silent.

The stars blinked, illuminating the silvery vines.

Ty sighed, giving over to the truth. "It's just that, like I said, there's something about her. For the last year and a half, I'd get these . . . I dunno, for lack of a better word, gut feelings that she needed help. And I didn't know what else to do, so I . . . I . . . well, I prayed for her."

"That's a new twist on pining."

He glanced at Gage. "Right? But that's just it. I do care for her—but it's deeper than that. I worry about her. I'm . . . *burdened* . . . for her. Like God put her in my heart."

Gage stood beside him, staring out into the night, silent.

"I know, weird. Maybe I'm just deluding myself. Just like I have been for the last two years."

"What are you talking about?"

"I don't belong on this team anymore, and we all know it."

Gage frowned.

"Ben said it best—if I'm not getting back in the cockpit, then what good am I to the team?"

"Actually, Ben didn't say that. He wasn't necessarily kind, but he hardly suggested you weren't good for the team. You are the one who found Chet—"

"*Brette* found Chet, I just followed my instincts, and we got lucky. Anyone with a map and a compass could do what I do."

"But they don't, do they? You show up, willing, and that's the point. So you're grounded—you helped with every significant search we've had in the last two years despite a bum knee and a few scars. That takes guts."

"Or it's because I have nowhere else to go." He shook his head. "Maybe you don't remember, Gage, but before the crash, I was a wreck. After my dad got remarried and Powers went to boarding school, I started getting into trouble. Drinking and smoking weed and . . . I was pretty messed up. Chet walked into my life and decided to take me under his wing. Taught me to fly, and he's probably the reason I didn't flunk completely out of high school. I even managed to get into Wharton and get a degree in Economics, but by the end I hated it, so I came back home." He brushed his hand across the railing. "I was the guy who spent every night looking for a party. I didn't need a job—my mother's inheritance took care of that, so . . ."

The shadows deepened as the night sank into the earth.

"I was still flying, though. That gave me a reason to stay sober, at least those days when I was flying for PEAK. And then came the night of the accident." He drew in a breath. "I'd been out drinking, and we got called up for a transport of an injured skier. I didn't tell Chet and he let me do the preflight check. It's my fault we ran low on oil pressure and dropped from the sky. My fault the guy broke both his hips."

Gage looked at him. "And your fault that Ben came home to take care of his dad. Your fault that Kacey and Ben reunited."

"That's a wild spin on it."

"I'm just saying that you should probably notice how God worked it out for good."

Ty made a face. "Yeah, he worked it out by my falling on my face while I was trying to save Chet's life. Wishing I could die, frustrated that I'd made a mess of my life. Thankfully, God showed up to save me."

"That Ty I remember, the one who suddenly stopped begging me to go out and started hanging out at church. Drove me a little crazy."

"That was me just trying to get my head back together. Still am. But I can't just sit around waiting for a callout. I need to—"

"Get back in the cockpit?"

Ty's mouth tightened, but he gave a grim nod. "Maybe."

"About time."

Gage turned, leaned against the railing, his arms folded over his chest. "You're worth more to this team than you can ever know. And it's not just because you show up with the pizza."

Ty wanted to receive his words, but, yeah, he was probably the best pizza fetcher they had. Still . . . "Thanks."

Gage gestured to the house. "We should get in there."

Ty followed him. But instead of everyone standing around the table, the searchers—from Ben's bandmates to the Marshall family, to the PEAK team to the extra family members—had formed a circle, jammed together to listen as Garrett Marshall prayed.

Ty found himself drawn in by Garrett's voice, the simple, raw words.

"Lord, we don't know where Creed and the others are, but you do. You are with them, just as you are with us, and we ask that you somehow show us where they are. We pray that you would provide for them—water and food and everything they need—until we can get to them. Heal them from injury, if they have any, and give them hope. Comfort them. Comfort us. And bring us all safely home."

Ty heard the screen door open and tucked a glance over his shoulder to see Brette walking away.

And shoot if his gut didn't give a familiar tug. Call it a burden, or an emotional need to fix things, but he surrendered to it and followed her.

She took a path away from the house, through the arching vines toward the big red barn.

The burden grew as she curled her arms around her waist.

Then, away from the lights of the porch, just outside the puddle of the floodlights on the barn, she stopped. Just stood there and lifted her face up to the sky.

That was when he saw her shoulders begin to shake.

Oh, Brette.

God, I don't know why you brought me—us—out here, but please give me the right words.

"Brette?"

He approached her quietly, but the ground snapped beneath his feet and she stiffened. Her hands went up to wipe her cheeks before she sniffed hard and turned.

The moonlight offered him a glimpse of her face. Her eyes were thick with . . . anger?

"What's—"

"I can't believe they're in there praying. *Praying.* As if God cares one iota about their problems."

The vehemence of her outburst stopped him cold.

"I just—it's so stupid." She lifted her hands heavenward. "God is the one who brought the storm, for Pete's sake. Why would they ask him for help?"

He took a step closer. "Why *wouldn't* they ask him for help?"

"Because clearly he can't be trusted!" She turned away then, as if shaken by her own words, and he longed to reach out to her. But she took off in a quick walk, then a full-out sprint toward the barn.

Running away from him, again.

But he wouldn't regret letting her go a second time, so he took off after her, speeding up to catch her just as she ran into the yard in front of the building. "Brette!" He caught her arm. "Stop."

She didn't jerk out of his grip, just shook her head and pressed her hands over her face. "Stay away from me, Ty. I'm a disaster."

"What? No, you're not. You're hurting, I get that. Really." He put his hand on her other arm. "Talk to me."

She lifted her face to look at him. Tears ran uninhibited. "I'm so tired, Ty. I'm tired of believing that God is good and that he'll swoop in and save the day. God doesn't care what happens to anybody."

"Anybody," he said softly, "or just you?"

Her jaw tightened, and her breath shuddered out. She looked away. "He took away everything. My father. My mother. My . . . my body. I have nothing, and he could have stopped it all. Made *none* of it happen."

"And then you would have naturally turned to him and thanked him for what he didn't give you?"

She looked up at him.

"How do you know that he didn't save you from much worse?"

Her mouth tightened. "I don't see what can be worse than . . . I'm hardly a woman anymore, Ty." And her eyes filled again. "Probably you didn't need to know that."

He refused to let her pain shake him. "Your body isn't what makes you a woman, Brette. It's your essence, who God made you to be."

"I don't know who God made me to be." Now she twisted out of his grip and walked away from him. She sat on a bench near the double sliding doors. "I used to think I was a journalist, one who wrote stories of hope. But now I see nothing but storms and destruction and . . . God isn't here. Or rather, if he is, then he's not a God I want to know."

"So you're saying that you're disappointed in God, because he could have stopped the storm."

She raised an eyebrow. "Yeah."

"Which means that you used to have hope in God, otherwise you wouldn't have been disappointed."

Her mouth closed and she stared at him. Blinked. "Maybe. Before my mother died."

Oh Brette. He longed to touch her face, brush away the tears.

Instead, he softened his voice, put all the emotion he dared into it. "I know you feel decimated, but don't let your circumstances tell you who God is. Let who God is tell you how to deal with your circumstances."

He knelt before her. "Brette, I've prayed for you nearly every day for the past year and a half. I have to believe that it's because God cares, very much, about you, even in the middle of your storm."

She looked at him, as if testing his words.

He took her hand. "C'mon."

He stood and opened the big doors to the winery, looked around, and found a light. Flicked it on.

The light illuminated the giant beams crisscrossing the ceiling. On one side of a great hallway, stainless steel drums held wine bubbling away in a fermenting cycle. To the other side, three tiers of oak casks held the finished, aging wine, three rows thick, three rows high.

The redolence of yeast, wood, and berries soaked the room.

He tugged her along the rows. "I was in Sonoma with a buddy of mine from Wharton, and he took me into his parents' wine cellar. Told me about the process of making wine. It's a real chemistry—you have to let the wine ferment just long enough to absorb all the sugars but not so long you let too much oxygen in. Then you rack it off and let it sit in barrels, aging. A good winemaker knows just how long to let the wine bubble and stew before it's ready to be put in barrels. But without the fermentation process, it won't be turned into wine."

"Are you saying that I'm wine?"

He had a firm grip on her hand. "I'm saying that storms happen—cancer happens. Accidents happen. We can either run from them, hide from them, or . . . go through them. God is with us in all of those situations. But yeah, some of his best people are pressed out, shaken, fermented . . . aged through circumstances or time."

She looked away. "I can't, Ty. I can't let myself lean on God—it's so—"

"Dependent?"

She pulled her hand out of his. "I have nothing to bargain with. Nothing to make sure—"

"It ends well?"

She nodded, her voice so low he barely heard it over his heartbeat. "What if he lets me down?"

"So the only outcome you'll accept from God is a good one?"

Her jaw tightened. When she wiped her hand across her cheek, it was everything he could do not to pull her into an embrace.

"I guess I just don't like this one," she said.

He couldn't stop himself. He reached out, and miraculously she came without hesitation. He held her, her body frail as it pressed to his, and tried not to let his desire to kiss her take control.

Just friends.

"God loves you, Brette."

She pushed away from him. "You're a good man, Ty. You care about people more than the average person."

Huh. "I don't know about that. I just know that if I were God, and I was chasing you, I'd do just about anything to get you to stop and listen to me. To show you that . . . that I loved you."

His words hovered there.

Yes, he could love her, if he let himself.

Maybe, in fact, he already did.

She had to keep walking. Because if Brette turned around, she'd do something crazy and humiliating like . . . start weeping. Or maybe just throw herself at Ty and never let go.

What was his problem that he wasn't furious at her? What kind of man just kept listening, caring? The compassion in his pale green eyes could turn her into a puddle right in the middle of the barn.

She pushed open the doors and headed toward what looked like a row of apple trees. The moon lit a trail between the orchard, and she just kept walking.

Because that was what she did when panic tried to choke her. Ran, far and fast and—

"Brette, slow down."

Oh, how she despised the weak, desperate, hollow person she'd become. Her body betrayed her, slowing for his voice.

It simply wasn't fair how quickly he'd gotten under her skin. As if he'd always been there, really, the memory of him lying dormant.

Well, not *so* dormant. She'd conjured Ty up plenty of times, remembering his smile, his dark whiskers, that tiny dimple he probably didn't even realize he had, the one that appeared when he tweaked up one side of his mouth. She could still feel his hands on hers.

His touch on her face.

"Brette!" His footfalls came faster, and she closed her eyes. "Listen. I know it's hard for you to hear that God loves you, but he does and—"

"I know!" She turned around, found him a few steps away. "I *know*—or I should—that he loves me. My mom was a believer, and she held on to her faith until the end. I'm just angry. I don't want to hear that God loves me, or that he's with me, or even that I might just survive all this and become a better person. I really just want to be angry."

For a second, he just stared at her. Then, "Right. Okay. I get that." He wore a strange expression. "Yeah, I get being angry."

He did?

His eyes shone for a moment, and then suddenly he looked around, reached down, and picked up . . . an *apple*?

He tossed it in his hand like a baseball. "My mom had this tradition at Christmas. Well, she made it a tradition. See, every year, she'd make Christmas dinner, and invariably she'd burn the dinner rolls. She made them from scratch, but by the time they were supposed to go into the oven, everything else was happening, and she'd burn them trying to get the turkey on the table. One year, I came downstairs, and I heard this screaming outside. I opened the door, and there was my mother, throwing the burned rolls into the field, yelling with each throw. She saw me standing there, handed me a roll, and said, 'Try it.' So I did." He held out the apple. "Try it."

She stared at the apple. Misshapen, brown, and hard, clearly worth throwing. She took it.

"Now listen, I want a real scream. Not some pansy, polite shout. From your soul. Just let it out and throw the apple as hard as you can."

Oh, this was silly, but . . . She leaned back, threw it, gave a grunt.

"That was pathetic." He found another apple. "You need to mean it." He turned, took two steps like some sort of shot-putter, and threw the apple into the night, letting out a deeply masculine roar that sounded like something out of *Braveheart*. The apple arched into the indigo sky and disappeared.

"You call that a scream?" She found an apple in the darkness and joined him. "A scream needs to be loud and angry and . . . like this." She wound back and threw the apple and let out something guttural and loud and *wow*, the sound swept through her like a wash of heat. As if she'd released something inside her soul, unlatched a darkness, and forced it from her body.

She let the scream linger until she was out of breath. Then propped her hands on her knees, breathing hard.

"Felt good, didn't it?"

"Let's go again."

He produced an apple, and she let it fly. Another loud scream tore from her soul, and the sound peaked in the higher ranges, sharp and focused.

She turned, her hand over her mouth.

He was grinning. "Nice. See, it works. Mom did it for the next three Christmases, and then, after she died, I . . . I don't know, it just helped sometimes. To let it out."

But she was caught on his words *after she died*. "You didn't tell me your mother died," she said softly.

He'd picked up another apple and tossed it in his hand. "Yeah. I was ten. We were driving through the mountains to Seattle when we hit a patch of ice. We spun, then hit the ditch and rolled." He threw the apple away, no screaming, but she sensed he might want to. "It was nighttime, and snow was coming down. I didn't know it at the time, but she was pregnant." He picked up another apple and tossed it, tight-lipped. "She ruptured her uterus and bled out. I was there the entire time."

"Your mom died right in front of you?"

"Not for a few hours, but . . . yeah. She died in my arms."

Oh, Ty. "You sat in a cold car, waiting for help, watching your mother die."

He drew in a breath, threw an apple underhanded into the thickness of the orchard. "I kept thinking that I should go for help, you know? But I had no idea where I was, and there was a blizzard—"

"If you'd left, you would have died too." She had somehow taken his hand.

"I know. But it doesn't make me feel any better. I still sometimes dream that I'm in the car with her, that I'm hearing her sing to me—she did that to make me less afraid—and I get out and run, screaming. Searching for help."

She got the running part.

But she didn't want to run so much at the moment. Something

about standing here with Ty rooted her to the spot. His fingers wove through hers, warm, solid, and when he turned to walk with her, she didn't let go.

"That's what made you want to be on the PEAK team?"

"I don't know. Mostly Chet, I think. My dad got married a couple years later to a much-younger woman."

"Oh great, a stepmom story."

"Naw, she wasn't evil. But she wasn't the mom type, and I missed my mom. Being thirteen and angry isn't a good combination. I got into trouble."

She could see him then, a good-looking kid with freckles and a troublemaker grin.

"I was a party boy, pretty much the textbook troubled kid with money." He glanced at her. "You wouldn't have liked me."

"Oh, I don't know." She winked.

And stilled. Was she seriously flirting with Ty Remington? She'd completely lost her mind. "So, you got into trouble in high school?"

"Yeah. Mostly drinking, but also some drugs. I was a lost cause. Until Chet started investing in me. But it didn't stop the drinking. That . . . well, after the chopper accident I had to face up to the fact that I needed help. So I started attending AA. There are days when I don't think about taking a drink—and others when the urge to find the nearest bar and dive into something easy and quick is nearly more than I can bear."

He lifted a shoulder. "So, I do understand the feeling of just needing to scream."

But the urge had left her as she'd been drawn in by his story and the fact that . . . well, maybe they weren't as different as she thought.

Maybe he did understand how it felt to lay on the floor and not know how you were going to get up. Suddenly her eyes stung.

"Brette, are you okay?"

Not at all. She made to break away from him but turned too fast and nearly tripped.

He caught her, his hand on her arm. "All this activity—I didn't even think about how exhausted you might be—"

"I'm fine."

Except, she might not be, not really. Because she hadn't gotten her test results back, and what was she doing out here for a midnight stroll with a man she couldn't—no, shouldn't—have?

She pulled her arm out of his grip.

He stepped away. "Oh. I'm sorry—this is about Jonas, isn't it."

"What?" Her brain shut down. "Jonas?"

"You two are . . ." He took another step back. "Listen, I'm not trying to get in the middle—okay, not that I wouldn't, but—"

"What are you talking about?"

But she knew, even before he answered.

The hug. Oh.

"The way you hugged Jonas today—I just assumed—"

"We're not together, Ty."

She probably shouldn't have said that if she hoped to keep him two feet or more away from her. But suddenly she didn't want him two feet away. She was tired of acting like Ty Remington hadn't made an impact on her life, as if she hadn't been thinking of him, too, for the past eighteen months.

As if seeing him hadn't turned her world inside out with a forbidden, terrible desire.

"You're not?" It was the way he said it, the tiniest hint of huskiness to his voice, that made her shake her head. Take another step toward him.

Oh, Brette, what are you doing? "We just work together."

He swallowed. "Oh."

She took another step. He didn't move; she was so close now

she could smell his aftershave, the husk of his skin, even hear his heart thundering. Or perhaps that might be hers.

Bad idea. But she couldn't move, caught in the aura of Ty, wanting him to wrap his amazing arms around her and—

"I'm not made of steel here, Brette, so either, um . . . well, I don't think I can be just friends with you looking at me like that."

"Whoever said that we were just friends?" she said softly.

And that was all it took. That and one long inhale of breath that shuddered out a moment before he wrapped his hand around her neck and pressed his mouth to hers. He was taller than she was, almost by a head, but when they kissed she lifted herself onto her toes, raised her chin, and let herself be surrounded by the strength and protection that was Ty. She closed her eyes and sank into the kiss, the way his lips moved over hers, the scent of this amazing man. He finished closing the gap between them, wrapping his other arm around her, and she encircled her arms around his toned waist, enjoying the feel of his body, muscled and powerful against hers.

Yes, there was a reason she hadn't let herself think about him for the past eighteen months. Had run from him like she might be on fire. Because when she was with him, she *was*—a blaze burning deep inside her, lighting every cell to flame.

He made her feel safe and whole, and for a moment, hope filled her chest. A hope full of dangerous tomorrows, and with one terrible swoop it had her trotting down the road of happily ever after. Building a life with Ty.

No. Oh *no*.

What if . . . She lowered herself back down, breaking their kiss, and he met her eyes, searching hers. "Sorry, I—"

"No, Ty, it's not you. It's me, it's . . ." She shook her head. "You made me laugh. And . . . I screamed, and it felt so good and . . ."

His thumb ran down her cheek. "What's going on, Brette? What are you scared of?"

The word emerged, fast, hard, unchecked. "Dying."

He stilled. But he didn't remove his hand. "Brette—"

She pushed his hand away. "I took another blood test a couple days ago, and the results haven't come back yet." There was more, of course, but she couldn't voice it.

I'm not the woman I used to be.

His expression turned earnest, his green eyes flashing. "It doesn't matter to me—"

But she was already backing away, shaking her head. "The more I hope, the harder it will be when that hope dies. I can't take it, Ty. I'm sorry . . . I shouldn't have . . . I can't . . ."

"Brette!" He advanced on her, backing her up to a tree. He braced a hand over her to touch the branch. His voice cut low. "Do you seriously think that I'd abandon you? So you're sick—we can go through it together." He touched her cheek, and she fought the urge to lean in.

"That's what friends—more than friends—do," he said, his eyes holding hers. "They stick around through *life*. They give each other someone to hold on to, someone to tell them that everything will be okay, even when it feels impossible."

Oh. But as much as she wanted to grab his words, hold on to them with everything inside her . . . no, she couldn't do that to him.

Because she could love him. Probably, a tiny, sad part of her already did, at least a little. And she couldn't watch him stand by her as her life wasted away.

So she put her hands on his chest, pushed. "No, Ty. I already went through that with my mother. I know what it does to a person to watch someone they love die, bit by bit, every day. I know you wouldn't abandon me. But I can't do that to you."

She ducked out from under his arm.

He stepped away, but she sensed he didn't want to. "You don't get to decide for me."

"Yes, actually, I do. Trust me, Ty. This is for the best."

He started for her, but she backed up, shaking her head.

"No, Ty. You're right. I might deserve a man who would love me unconditionally, but you deserve a woman who won't die in your arms."

"Brette!"

But she'd already turned, already started running.

And this time, she wasn't looking back.

7

HE'D SPENT TWENTY-FOUR HOURS in a storm drain, and the hospital wasn't even admitting Chet for observation. Despite dehydration and an elevated blood pressure, the guy had spent most of the past two hours charming the nurses, after he'd gotten off the phone with his girlfriend, Maren, back in Mercy Falls.

Ben stood outside the hospital, just needing some air. Night had fallen, and the clear sky held a scattering of stars and a waxen moon. Summer freedom, the smell of cut grass, and a hint of the heat of the day radiated off the parking lots, now puddled with overhead lights. A car drove by, its radio thumping out hip-hop.

Ben leaned back against a pole near the front doors, the cement cool on his back. Maybe he needed to be admitted for observation the way he couldn't get the adrenaline out of his body. He just needed to breathe, let the fact that they'd found his father alive calm him.

It wasn't too late to get his life back.

Call him crazy, but in this moment, more than anything, he just wanted to grab Kacey and find a preacher. Run away and spend a week holding on to her, reminding himself that his life hadn't completely blown up right in front of his eyes.

"There you are." Kacey came out through the sliding doors. "Audrey said you went to find some coffee."

"The coffee shop is closed," he said. "I just needed a break. My dad seems to not realize how close he came to dying."

"He knows. It's just his way of dealing with disaster—joke, pretend it didn't happen, remind us that he's invincible."

Driven by the need to feel her arms around him, he pulled her into an embrace.

She came to him like a friend, wrapping her arms around his shoulders, laying her head on his shoulder. "It's going to be okay."

He needed more than okay. He slid his hand to her cheek, caressed it, wanting her eyes to find his. But she backed up, looked down.

"I'm so glad you're here," he said, trying to reach out, draw her back in. "I couldn't go through this without you."

"I know. And like I said, I will always be here for you, Ben. That's not going to change, ever." When she lifted her head, her beautiful eyes had filled with an emotion he couldn't place. "But I'm so mad at you for talking to Audrey without me. You should have waited. We should have done it together."

He stared at her. "I don't understand . . ."

"About us. Our future. You shouldn't have involved her."

He frowned at her. "You *know*?"

"Of course I know." She shook her head. "How could I not know? We talked about it. Just never . . . I mean, I figured you thought we needed to be face to face. And we probably do—that was a good call. And yeah, I get wanting to explain it to Audrey, but not without me, Ben!"

He just stared at her, the words stripping a response from him. "What are you talking about?"

"What do you mean? What you said before. How you're never at home, and your trips get longer and longer—"

"That's why we have to do something about it. That's why I planned this weekend!"

"Yeah. But you told Audrey before you even talked to me?"

Wow, had he pegged this one wrong. "Okay, yeah, maybe I should have talked to you first, but . . . she was so excited. She wanted to help plan everything . . . I'm sorry, babe. I thought you'd be, I dunno, surprised."

She wore a sort of horror on her face. "What are you talking about? Why would Audrey want to help plan our *breakup*?"

His heart slammed into his ribs. *"What?"*

"You involved our daughter in the worst moment of our lives?"

He just stared at her, his breath hot in his chest. "You want to *break up* with me?"

She folded her arms. "Isn't that . . . don't *you*?"

"No!" He advanced on her, but she stepped back, so he stopped, cut his voice low. "I planned this weekend to elope with you. You were supposed to show up after my gig on Friday night. I had a preacher all lined up at this B & B outside Duck Lake. That's why my dad was headed there—to make sure the preacher could stick around with the bad weather."

Her eyes widened.

"I have the next four days off, and I wanted to spend them with you, as husband and wife."

Silence. She drew in a shaky breath. Swallowed. "You planned on us eloping."

"Yes." He curled his hands around her arms. "I hated canceling our wedding in December. Every day that I spend away from you and Audrey eats a hole through me. I just thought, if we got married—"

"How does that solve *any* of our problems, Ben?"

His mind went blank.

She shrugged away from him. "You'd still be on the road, traveling all the time—"

"But we'd be *married*."

She quirked an eyebrow. "And that means . . ."

"We could at least *be* together, for one." He didn't know why he'd led with that; he clearly needed to back up, start again.

"That's what this is about? The fact that you—"

"No! Yes, maybe a little, but . . ." He came after her again, but she stepped away, held up her hand to stop him.

He took a breath to stop the rise of emotions. The last thing he needed was for some fan to catch him breaking up with his fiancée and leak it to TMZ. He schooled his voice, found the right words. "Listen. I want to marry you so we can be together, yes, but also so we can start building that family, that home that we talked about back when we were teenagers."

Her jaw hardened. "I want that too. But even if we get married, it doesn't solve the basic problems we have. Like you deciding what's best for us."

"What?"

"You just assumed I'd want to elope, Ben. Yes, I want to marry you too . . . more than you can imagine. But your life is . . . it's all about you. It's about your career, your music—even back to the day when you left Mercy Falls. You made a decision that changed our lives without even talking to me."

Her words found the wounds in their past, and he flinched. The hurt roused something he'd thought he'd locked away. Forgotten. Heat slipped into his tone. "*I* made a decision? You were the one who decided to hide my own daughter from me for thirteen years, Kacey. Thirteen. I missed everything—her first smile, seeing her walk, her first lost tooth, helping her learn to read—I missed it all. *You* made that decision."

Kacey recoiled, as if stung. But she rebounded like the soldier she was. "Yeah, well, you didn't want us, remember?"

Huh? "No, I *don't* remember that because I wanted you with

everything inside me. You and Audrey. I thought you didn't want *me.* I loved you, Kacey." He cut his voice low, gravelly. "I still love you. There's never been anyone for me but you, and you know it."

A tear streaked down her face, and she wiped it away, her jaw so hard it seemed she might be breaking teeth. She closed her eyes, as if pained.

It wasn't supposed to be this way. He closed the gap between them, put his hands on her shoulders. "I love you, Kacey, and we found each other again. I don't want to lose you. Or Audrey. Maybe I made a mistake in planning an elopement, but . . . please. Don't break up with me. Let's get married."

She let out a shaky breath. Opened her eyes, and the agony in them unlatched his heart, dropped it down to his gut. "The real problem is that I don't fit into your world, Ben. I'm not a glitzy, pretty, country music star wife. I fly choppers. I'm more comfortable in a jumpsuit than a dress and I just don't clean up well. I don't belong in your world. It's too big for me—I'm just going to get lost."

"You're the most beautiful woman I know." He caught her hair between two fingers, curled it behind her ear. "And you won't get lost in my world—you're the center of it."

For a moment, she leaned into his touch, and he thought she'd changed her mind. Then she shook her head. "You are a master of charm, Ben King. That's why you have so many fans who love you."

"I just need the one. Or rather . . . the two." *Please.*

The doors behind them opened, and Kacey looked up, past him, and in a second, her countenance changed. A bright smile, a quick wipe of her tears. "Hey, honey."

Audrey was walking out with Chet, his arm around her shoulders. "We're escaping," she said and looked up at her grandfather with a conspiratorial expression. Then her gaze fell on Ben, and she raised an eyebrow, as if in expectation.

Oh, he couldn't break her heart. Clearly, she had no idea the craziness stirring in her mother's mind. So he smiled back, feeling like a liar. Or a charmer, like Kacey said. "I'll get the truck." He ran out into the parking lot.

"But your life is . . . it's all about you."

Shoot, maybe it was. But he didn't know how to fix that. Not without giving up his career.

He climbed into the truck, Kacey's words sinking in. *"You didn't want us, remember?"*

He did want them. With every cell inside of him.

But he wanted the music too.

He pulled up to the circle drive of the hospital and got out, and by the time he came around, Kacey was climbing into the backseat with Audrey. He held the door open for his dad.

"I don't need any help," Chet said. "I'm going to be just fine. I just need a burger and a good night's sleep."

Kacey laughed, something forced, for Audrey.

Ben dragged up a grin.

But maybe he should just be glad that someone would be okay. Because he wasn't sure how he'd live through the wreckage of this particular storm.

Ty didn't need saving. Or protecting. Not from Brette. He ran down the path from the apple orchard, toward the Marshall family farmhouse, watching as Brette entered through the back porch, letting the door slam behind her.

He slowed to a quick walk, not wanting to come blazing in on her heels like he might be a stalker.

"You deserve a woman who won't die in your arms."

For a blinding, raw second, he saw in his mind's eye exactly what that might look like. Brette in a hospital bed, him by her side, trying to be stoic as the life waned from her body.

Yeah, he could agree that he didn't know if he had the strength for that either. But maybe by the time they got there—*if* they got there—he would.

He refused to make a decision today based on a fear of tomorrow.

Or, rather, to let *her* make the decision, regardless of her words.

Because he wasn't dreaming the way she'd surrendered into his arms. How she had, for a moment, fit perfectly, kissing him as if she'd missed him just as desperately.

Brette. He could still taste her, smell the fragrance of her skin, her hair, and with everything inside him he wanted to chase her down and tell her that no, he wasn't going to let her fears keep him from showing up in her life, now or . . . well, maybe forever.

He stalked into the house and found the main room quiet, the kitchen area dark, only a light over the table illuminated. Garrett was bracing himself over the map spread out over the table. His dark eyes roved over the possibilities, the nooks and crannies where a group of high school students might be hiding.

Garrett looked up when Ty came into the room. With dark hair, graying at the edges, and the faintest stubble of gray-white beard, he reminded Ty of an older Liam Neeson, including the stern expression.

"Did you see Brette come in?" Ty said, feeling like a high school kid being dressed down by a ruffled father.

"She headed up the stairs," Garrett said. Returned to looking at the map.

Shoot.

Ty walked over to the map, noticed that the cookies and salt and pepper shakers had been replaced with Monopoly pieces, and the tornado's path etched in with marker.

"You should get to bed," Ty said to Garrett. "You need your sleep."

Garrett looked up at him, frowned. "Even if I tried, I won't sleep until my son is safely at home."

Oh boy. Ty had been on the dark side of SAR enough to know that sometimes body recovery was all they could hope for.

He kept that to himself. "Agreed. Still, you need to get enough food and rest or you'll be in jeopardy too. We're not going anywhere until we find Creed, I promise."

Ty didn't know why those last words spilled out—he couldn't vouch for the rest of the team. But seeing the look on Garrett's face, yeah, Ty made that promise with every cell in his body.

Garrett blew out a breath, leaned forward, and ran his hands down his face. He walked over to the window, staring out at the porch. "Creed hated it here when he first arrived."

Ty frowned.

"He came from a pretty tough neighborhood in Minneapolis, and when our pastor called and asked if we would be willing to take him . . ." Garrett shook his head. "Jenny said yes almost immediately. She just knew that he needed us, and frankly, we probably needed him." He sighed. "I was looking forward to our empty nest, but Jenny said we had plenty of good parenting left in us, so . . ."

He curled a hand behind his neck. "Creed was so angry. He'd seen his brother shot right in front of his eyes, never knew his dad, and his mother . . . she just walked out of his life. He was ten. The last thing he wanted was a life out here on the farm, or us telling him that God loved him."

Ty found himself joining Garrett at the window. He stared out into the darkness, at the stars glittering against the pane of the night.

"He absolutely refused to let us rescue him. Tried to run away twice before the local police brought him home. Got in fights at school. Started stealing from us."

"What did you do?"

"Jenny just kept praying for him. Once, he threw one of her heirloom dishes across the room, and I wanted to end it. Just kick him out. But Jenny reminded me of my cowboy days in Montana, when my dad would break a horse. He was a whisperer . . . he'd work with the horse until it trusted him. Then he'd ease right up to the animal and climb onto his back. Sometimes the horse would buck at first. But once it got used to my dad, he'd obey him. He felt safe, and that was my dad's trick. A horse bucks out of fear, and so did Creed."

Ty glanced at him.

"He just wasn't used to grace. Or mercy. It scared him—mostly because he was afraid of embracing it, only to lose it. He wanted to hold us far enough away that we couldn't hurt him. Or worse, to figure out how to pay us back before he let us or God in."

Garrett put his hands into his pockets. "We can't bargain our way to God's love. Even if we wanted to, God would say, I already love you. It's done. The problem is that most people have pride in their own abilities, their strength, their ability to provide for themselves. They'll give until they bleed, sacrifice everything, but reaching out to God—that's too humiliating. We enter into salvation through the door of destitution. And Creed had too much pride to let that happen."

Garrett offered a small, sad grin. "Sorry. Long days herding cattle with my dad made for theology lessons."

But Ty couldn't get Brette's words out of his head. *"The more I hope, the harder it will be when that hope dies."*

"How did you get him to realize that you meant it? That you loved him?"

"That was the hardest part. I wanted to shake him and tell him not to fight us, that we were on his side. But he'd been hurt, and he wasn't letting us in, no way, no how. So we had to back off, let him see it at his own pace. Jenny just kept making cookies. I kept driving him back and forth to school. We just kept loving him. And one day, he just got it. Realized I wasn't going anywhere, and that I loved him, period. I'll never forget the day he asked if I'd adopt him."

Garrett ran his thumb under his eye. "I said yes." His breath tremored. "Creed is every bit my son as my other kids are. I love him and I can't bear to think of him out there, injured or . . ."

"We'll find him," Ty said, his voice soft.

"We just kept loving him."

Not unlike Chet had loved Ty, had stuck by him before, during, and after the accident.

Hadn't blamed him for his colossal mistakes.

Had treated him like he still belonged on the team, even if Ty knew the truth.

Yes, grace was terrifying when you knew just how much you didn't deserve it.

Garrett glanced at Ty. "I'm so grateful that you and your team are here, Ty. The Red Cross is sending a team in, so maybe tomorrow we'll have more help, but you've been . . . well, you gave us hope when you found Chet and the middle schoolers."

"It wasn't just me."

"I know. But you think on your feet well. The fact is, we're all just trying to stay standing here. We can't think, we can hardly breathe. We need someone like you and your friends to come in and give us what we don't have—the energy to hope."

Ty just stared at him.

"Even if we can be a little grumpy about it." Garrett let one side of his face tweak up. "Maybe I'll try and get some shut-eye."

He pressed his hand on Ty's shoulder as he turned away. "Turn off the light when you hit the sack." He headed toward the stairs.

"We need someone like you . . ."

The front door opened, and Ty's gaze went to the group entering.

Kacey. Ben. Audrey and . . . Chet.

The sight of his old boss nearly rendered Ty to tears, especially when Chet met him with a smile.

Ty crossed the room, holding out his hand to Chet.

"Not hardly," Chet said and pulled him into an embrace. He seemed more fragile than Ty remembered, but he slapped his hand onto Ty's back. "You did good, kid."

Ty swallowed the burr in his throat, pulled away.

Kacey headed upstairs while Audrey made for the den.

Ben glanced at his dad, looking tired and defeated despite tonight's somber victory. Yes, well, Ty got that.

"Let's get you settled, Dad."

Chet glanced again at Ty. "I always knew that keeping you around would pay off."

The words settled in his chest as Chet followed Ben into the main floor den, just off the kitchen.

Ty stood there for a moment, then walked over to the map.

His gut said Creed was out there, still alive.

And his heart said that someday, Brette would stop running. And when she did, he'd be standing there, waiting.

+

Brette tried to convince herself that she hadn't just repeated the worst mistake of her life.

Walking—no, *running*—away from Ty Remington.

She closed the door behind her and leaned back, closing her eyes. *"I might deserve a man who would love me unconditionally, but you deserve a woman who won't die in your arms."*

She leaned up from the door, flicked on the light, and noticed that someone had put a backpack at the end of the other twin bed. But no one was huddled under the covers, so, for now, she had a little privacy. Brette walked to the dresser and stared at herself in the mirror. Haggard face, deep wells under her eyes. Her hair stuck straight up where the wind had its way with it, and despite her best efforts, she looked practically skeletal.

In fact, without her prosthetic, she resembled a teenage boy more than a thirty-year-old woman.

She opened her duffel bag and pulled out an oversized blue T-shirt with the words "Middlebury College" on the front. Ragged and thin, the old shirt bore the texture of overwashed, soft cotton. She changed into it, leaving on her prosthetic, then, with her shirt on, she worked off the sculpted size Bs.

Her shirt fell flat against her barren chest, and for a moment, she simply stood there. Then, softly, she ran her hand down the emptiness, pulling the shirt tight against herself.

Yeah, full-on junior high boy. Her jaw tightened against the sting in her throat. For a moment, her thoughts ran back to Ty, in the orchard, his arms around her, pulling her close. She didn't want to ask if he might sense the difference, the pillows of the prosthetic pressed against his chest instead of real body parts—that seemed way too intimate.

And that was where her thoughts caught. Because if she allowed Ty any further into her life, if she truly let her heart unwind into his embrace, and if he loved her back, then someday they might find themselves married.

Becoming man and wife.

And yes, she'd already sort of warned him of what the cancer stole from her, but in her mind, she saw him on their wedding night, realizing her words for the first time.

At best, trying to mask his horror.

At worst, well, he'd already said it once. *"Oh my gosh, Brette, what happened to you?"*

It was bad enough that she'd have to enter her marriage with the emotional scars Eason left on her soul. Baring her physical scars . . . well, she didn't have enough screams, enough apples to expunge that.

Running remained her only option.

She was turning, the prosthetic in her hand, when the door opened.

Kacey Fairing stood in the frame.

Brette stared at her like a deer in the headlights, the offensive garment in her grip.

Kacey shut the door behind her. Met Brette's gaze. "Sorry. I didn't realize you were here."

Brette dropped the prosthetic into the duffel bag. "It's okay. I . . ." And then she didn't know what to say because Kacey pressed a hand to her mouth as if trying not to cry.

"You okay?"

Kacey nodded, but her eyes filled.

"So that's a no then."

"I think I just made the biggest mistake of my entire life."

"Really, you too?"

Kacey just stared, and Brette shrugged. "You're in good company. I just walked away from Ty Remington again, one of the best guys I know." She sighed, not sure why she'd shared that.

"And I just broke up with America's sexiest man, or at least one of the top 100, according to *People* magazine."

"You broke up with Ben King?"

Kacey crawled onto the bed and buried her face in her arms. "My daughter doesn't know, so don't say anything."

Brette crossed her heart. "Why?"

Peeking up at her from her nested arms, Kacey said, "Because he's one of America's sexiest men, and I'm just . . . I'm . . . I don't fit into his world."

Brette sat on her bed. "He thinks you do. He moved to Montana to be with you."

"And he's on the road constantly. I miss him so much my bones ache, but . . . music is his life."

"I thought you were his life. At least that's the vibe I got from Gage and Ty."

A sad smile lifted up the side of Kacey's mouth. "I am. Or at least that's what he said tonight. But . . . I thought he brought me here to break up with me."

Brette frowned. "I'm not following you. I thought you said you broke up—"

"He wanted to elope. Begged me to marry him, tonight. I turned him down."

Brette stared at her, an unnamed darkness roiling inside her. "Why?"

"Because . . . well, because . . ." Kacey blinked at her. "Because Ben is always planning our lives for us, and . . . okay, right now I'm not sure why!"

But the darkness stirring inside wouldn't subside. "So, you're saying that the man begged you to marry him and you said no?"

Kacey wore a stricken expression. She sat up. Nodded.

"Okay, I'm sorry, I'm just not tracking here. You have a perfect life. A beautiful daughter, you're tall and beautiful and loved by a handsome, successful, romantic country star, and I quote, 'the sexiest man alive,' and you turn him down because he had the audacity to *plan your elopement*?"

Kacey's mouth tightened.

Brette didn't care if she might be offending her. "No. You don't get to do that." She stood up. "The world is full of people who have bigger-than-life problems, and you don't get to take something perfect and throw it away."

A frown creased Kacey's face, but Brette was too far down the rails. "I'd give anything to have your problems. To have a career I loved, helping people, a beautiful daughter, that amazing long red hair, and a body that was . . . well, didn't have a few essential parts carved out."

Kacey swallowed.

"And especially to have a man who cared enough to chase after me, to . . ."

And there it was. The excruciating truth. Her voice turned low and bereft. "To be able to give the man you love—or want to love—all of yourself without horrifying him." To add insult, her eyes filled.

Kacey hit her feet, took two strides over to Brette, and folded her into a hug.

Brette just stood there, not knowing what to do. What was with this PEAK team that thought they could invade her personal space?

But she didn't move. Her body betrayed her, leaning in to the embrace, and yes, maybe she yearned to have a friend reach out to her.

Even if Kacey couldn't possibly understand what she'd lost.

Kacey let her go. "When I came back from Afghanistan, I couldn't sleep through the night. I had a bad case of PTSD and had to take meds to get any sleep. I was raw and angry and knew that if Ben got close enough, he'd see, and hear, some pretty ugly things. But I couldn't stop him—see, Ben knew me before I was a wreck and loved me even more when I told him what I'd been through."

She wiped a hand across her cheek. "You're right. I am an idiot. And maybe Ben and my problems are minuscule compared to what other people—what you—have gone through. But I can guarantee you that Ty—and that's who we're talking about here, right?—is going to love you in whatever, uh, *form* you love him back in. He's that kind of guy."

Brette blinked hard against the heat in her eyes. "Yeah, I know."

"Then—"

"I just . . ." She squeezed her eyes shut. "I feel disgusting. Ugly."

Silence, and she finally looked at Kacey. Who simply nodded even as she stood there.

Huh?

"Nothing Ty, or any other guy, says will change that. You have to stop seeing yourself through the eyes of your disaster and start seeing the woman you've become. Our scars—my scars—are part of the beauty that makes us not only survivors, but beautiful. Stronger. Only then will you be able to accept Ty's words."

Brette didn't feel beautiful, or strong. Still, she reached for Kacey's words. She sighed. "I can't face him."

"Ty."

She nodded. "I kissed him. Then ran away from him."

Kacey sat on her bed. "I told Ben that he was the master of charm."

"He is. I love his songs, and he has the most amazing voice."

One side of Kacey's mouth lifted up. "I know. He's beloved by the whole world. The problem is, he doesn't have room for two more in his life."

Brette opened her mouth to argue—not sure why, because she certainly didn't know what to say—when the door opened.

In a second, Kacey transformed, her face lighting with a smile. "Hey, honey. Did you get Grandpa settled?"

Audrey nodded, but she came in and sat down next to Kacey on the bed, her face in a snarl.

"What's the matter?"

"I just don't understand Dad. While we were down there, his manager texted and asked if Dad would be willing to go to Wisconsin for some country music festival. She said one of the acts backed out and Dad would get prime billing on the last night."

Kacey put her arm around Audrey. "Your dad lost a lot of money in the destruction of his equipment and merchandise after the tornado. He's just getting started with the insurance company, so my guess is that he needs the gig to fill in some of the gaps—"

"He's leaving *tomorrow*, Mom." Audrey looked stricken. "We had plans. I thought . . ."

Brette had to give Kacey points for her composure, probably the soldier in her, because Kacey framed her daughter's face with her hands, her expression gentle. "Breathe, honey. It'll be okay."

"But you and Dad are supposed to be getting married. That's why we're here."

Brette looked away, even as Kacey pulled Audrey into her arms. "Sometimes life just doesn't work out the way we want it to," she said softly. "But I promise, your dad and I love you. Everything is going to be okay."

Brette's gaze fell to her prosthetic, and Ty's soft voice found her. *"That's what friends—more than friends—do. They stick around through life. They give each other someone to hold on to, someone to tell them that everything will be okay, even when it feels impossible."*

She closed her eyes and curled onto the bed.

The sooner she left, the better.

Except, for the first time ever, with everything inside her, she longed to stay.

8

TY WOULD FREEZE TO DEATH before the pain consumed him. Maybe. Because the agony of his fractured knee still made him cry out with every step.

He'd fought, and lost, the battle for bravery long ago. Sheer desperation pushed him now, as the snow scoured his eyes and his body shook all the way to his core.

But his gut said he was still headed in the right direction, following the river cast off the mountain deep in the Swan River range where they'd crashed. The river, a mere stream in the summertime, turned into a torrent of crashing whitewater, foam, and destruction this time of year.

However, it made for a clear path that led him straight west, across Morrell Creek to Morrell-Clearwater Road.

Please let there be a car, a plow, even a dogsled trekking the county road. That thought pulsed through Ty's head, a feeble hope dying with every breath-shattering step as the sun fell beyond the western horizon.

Around him, the forest rose, pine, alder, and birch running shadows across the lethal powder that hid tangles, bushes, and even drop-offs that could cast him into the deathly clasp of the river.

His foot came down hard into a nest of branches, jarred his

knee, and he pitched forward. Catching himself against the trunk of a whitened paper birch, he gasped, breathing hard.

A whimper tunneled through him, and it roused a fear, long buried.

How had he ever thought he could rescue anyone—he couldn't even rescue *himself*. The thought seared through him, a fire that singed his core even as the cold turned him numb.

He forced himself to his feet and trudged through the snow, but he couldn't stop shaking. With each step the whimper grew, thundering through him until it turned into a high-pitched keening.

He shook his head, fighting through it, but it was now a shriek. He pressed his hands over his ears, ducked his head as the branches slapped him, pushed him back.

Get to the road. Get to the—

"Ty, wake up. You're dreaming."

Hands clutched him, and he struggled, fighting, even as the voice broke through the pane of the dream. He fell back, came up thrashing.

Ty opened his eyes to see Gage standing over him. Gage backed away, hands up as if in surrender.

It took a long second to orient himself. To realize he'd fallen asleep on the Marshalls' sofa.

He reached for a knitted afghan, pulled it over his shoulders.

"You okay, dude? You were making the funniest noise."

The shrieking hadn't abated, and Ty winced even as he searched for it, frowning, sitting up.

He spied Jenny Marshall in her kitchen, removing a teakettle from the heat of her stove.

Oh.

His gaze landed, however, on the woman sitting in the corner, typing on her computer. Brette.

Who'd heard him whimpering like a three-year-old.

Perfect.

"I was dreaming of the accident," he mumbled.

Gage nodded. "I thought so. You make those sounds sometimes at home, so . . ." Gage lifted an eyebrow. "I figure you're remembering being out there in that storm, huh?"

"Something like that." Ty looked out the window, at the somber drizzle that hovered over the day. The wet breeze wafted into the room, and he got up and shut the window. "We would have died out there if Sam and the team hadn't found us."

Gage stepped up beside him. "But we did. And you did everything right. Headed for a road, blew your whistle—"

"I was desperate and made a stupid decision based on fear. I should have never left Chet. He nearly died."

"Sometimes there are no good choices. You followed your instincts—"

"Which is a pretty poor way to manage a search," Ty said.

"Your gut led you to the road. To us."

His gut. Ty was tired of listening to his instincts. They only broke his heart.

He dropped the afghan on the sofa. "We need to rouse everyone, start looking for Creed and the others. We're going to find them today."

Gage hadn't shaved this morning, had tied his long hair back into a black bandanna. "Yes, we are."

"We can't screw this up." No, *he* couldn't screw this up. He might have found Chet, but there were too many people depending on them. On him. Ty hardly had the credentials to lead a callout, but with his finding of Chet, he'd somehow become the de facto leader. Ty headed over to the table.

"I spent most of the night mapping out a search strategy, starting from the school and moving out past that in a grid. But truthfully, we need to talk to the other parents, see if they had an idea of where the students might have gone for practice, then start a grid from that last known point too."

Gage stood over the map for a moment, then headed to the big island, where Jenny had poured him coffee.

"You want a cup, Ty?" Jenny said, looking ragged and red-eyed. But she offered a smile, as if grasping for hope.

Oh, he wanted to give it to her. So, he met her smile with one of his own and nodded.

He couldn't bear to look at Brette.

The coffee poured life into him and he headed upstairs for a quick shower.

He stood under the hot water, shaking away his nightmare, and emerged at least a halfway new person. He was charting out the search grids in his mind by the time he headed downstairs.

Garrett, Jonas, Ned, Ian, Shae, Kacey, Audrey, Ben, and his bandmates had risen and were eating muffins and downing coffee.

Chet even shuffled out and took a seat on a high-top at the bar.

"No one expects you to go out looking today," Ty said as Chet poured himself a cup of coffee.

Chet just peered at him over the rim of his cup, giving him a look that a man who hadn't grown up under Chet's tutelage might interpret as a challenge.

No, it was a challenge, but Ty wasn't up to a fight. Today, he just wanted success. Hope.

Wanted Brette to see that not all things ended badly.

He finally glanced at her out of the corner of his eye. She got up and grabbed coffee and a freshly baked bran muffin. Then she sat back down at her computer at the breakfast table, neatly ignoring him. She wore a peach headband, her short blonde hair poking out of the top, along with a gray Vortex.com T-shirt and a pair of cargo shorts.

For a moment, all he could think of was the way she came

alive in his arms, how he'd wanted to pick her up and run away from this nightmare.

Except, as she pointed out, her nightmare would keep following them.

Somehow, he had to show her that he wasn't ditching her into its clutches. Ever.

Which meant, right now, not giving up hope.

He got coffee, then walked over to the table and called the group together. "I spent some time last night mapping out a search grid. We should assume that for some reason, after Creed texted his mom he had decided to go back to school. So, we're going to start at the school and work our way out. Meanwhile, Jenny, you get on the phone to the other parents and ask if they heard from any of their kids before the storm."

"I will. I got a call early this morning that the Red Cross is setting up in town. They're sending a man over to help with the search."

"Good." Ty glanced at Garrett, who stood with his arms akimbo, frowning.

As if thinking.

"What?" Ty said.

"It's just—we assumed that Creed rode in the coach's van. But if he was with his team, what car did he drive? If we find his at the school, could he have ridden with someone else?"

"He sometimes rides with this girl he likes," Jenny said quietly. "Addie Ridley. She drives a red Impala."

Ty stared at the map. "Or, he drove and they made it back to the school . . ."

"We know they're not there," Ned said.

Shae came up behind Ned, her arms folded across her body, her mouth in a grim line. "We were there when they pulled out the teacher and that janitor."

But Garrett's words burned inside Ty. "Are we *sure* they didn't go back to the school?"

"The school is an empty lead." The voice came from behind them, and it was familiar and just bossy enough for Ty to place it immediately.

Ty didn't even have to turn to confirm the identity, to know it belonged to a tall blond with confidence in his swagger and command in his eyes befitting an incident commander.

Former PEAK team member Pete Brooks.

For a second all the air left the room. Pete walked in, wearing his white, collared Red Cross shirt and a pair of black jeans, but Ty couldn't tear his eyes off Pete's hair, which was cut short to match his nearly clean-shaven face, as if he had joined the ranks of responsibility. Pete's gaze scanned the room a long second before it landed on Gage.

His fellow EMT. "Hey," he said to Gage, but really to everyone, Ty guessed. "I see you've started without me." He shook Gage's hand, came in close for a thump on his back, turned to Ben, met his grip, then Chet, who he pulled close. "So glad you're okay," he said, a little husk in his voice.

He gave Ian a fist bump, Shae a half-hug, Kacey a firm embrace, and finally turned to Ty, offered him a smile and a tight grip. They'd never been close, but they had worked together.

Pete turned to Garrett and the rest of the Marshall family. "Pete Brooks. I'm here with the Red Cross."

"Oh, thank you," Jenny said and wrapped her arms around Pete's neck. He leaned in for a hug like it might be a practiced move. Maybe it was—Pete had traded in his small-town SAR stats for a national gig over a year ago. A special, elite search and rescue team put together by a senator, the SAR team assisted the Red Cross disaster relief teams. Pete was their first national incident commander. No doubt he'd seen plenty of tornado-damaged disaster zones.

Probably knew exactly what he was doing.

Ty couldn't decide if his sigh contained relief or just the slightest edge of disappointment. Still, he stepped back, folded his arms over his chest, and made room for Pete to scan the map.

"So, this is the area you already searched," he said, fanning his hand over the roads to the west of the school. "And this is your new search grid?" He traced the areas. "Good job."

No one mentioned it was Ty's handiwork.

"We'll start in vehicles along the tornado path. Kacey, can you do a flyover?"

"Of course," Kacey said. Ty noticed that she hadn't gone to stand by Ben, who had his hands shoved into his pockets and was standing a little behind everyone else, as if he might be debating bolting.

Better not—Ty had made this family a promise.

Ben wasn't the only one who had a skittish aura. Brette was working on her computer, as if barely listening, her attention elsewhere.

Ty suppressed the urge to walk up to her, to ask . . . maybe simply if she was okay. And fine, it burned him that she could occupy the same airspace as he did without a blink in his direction, as if he might be a piece of furniture, or an afterthought.

Maybe he was.

"Let's break into teams. I brought walkies for everyone, along with a GPS device that will monitor where everyone has searched," Pete was saying, clearly taking over. "We've set up a base in town, at the fire station, and we'll coordinate from there."

Ty turned back to the table. "What about the school?" He couldn't stop the niggle in his head that maybe searching for Creed's car might be a clue they couldn't ignore.

"According to local EMS, they searched the school," Pete said. "I don't want to use valuable manpower digging up a dead end." He sighed, glanced around the audience. "We're coming up on forty-eight hours past the event, which means we're running out of time. Let's get moving."

Running out of time.

Pete led the group out of the kitchen.

Ty gave a quick glance at Jenny. "We'll find him." Scooping up a walkie, he followed Garrett and Kacey out to the truck.

Chet and Ben left, and Ty noticed Brette following Jonas. He couldn't shake the sense that their search had taken a turn in the wrong direction. And for a second, he was standing in the snow, the wind howling around him as he stared into the gray sky.

If they didn't get this right, kids would die.

"You getting in?" Kacey said as she stood at the truck. He glanced at her, then at Ben, who was taking the wheel of one of the Marshall Vineyard SUVs.

"No," he said.

Kacey frowned at him, but he ran up to Ben, catching the door a second before it closed. "Ben—I need you to go with Kacey. I . . . I need to check on something."

Ben frowned, glanced at Kacey. Swallowed. "Okay." He got out.

Ty slid in. Chet sat in the opposite seat.

"What's up?" Chet said.

Ty turned the SUV over, put it into drive. "I hate to tell you this, but—"

"Your gut is at it again?"

He glanced at Chet. "Pray that I'm right."

Ty was pulling out of the driveway when he noticed movement in the backseat. He glanced in the rearview mirror.

Brette offered him a slight smile. "So, where are we going?"

+

While Ty barely noticed her, Brette was aware of every breath he took.

Especially the way his eyes widened, just for a second, at her question. Or maybe by her appearance in the backseat of the SUV.

As if he'd forgotten she existed. Okay, that might be overstated, but he'd barely looked at her this morning.

Whereas she'd been watching him since the first fall of rain, somewhere around 4:00 a.m. She'd listened to the patter on the roof, her instincts finally compelling her from the bed to see if she could get a glimpse of the horizon. She'd dressed, grabbed her camera, padded downstairs, and gone out onto the porch.

Not a torrential downpour but a sad weeping from the sky, as if it was mourning the advent of a new day with five kids still lost somewhere out in the razed landscape. The humid air rose through her, and the smell of a damp morning—mud, grass, moistened wood—stirred memories through her.

The kind that could make her collapse into a puddle if she let them. In a blink, she saw her mother sitting in an Adirondack chair, a blanket wrapped over her shoulders as she cradled a cup of coffee. She was bone thin, weary, staring at one of her final sunrises. *"Isn't it beautiful, Brette? Sunrises are meant to be shared."*

Brette shook the voice away and instead took a shot of the awakening horizon, a narrow burst of light against the darkened clouds, a sliver of fire that fought the night.

She went inside and opened her laptop, loaded the shot in, and posted it on her blog.

That was when she heard the sound. A huff of breath, the slightest groan, or maybe a cry of pain, and it raised the hairs on the back of her neck. She froze and cast a glance around the room for the source.

She found it in the huddled form of Ty sleeping on the sofa. He wore last night's clothing, and his arms were curled around him as if attempting to warm himself. She had the urge to get up, pull the knitted afghan over him, but she feared he'd wake and see her standing there.

And if he even just looked at her, she might find her resolve dissolving. So instead she simply watched him.

Then he began dreaming, and it wasn't a happy dream. The urge then to wake him from the nightmare, to pull him back from whatever abyss threatened to yank him down, caused her to push her chair away from the table.

Before she could rescue him, a creak sounded on the stairs and she spied Jenny Marshall coming down into the kitchen. Jenny paused, taken by the sleeping man on her sofa, then turned to the kitchen and reached for her teakettle. Filled it and popped it on the stove.

Still, Ty seemed fitful.

Jenny had likewise shot a look at Ty, a bit of worried mother in her gaze. The teakettle began to whistle, slow at first, then building.

Brette stood up just as Gage came down the stairs. She watched, the knot in her stomach unraveling as Gage went over, shook his friend awake.

Jenny opened the refrigerator and pulled out a bowl of batter.

Brette had focused on her computer, refusing to be an interloper in the conversation between the two guys. While their backs were to the window, she got up and poured herself coffee.

"Good morning," Jenny said quietly. "Muffins will be ready in about ten minutes." Jenny's eyes appeared cracked and red, as if she'd spent the night crying. Probably few people actually got any real sleep last night under the Marshall roof.

Ty headed upstairs as others began to appear—Ben and his crew, Kacey and Audrey, Jonas and Ned. She uploaded her pictures from yesterday's rescue and began to sort through them.

The teenager wrapping her arms around Ty. Chet and Ben.

The fireman and his little sister. A picture of the mangled house enshrouding the van. A few of the torn countryside.

But it was the shot of Ty and Chet that caught her attention. The way Ty held him, his eyes closed, such a vivid, pained relief on his face it made her wonder at the depth of their friendship.

The photo montage could make for a good story. And she hated how her brain turned to that, but . . . it was her livelihood. Capturing the tragedy . . . and the triumph.

"Those are good," said a voice, and she turned to see Audrey catching the crumbs of her fresh from the oven muffin.

"Thanks. I thought I'd send them to my editor at *Nat Geo*. See if he thinks they could work for a photo essay."

Audrey's eyebrow went up, but she nodded. "Cool."

Ty returned, his dark hair wet and curly around his face, a few droplets of water on his gray T-shirt.

She got up and refilled her coffee, grabbed a muffin, and escaped before he wandered over to the kitchen bar.

Averting her eyes as he called the group together, she opened her email and jotted a quick note to her editor at *Nat Geo*. She attached a few of the photos and had it sent by the time Pete Brooks walked in.

She remembered him too well from eighteen months ago. Bossy, a little arrogant. In the end, he'd brought her flowers in the hospital, offered to tell her his story, and turned out to be a charmer. But today he was all business.

She watched as Ty stepped back and let Pete take the reins of the search. Ty wore an odd expression, as if he wasn't quite buying what Pete said. She knew from Ella that Pete fashioned himself as some kind of national hero, the way he jumped into a rescue with both feet, but she'd seen Ty in action too.

Ty's hero stats could stand up to Pete's any day. And he had Pete's good looks beaten, hands down. Sure, Pete was wide-shouldered, blond, and resembled a Marvel-inspired Norse god. But Ty had tall, dark, and handsome written all over him, with that tousled dark hair, the solemn face, those pale green eyes, his biceps thick against his shirt.

Yeah, Pete Brooks had nothing on Ty Remington.

What was she thinking, running *away* from this man who so clearly wanted to be in her life?

When the group disbanded, Brette had gotten up, tucking her camera into her satchel. She didn't quite have the stomach to ride with Ty in the chopper again, so she followed Ben and Chet out the door, toward the SUV.

Climbed in the back.

And had tried to be perfectly fine, not bothered at all that Ty hadn't even said good morning, that he hadn't stopped for one millisecond to see how she was.

Then . . . "Ben—I need you to go with Kacey. I . . . I need to check on something."

His voice had stopped her heart cold in her chest, and when he slid into the front seat, she couldn't breathe.

When Ty put the SUV into drive and tore out of the driveway, she knew something was up.

That was when he noticed her in the rearview mirror. His eyes widened, as if shocked to see her. What could she do? She flashed a quick smile. "So, where are we going?"

"Oh, uh . . ." He glanced at Chet as if he might be debating stopping and leaving her in the driveway, and for a second, she wondered if she'd reduce herself to begging that he take her along.

No, she didn't recognize herself at all anymore.

But he met her gaze again in the rearview mirror. "Everyone else is searching the surrounding roads. But I can't get past the feeling that we need to go back to the school. That maybe they're still there."

The school. "But—"

"I know what Pete said. But I . . ." He made a face, stared back out onto the road. "I get these gut feelings that something isn't right, and—"

"Like you had with me this past year?"

She didn't know why she said that, why she suddenly yearned for the answer to be yes. *Yes, I thought of you. Yes, I couldn't forget you no matter what I tried.*

He caught her gaze in the mirror. "Yeah. I'd get these . . . feelings. That you needed me." He looked away, as if he might be regretting that admission.

But his words had reached in and took ahold of her, warmed her body to the core.

"And you were right," she said, so softly she doubted he'd heard her. So, she cleared her throat. "I get it. We reporters have hunches too. And the first rule of being a journalist is . . . always follow your hunch."

And her particular hunch said to hold on to Ty Remington for as long as she could, no matter what it cost her.

He who hesitates is lost. That thought alone rippled through Ben's brain as he watched Kacey drive away with Garrett.

He could have climbed into the backseat of the truck, could have spent the day with Kacey, and despite the chaos of the chopper noise, maybe figured out a way to talk to her. Beg her not to run away from him.

Give them another chance.

He could have even suggested that they find a quiet corner somewhere in the middle of all this trauma to talk about their future. Audrey.

The fact that Kacey had broken up with him.

But he stood there, watching her drive away, and the loss left him unraveled.

Because, in that moment, he saw it. For some reason, he just kept hesitating. Sure, he said he wanted to get married, but it hadn't been Kacey who canceled their nuptials, twice.

Worse, he couldn't put a finger on why. He blamed his busyness. But that was the easy reason. Something else niggled at him, something—

"Ben, you need a ride, buddy?" Pete had pulled up behind him, and he turned at the question. Pete drove a black Hummer with the Red Cross emblem on the door. Gage and Ian were tucked inside.

"Yeah," he said and climbed in back. Gage scooted over. Ian sat in the front seat and glanced back at him.

"You okay? I thought you were headed out with your dad."

"Ty got into the truck and said he needed to follow a hunch or something. I . . ." He glanced out the window. "I was going to ride with Kacey, but it looks like she's got it covered."

Pete pulled out, following the caravan—Ty in front of him, and Jonas and his brother, along with Shae, in the Suburban out in front. His bandmates had headed out with yet another vehicle to scour the festival site. And check on the towing of his RV to Minneapolis for repairs.

Hopefully they'd also finish salvaging the rest of their equipment. They'd have to rent their instruments for the gig in Wisconsin, but . . .

The gig in Wisconsin. Ben tapped his fingers on his knee, thinking through the text from his manager. And his stupid slip in front of Audrey. He should have never mentioned the gig—the look on her face had opened a wound that was still throbbing in his chest.

But in truth, it tugged at him, the temptation to fall back into the music, wrap himself into the words, the beats, the familiar, and forget, at least for two hours, the fact that somehow he'd blown it again.

He hadn't a clue how to woo Kacey back into his arms.

"I wish you'd called me when Chet went missing," Pete was saying, glancing into the rearview mirror as he drove. "I would have been here earlier."

"Sorry. I called PEAK. I didn't know what else to do."

"We should have called you," Ian said quietly. "Sorry. How is the Red Cross working out?"

Pete lifted a shoulder, strangely noncommittal. And then, "So, Jess isn't here." His voice was casual, as if he could fool any of them into thinking that it might be a random, meaningless observation. Right. Even Ben had heard about the altercation in some hospital in Miami when Jess's past charged back into her life, one that included a fiancé. Apparently, despite Pete's inclination to level the fancy pants Frenchman who'd tried to claim Jess, Pete had simply walked away, left the choice to Jess.

"She's still in New York," Ian said, matching Pete's casual tone. "I saw her a month ago. Apparently, her mother is thinking of selling their home, and Jess decided to stick around and help."

Ian said it as if Jess's home wasn't the entire penthouse floor of a high-rise in Manhattan, worth eight figures. They probably had an armada of real estate brokers working on the sale.

Pete's mouth tightened into a line. Quiet filled the cab until he said, "I should have punched him in the mouth and thrown her over my shoulder."

Gage suppressed a smile and glanced at Ben. But he agreed with Pete.

"There's a reason I married Sierra as soon I could. I was afraid she'd come to her senses," Ian said.

Pete glanced at him. "Really?"

Ian held up his hand. "I'm not saying you and Jess aren't the perfect match, but a year of waiting for an answer . . . I'd lose my mind."

Pete's mouth tightened, as if yes, that's exactly how he felt.

"You waited seven years, dude," Gage said. "You've been crazy over Sierra for as long as I've known you."

Ian's face twitched with the truth.

Tires ground out the dirt road, wet gravel from the rain pinging against the tailgate. They'd have to go off-road today to follow the tornado's path to find the missing red Impala driven by Creed's teammate.

"Jess needs time to figure out what she wants," Pete mumbled.

The stretched silence suggested that maybe Jess had found it.

"Maybe I'm an idiot," Pete said, as if reading their minds.

"By Kacey's standards, you're a gentleman," Ben said before he could stop himself. "I was planning on eloping this weekend, and when Kacey found out, you would have thought I'd kidnapped her into a forced marriage." He didn't exactly mean his tone, but . . . okay, maybe he did.

"You were going to elope?" Ian said. "And you didn't tell any of us?"

"It was a surprise. That's why my dad was here. And Audrey. We had the whole weekend planned. And then the storm hit."

"That's some rotten luck," Ian said. "So, Kacey found out and she wasn't thrilled?"

Ben stared out the window. "She broke up with me."

"She broke up with you?" Gage said. "Kacey?"

"No, Taylor Swift. Of course, Kacey." He took off his hat and scrubbed a hand down his face. "But maybe it's for the best."

He could barely believe his own words—and by the silence in their wake, neither could the rest of the car's occupants. "Maybe I'm just fooling myself that this could work out. I've been thinking about why I've put this wedding off so many times and . . ."

"Is it because you're busy trying to keep your career alive?" Gage said. "That means commitment and sacrifice and—"

"And I've already messed up Kacey and Audrey's life once," Ben said. "I love being Audrey's dad. And I love Kacey, but I watched my parents struggle for years on my dad's here-and-there income and . . . I don't want that for Audrey. Being a musician takes total commitment—and these days, I need to tour to make money if I hope to keep the studio alive. But if I tour, I'm never home. Audrey deserves better."

Gage stared at him as Pete turned onto the main highway into Duck Lake. "So, let me get this right. You'd let some other guy marry Kacey? Be a stepfather to Audrey?"

Ben just blinked at him. Gage's words were like a fist to his gut. No.

"Because if you let Kacey walk away, you free her to be with someone else."

The thought made him physically ill. Still . . . "At least this way I can still provide for them. If I walk away from music for Kacey, we could end up with nothing."

"Or everything." Ian hiked his elbow over the backseat. "Sheesh, Ben. I have a little experience with losing everything. First, my wife and son, and then, did you happen to read the article in the *Wall Street Journal* where the IRS fined me over ten million dollars? Yeah, that hurt."

Ben looked at him. "So that's why you sold your house."

Ian nodded. "But out of the two losses, only one took me to my knees, made me want to stop living. And it wasn't the money. You don't know what the future holds—you could lose your voice, your entire career could implode, but Kacey and Audrey are *real*. They're not going anywhere." He glanced at Pete, then back at Ben. "It matters who you choose to spend your time—and your life—with. And when it's the person you love, then you can't fail."

He looked at Pete. "Jess loves you, man. You'd have to be blind not to see that. Have a little faith." He grinned, and his gaze spanned the backseat. "I learned that bit from Sierra."

"You're way too happy, man," Gage said.

"You should talk," Ian shot back. "When are you going to stop goofing around and propose to Ella?"

Gage lifted an eyebrow, looked out the window.

Ben's phone buzzed, and he dug it out of his pocket. A text from his drummer. *Are we headed to Wisconsin?*

He shoved the phone back into his pocket.

9

Please let this work.

Ty glanced at Brette through the rearview mirror, way too happy about the way she offered him a tentative smile at his bold idea to search the school.

He didn't know what he'd done over the past twelve hours to make her want to be in the same vehicle as him.

And she listened with a sort of eagerness in her eyes as he revealed his hunch about the kids at the school. As if she believed him.

Which meant he couldn't let her down—couldn't let any of them down, really—but especially Brette, who looked at him the way she had eighteen months ago . . . like he might be the kind of man she'd been looking for her entire life.

"The more I hope, the harder it will be when that hope dies."

Please, God, help us find Creed today. The words bubbled up inside him, and he couldn't cap them, just let them seep through to him and light him on fire with hope. *Only you know where they are. Please keep them alive until we can find them.*

Ahead of them, Pete kept driving past the school, as did Jonas, but Ty tapped the brakes and turned at the Duck Lake school entrance.

Or what remained of it. The broken debris of the sign littered the ground as if a giant foot had come down hard, turning what had been a sculptured stone sign to rubble. The twister had torn through the parking lot, upending light poles that now lay toppled like matchsticks across furrowed pavement and on the sunken remains of the roof.

The destruction indicated the path of the twister, from the destroyed classrooms on the northwest side, through the middle section, and out the following southeastern corner. Nothing of structural significance remained of the elementary area; it looked as if God had picked it up in two massive hands and torn it asunder. Adding insult to injury, the roof from the high school section pancaked the entire mess.

The sun blinked off shattered glass in the yard. Cars were strewn against the far side of the building as if a broom had swept them carelessly aside.

Ty pulled up slowly, not wanting to pop his tires on the debris. Silence clung to the occupants.

As they got out of the SUV, Ty could barely make out anything but the chaos of rubble. Classroom desks lay twisted; he recognized a broken round lavatory sink atop a pile of bricks. A basketball had rolled out past the muddle, as if trying to escape.

A lone football helmet was embedded in the mud of the front yard.

Brette picked up a pink backpack. "I hope this was in the lost and found."

Ty stepped on a tattered, grimy US map.

Chet just stood by the Suburban, his eyes wide.

Ty glanced at him. "You okay?"

"I heard it go over us and thought, wow, that's a doozy. But I had no idea." He pressed his hand on the hood.

"Why don't you get Pete on the walkie, tell him that we're going to stick around here and see if we can find any clues."

Chet nodded and slid back into his seat.

Ty walked over to Brette. Touched her shoulder.

She turned, almost jumping. "We stopped by the school right after it happened, but we were so consumed with getting home . . . we should have looked harder." She lifted her camera and took a picture of the backpack, then turned and grabbed more shots.

Then she unhooked the camera from around her neck. "Do you think one of these cars might be Creed's? Let's find it."

She started for the pileup, and Ty followed her. He counted maybe five cars in total, covered in mud, the front lights ripped out, roofs sagged in, and the entire lot of them wadded up like paper and jammed together.

"He has an orange Subaru, according to Jenny. And we're looking for a red Impala—Addie's car."

She pointed at an orange, crushed station wagon on the top of the heap, and he nodded. But when she headed for it, he grabbed her back. "The cars could shift on us."

He left her there before she could argue and scrambled onto the hood of a white Jeep. Oddly, his gaze fell on a sticker of a paw in the front windshield. He kept climbing, balancing on the remains of a red pickup and crawling along the bed to the Subaru. It had landed upside down, and he braced himself just for a moment before peering inside.

Empty.

His lungs released his relief. "He's not here."

Brette edged up to the pile. "Good, now get down."

"In a minute." Because he'd seen something—there, wedged in the gap under the passenger seat, a small, tie-string athletic bag. He leaned in, balancing himself on the shattered window—

The car creaked, shifting its weight toward him.

"Ty!"

His fingers brushed the fabric.

The car rocked.

"Get out of there!"

He snagged the bag and backed out. But not before the car listed hard toward him and began to roll.

He took two steps and leaped from the bed of the truck just as the car careened down the side of the pile and crashed behind him.

Bending over to grab his knees, he let his heart find his chest.

"Are you crazy? You could have gotten killed!" Brette grabbed his arm, bent down to meet his gaze, her eyes big. "What did you find?"

He opened the bag. "Shoes." He pulled them out. A fairly new pair of orange New Balance running shoes. "The kind a cross-country runner might wear to practice."

"And take off after practice before returning to the school," she said. "This feels like good confirmation to a hunch."

"But it's not proof. Maybe he wore a different pair that day."

"Help! Help me!" The voice rose from beyond the debris, behind or perhaps inside the building.

Ty glanced at Brette, his heart banging hard against his ribs.

No—it couldn't be that easy.

He scrambled toward the entrance. "Hello? Where are you?"

"I'm in the school!"

The voice seemed to be coming from the center of the U, past the maw of the main double doors. Ty headed inside the building and reached out almost on instinct for Brette's hand.

She took it and held on.

Mud and debris clogged the main hallway—twisted metal, wood, flooring, bricks, papers, an announcement board torn from the wall. A display case of trophies had toppled, and glass littered the hallway.

"Careful," he said and tightened his hold on her hand. They crunched through the carnage. "Hello?"

"Back here!"

They climbed around a tumble of desks in the hallway. "We're coming!" Brette yelled, so much life in her voice it made him want to haul her up in an embrace.

In fact, he did as she nearly fell through the linked legs of the desks. So much easier to just lift her over the mass.

She weighed nearly nothing now—and he knew that because he'd picked her up before, when she'd needed her appendix out. Now, she grabbed on to his arms just for a moment as he put her down, as if needing balance.

He held her back. "You okay?"

Her face was flushed, her beautiful eyes big. "Yeah."

"Over here!"

She took off, searching for the voice, Ty on her tail as they ran up a hallway, over papers and mud and lunch trays and even a smashed globe.

They rounded the corner and found a man standing near a pile of debris that leaned against a metal doorway. Inside the thin slip of safety glass, the room was dark. A big man with an athletic build, he wore his brown hair short, capped with a Twins hat perched backward on his head. He looked at them with such wide-eyed desperation that Ty fought the instinct to take Brette and put her behind him.

"Are you hurt?"

He shook his head, his face contorting before he drew in a breath. "I can't find my wife. I think the school locker room is behind these doors, but I can't wedge them open."

Ty just stared at him. "What?"

"My wife April is missing. I was out of town, but . . . her apartment building is destroyed, and I thought maybe she would've come to the school."

He pushed again on the door, but it didn't move, and Ty ran

his flashlight into the dark crevice. "There's a beam down on the other side. We'll never get it open from here."

The news seemed to undo the man, and Ty guessed his adrenaline might be running low because his hands trembled, and when he stepped away, he tripped.

Ty grabbed his arm. "Steady there, pal. Let's just take a minute. Maybe get you a drink of water."

But to his horror, the man collapsed, right there, onto the pile, his head in his hands. "I tried to get here . . . I tried, but . . . and now she's just *gone.*"

Ty knelt in front of him. "Who are you, and who is your wife?"

He ran his palm across his cheek. "April Maguire. She's the new science teacher and cross-country coach."

Ty couldn't move. "Cross-country coach?"

"She moved here just a week ago to get settled in. I was out of town when I heard about the tornado. I got here as soon as I could, and I went to our apartment, but . . . it's gone. It's just *gone*. And she's not answering her cell phone. I thought maybe she'd be here, but . . ." He looked like he might unravel again, and even Brette must have sensed it because she crouched next to him.

"We'll find her. When's the last time you heard from her?" Her voice was gentle, as if she might be talking to a child.

"We texted before the storm. She was going to work out with the team. She mentioned a park they were running at . . ." He looked away, his eyes thick with moisture.

"He could go into shock," Ty said to Brette. "Let's get him to the Red Cross area. They might have heard from his wife." He turned to the man. "What's your name?"

He swallowed, his lips barely moving. "Spenser."

"Let's see what we can find out about April," Ty said. "It's possible she simply lost her phone. Let's not jump to conclusions." But he glanced at Brette, who'd come around beside him, looped her arm under Spenser's. Ty did the same, and they hoisted Spenser to his feet. He seemed almost disoriented as they led him through the rubble back to the car.

Chet opened the door for them and Ty settled Spenser into the backseat. Chet climbed in beside him, introducing himself and talking to him in low tones.

Brette pitched her voice low. "Do you think April was with the team?"

"He mentioned a park. Maybe they met there, took shelter, and got trapped." He reached out for the driver's door, but stilled when her hand landed on his arm.

The softness in her eyes eased the wounds raked up by her fleeing from him last night. "Good hunching."

"Is that a word?"

"I'm a journalist. I get to make words up." Then she winked and let go, running around to the passenger side.

Huh.

So this was the substance, the taste of hope. Brette almost didn't recognize it, this sweet, warm welling in the center of her chest, that anticipation of a longing about to be answered.

She could get drunk on it, the way it seeped into her bones, made her yearn for more.

Or maybe that was what being around Ty did to her. Made her loosen her grip on despair, shattered the darkness so light could crack through.

"What park did April go to?" Ty was asking Spenser, who stared out the window almost hollowly as they motored into Duck Lake. The town had accomplished little in the way of cleanup over the past two days. She spotted the bowling alley, the roofless houses, and then Ty turned on some unnamed street and she made out a huddle of Red Cross tents spanned across the dirt parking lot of the fire department. Four tents in total, imprinted with a red cross on the white roof. Red Cross vehicles—a van with the words "Disaster Relief" written on the side, an ambulance, an RV, and a Hummer—jammed the parking lot. A school bus had just pulled up, letting off adults wearing T-shirts—Minnetonka Baptist Church—and Brette guessed them to be bussed-in volunteers. They headed toward one of the tents. The flaps of another tent opened, and a worker dressed in a red vest came out carrying a crate of water bottles.

Ty pulled up to the curb. "I'm hoping that's Pete's Hummer."

Brette got out as Ty opened Spenser's door. She ran toward the woman carrying the water bottles. "Can I get one of these?"

Brette returned in a moment as Ty brought Spenser around, set him down on the curb. She crouched before Spenser and handed him the bottle.

Spenser guzzled it down.

"Easy there, champ," Ty said and eased the bottle away from his mouth. "Let's see if we can find a medical center."

Brette pointed toward yet another tent, this one with the flaps propped open. "I see some cots and blankets in there."

"Perfect." He helped Spenser to his feet, but Spenser shook away, clearly coming back to himself. "I don't need medical attention. I need to find my wife!"

Brette stepped back as Ty edged up to Spenser, even took a step between them. But the voice that emerged bore patience, even understanding.

"Dude, I gotcha. And I agree. Listen, I got a buddy here who's heading up the search and rescue. Let's go find him, okay?"

Spenser took a breath, nodded.

Ty reached out again for Brette's hand, and like it belonged there, she slipped hers into his grip.

He had warm, strong hands, and she wanted to hold on forever.

Ty headed for the RV, a long white slide-out with the words "Mobile Command Center" on the door. Pete's voice spilled out from the screen door as he checked in with one of the teams . . . no, with Kacey, who was scouring the area by air. "Roger. Just keep doing a sweep of the area. The storm isn't due until a little later today."

At his words, Brette cast her gaze to the sky, and yes, in the distance she noticed the slightest gathering of Cu. But it seemed harmless, a little trickle of moisture at best.

Although challenging for a search and rescue operation. She gave Ty's hand a squeeze before he released it.

"Hey, Pete, got a second?" Ty said.

Pete came down from the RV. Brette glanced over his shoulder inside and spied a bank of computer screens, some with grids of the area with blinking GPS lights. Another played the Doppler weather screen, which was blinking every two seconds with an update. She noticed a hot cell drifting northeast out of Colorado.

Yeah, that might be a twister by the time it hit Nebraska, or even Iowa.

"You're supposed to be searching the northern grid," Pete said without greeting.

Ty ignored him. "This is Spenser Maguire. His wife April is missing."

Pete grabbed his phone and scrolled. "She's not on the list of missing."

And for a brilliant, wild second, hope took on physical form. Spenser's intake of breath, the way he turned, cupped his hand over his mouth, as if trying not to cry. Brette wanted to touch his back, maybe grab a piece of all that overwhelming relief.

"She's alive." Spenser turned back to Pete. "She's *alive.* Where is she?"

Pete turned back to the operations team. "Guys, track down an April Maguire. Look on the survivor list."

Please.

Ty had found her hand again. This time she wove her fingers between his. She glanced at Spenser.

"Nope," came the voice from inside.

Everything stilled inside Brette. Oh no.

Pete climbed back inside the command center. His voice lowered, but she caught it. "Check again."

Spenser braced one hand on the RV, as if trying not to sag.

And then Pete returned.

She wanted to reach out, catch Spenser before he fell, but Ty beat her to it.

"She's not on the survivor list either," Pete said.

"Are you sure?" Brette asked, not able to stop herself.

"We've kept a tally of everyone who is accounted for. The only ones still missing are the five from the track team and a woman named Hattie Foreman."

"And my wife," Spenser said, barely above a whisper.

Pete nodded. "We'll add her."

Spenser leaned against the RV. Closed his eyes. "I should have never let her move here alone." He opened his eyes, his gaze on Ty. "She just insisted." He pushed off the RV, stalked away, and Brette winced when he made a feral sound and threw the water bottle across the parking lot.

Pete looked away.

But Ty walked right up to him. Stood beside him. And when Spenser turned, he grabbed him by the shoulders and met his eyes. "We'll find her, man. We'll find her."

Why, oh why, had she ever run, not once, but twice, from this man?

Ty returned to Pete, Spenser behind him. "Pete, April is the new cross-country coach. Spenser seems to think she was—is—with the team and that they didn't go out to Duck Lake but were training at a park in town. I think it's worth checking out."

Pete glanced at Spenser, then back to Ty. "Right. Okay, which park?"

Ty shook his head, and Pete invited him inside the RV. Brette followed them into the cramped space.

Two men manned the computer stations and were talking on walkies. Out of the window, she spied the Baptists hiking away in groups, armed with wheelbarrows, gloves, and shovels.

A map of the town, gridded and numbered, lay across a table. The group leaned over it.

"Her apartment is—was—here," Spenser said, pointing to a building just off Park Avenue. "And here's the park she often mentioned."

A small square of green off Park Ave, labeled Heritage Park, maybe a mile from the fire station.

Right in the center of the tornado's destruction, according to Pete's markings.

Spenser saw it too, because his voice quavered. "She liked to go there—people walked their dogs and played Frisbee and . . . oh . . ." He pushed a fist to his mouth. Cleared his throat. "She would run the loop around town, about seven miles."

"So, the team could have driven to the park, then run the loop for practice," Brette said.

"Let's go." Ty glanced at Pete, who gave him a grim look. "What?"

Pete shook his head. "You'll see. But . . . here's hoping."

Brette landed behind Ty, with Spenser on her tail as they ran to the SUV. Chet was standing next to the car and now got in as he spied them heading his way.

In moments, Ty had them back on the road, heading north, back to Main, then west toward the park.

As they neared it, Pete's tone took on meaning. The debris thickened the farther they drove down Main.

Ty found Park Ave and turned north.

A war zone. The trees lay dying, uprooted and smashed on the bungalows. Tudors and Victorian homes built in the last century were now reduced to ruin, their chimneys half toppled. Muddy, tangled roots blocked driveways. Some of the tree trunks had been split down the middle, the two halves falling away from each other. The thick bodies took out roofs and power lines and rammed through car windows.

It created a tangle of jungle they hadn't a hope of driving their car through. Ty parked and they got out. Spenser ran toward the park, or what remained, and Brette followed, drawn by that ember of heat she called hope.

Ty caught her eye with a grim look but then offered a smile.

As if trying to keep the flame alive.

They climbed over trees, and Ty grabbed her arm, pulling her away from a live wire. "Careful."

Ahead of them, Spenser had found what remained of a pavilion. He stood there, pale, his gaze fighting to land on something familiar.

Brette saw it before anyone else.

"Ty, is that a red—a red Impala? Or what used to be?"

A fire had consumed the vehicle. Only the trunk area, a dark, albeit grimy red, hinted at the car's make.

Ty ran over to it, peered inside. "There's nothing left. I'll bet it was hit by one of the electrical lines." Ty backed away, catching Brette before she could get too close.

Spenser stood a little ways away. "That's not April's car."

"No, it belongs—or could belong—to one of the runners," Ty said. "I'm sorry."

"Don't be sorry!"

Brette turned just in time to see Spenser backing up toward the SUV.

"We just have to find them!" He took off in a run toward the vehicle.

"This is horrible," Brette said softly.

She could have predicted that with her words, Ty would put his arms around her. His embrace seemed to possess just enough strength to keep her upright.

Despite the odor of char and creosote and stripped foliage and even a hint of rain in the air, Ty could turn her weak with the very real redolence of comfort, safety. Hope.

Shame on her, but she just wanted to lift her face to his, put her arms around his neck, and draw him down in a kiss. Something that might make her forget, just for a moment, the chaos and pain and ache and downright fear that had seemed to dog her for the past year.

No, most of her life, really.

His chest rose and fell; his hand cupped the back of her neck. "It'll be okay, Brette," he said quietly, then leaned down and kissed the top of her head.

Ty. She lifted her face.

But he let her go.

He did grab her hand again, as if now they simply belonged together, and led her back to the car.

And she held on. Because she couldn't do anything else.

10

THEY COULD BE SAVING LIVES. Uncovering the debris at the Duck Lake high school, digging to find the lost cross-country team.

Instead, all the precious machinery—two excavators, a bulldozer, and all the engineering manpower—was being routed to pry trees, debris, and broken fencing from the power transformer station east of town with the hopes of restoring electricity.

Ty couldn't even look at Spenser pacing outside of the mobile command center.

Despite searching every damaged car, rooting through empty houses, and scouring fields for clues, no one had surfaced a hint of April Maguire, Creed, or any other member of the team.

They'd simply vanished.

And with the sinking of the sun into the backside of the day, Ty could feel the tenuous hold they had on hope slipping.

"There has to be *someplace* else we can look," Spenser was saying to Pete, who'd come out of the RV with another dismal report. After the park, Spenser had convinced Ty to return to the Park Avenue apartment complex—or what remained of it—to search. Spenser had climbed through the skeletal frame of the eight-unit, two-story building, calling April's name. Ty searched the nearby cars while Brette and Chet shifted through the debris—two-by-fours,

Sheetrock, appliances, broken furniture—just in case April had been thrown from the flat.

Three hours later, Ty finally convinced Spenser to return to the Red Cross area. Mostly because he could see the man physically unraveling.

Not to mention the pain etched deeper into Brette's face as the day spiraled out. Ty kept wanting to return to the moment in the park when he pulled her close, only to have her hang on. Like she meant it.

"We're scouring the countryside," Pete said.

Ty couldn't take it. He stalked up to Pete. "We could—*should*—be searching at the school."

Pete set his gaze on him, raised an eyebrow.

"You're making a mistake not searching the school again," Ty said. "Creed's car is there—and we found his running shoes in it, which could mean he went there after practice. And maybe that's a reach, but—"

"It's a reach that could cost us their lives," Pete said tightly. "I can't base a search grid on your gut, Ty. We don't have time or resources to haul everything over to the school and start digging. We're past forty-eight hours since the tornado touched down. Even you know the window for rescue is closing."

Spenser's eyes widened. He took a breath, turned away.

"Nice, Pete," Ty said quietly. He shook his head. "Maybe you've forgotten what it feels like to lose someone—"

Pete advanced on him until he was inches away. "I haven't forgotten anything." His blue eyes darkened. "I remember *exactly* what it feels like to hold on to hope way too long."

Ty knew it was cruel to bring up the accident that caused Pete's father's death—a skiing tragedy that occurred when Pete and his father went off slope and got lost. But he was desperate for anything he could find to make Pete hear him.

Pete's voice turned tight and sharp. "People should have been honest with me and Sam from the beginning. My dad probably died—suffocated—within ten minutes of falling into that tree well. By the time the blizzard hit, he was long gone. But everyone rallied around hope—and so did we. Maybe if someone had told me the truth, I wouldn't have suffered years of nightmares about him freezing to death. Or the ones where I'm trying to dig him out, hearing him scream only to wake up and discover it's my own voice." He cut his volume down to just above a whisper. "So yeah, maybe I'm not keen on fabricating hope for something that is probably going to end tragically."

"Not if we search in the right place—"

"What is your problem?" Pete backed away from him, shaking his head. "Give it up. They aren't at the school. Leave it, Ty. This is you getting in the middle of something you don't belong in again."

Ty blinked at him, untangling his words. "Wait—is this about Jess? And . . . her pretending we were dating?"

Pete's jaw tightened, and Ty could read the blame in his eyes.

"You think it's my fault she went back to her life in New York City."

"If you hadn't stood between us then she might have told me the truth. And then we could have faced her past together instead of her having to choose between me and French fancy pants."

"She didn't want to tell you!" Ty shook his head. "She wanted you to leave her alone."

"Because she was scared that I wouldn't understand why she testified against her father, why she sent him to jail. She was afraid I'd be hurt or angry or even walk away from her," Pete said. "But guess what—I *love* her. Or . . . I did. And I do understand."

"And yet you still walked away."

Ty didn't know why those words came out of his mouth. Maybe because he still couldn't believe that Pete, after asking Jess to marry him, could abandon her to sort out the mess in New York on her own.

Pete's eyes turned sharp, his hands closing into fists. But his voice remained incongruently calm. "Believe me, I didn't want to. But Jess needed to figure out what—and apparently *who*—she wanted."

"She wanted someone to lean on. Which left Felipe, who has been there for her. It's not been easy—their engagement—"

"They're engaged?" Pete went white at his words.

Shoot. A heartbeat, and the truth sank in. "You didn't know."

Pete swallowed.

Pete wasn't supposed to find out like this. "I'm sorry, man. I thought—"

"I don't want to talk about it!" Pete snapped. He drew in a breath and turned away from Ty. "It doesn't matter. We've been over for a while now. I'm moving on."

Ty just stood there, Pete's words ringing in his ears. Over . . . for a while? Um, not according to Jess.

But none of it was Ty's business, really.

Pete shoved his hands into his pockets and looked at Spenser.

The man was slumped against the side of the RV, his head in his hands, his shoulders shaking. Pete watched him a long, brutal moment, then turned, his eyes hard. "Get me more proof that they could be there—not just a *hunch*—and we'll start digging." Then he walked back into the RV, slamming the door behind him.

A hand touched his back, and he was surprised to see Brette standing there holding two water bottles. "That was ugly." She handed him a water bottle. "You okay?"

He nodded.

"For the record, I thought you were dating Jess too."

"I know. Jess needed . . . protection. She just wasn't ready to tell Pete about her past, and since I already knew it . . ."

Brette took a drink, then wiped her mouth with her finger. "You stepped up to offer it."

Ty frowned but nodded. "We are friends and—"

"And you just can't help yourself." She offered a wry smile.

"In my worst nightmares, someone needs me and I'm not there." He didn't know why he'd revealed that, but—

"Like me?"

He nodded, wanting very much to reach out and cup her cheek, draw his thumb down her beautiful face.

"Why do you have to save everyone, Ty?" She said it softly, without accusation, a reporter's question.

"Because I didn't save *anyone*, Brette. Not my mom. Not Chet. *Not even myself.*"

And he just wanted to grab all that back. Because this was not about his past . . . except he was right back to the frustration of being lost, alone, and desperate.

So, maybe it was.

She blinked, then caught up to his words. "Are you referring to the chopper accident? Ty, you hiked out—"

"No. I didn't make it to the road. I collapsed in the snow and I would have died there if it weren't for God intervening. Sam says he heard my rescue whistle, but . . . truth is, I have no idea how he found me. I'm very aware that without God, I would be dead—and so would Chet. I'm not a rescuer. I'm *barely* a survivor. Maybe Pete is right. What do I know?" He cupped his hand behind his neck, kneaded a muscle there. "I have hunches—that's not a way to lead a callout. I just hate being helpless. I work better when I have something to do."

"Someone to protect. I know," she said. "But you're about the least helpless man I've ever met."

Then, she stepped up to him, caught the front of his shirt in her grip, and lifted herself on her tiptoes.

He recognized the intention in her eyes a second before her lips parted.

Oh.

And, *yes.* Every other thought left his head as he released himself into the invitation. She kissed him sweetly, her lips gentle against his, and for a moment, the world stilled. All the chaos, the fear, the frustration, even the anger, dropped away.

She tasted fresh and sweet, smelled of the sunshine on her skin, and something he hadn't sensed before. Nothing dangerous or dark, but filled with warmth and hope and—*and that was it.*

Hope.

As if she wouldn't run from him this time.

That thought sank into him, and for a moment he simply breathed her in.

Brette.

And he might have let himself relax, but he couldn't stop himself. Wow, he needed her. Hadn't really realized how much until this moment.

He somehow wrapped his hands around hers and came back to himself, to the fact they were standing in the middle of a crisis zone, and drew back, finding her eyes.

She had her gaze on him, and he didn't know what to say.

So, "All I know is that helping others helps me live with myself just a little longer." It was the only thing he could think of in response to her comment.

And that kiss.

She smiled. "And you do it well."

He smiled back, completely, happily flummoxed.

"I have an idea," she said, glancing at Spenser. "I keep thinking about that other missing person—Hattie Foreman. What if we tried to retrace *her* steps? She's probably not with the team or April, but . . . well, it seems strange that they haven't found her yet, either."

He wanted to kiss her again.

And that really had nothing to do with how amazing and brilliant and resourceful she was. Or maybe it did, but—

Okay, he could kiss her for no reason at all.

"That's a great idea." He reluctantly let her go and headed back to the RV. Pressed a hand on Spenser's shoulder right before he climbed up the steps. "This isn't over yet."

Ty was clearly rubbing off on her because Brette never wanted to be the voice of hope, the voice of inspiration more than when she stepped up to Ty, silenced the voices in her head, and kissed him.

She'd meant it as something sweet and encouraging.

Not life-changing and soul-deep. But he'd kissed her back like he'd needed her. Almost as much, maybe, as she needed him.

She might survive the future if she could hang on to Ty.

"You're about the least helpless man I've ever met."

She smiled at her corny but oh-so-true words as he disappeared into the RV. She had a mental image of Ty, pretty much all the time, hiking through some whiteout on a busted knee, refusing to go down.

"In my worst nightmares, someone needs me and I'm not there."

She didn't know why she'd let the tiny "like me?" trickle out.

The look he'd given her had turned her heart to butter, and right then the pieces of the woman she'd been fell into place. Once upon a time, she'd been a journalist who found the good, the *right* in people, and told *that* story, the one that might inspire the world to be a better place.

A place she wanted to stay alive, even fight, for.

Ty emerged from the RV. "C'mon," he said to Spenser, who had risen to his feet.

Really? Spenser could hardly be of use the way he kept unraveling.

She must have asked the question with her eyes because Ty walked right toward Brette, nodding. "He needs to come with us. Trust me."

She glanced at Spenser, who seemed to come back to himself with Ty's invitation. He fell in line behind Ty.

"I have Hattie's address. She lives with her sister. Their house is still standing, just north of town." He stopped in front of her. "Just off Park Avenue."

Huh.

"I like how you think, Ace," Ty said and pulled out his keys.

She slid into the front seat as Spenser climbed into the back. Ty turned them north, back to Park. "Hattie lives with her sister, Lottie. Lottie called in Hattie's disappearance not long after the storm hit, maybe from her landline, because the cell towers are still down. Hattie is in her late sixties, medium build, and was last seen wearing a blue T-shirt and jeans. Apparently, she'd gone out to walk her dog."

He turned off Main Street, and Brette noticed that work crews, dressed in the white Red Cross volunteer shirts, had begun to pile debris onto street corners. Belongings—a guitar, a rocking horse, a grill—were propped up next to the front steps of various homes.

They passed through the most dismantled neighborhoods and came to a formerly heavily wooded street. The trees were stripped, broken, and uprooted across front yards, a couple roofs. A bulldozer had cleared a path through the center of the road.

Ty was trying to read house numbers, but the effort was laughable. Brette finally rolled down her window and flagged over a young man with a Duck Lake Flyers T-shirt who was hauling branches from his front yard. He looked about seventeen. "Do you know where Hattie Foreman lives?"

He pointed to a tiny ranch house two doors down. Branches littered the cement walk; a peony bush lay in tatters.

"Brette!" The voice came from behind the car, and in a moment Geena appeared next to their SUV, dressed in work clothes, her dark hair tied back in a bandanna. "How's Jonas? We tried to call him."

"His brother's still missing."

Nixon came up behind her, his dark skin glistening in the heat. He wore a bandanna over his balding head. "That's not good."

"I don't suppose you saw the long-range Doppler radar?" Geena asked. "The SPC is tracking a system out of Colorado, heading northeast into all this heat. They've issued a moderate risk of severe weather, but Nix is pretty sure that something is going to go up tomorrow, in Iowa."

Geena bore that look, the one she got right before she charged into a wall of clouds.

"Geena, I can't go right now." Brette glanced at Ty, who regarded her with a tight, expressionless look.

The kind he gave her when he was trying to not get involved but ached to.

Interesting that she knew him that well already.

Brette turned back to the duo. "We have to find Jonas's brother and the other kids. I'm sorry—you'll have to go without me."

"Are you sure? We've got another week of tornado season, and one more probe to deploy to fulfill our grant . . ."

"I'm needed here."

Ty's grip covered hers and squeezed, and warmth bloomed through her entire body.

"Okay," Geena said, stepping back from the car. "We're leaving first thing in the morning. Let us know if you change your mind." She patted the car, and Ty eased away.

Silence.

Then, from the back, "You chase storms for a living?" Enough darkness laced Spenser's voice to suggest his opinion.

"Listen, it's a job—"

"A dangerous job, one that gets people killed unnecessarily. Don't you have any respect for the power of nature?"

Ty's mouth tightened. Fine.

"First off, we don't put ourselves in harm's way." Much. Or, rather, Jonas didn't, but she held that back. "Second, what you don't know is that the only way the weather service can issue a warning is from a firsthand sighting. They can't tell from the radar if a mesocyclone has dropped. So they need people like us on the ground, calling it in. They're called spotters, and they've been chasing storms for over a century. We give people a chance to live." She looked at Ty, who'd eased up to the curb in front of Hattie's house. "We save lives."

A tiny smile sparked on the side of Ty's mouth. "So, you're a rescuer too."

She didn't nod as she reached for the door handle, but that thought stirred inside her.

Ty kicked away a few branches as they headed up to the door. He stopped, knocked, and then opened the unlocked door. "Hello?"

Nothing. He stepped over the threshold, Brette on his tail.

"Hello?"

"In here!" The voice emerged fractured, on a breath of air, and Ty hustled toward it.

The front door opened into a main room, with a tiny kitchen and dining area in the back. Simply decorated with a bookcase filled with family pictures and basketball trophies, an overstuffed sofa, a couple fabric chairs. A dog bed lay in the kitchen.

Ty headed down a short hallway, Brette on his heels. He ducked his head into the first room, a bedroom, then pushed the door open. "In here," he said, tossing the words over his shoulder, to Brette and Spenser.

A woman lay on the carpeted floor next to her bed, a broken milk-glass lamp in shards beside her, a cotton bedspread folded under her head. Near the door, her walker was upended and out of reach. Brette put her in her early seventies. Her short silvery-white hair was matted, her eyes reddened, and by the looks of her attire—a long cotton nightgown—she'd been on the ground for most of the day.

"Oh, thank the Lord," she said, her eyes shiny with relief as Ty crouched beside her.

"Are you Lottie Foreman?" Ty asked, and Brette saw him give her a once-over with what she assumed was a medical eye.

Lottie gripped his arm with bony fingers. "Yes. I tripped getting out of bed. I was reaching for my walker, and it slipped out of my grasp." She lifted the edge of her nightgown to reveal a grotesquely swollen ankle and an equally engorged knee.

Brette winced.

"Is Hattie okay? I haven't heard anything since I called 911 right after the storm hit. But then I couldn't get through to anyone . . ."

Only then did Brette notice the old flip phone clutched in her hand.

"Let's get you off the floor and see what we can do about that leg," Ty said. He slipped his arms under her and lifted her almost without a grunt. He set her on her tousled bed. Turned to Spenser. "See if you can get ahold of 911. Or any emergency services. If not, we'll have to drive her to the ER."

"I'll get some ice," Brette said.

"Um—"

But she was already out of the room, her heart slamming against her ribs.

That could be her. Alone and helpless on the floor. No, it *had* been her. Brette found the kitchen, braced her hands on the Formica counter, and took a couple big gulps.

That could be her again.

Hands pressed onto her shoulders. She looked up.

Ty wore a frown. "You okay?"

"Mmmhmm," she said, but she blew out another long breath.

"She'll be fine. It looks like a couple bad twists, but she can move her foot, so I'm guessing it's not broken." He squeezed her shoulders, then opened the freezer. "Shoot. The ice has all melted." He closed the door and walked out into the living room. "Spenser, any luck with 911?"

"No. I think we'll have to drive her." He had a new energy, something urgent in his demeanor as he followed Ty back to the bedroom.

And she got it then. *"All I know is that helping others helps me to live with myself just a little longer."*

Ty was trying to keep Spenser from folding in on himself by making him take his eyes off his own pain.

In moments, Ty emerged with Lottie swaddled in the blanket. Spenser held open the door and Brette scrambled through to grab the car door.

Ty set Lottie in the backseat and Spenser climbed in beside her, gathering the woman into his arms.

"You're going to be okay," he said.

Huh.

Brette got into the car. "The nearest hospital is in Waconia." She turned in her seat as Ty worked his way down the street. "Lottie, we're searching for your sister. What can you tell us about the day of the tornado? Do you have any idea where she might have gone?"

She had pretty eyes, blue-gray and alert despite her pain, and now Brette saw her muster herself.

"Yes," she said. "She went to the park, like she did every day at 5:00, to walk Walter."

"Walter?"

"He's her labradoodle. He's a rather smart dog, and loyal. He wouldn't abandon Hattie if she were hurt."

"She was at the park when the tornado hit?"

"Yes. I expected her home, but . . ." She pressed her hand to her mouth. "She's all I have, you know. We never married, so we only have each other and . . ." Lottie fought for a smile. "She's going to be okay, I just know it. My heart says so."

Brette glanced at Ty, who lifted a shoulder.

"And what if she's not?" Spenser asked. He had his big arms around her, propping her up on his chest, his breath rising and falling hard with the emotion burled up inside.

Brette wanted to nod, because yes, what if . . .

"I will hold on to my faith to carry me through."

Brette drew in her breath, wishing for something more . . . something tangible.

"At first, I was so afraid. Filled with dread," Lottie said quietly. "Except, dread is produced by the fear of going through something alone . . . and I wasn't alone. God doesn't promise to keep the storm away, but he says he'll be with me through it. My faith won't protect me from the loss, but it will carry me and keep me from despair."

Oh.

Brette turned back in her seat, not sure why her eyes burned.

"We're missing a team of high school students who we think were running near or in the park," Ty said.

"And my wife, who is their coach," Spenser mumbled. He was looking out the window now, as if also trying not to cry.

Lottie curled her hand around Spenser's. "I'm so sorry. But if Hattie was with them, somehow, during the storm, she would have gotten them to shelter."

"Where?" Ty looked at her in the rearview mirror.

"The warning sirens went off just a few minutes before the storm hit. I kept waiting for Hattie to come home, but . . . maybe she went someplace she thought was safer than our bathtub."

"You don't have a storm cellar?"

"The house is too old. When I was a kid, they'd tell us all to go to the school. Of course, it was a different building back then, but it had a storm shelter, so—"

Ty's hand came down on the steering wheel. "I knew it. What if Hattie hooked up with the kids, and for some reason they headed back to the school?" He had turned onto the highway and headed east, toward Waconia.

"She still works at the school. She's been the lunch lady for nearly fifty years. Knows all the kids. And the school. It's generations old, and she's been there through all the remodeling phases."

Brette turned in her seat. "Lottie, where would she take the kids to shelter there?"

Lottie shook her head. "I don't know. The locker room? I haven't been to the new school, so I don't know, but . . . maybe the lunchroom?"

Brette had seen the lunchroom, or what was left of it. But she made no comment.

They turned north, following the signs to Waconia, and she could almost see Ty's brain churning over maps of the school.

When they pulled up to the ER, he helped Spenser ease Lottie out of the car, then carried her inside.

Brette got out and stood under the canopy in the heat of the waning day. The sun had gathered itself against the western horizon, a brilliant blaze of yellow and orange, pressing fire into the gathering cumulus in a lavender sky.

"Even you know the window for rescue is closing."

Hands on her shoulders made her jump. She turned, found herself in Ty's arms. "Spenser is getting her checked in. You okay?"

She pressed her hands against his chest, feeling his heartbeat against all that muscle. "That's my worst fear—that in the end, I'll just be alone."

She closed her eyes, wincing that she'd admitted that, so she swallowed and followed up with, "Lottie could have been there for days before help came."

He put a hand under her chin and nudged her face up. "Yeah, but help *did* come. Because you suggested that we find Hattie."

Huh. She hadn't connected those dots.

"See, you *are* a rescuer."

She made a face, trying not to cry or let out some hysterical laughter. "Oh, Ty, once upon a time I thought I was. Or at least someone who tried to see the good in the world. But ever since . . . ever since I got sick, I just . . . all I felt was dread, just like Lottie said. I couldn't see past the darkness. I was scared all the time. Dread is so insidious—it gets inside your bones and it steals every thought, every happy moment, every morsel of hope. It steals the person you were. I used to be confident and pretty and not scared of anything. I want that person back."

"I don't know—this Brette is pretty cute." He touched her face, desire gathering in his eyes.

Oh. Uh . . .

"But I understand," he said. "Dread makes you take a good look at yourself, hoping that you're enough to face whatever is out there. And when you only have yourself to save you, then it does get pretty dark. I spent a lot of time looking for rescue in the wrong places. You're not alone, Brette. And you don't have to feel that way ever again."

"Because you're with me?" she said, not quite believing her own words.

"For starters," he said softly. Then he winked, and oh, she wanted whatever he had that gave a person strength, helped others see beyond themselves to who they could be.

His gaze was roaming her face, and her heart thundered.

Ty.

He leaned down and pressed his lips to hers. Softly at first, but then he deepened his kiss, drawing her into the cradle of his arms, even as the night cocooned them—cicadas, the rush of the wind in the nearby elms, the scent of cut grass, the fragrance from the viburnum edging the landscaping.

She moved in his arms, stepping up on the curb behind her to prop her arms over his shoulders, twirl her fingers into his hair. He was solid and strong, and at his touch, fire consumed her. She turned alive, bold, even beautiful.

He released her and met her eyes, his gaze warm. "I can hardly breathe around you, Brette. I know you're scared, but I'm not going anywhere. We'll face—whatever—together. I'll keep you safe, with everything inside me."

She touched his face, her fingers scrubbing the edging of dark whiskers that had deepened with the day. "I'm not so scared, at least not right now."

He smiled, something slow and sweet, then he dove back in, his kiss urgent and bold and everything that was Ty.

And she found the courage to meet it, letting free the holds that kept her from believing, from wanting, from loving.

From receiving.

"You're not alone, Brette. And you don't have to feel that way ever again."

The doors behind them opened, and Spenser came out.

Ty loosened his grip on her.

She ducked her head, her face heating.

But Spenser seemed oblivious or perhaps just uncaring at their ardor as he glanced at them. "Do you think we have enough proof now?"

Ty raised an eyebrow. But he took Brette's hand and headed toward the car. "When I tell Pete about the car I saw today at the school, with the dog paw sticker pasted in the window, we will."

11

HE MIGHT NOT BE a chopper pilot anymore, but that didn't mean Ty couldn't search for—and find—the lost. He couldn't help but reach over and take Brette's hand as they pulled up to the Marshall family winery. He'd called in an update about Lottie on the walkie to Pete, who'd sent them back to the family base.

He needed to have the conversation about his latest hunch in person, really lay out the proof—solid proof, from his angle.

Hattie, the dog lover, driving a vehicle with a paw print sticker, which now sat in the rubble of the school. His best guess was that she'd met the team at the park and driven them in her Jeep to the school for safety. Maybe Creed had even followed her.

Leaving the red Impala to wait out the storm at the park.

As if she could read his mind, Brette squeezed Ty's hand.

They'd made a good team today. He hadn't realized how involving Brette in the search might pull her away from her fears. It worked the magic he'd hoped. *"I'm not so scared, at least right now."*

You don't have to be, Brette. Ever again.

He let those words sit in his head as he pulled up and noticed Pete's Hummer in the driveway. Ty got out and nearly sprinted to the door with the adrenaline of his news.

But his step stuttered just a second before he reached for the handle.

"I'm so sorry to have to tell you this. It's the last thing we want to admit, but . . ."

Oh no.

Ty yanked open the door and spotted Pete standing in the middle of the room, the Marshall family staring at him, agony in their expressions. Jenny had her hand pressed to her mouth. Garrett stood with his back to Pete, and Jonas and Ned glared at Pete as if they'd like to turn him to ash.

Gage examined the floor, shaking his head.

Ian paced the terrace outside, on his cell phone.

"This has gone from a search and rescue to a search and recovery."

"Pete!" Ty couldn't hold back as he strode inside. Pete glanced over his shoulder at him, narrowed his eyes, then quickly shook his head.

He turned back to the family. "We need to look at the facts here. They've been missing for over forty-eight hours. Even if they have mild injuries, if they don't have any water, it's likely they are . . ."

Jenny made a noise, a sharp intake of breath. Garrett went to his wife. Ned slammed his hand on the table.

Jonas found his voice. "What are you talking about here? Recovery? You think they're *dead*."

Pete drew in a breath. Nodded. "It's . . . likely."

"Possible. It's *possible*," Ty said, stepping up beside Pete. "But we don't know—"

"That's right. We don't know." Jonas let out a growl. "And we're not giving up."

"Stay out of this, Ty," Pete said quietly, shooting him a look.

Ty didn't move.

"What does that mean, *recovery*?" Jenny said, her eyes glistening.

"It means that we divert resources to getting systems up and functioning. Electric. Gas lines. Cell towers. We start putting Duck Lake back together again."

"Does this mean you're going to stop looking?" Garrett said, and even Ty felt a little sorry for Pete right then.

Which made him step in, despite his common sense. "No, Garrett," Ty said. "It means we look with a smaller crew, but . . . listen to me. I think I know where they are."

"Ty—" Pete started.

"No, listen. I've spent the day looking for them, and I found—well, you wanted proof, right?"

Pete folded his arms over his chest.

"Remember we went to look for Hattie Foreman? We went to her house, and her sister was there. She told us that often Hattie walked her dog in Heritage Park—where the kids were practicing."

"That's a pretty big leap. We don't even know if the kids went there."

"If they were with my wife, they did," Spenser said, and Ty had forgotten that Spenser was behind him. If Pete gave up on the kids, he was also giving up on April. Pete should probably be a little more grateful Ty had shown up with this new lead.

"We don't know if your wife was practicing with them today," Pete said.

"What about the red Impala we found at the park that belongs to Addie Ridley?"

"What *looks* like an Impala."

"Creed's car is at the school," Ty said. "And, did I mention that we also found a Jeep at the school with a dog sticker in the window—Hattie's Jeep."

"Are you sure it's Hattie's?" Pete asked. "And I just gotta ask, if they were at the park, why would they all go five miles down the road to the school, with a tornado on their tail? It doesn't make sense."

With Pete's words, the entire premise suddenly seemed flimsy.

Except for . . . aw, shoot.

Pete raised an eyebrow, almost asking for him to say it.

"My . . . instincts tell me they're there."

Pete let a moment pass. "So, you want me to pull everybody off their duties, haul over all the equipment, and start digging around the school?"

"Tonight, with lights. Yes."

Pete's mouth tightened. "Listen. There is no electricity in the town of Duck Lake. No power, no gas, no phone lines . . . If someone in town should get injured, we wouldn't even know about it. It's a war zone over there right now. We don't have the equipment or the people to go on a wild-goose chase."

"And Creed, and his team—" Garrett said.

"And April—" Spenser interjected.

"Are all casualties of war," Garrett finished, his words putting a sharp and dark finale on Pete's proclamation.

Pete looked down. "No. I don't know."

And that was just . . . *enough*. "Are you kidding me?" Ty let the frustration leak into his voice, and didn't care. "C'mon, Pete, have some faith! You were on the PEAK team. You know we can't give up—why don't you stick around and fight? Or are you a coward in this too?"

Pete's head snapped up. Ty stood there, his gaze hard in Pete's, seeing him struggle with his response.

Ty never wanted to hit something—*someone*—more in his entire life.

It seemed, maybe, that Pete shared his feelings. Pete's jaw tightened, and a darkness rose in his eyes.

But a brawl, right here in the middle of the room, would only add to an already open wound.

Pete's gaze flicked off Ty to Gage, then Chet. Finally, away to Jenny and Garrett.

"I'm so sorry," he said, stepping away from Ty. "I have to get back to the staging area."

Then he turned, pushed past Spenser and a white-faced Brette, and headed outside.

The mood in the room darkened with the silence in his wake.

Brette drew in a shallow breath, turned, and ran up the stairs.

Spenser just stood there, staring at Ty. "What just happened?"

Ty couldn't speak.

Behind him, Ned let out a dark word. Ty turned to see him slam his way outside.

Jonas sank against the table. Jenny turned into Garrett's chest, and his arms curled around her.

Ian came into the room, pocketing his cell phone. "Pete left?"

Ty glanced up the stairs, intending to follow Brette, but Ian caught up to him. "Let's talk about this."

There was just enough steel-edged determination in Ian's eyes to make Ty listen.

"I don't have the resources I used to, but I do have leverage, favors, and a few strings I could pull. I could get excavators and any other equipment we needed here by morning. We don't need Pete's permission to dig through the debris of the school, if you really think they're there."

Ty should have known that Ian wouldn't give up a search. Not when he'd lost his own family, had searched for them in the chaos of Katrina for a week. And he'd formed the PEAK team and spent four years searching for his niece.

No, Ian might not have the financial resources he once did, but Ty did. Finally, a good use for his mother's inheritance. And with Ian's connections . . . no, they *didn't* need Pete's okay to dig out the school.

Ty met Ian's gaze. "You believed, without a doubt, that Esme was alive, that she would someday come home. Which she did. I believe these kids are still alive and are trapped inside this school. You find the equipment and I'll pay for it to get here."

"That's the yes I needed." Ian pulled out his phone.

Ty moved toward the stairs again, but Ben came down, cutting him off. He carried a duffel bag over his shoulder.

Ty stared at him. "What are you doing?"

"I can't stay. I got a gig. I was upstairs talking to Audrey." He didn't meet Ty's eyes.

Incredible. "Does Kacey know?"

The answer lay in Ben's tight expression.

"You gotta talk to her, dude. That's not fair."

Ben's face hardened. "Leave it, Ty."

Wow. Well, he couldn't save everyone. He started up the stairs.

"Ty."

Ben's voice pulled him back. He motioned to the foyer, and Ty considered a moment, then acquiesced. "What's up?"

"Audrey told me that Brette had a bunch of pictures from when we found my dad."

"Really?" He knew she'd taken some shots of that day, but nothing personal.

"Yeah, and I realize she's a journalist and I'm a public figure, but that's a pretty private moment. I'd really like it if TMZ didn't get ahold of them."

"I don't think she's going to sell them to a magazine."

"Maybe not, but even if they ended up on her blog, I don't want my family pulled into the limelight. Can you ask her to destroy them?"

Ty nodded. "No problem."

Ben held out his hand. "Thanks for showing up. For finding my dad. You mean a lot to him, Ty. I'm grateful to you."

Huh. He met Ben's grip, then let the man pull him in for a quick one-armed bro hug.

Then Ben let him go and escaped the room.

And Ty headed upstairs.

Every bone in her body vibrated. Kacey cast a glance at the horizon, where the sun spilled its last rays into the deepening twilight, turning the clouds to tangerine against a purpling sky. The ceiling hung low, but she'd managed to keep her bird in the air all day, with four fuel-ups from the local fixed base.

Still, her arms ached and she would have appreciated a copilot today.

Someone like Ty, who needed to stop letting his fears keep him from stepping back into the world that belonged to him. Or once had.

Although she understood too well the fear of grabbing for something you longed for only to discover it didn't belong to you anymore.

She locked the chopper, then waved at the black pickup in the lot. Garrett Marshall, her ride back to the winery.

Where Ben would be waiting for an answer to last night's plea to give them a future and marry him.

Somewhere around 3:00 this afternoon, after hearing his voice on the walkie as he reported in the dismal results of their search, she realized the truth.

She'd let her fear of not belonging in Ben's world keep her from stepping fully in it. She hadn't once asked to attend any of the country music events, didn't join him on stage, and though she'd attended all his concerts in Mercy Falls and had flown out to a few on the road, once he left Montana, their lives separated.

"I'm not a glitzy, pretty, country music star wife."

Her words rattled in her tired brain as she approached the truck, her helmet under her arm.

Maybe not. But maybe she could be.

She could try.

The other option would be to let him walk out of her life, this time for good.

She opened the door. "Hey, Garrett."

"Sorry," Shae said. She sat in the driver's seat. "I offered to pick you up. Pete's coming out to the house to give them an update."

Shae Johnson, aka Esme Shaw, the girl who'd come back from the dead. Or at least from the forever-missing list. She wore her hair in a long blonde braid and looked impossibly young in a pair of short jean cutoffs and a T-shirt. The massive seat dwarfed her as she put the truck into reverse.

"Tough day," she said as she pulled out. "Ned is pretty upset."

Kacey nodded. "Yeah. People can lose their minds searching for their lost loved ones. Especially when the search starts to . . . well, look like it won't end well."

Shae glanced at her. "Are you saying—"

"No. It's just that it can be pretty hard to keep a lid on your emotions. You go from hope to dread to despair and back again, sometimes all in one moment."

Shae pulled out onto the main drive. "Is that what happened to Uncle Ian after I left? I worried about him a lot. I even called him a couple years ago, telling him not to worry."

Kacey didn't mean to emit the harrumph.

Shae looked at her, eyes wide.

"Sorry. It's just, when you love someone, you never let them go. You never stop thinking about them, worrying about them. You probably only fueled the fires with that call."

Shae nodded, but Kacey's own words found soft soil and dug in. *"You never stop thinking about them."*

No. Ben never strayed far from her mind.

And yes, she saw the Twitter feeds, the Instagram pics, the Facebook posts, the—

Oh no. She was *jealous*. Jealous of every single woman who took a picture with Ben. Every concertgoer who got to hear him sing the songs he'd written for her. Every band member who laughed with him after the show.

"I wanted to come home, more than you can know," Shae was saying as she turned onto the Marshall family road. "I was afraid—of getting hurt. And of hurting Uncle Ian."

Yeah, she got that too. Every time Ben had postponed the wedding, the wound deepened, that fear that he didn't truly want her. Maybe that was why she so easily believed that he wanted to break up with her, reading into his words, expecting the worst.

"You're the most beautiful woman I know."

Maybe she should start believing that, start showing up and being a part of his star-studded life. So it was big—so big that it scared her sometimes. Clearly it was big enough for the both of them.

Yes, Ben. Yes, I will marry you. The words formed in her chest, bloomed through her tired, aching body.

She could fix this, turn it around.

End up married to the man she loved.

They turned into the driveway.

The trucks, along with a number of Suburbans, were all lined up, but her gaze went to only one. A large black Escalade with the back hatch open.

Ben stood at the end, rearranging duffel bags.

Kacey had the door open even before Shae stopped the truck. "Ben!"

Panic sharpened the edge of her voice without her permission.

Ben turned, and in a flash, his expression tightened. He held up his hand. "Stop, Kacey. Before you start, yes, I've already told Audrey. I didn't know when you were getting back, and we need to get on the road."

Get on the road.

She tried not to let those words tear like a blade through her heart.

And she absolutely refused to let him see her cry.

"You're leaving?"

His face gentled. "I'm sorry, Kace. We got offered a gig in Wisconsin, and we need to be there first thing in the morning. We could use the ticket sales. We gotta go."

"But . . . what about Creed, and the other missing kids?" And no, that wasn't what she wanted to say, not at all.

Ben shook his head, looked at the house, then at the ground. "Pete just left. He came over to tell them . . . well, he's downgraded the search from a rescue to a recovery."

Oh. She closed her eyes, turned away, took a breath.

And maybe fearing she might collapse, Ben put his arms around her and pulled her to himself.

Heaven help her, she leaned into him, putting her arms around his torso, leaning her head into his amazing shoulders. The labor of the day lifted off him, but it reminded her of his scent after one of his concerts when he'd left all of himself on stage, the stars still vibrating with the sound of his voice.

She *was* his biggest fan, and that realization welled up inside her, took root. She could live in his world because he was her world too.

Please, don't go, Ben. The words rose to her lips—

"Ready, boss?" The voice came from his drummer, Moose, who got in on the driver's side.

Ben sighed, and for a second she thought, *Just hold on. Just . . . hold on.*

But Ben released her. For a moment, his gaze held hers, roaming her face, as if he longed to kiss her.

"I'll call you." Then he smiled, something sad and tight, and turned for the SUV.

He didn't even look back as he climbed into the passenger seat.

And she didn't have it in her to wave as he drove out of her life yet again.

Breathe, just breathe.

Brette closed the bathroom door behind her and leaned back on it, listening to her heartbeat.

Recovery.

Not rescue.

God, please, it can't end this way. She didn't know where the thought came from, but she let it linger, even lifted her gaze to the ceiling, hoping that someone—the One—might hear her.

Please don't let them be dead.

Her jaw tightened against a rush of heat in her eyes, and her throat thickened at the memory of Jenny's face slowly morphing from fear to horror, as if the news seeped through her like poison.

And poor Garrett—the way he trembled, those wide shoulders about to give.

She'd suppressed the urge to go to Jonas, to tell him that they had a hunch about the school—and then it didn't matter because Pete had shot so many holes in Ty's theory that it turned Brette thin and brittle herself.

She should have known better. Hope did nothing but veil the truth. Turn them into fools.

And she'd reached out and invited it into her body, again. Let it sit in her chest and warm her. Again. She'd neatly, completely, too easily forgotten that it could burn her right through, leave her singed, scarred, and bereft.

She wiped her hand across her cheekbone.

Her phone buzzed in her pocket. She pulled it out and stared at the number.

A fist slammed into her gut.

No. She thumbed the call away to her voicemail but couldn't look away, waiting for the icon to buzz.

Sure enough. She pressed the icon and listened. "Hello, Brette. It's Dr. Daniels. I need you to call me. Your test results are in."

A pause, then, "It's not urgent, but we need to talk."

Not urgent? Maybe because there was nothing they could do.

She stood at the window, watching the very last wink of sunlight across the tattered horizon. No rain, not yet, and the sky was a brilliant tufted red. She spotted Ned walking out through the vines of the winery, maybe hoping to lose himself in the maze.

Not a terrible instinct.

"We're leaving first thing in the morning. Let us know if you change your mind."

Geena's voice found her and edged under her skin.

Brette released a breath, splashed water on her face, then emerged from the bathroom and headed across the hall.

As she pushed open the door, she nearly ran into Audrey, whose face was red, her eyes shiny.

"Whoa, Audrey, are you okay?" Brette caught the girl by the arms before she plowed her over.

Audrey stumbled back, as if in a haze, but in a moment she found her bearings. "My dad is leaving. He's going back out on the road." She said it just above a whisper. "I . . . I can't believe it."

Oh, Audrey. She didn't know the girl well, but the look on her face made Brette want to reach out and give her a hug.

And how crazy was that? Because she hadn't comforted someone else in . . . well, not since her mother lay dying, probably.

Brette softened her voice. "I'm sorry."

"Yeah, well . . ." Audrey wiped her hands across her cheekbones, her voice gaining strength. "I guess I should be used to him leaving by now. It's just . . . I thought they were going to finally get married." She wrapped her arms around her waist. "This is the third time they've called off their wedding."

"And you think they're going to break up."

"No!" She flashed a look of horror at Brette. "I . . . do you?"

Oh. Brette scrambled for the right words, the ones that wouldn't betray Kacey and last night's conversation. "I just . . . well, three times calling off a wedding is a lot, so . . ."

Audrey didn't move. "It *is* a lot."

"Uh, well, not if you're busy?"

"Nothing *ever* works out." Audrey whirled around and headed to her mother's bed. Threw herself on it, her head in her arms. "It's not fair."

Yeah, well, she got that. Brette sat at the edge of her bed, not sure whether to reach out, what to say. Because a not-so-tiny part of herself wanted to do exactly the same thing. *"It's not urgent, but we need to talk."*

Yeah, life wasn't fair. Not at all.

"Just when you think that finally, everything is going to be perfect, something happens. It's like God doesn't *want* me to be happy."

Brette stared at her. Yeah, it felt *exactly* like that. No matter what she did, she couldn't escape the devastation of her life. She very much wanted to curl her legs up, roll into the fetal position, and simply let the storm take her, even if it left her wrecked and washed out.

In truth, she didn't have the strength to fight it anymore.

"I wish we'd never come to Minnesota." Audrey caught the pillow up in her arms.

"Yeah," Brette said. Because she too just couldn't stay one moment longer to watch the cruel ending of this story. She had enough tragedies playing out in her life.

Brette pulled her computer from her bag and set it on the bed. Opened it, and in a moment her screen flashed on.

"What's that?" Audrey looked over. Sat up.

"That's a Doppler weather map. We use it to track storms. See this cracked-egg-looking image here?" She traced her finger across the cell, the edges a bright green, then yellow, orange, and finally red in the center. "This is a storm moving across Nebraska. It's not big enough to be a tornado yet, but if a hook forms in the lower left quadrant, that's called a mesocyclone and can turn into a tornado. Storm chasers watch for these and try to predict when and where they'll hit the ground."

"This is what you use to chase the storms?"

"We try. It doesn't always work. Sometimes the storm just dies out. Other times it drops in an area you don't expect and you miss it completely. But then there are the times you get it right."

"And you get an epic picture?"

"That's the hope."

"It's dangerous, though."

"Yeah. We get as close as we can, then I take pictures while our videographer, Nixon, grabs footage. Jonas is our meteorologist—he tells us where to drive and predicts where the tornado will land. And a girl named Geena drives. She's . . . pretty cool."

"Have you ever gotten caught in a tornado?"

She tamed her answer. "Almost."

"Wow," Audrey said, wiping her face clean. "Were you scared?"

Was she scared? "Yes, but . . . well, I was in this ditch and Jonas was with me, so that helped, to have a friend there."

"We'll face—whatever—together. I'll keep you safe, with everything inside me."

She shook Ty's voice away.

He couldn't keep her safe from dread. Not when dread could snake under her skin, around her bones, take root in her cells. *"Dread is so insidious . . . steals every thought, every happy moment, every morsel of hope."*

Her future.

"Why do you do it?" Audrey asked.

"Chase storms?" She minimized her windows until her wallpaper showed, revealing the picture that had landed on the cover of *Nat Geo*. "Because of this."

"Wow. That's cool."

"See how the funnel is on the ground, but up here, in the sky, it's so blue? It's amazing, isn't it? It reminds me that inside the tornado, everything is in chaos, but outside, there's still blue skies." She looked at Audrey, not sure where the thought, the words, came from. "Maybe we just have to figure out how to survive the tornado, if—when—it hits."

"Yeah. Like hold on to something really hard."

Brette nodded, the smell of Ty's shirt heady in her memory.

"Or maybe just run away?"

"That's always an option."

Audrey sighed. "Apparently." She got up. "Thanks, Brette."

"For what?"

"I'm not going to give up. My dad *will* marry my mom. They love each other—what else can they do?"

Sweet. "I'm sure you're right."

Audrey left, closing the door behind her.

If only it could be that easy. But love didn't solve problems, didn't protect anyone from despair. It couldn't take her cancer away, save lives.

Love just got in the way. Kept people from making the brutal but wisest decisions.

Brette pulled up her email and found a reply from her editor at *Nat Geo*.

Brette—

Love the pictures, and the concept. Would consider running a spread on the summer of storms if you were to get a few more storm/tornado shots. Was that country music singer Benjamin King in one of your photos? Great personal angle. Let me know when you have more.

Gordon

More shots. They maybe had one more week of storm season. Unless . . .

A knock came at the door, and she expected Kacey to walk in. "Hello?"

"It's me, Ty. Can we talk?"

She closed her eyes, grimacing. Not what she needed if she hoped to make a quick and quiet escape.

That thought hit her broadside. Really? Leave now, with Creed still missing?

Except, really, what could she do? She didn't want to stick around to watch the grief. Worse, she'd willingly been wooed into a happy ending that didn't exist, and the only way out was to leave, before she lacked the strength.

"Not right now—"

"Brette. Please. Listen, the search isn't over yet. Don't give up."

She shook her head, despite the fact that he couldn't see her. Got up and stood on the other side of the door, pressed her hand to it. "It is for me."

"Brette—"

She opened the door, her jaw set.

He stood there, looking fierce and not a little undone, his whiskers dark across his tight jaw.

She should have kept the door closed.

"Ty—"

"I see it in your eyes, Brette. You're scared and you're letting it take over. But Pete's wrong—they're still out there. I have to believe they're alive—"

"What is it with you! You don't give up." She grabbed his arm and yanked him into her room, shut the door. "You can't keep doing this. Giving people—Jenny and Garrett—false hope. It's cruel."

"Hope isn't cruel—"

"It is when it's a lie."

"Is that what you think I'm doing? *Lying* to everyone?"

The earnestness, even the hurt, on his face made her look away. Soften her voice. "I just think you don't like being helpless, so you keep reaching—"

"So, lying. *Dreaming* up a happy ending."

She'd didn't want to wound him. "It's a way of denying the inevitable—"

"Or it's called faith. Believing in miracles."

Oh Ty. She shook her head. "Faith hurts too much."

Silence.

"Brette, what's going on?"

His eyes caught hers, so much worry in them she had to look away. Clench her jaw to keep the words from spilling out. *My doctor called* . . . No, the last thing she needed was him swooping in, holding her hand, telling her that they'd fight this thing together.

"I'm taking off. First thing in the morning—"

"What—no. Why?"

She met his gaze, straight on. "Because I'm *not* a rescuer. *You* are. I'm a storm chaser, and there are storms coming."

"C'mon, Brette, that's just an excuse."

"Okay, how about this—I can't sit here and watch the Marshall family grieve. I've seen and done enough grieving in my life, okay?"

His mouth tightened to a grim line.

"I have a life. A job. I don't have an inheritance to fall back on. Someone has to show up to pay the bills. And that's me."

He made to reach out for her, but she stepped away, and his

hand dropped. "Brette, come back to Montana with me. There are plenty of photojournalist jobs, I promise—"

"And in the meantime, you'll take care of me?"

His expression suggested that he'd do just that.

"Listen. I appreciate your friendship—"

"Friendship? An hour ago, you were kissing me as if I'd just come back from sea. That's not just friendship." He took a step toward her, his eyes raw. "Brette, I don't quite understand what's going on here, but please don't leave. I don't know how, but God brought you back into my life for a reason, and I'm not letting you go!"

She took a step back, swallowed.

He released a shaky breath. "I didn't mean it like that. I mean, I don't want you to go, but . . . aw, shoot. You know what I meant."

She nodded but didn't close the gap. Because finally they were back to the truth, clearly free of the haze of hope. "I know that you would do anything to protect me, to take care of me, to make sure I had everything I needed. And I'd depend on you more and more, even start hoping, like I did today. And then something would happen—"

"And you'd be left with nothing, like your father was. Or worse, forced to be beholden to me."

She swallowed. "Alone is better. Trust me."

It took a second, but his voice dropped, low and pained. "Oh my gosh, this is about the cancer."

She must have flinched despite herself because his eyes grew large. "Did you get a phone call? Are your tests back?"

"It's no big deal. The doctor left a voicemail to call him back."

A beat, then, "And? Did you call him back?"

"No. I'm not going to."

"Brette—"

"No! I'm tired of fighting. Tired of picking up the pieces. I just want to—"

"Run away."

She folded her arms. "I need to go on with my life, whatever I have left."

"You don't know that it's bad news!"

"It's bad news." She stared at him, hating how her eyes filled. "Of *course* it's bad news. That's the only kind of news I get."

She hated how pitiful she sounded, but . . . well, there it was.

"You still don't need to be afraid." He advanced on her, but she stepped away from him.

"Why? Because you'll be there?"

"Yes. *Yes.*" His eyes had actually filled.

And if she needed any proof that her illness would destroy him, it was watching Ty, the man who didn't give up, crumble in front of her.

"No, Ty. You can't rescue everyone."

"Maybe I just want to rescue you!"

Oh, the man could break her heart. "I can't let you do that. For your own good. For *my* own good. I can handle my own broken heart. I can't handle yours too."

"Brette—"

"Trust me. There will come a day when you can do nothing for me. You'll be helpless. You'll have to stand there while I suffer. And then what are you going to do, Ty? What?"

He swallowed, took a breath, and the tear escaped without him trying to stop it. "Suffer with you. It's what people do when they . . ."

And she waited for it, saw the word bloom in his eyes a second before he snuffed it out.

"When they care about each other."

Right. Well, she *cared* about him too. And that thought gave her the courage to say again, "No."

His jaw tightened.

"Can't you see that it's time to give up?" Her throat burned, but she refused to flinch.

"Apparently not." His eyes flashed. "I have done nothing but prove myself to you. Try to show you that you can trust me. But you just can't depend on anyone but yourself—your scars run too deep." He reached up now and ran his palm across his jaw, his eyes dry and fierce. "This has nothing to do with your cancer, not really. That's just a convenient excuse. Truth is, you got in too far, didn't you? You wanted to believe me, and it freaked you out. You're so scared that I will hurt you, that I might let you down that you'll run away, even if you don't want to."

"And you always have to be in control—even if you have to call it a *hunch*. I call it being a bully."

He recoiled.

She ached, all the way to her bones. But she couldn't seem to stop herself. "Yeah, I *am* freaked out. Because I know that storms take people out, and you can't stop them. This . . . thing between us, it's not going to save me. It's only going to make everything worse. I'm beyond saving, so stop trying to rescue me."

"I don't believe that."

"I don't care. You're too far into my life, Ty. Back out."

He stared at her, his eyes dark and hard. "Fine."

Although she expected it—wanted it—the word drove a fist into her gut. She managed to step away as he headed to the door. *Don't cry. Not yet.*

He stopped when he reached the door, though, and for a moment she thought he might turn.

Beg her one more time to stay, or perhaps to go with her, but most of all not to give up on them. On life.

And oh, heaven help her, if he did, she would. Because despite her words, a much, much larger part of her wanted to stumble toward him, let him pick her up.

Carry her.

Don't go.

"By the way, Ben told me about the pictures you took of him and Chet. Delete them."

She blinked. "What?"

"You have no right to invade their privacy." His voice emerged hard, sharp.

"I need those—"

"Delete them."

"Get out."

"I'm serious—"

"Get *out*!"

His shoulders rose and fell. Her heart banged into her ribs.

Then he opened the door and closed it with a soft click behind him.

And she sank onto the carpet, her head in her hands, and let the darkness have her.

12

TY SIMPLY COULDN'T BE WRONG. "According to the blueprints, the locker room is in the middle of the school, behind the administrative area." Ty glanced at the excavator operator, the small group of searchers—the Marshall family, the PEAK team, Shae, Audrey, and a few parents along with Spenser—all wearing gloves and hard hats, and bearing flashlights and shovels. "Our best guess is that they headed there. It's an inside room, and maybe they took cover in the shower stalls."

Garrett had somehow procured a copy of the recent remodeling blueprints of the school, and Ty had spent much of the early morning scouring them.

Not that he could sleep, anyway. *"You can't rescue everyone."*

Maybe not, but he could try.

He had nearly leaped in front of Brette this morning as she dragged her bag downstairs just in time for her ride to show up. Yesterday's raven-haired girl and her boyfriend, riding shotgun in the front of their Toyota Highlander. The man got out and tossed Brette's bag in the back.

Ty had wanted to run out then, beg her not to give up—on herself. On them.

Apparently, he could be very, very wrong. Because when she'd kissed him in the parking lot at the hospital, he practically had them to the altar. At the very least, she'd ignited inside him all the reasons why he'd done the right thing in not giving up on her.

"Faith hurts too much."

Indeed.

"Can't you see that it's time to give up?"

Yep. He'd let those words fortify him, turn him away from the door, stop him from raising his hand in farewell.

But it didn't prevent the ache from digging into his chest and squeezing.

At the first dent of light, Ian came downstairs with an update on the equipment. Then Garrett and Jenny, who'd whipped up a batch of pancakes, put on coffee.

Ty had assembled an excavation plan by the time the rest joined them.

Now, he surveyed the building as he sipped the last of his coffee. He prayed that his hunch wasn't just desperation, or a need to be in control. *Thank you for that, Brette.*

"The roof is still intact over the weight room, so if we can clear away the debris near the door, we can get inside. The locker room area has some damage, but we can't get to the debris without getting a crane in here, so we'll have to do our best to cut through the weight room. Watch for broken glass, and although the electricity is still out, there's jagged wire and plenty of razor-sharp metal."

He turned to the drivers of the excavator and the bulldozer. "I'm going to send a team with you, just in case we find something while you're taking away the debris. Be careful."

He glanced at Garrett, who met his eyes with a grim expression. "Let's go."

Garrett, Spenser, Jonas, Ned, and Gage headed inside, Ty behind them, leaving Ian to supervise the heavy machinery.

The school reeked of old milk, dirt, and decaying cement, arid and cold. Jonas and Ned cleared away the clutter of chairs in the hallway as Spenser led them toward the back of the building. Light glinted through the expansive gymnasium. Boards were ripped up and scattered into the hallway, flags from past championship wins lay tattered, and another trophy case spilled glass and achievements across the cement floor.

Ty held his phone, checking the photo of the blueprint. "To the right."

Twisted, galvanized metal blocked the path to the locker room, but a small office off the hallway—perhaps the athletics office—led through to the weight room, albeit once the wood, cement, desks, filing cabinets, Sheetrock, and ceiling tiles were cleared away.

The group stepped up without a word and began to dismantle the mess. Outside, the engines on the equipment fired up, ricocheting the noise through the hallways.

Behind it all, Ty thought he heard a dog barking. Maybe just wishful thinking, but he clung to it.

They pried off Sheetrock, lifted the heavy filing cabinet from the room, and moved a metal desk. "We'll need a chainsaw for some of these wall joists," Garrett said. "They're too heavy for us to lift. I have one in my truck."

"I'll get it," Ty said and headed back down the hallway.

Outside, the excavators had begun to sift through the pileup of cars along the far edge of the school. The oldest part of the building, it now contained the theater. Or what remained of it.

As Shae, Jenny, and some of the other parents searched the cars, Kacey and Ian led the team that eyeballed the debris before it was extracted.

Ty headed to Garrett's truck. Footsteps behind him made him turn—Gage ran up. "We need a crowbar too."

Ty took down the tailgate and climbed onto the bed, then

opened the box in back and dug out the chainsaw and a crowbar. He handed both to Gage, who took off for the building.

Ty jumped down, noticed Chet standing nearby, hanging up from a cell call. He came over. "Pete said he's sending over some volunteers."

Ty just stared at him.

"He's trying to help, Ty. Don't throw it away."

"Of course not," Ty said. He shook his head. "I just thought he thought . . . well, I know my hunches aren't that popular—"

"Your hunch saved my life," Chet said.

Ty frowned.

"After we crashed, you knew the storm was coming. You had a gut feeling about which direction to hike . . . I put every last smidgen of faith in your hunch, Ty, and you brought us home." Chet pocketed his phone. "Of course, I did my fair share of praying for those two days."

"I didn't leave because I had a hunch. I left . . . I left because I was afraid you were going to die."

"I nearly did."

"Yeah, but . . . listening to you . . ." Ty blew out a breath. "Truth is, I was probably more coward than brave. I just couldn't listen to you suffer. Not if I could do something about it."

"There will come a day when you can do nothing for me. You'll be helpless. You'll have to stand there while I suffer. And then what are you going to do, Ty?"

Maybe she'd been right in leaving. Because maybe he wasn't the hero he hoped to be.

Truth was, he so feared the world falling apart underneath him, he simply refused to let it happen. *"I call it being a bully."*

Maybe, but he called it fear.

Fear of the storm. Fear of what could happen. Fear of collapsing in the snow, or worse, watching the people he loved die in his arms.

In fact, perhaps he lived in dread more than Brette. At least she had the courage to acknowledge it.

He spent his life dodging it. Controlling it.

Refusing to admit that most of the time, he just hoped he was enough to face whatever lay ahead.

Chet was still talking. "That's why I knew we'd make it—I had faith in you. Because you don't give up. You keep fighting—from staying sober every day to not letting that busted knee stop you. You've got what it takes, son. That's why I keep holding out hope that someday you'll get back in that chopper."

"You do?"

"You're a born pilot, Ty. You have the ability to think clearly under pressure, good instincts—yeah, you belong on this team, and even more, in the cockpit."

Heat filled his chest.

"You belong on this team."

"Let's just find these kids," he managed.

It could have been a good day.

"Give me the map, for Pete's sake!" Brette leaned up between the seats of the Highlander—Nixon's parents' car, a loaner for this round of storm chasing.

Nixon sat with his computer on his lap, trying to read the amoeba writhing on the screen, overlaid upon a grid of the area. He examined it as if it might hold the hidden secrets of the universe.

She only wanted a tornado.

Brette smoothed the map out on her lap, then folded it so she could study the section.

They could practically see to Des Moines. The prairie was dry, brown, and dismal save for the mushroom of gray clouds. One in particular had puffed up and exploded outward from the congestion of clouds, its underside darkened and menacing.

They'd been following the radar for hours, taking back roads and highways, then back to gravel. Driven through two rainstorms—the forward scouts of the storm. Punched through to the other side to find an anvil Cu hovering, a cloud with a flat bottom and top, leveled by the higher atmosphere winds.

And still, no hook, no churning.

No drop.

The air smelled of rain, and somewhere at the base of the storm, in the distance, lightning flickered. "I'm hot, hungry, and I think I stink," Geena said. "We'd better get some action soon or I'm finding a Dairy Queen."

"I think we're about a hundred miles southwest of Des Moines," Brette said.

"Just tell us if there's a road between here and that storm," Nixon snapped.

"I hate the word *rerouting*," Geena said, pulling over. "I'm not driving one more mile until we know if we're heading in the right direction."

"The right direction is directly toward that big black cloud," Nixon said, not looking up from the computer.

Probably he was right. They could simply keep moving through the farm fields, working their way west, closing in on the bank of clouds.

Rain began to spit on the Highlander, a light spray from an overhead renegade, just a toddler compared to the massive front moving east.

"Okay, I think we're coming up to a farm road. If we take it north, it should intersect a county road that'll drive us right into the core."

"I hate getting wet," Geena said but put the car into drive. "We shouldn't have done this without Jonas."

"I can figure this out, Gee," Nixon said, and Brette heard restraint in his voice. "I've been doing this with Jonas for years."

"It's different with Jonas," Geena said. "He knows weather. Can read the clouds." She braked as she came up to the road. "You are an excellent videographer, but you don't know how to read the sky. Jonas can *feel* weather, it's in his genes. No offense."

Nixon said nothing, and Brette picked up her camera. From here, the storm looked immense but still unorganized, showers pinging the earth in dark patches.

The rain thickened.

Hail.

"Now we're talkin'," Nixon said, glancing back at Brette.

She white-knuckled her seat belt. Swallowed. Forced a smile.

Geena said nothing as they came up to the intersecting road. She turned right, pointed the Highlander at the storm, and hit the gas.

"The radar suggests something is forming, but—"

A branch skittered across the road, and Geena hit the brakes, scooted around it. "Are we heading into the core?"

Brette leaned forward, Jonas's words on her lips. *Do not punch the core.*

"No. These are probably the RFDs—rear flank downdrafts. Just keep it steady."

The heavy overlay darkened the road, and Geena flipped on her lights. Brette lifted the camera and shot pictures of the stray shafts of light punching through the layer of black like fingers from heaven.

More hail, thunder on the roof, and Geena eased up. "I can't see. The wipers are going too fast."

"Pull over," Nixon said.

"No—we have to keep going!" Brette leaned forward. "Listen,

we've been tracking this stupid storm for hours, and if all we get is a few storm clouds, then . . . we should be back at home, trying to find Creed."

And there it was. The source of the churning of her gut. Why she hadn't eaten at the last convenience store. Why the smell of Nixon's sunflower seeds and Geena's coffee turned her nauseous.

She shouldn't have left.

She knew it even before Nixon had grabbed her duffel bag this morning. Knew it even before Ty left her room last night, his words radiating inside her. *"You're so scared that I will hurt you, that I might let you down, that you'll run away, even if you don't want to."*

She closed her eyes.

She just couldn't live like Ty, with faith and hunches and the blind belief that everything would work out. God might have rescued him, but he hadn't done a thing to save her.

Geena pulled over. "I can't see anything. I think we need to ride it out."

"The radar is frozen," Nixon said.

Around them, the sky had turned a murky pea green, the fields almost black. Wind shook the car.

Geena reached out for Nixon's hand.

Brette folded her hands on her lap and leaned her head into the seat.

"It's behind us!"

Nixon's voice raised her head, and she turned around.

There it was, out of the storm, dropping like a rope, a skinny side-winding funnel, white where the sun hit it.

It dropped right behind a farmhouse, in a field heading northeast, a hundred feet from the car.

Brette scooped up her camera and, without a moment to think, opened her door.

"What are you doing?"

"Getting the shot!"

The hail had stopped, but the rain pelleted her, slammed her against the car, soaked her through, icing her skin. She tried to focus the camera, but water bled down the lens.

The twister snaked, spiraling through the field, churning up the dirt.

And on the far side of the storm, the sky bled out into a pale, calm blue.

The roar of the funnel billowed up, but she snapped the shots, capturing the twister as it writhed across the field.

Then lightning flashed, a splinter from heaven with arms that crackled down and seared the earth.

"Please tell me you got that!" Geena said, opening her door.

"Yep."

"Get in! We'll go after it."

Brette threw herself in the car, and Geena gunned the Highlander into a tight circle.

"Where'd it go?" Nixon peered out the windshield toward the funnel that was suddenly dissipating. "Are you kidding me?"

Brette watched, her heart sinking as the funnel twisted out into a thin curl and faded into the atmosphere.

He turned off his camera, dropped it on his lap. "Eight hours of driving for a three-minute funnel? And there's probably hail damage to my dad's car."

"I can't believe it dropped down behind us." Geena met her eyes, but Brette couldn't smile. She agreed with Nixon. They'd spent hours bracing themselves for a storm that barely materialized.

They drove past the farmhouse and spied a family emerging from a storm cellar in the front yard. A couple youngsters, their mother. Her husband, now surveying the damage to his field. The woman came up and took his hand. Brette turned to watch them.

It could have been much, much worse. But that was how it was—you saw the storm coming and hadn't a clue how it might hit, how bad the damage might be, how you'd survive.

She settled back into the seat, checking her shot.

The water on her lens had flared out against the light of the storm, causing a rainbow effect into the receding tornado.

Or maybe the rainbow had been there and she hadn't noticed it until now, because as they headed east, she glimpsed the faintest arch over the horizon.

"Can we get a sundae now?" Geena asked.

"Not quite yet, Gee," Nixon said. He had pulled up his Doppler. "Look at this."

Geena pulled over, and Brette leaned up.

"There's another storm heading across South Dakota. We might be able to connect with it east of Sioux Falls, if we hurry."

Geena collapsed her head back against the seat. "I just want some stinkin' ice cream!"

But Brette's gaze glued to the screen. "So, it's heading straight east."

"Well, it could deviate. But . . . yes."

Brette ran her fingers across the screen. "Pan out."

He widened the screen, and her finger continued until it hit . . . "Chester. If it doesn't deviate, it'll hit near Chester, maybe even dead-on."

Silence.

"At this rate, it'll hit in the night. Around midnight," Nixon said.

"There won't be any storm chasers to call in a funnel if it hits the ground," Brette said.

"People will be in bed," Geena added thinly.

Brette leaned back. "I'll text Jonas."

"Who is trying to find his brother." Geena sat up, put the car into drive. "Is there any chance we could hit a drive-through?"

"We haven't come this far to give up." Ty said the words to himself twice before he uttered them to Garrett.

Grimy, strung out, and on edge, Garrett stared at the header beams of the weight room, now wedged against the locker room entrance. He looked like he'd like to hit something.

Likewise, Jonas stood not far away, finishing off the last of his water, his face streaked with sweat and cement dust. Four hours into the excavation and they'd managed to wedge open the door to the weight room, only to discover the roof had collapsed near the entrance to the hallway that led to the locker rooms.

Another two hours and they'd managed to dig a path to the door, which was blockaded by a web of steel girders.

"Will this help?"

Ty turned to see Pete picking his way through the rubble. He held what looked like a tire with hoses attached.

"It's an airbag. I was thinking, maybe we just lift it and send someone in."

Pete had arrived around lunchtime with food, water, and the local volunteer fire department. He'd helped the crew dig through the last of the debris, unearthing the girders.

"It's an airbag jack. But it'll lift three tons, so hopefully the girder mess isn't more than that."

He looked as grimy, as sleepless, as raw edged as the rest of them, and Ty tried to forgive him, even just a little.

Pete wedged the lift under the tangle of girders.

"Careful," Ty said. "We don't want it to fall and collapse the inner wall. There could be kids on the other side."

Pete nodded, no animosity in his agreement. "We also have a stabilizer." A young woman with blonde hair and wearing gloves and a T-shirt with the Red Cross logo brought over something that looked like a jack. Pete affixed it to the floor and tucked its U-shaped end into an arm on the girder.

"Katie, you work the stabilizer while I turn on the air hose."

Pete had snaked out the hose to a compressed air tank. He now picked up a handheld gauge. "Stand back."

He released the valve, and Katie worked the hydraulic pump as the bag filled. Garrett stepped back, casting his gaze overhead.

The girders creaked, something tore free, and cement crumbled to the ground. But the girder mass moved, a foot, then two, finally three feet off the ground, the maximum height.

Ty hit his knees. "I see the door on the other side. It's open."

Pete too knelt and grabbed his Maglite off his belt. Shined it in. "Hello! Anyone in there?"

Darkness echoed back, and the light pushed away nothing but emptiness.

"I'm going in," Ty said. He reached for his own light, which was smaller but perfect to put in his mouth and hold there as he wiggled through.

"Ty—" Pete started, but Ty rounded on him.

"This is my rescue."

Pete seemed to assess his words.

"Fine. Don't get killed." But something shifted in his eyes. A hint of friendship, perhaps, and Ty offered a quick, wry smile.

"If the wall comes down, don't leave me to die," Ty said.

"We'll see." But Pete grinned.

Ty hugged the rubble and noticed that Garrett had knelt next to him.

"Find them."

Ty headed into the darkness, trying not to think of three tons—okay, probably less, but his brain had that number lodged inside—of steel above him as he struggled through, careful not to dislodge the precarious lift.

Please let it not crash down over me, crush me, paralyze—

He reached the door and slipped inside, his Maglite cresting through the hallway. The beam revealed two doors, both accessible. One to the men's locker room, the other to the women's. He got onto his knees and crawled toward the men's entrance.

Not as demolished as he imagined it might be. He moved toward a trickling sound, his light casting over wet towels, shoes, soap, and other locker remnants. The beam spilled into the shower area. "Anybody here?"

Water puddled on the floor. He scrabbled farther into the room and cast the beam over the individual stalls. "Hello?"

He checked each stall, their tiles torn and spilled like teeth on the floor. Then he tunneled back out to the other side.

Please.

The women's locker room fought his entry, something blocking the door. But he pushed the door halfway in and squeezed through. "Hello?"

This room had suffered more damage. A wall had crashed in from the weight room, and more litter had showered down from the ceiling. He panned his light across the room, over sheared lockers and shattered benches, finding the shower area.

Still intact.

And . . . oh no.

A leg. It protruded out of a shower stall, unmoving, the skin shiny as if old, the body still in death.

No, *no*. He scrambled over the benches and dumped out onto the floor.

He cast his light again toward the body, saw the feet, the odd angle of the legs, and he tried not to be ill. Still he pressed on. *God, please.*

He reached the stall and forced himself around the edge.

His heart snagged in his chest. He flicked the light over the body again, just to make sure.

A CPR mannequin. Full body, the kind students might practice on.

He leaned back against the wall, breathing hard.

Not a body. But still, the locker rooms . . . empty.

His entire body ached; he just wanted to sit here, listen to his heartbeat and wail.

He'd dragged everybody out here, made them all believe that he could find these kids . . .

"I just think you don't like being helpless, so you keep reaching—"

"So, lying. Dreaming up a happy ending."

Brette was right.

There were no miracles out there. No happy endings.

He scrubbed a hand down his face, hating the wetness there. How could he tell them that he'd found nothing? He worked his way out of the shower, over the wreckage in the locker room, and was just wedging himself into the hallway when Pete's voice punched through.

"Ty—don't come this way! The wall is collapsing!"

He dove back inside the locker room.

A blinding white pain streaked up his leg as his knee hit something hard—cement or a board—but he ignored it and curled into a ball just as the weight room wall collapsed inward. Cement chips, dust, and debris clogged his mouth, his nose. He lost his Maglite, and darkness fell.

Then everything went deadly silent.

13

AS USUAL, THE MUSIC HEALED HIM. Ben stood on stage, pouring himself into the last song in his set, reluctant for the melody to fade, to return him to earth.

To stop the heady sluice of hope and romance that filled his veins when he heard his voice twine out through the massive sound system that framed the stage.

We said goodbye on a night like this
Stars shining down, I was waitin' for a kiss
But you walked away, left me standing there alone
Baby, I'm a-waiting, won't you come back home

And yes, the words could tear him asunder if he let them return him to the moment just before he left her, when he pulled Kacey into his arms, her body melding to his like it belonged in his embrace. To the memory of the sweet fragrance of her hair, the longing that swelled inside him to lift her chin, press a kiss to her lips.

The lyrics stirred that ache, the hunger of needing her.

He let his longing bleed out into the bridge.

I need you, I need you, I need you
Don't say goodbye
I need you, I need you, I need you
Can't live without you
I need you, I need you, I need you
Come back to me tonight

The crowd before him went wild at the sorrow in his voice, as if he might be singing to every teenage, college girl and single mom in the audience.

They had a good turnout for the festival. RVs and pop-ups and even a glamping area with canvas tents jammed the fields around the four stages. Even on the last night, the crowd seemed jazzed, ready for an evening of love songs, country rock, and stories.

He'd landed the 6:45 slot, warming up for Chase Rice, and the finale, Keith Urban. Twilight bruised the sky, tufts of fiery orange against a template of purple and deep indigo. An orange moon hung low on the horizon, a hint of a starry night ahead.

The kind of night where, if he were back home in Mercy Falls, he might drive out to Kacey's house that she shared with her parents, cajole her into taking a ride in his pickup. He'd find a spot that faced the mountains and watch the granite peaks reach for the heavens.

Among other things.

Turn around, listen to your heart
I need you so much, don't tear me apart
I was wrong, you were right
Nothing between us but this darn fight

He cast a look at Moose, his drummer, who caught his eye with a nod. He'd run the chorus twice at the end and queue up their encore song, the single that still hung on the charts, the last one he'd recorded with his former partner, Hollie Montgomery. The one that reminded him that he'd wanted to live a different life. A simpler life.

Right.

Ten years gone by, my eyes are dry
But the echo of my heart won't tell a lie
I'm coming home to the one I love
Second chances, given from above

He launched again into the chorus, added a guitar solo, and fell into the final line, let it hang for the crowd as the music fell.

A life I never knew . . . until there was you

He stared out, meeting eyes, and the crowd roused to the flirt in his smile, the way he pointed to a few cheering fans.

Then with a nod of his head, Moose brought it back to life, and he repeated the chorus.

I need you, I need you, I need you
Don't say goodbye
I need you, I need you, I need you

He walked to the front of the stage, knelt, and held out his hand. The ladies in the front row freaked out, grabbing at him. He grinned, winked, and took a couple steps back.

There was flirting with the audience, and then there was trouble. But the crowd loved it, and he glanced at Buckley on keyboard, then Duke, bass guitar, finally Joey, lead guitar, and they got the message. The backup music dropped out on cue.

He finished the song on his own, with his guitar slung behind him, his golden voice lonely and pleading through the speakers.

Can't live without you
I need you, I need you, I need you
Come back to me tonight

The crowd screamed his name and he lifted his arm and waved.

His entire body ached with the gnawing hollowness of missing Kacey.

They shouted for the encore, and of course he gave it to them, smiling the entire way through "Start a Fire."

Golden tan, a laugh for the band
I see you in the crowd, waving your Coke can
I like your smile, stay for a while
Huddle up around the fire
It's all right, stay for the night
Let's chase away the cold and do it right
C'mon, baby, let's start a fire

He left the stage under the thunder of the applause, running off fast to meet up with the band, high-fiving them even as they gathered to catch their breath. Sweat ran down his spine, his stomach growled, and he just wanted someplace quiet.

Maybe.

Because quiet also meant the voices might find him, shout out his regrets, make him take a good look at his stupidity.

Moose hung an arm around his neck. "I needed that, man, after the last few days." He thumped Ben on the chest. "Let's get back to the motel, clean up, and see if we can find any good music in this town."

Moose fist-bumped Joey, gave a nod to Buckley, and tossed his keys in the air.

Normally they'd head back to their RV, maybe set up lawn chairs on the roof and listen to the next act.

No, normally Ben would shut himself into the air-conditioned quiet of his room and call Kacey.

He packed up his guitar, a new Gibson sent to him by his manager, then followed the band out to the Escalade they'd rented.

The festival grounds were situated ten miles from the tiny town of Colvill, a sleepy farm town tucked into the western border of Wisconsin. Population 1,500 during the winter, but with the hub of festivals in the summer, the population swelled into the ten-thousands and the two motels in Colvill couldn't handle the explosion of guests. Still, somehow his manager Goldie had managed to land them two rooms at the Village Motor Inn, a two-story motor lodge with 1960s throwback decor. The complex surrounded a bean-shaped pool with a high dive at one end and ancient loungers with floral padded seats for sunbathers. His own room, the one he shared with Moose, faced the pool and offered a tiny sitting room along with the one bedroom. The bedroom sported a stuffed fish between the two double beds, which were both fitted with quilted floral polyester covers, and included a television armed with rabbit ears and an in-room Jacuzzi.

The deluxe suite.

But it was clean and came equipped with Wi-Fi, and he flopped on the bed after throwing off the cover and listened to Moose hum as he showered.

Ben wasn't the least interested in the band's plans. Not that he had any other options.

Except the one that he couldn't get out of his head.

Return to Minnesota. Chase down Kacey.

Just like that, she sat down on the bed and reached over, running her fingers over the five-o'clock shadow he'd saved for his audience. For her.

Her beautiful eyes caught in his. "I love to hear you sing. It reminds me of when we first met and you'd try out your songs on me."

"You were my inspiration." He wove his fingers through hers. "Still are."

She smiled, and it hit him full blast, the desire aflame inside him. Oh, he needed her, and if she were here, he'd pull her into his arms, lean back, and . . . well, there was a reason he'd stopped inviting her on the road. He was keenly aware of his own frailties. Postponing the wedding twice certainly hadn't helped either.

He ran his hand over his face, pushing the image, the longing away.

As if.

Oh, he was a mess. He longed for Kacey, but not like this. Not in a world where everything could go south, not in a world where their worlds never intersected.

And that left them without options.

Ben closed his eyes, the truth burrowing deep. He wanted it to be perfect—their life, their future. He wanted what he sang about on stage. And until he could give that to her . . .

Still, the thought of anyone else coming home to Kacey, holding her in his arms . . .

Moose came out of the bathroom dressed in a clean pair of jeans and pulling on a black T-shirt with the words "Start a Fire" imprinted on the front.

"Are you looking for trouble?" Ben asked.

"Maybe." Moose had trimmed his dark brown beard down to a fine scruff, pulled back his curly hair, and donned a red baseball hat turned backward. "And so should you be."

Ben pushed himself off the bed and headed over to his bag. "I don't think so."

"I heard what went down between you and Kacey, man. I'm sorry. Come out with us, blow off some steam, just have some fun."

Ben rifled through his clothes, looking for a clean pair of jeans, a T-shirt, anything, really, to wear to get a bite to eat.

Or maybe he should just order room service. "I don't think so, Moose."

"C'mon, dude. You heard that audience tonight. They're crazy for you. I'm not suggesting you hook up with anyone, but the first step to getting Kacey out of your system is to do a little flirting, see that you've still got it. And you do, man." Moose grabbed his wallet, shoved it into his pocket.

"I don't want to get Kacey out of my system!"

Moose held up his hands in surrender. "Step back. I'm just trying to help."

"I don't need help."

"Yeah, actually, you do but—fine." Moose shook his head. "You used to be fun."

Ben frowned and headed to the bathroom.

After taking a hot shower, he got out, didn't bother to shave, and emerged from the bathroom in a towel. He searched for a room service menu and even called the front desk, but the girl there paused long enough at his request for him to apologize and hang up.

He got dressed, grabbed a hat, shoved on his cowboy boots, and headed outside. A couple kids were running across the cement deck, cannonballing into the pool. Their mother lounged on a deck chair, reading.

He searched for the Escalade, then realized Moose and probably the rest of the band had taken it, so he headed to the lobby and asked about the nearby restaurants.

Across the highway and down the road, he could land a gourmet nuked burrito at a 7-Eleven.

Perfect.

But his stomach said yes, so he walked in the grassy ditch down the road, under the starry night, and entered the store.

He stood for an eternity at the hot lights, debating between crispy taquitos and a lone piece of pizza, before moving on to the refrigerated sandwiches and burritos. He finally chose a bag of popcorn and a Diet Coke and headed back to the motel.

He spent ten minutes flipping through the TV channels, all eleven of them, pausing for a moment on the final innings of a Cubs game.

"You used to be fun."

No, he used to be lonely. Hollow. Broken.

And then he'd found Kacey again, and she'd introduced him to the daughter he never knew he had, glued him back together, reminded him that it wasn't too late for a second chance.

That he could have the life he'd longed for—with her.

"If I walk away from music for Kacey, we could end up with nothing."

His stupid words to Ian. But that fear dogged him, kept him on the road.

Yet he'd ended up right back here, eating dry popcorn in a ratty motel.

"It matters who you choose to spend your time—and your life—with. And when it's the person you love, then you can't fail."

Ian, back in his head, but with his words came the memories. Kacey, sitting on her stool at the Gray Pony, singing along to his songs, her eyes lighting when his gaze landed on her. Kacey, waiting for him after a gig on the bed of his pickup, hopping off to embrace him, her fragrance calling him back from the heights of the music to home. Kacey's voice on the other end of the phone, refueling him, healing his loneliness.

He sang for his audience, to fill them up, make them dance, keep them young, remind them that summer nights could last forever.

But Kacey was *his* song. The tune that lingered, the soundtrack to his life.

A life that could be much simpler. Without the riffs and solos and backup singers.

It could be an easy, beautiful melody.

Him on stage at the Gray Pony, playing for his girl.

Ben reached for the phone, the words already forming. *I'm sorry, Kacey. You're right—it shouldn't be about me, it needs to be about us. I'm nothing without you.*

The phone rang. Three, four, five times.

Finally switched to voicemail.

He called again. Listened to her voice.

Called a final time, debating whether to leave a message.

Let the beep pass without a word.

He hung up and stared at his phone, at the wallpaper of Kacey and Audrey.

Shoot.

Laughter from outside spilled into the room. Footsteps and then the key in the lock and the door opened.

Moose stood at the door, his arm around a pretty country fan in a sundress and boots, her blonde hair long and curly. "There he is, girls. Our job is to cheer him up."

Ben found his feet. "Moose—"

"Nope. Not listening." Moose came in, and two more girls, along with Joey, followed him. Young and talented, classically handsome with blue eyes and dusty blond hair, Joey had future written all over him with his ability to improvise, to keep up with Ben's guitar licks, add that slightly husky baritone to Ben's tenor.

Joey could be his own star, if he kept away from the influence of the drummer. Joey fell into one of the two chairs, and one of the women followed, landing in his lap, looping an arm around his neck. He grinned, and a slight blush suggested he might not quite be accustomed to Moose's after-gig parties.

"This is Madison," Moose said. "Which is super-ironic because we're in Wisconsin."

Ben rolled his eyes but shook the hand of the cute brunette. Of course, she wore a "Ben Is King" shirt, the pink V-neck version. "Nice to meet you."

"All right, so we're all friends here. Let's go—we found a honky-tonk down the road with a decent cover band. Buckley and Duke are holding a table for us."

"I'm not—"

"And they have amazing burgers, don't they, Lucia?"

The blonde nodded. "I'm a waitress there."

Of course she was.

"Let me at least feed you, boss," Moose said, casting a look at the popcorn. "Nothing else on the agenda. I'll bring you right back afterward and tuck you into bed."

Funny. But Ben glanced at Madison, the fan gleam in her eyes, and managed a smile. "Just a burger."

"Mmmhmm," Moose said. "Just a burger."

"Ty, can you hear me?"

Pete's voice penetrated the shadows, the darkness that pressed into every pore of his body. Ty had lost his flashlight and had spent the past two hours breathing through his shirt, praying that he hadn't coated his lungs with cement dust.

"Mmmhmm," he said. "I'm here somewhere."

"We're digging you out. Hang in there."

He'd already checked all his limbs—everything seemed intact except for his knee, which had blown up, the skin spongy and hot. His dive back into the locker room had saved him from being crushed by the wall, but he might not be able to walk for a couple weeks. And he'd scraped his back when he'd wedged himself next to a bank of lockers. Maybe *in* a locker, for all he could tell.

Kind of made him think of his middle school days. He'd never been the guy to be shoved into a locker. But he'd done plenty of shoving.

A lot of anger back then, pent-up grief, frustration.

The kind that pushed him into dark choices to ease the persistent ache.

Or perhaps he was just stubborn. Driven by a need to prove himself.

Prove himself to whom? Himself? The PEAK team?

God?

Maybe. Or maybe he wasn't proving himself to God.

Maybe he hoped desperately that God would prove himself to Ty. That he'd show up again, that it wasn't a fluke the first time, as Ty lay collapsed in the snow.

He longed to believe that hoping and reaching out in faith resulted in God reaching back, but he couldn't shake the idea that he had to do enough, *be* enough to make the Almighty care enough to show up.

"Ty! Any sign of the kids?"

Garrett's voice echoed down the clogged corridor, and Ty wanted to weep anew.

"No," he said softly, but apparently loud enough because Garrett didn't reply.

I'm sorry. He tried to straighten his leg and nearly howled with the sharp-edged pain that turned him into a coward.

"As long as we think we're enough, God can do nothing for us. We enter into salvation through the door of destitution."

Apparently, Garrett had decided to stick around in his head.

Ty counted his heartbeats, now beating in time to the banging ache of his knee. Perfect.

Not far away, voices lifted, the sound of shovels, and behind it all, a dog barking.

Pete, probably bringing in the K9s. Talk about upping the game.

But he should have probably left the search and rescue to Pete in the first place. Now everyone was risking their lives for *him*.

And his stupid hunch.

More movement, and scattered light hit the opening, flashed across his face.

He winced.

"There you are," Pete said, shining the light on his own grimy face. "Are you hurt?"

"I'm fine," Ty ground out. Or, he would be. He just needed to get out of this tunnel and put some ice on his knee.

"Hang tight. The good news is that we were able to dig down through the roof. We've got the fire truck bringing in a cable to hoist you out."

"What's the bad news?"

Pete's face turned grim, and even Ty recognized grief in his expression. "I think you know the bad news."

He did. The search was over.

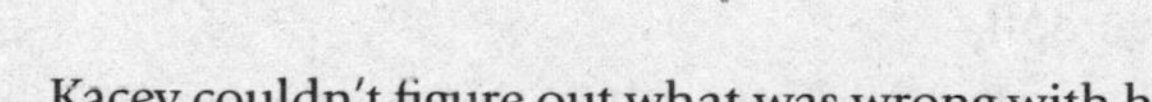

Kacey couldn't figure out what was wrong with her. She hadn't been the one caught in the cave-in. This time. Hadn't been the one dragged out of the bowels of some dank room, shaking, dirty, damaged.

And yet here she stood, trembling, feeling like she might just fly apart, wing off in every direction. Kacey ground her jaw tight as she watched Gage crouch in front of a very in-pain Ty.

"You should go to the hospital and get this knee looked at," Gage was saying as he wrapped Ty's knee in a cold wrap. Pete had pulled him out, finally, after hours of digging with Gage and the Red Cross SAR team. Despite Ty's protests, they carried him out on a gurney, and now the lot of them clustered around him, watching as hope dissolved into the darkening sky.

"No. We gotta keep looking . . ." But Ty's voice emerged broken, feeble, an old mantra that he probably realized fell on dubious ears. Especially those of Pete, who stood with the city engineer, talking through the stability of the building.

Kacey wrapped her hands around her neck and turned away, feeling a little woozy. She walked over to the Duck Lake fire truck, sat on the back, and leaned against the metal frame, needing something sturdy to fight the dark roil inside her.

She refused to surrender to the ancient nightmares.

But wow, she needed Ben.

Oh, *c'mon*. She was a capable, strong, smart chopper pilot who'd seen and experienced worse—much worse—than a cave-in that half-buried one of her teammates.

Try an ambush in the mountains of Afghanistan that had cost her the lives of her navigator and copilot, while she fought with five brave Army Rangers to stay alive.

Or even her own cave-in at her friend Sierra's house. Kacey had been trapped in the cellar, injured, reliving every moment of the Afghanistan standoff.

But both times, Ben had been there. Via his songs, on that mountaintop, and in person in the cellar, as he descended through the shattered house to find their daughter. Then, her.

Ben was always there, swooping in to catch her up, carrying her out of the darkness, his strength radiating through her. Reminding her that she didn't have to be strong, not all the time. He would rescue her.

She closed her eyes, the fatigue pressing through her. If he were here, he'd be telling her to take a nap, or better, be sitting behind her, his strong, musical hands kneading free the knots in her shoulders.

Tears burned her eyes, and her own voice bombarded her, left her bruised. *"But your life is . . . it's all about you."*

Oh, Ben hadn't deserved that because even she knew he'd moved to Mercy Falls and opened up Mountain Song Records for her. For them.

Had hit the road to pay for the life he envisioned for them.

Still, she couldn't help but feel like second place to the music.

A presence beside her made her open her eyes, just as Chet sat down beside her. He appeared as wrung out as she felt, the wisdom lines on his face deepening as the sun fled the day. Shadows cast over the school, and soon they'd need lights if they hoped to keep searching.

"How are you doing?" Chet asked.

She lifted a shoulder. "I can't believe we can't find these kids."

Chet nodded. Let silence fall between them.

"If it were Audrey who was lost, I couldn't stop looking, ever," Kacey said.

"No. I don't think you would. And neither would Ben. It was hard for him to leave."

She didn't mean the noise that emerged. But, well, there it was.

Chet frowned. "He didn't want to leave, Kacey. It's his job—"

"Believe me, I know." She was full of inadvertent tones today. "I'm sorry. I just . . . I should be used to it by now. Ben leaving me."

Chet blinked at her. "He hates leaving you and Audrey. He probably would have stayed if you'd asked."

She looked at Chet. "That's not true."

"Really? Because it's always been that way, Kacey, starting when you gave birth to Audrey."

What? "He got in a fist fight, landed in jail, and left town without even talking to me!"

Chet held up his hand. "Let's not debate the specifics. There's no doubt there were hurt feelings on both sides—"

"Hurt feelings? He missed thirteen years of his daughter's life."

She looked away. "And I know it wasn't his fault, but I just can't believe he's missing more."

"Kacey. He does this all—everything—for you. From the day Ben met you, he's been trying to impress you. Make something of himself so he could provide for you. He loved music, sure, but he would have chucked it all and worked at the local lumberyard if he'd thought you wanted him."

Chet's words turned her mute, even as they strummed through her. Because yes, Ben would have—in fact, that had been his very plan when he'd proposed, his hand resting on her swollen stomach, so much love in his eyes that of course she'd said yes.

"He's wanted to marry you since, well, since the day you got lost together in the Glacier mountains," Chet said, his voice gentling.

"We were thirteen," she said softly. "He made me feel like every song he wrote was for me."

"They probably were," Chet said, offering a small smile.

"It's just that every time he calls off our wedding, I feel . . ."

"Like you're not important. Like that adopted child who feared her parents would give her back."

She drew in a breath. She'd forgotten how well Chet knew her.

"You've always been Ben's first choice. Music is just his default. And right now, it's his solution to pay for the life he wants you to have."

"I don't want that life. I just want him."

Chet nodded, his eyes kind. "Does he know that?"

She stared at him as he pressed his hand to her knee, squeezing.

"You might consider that deep down, Ben is still that skinny kid who used to get beat up because he was poor. And yet, he was still willing to be poor, for you."

His tone was soft, but it contained barbs that made her wince with their accuracy. She might feel like second place to his music, but she'd stood on the sidelines, not willing to enter his world.

Making him feel like he had to choose.

And he *had* chosen. He'd pursued her all the way to Montana, uprooted his life for her, and yes, even planned their elopement. And frankly, she *did* need a man who was strong enough to take over, to see the frailties she kept hidden from everyone else.

She needed his arms around her, his golden voice in her ear and threading through her. The sheer charm of him to make her feel beautiful. *"You're the most beautiful woman I know. You won't get lost in my world—you're the center of it."*

And he was the center of hers.

But they needed a world together. Ben had already stepped into her world. Time to step into his.

"The rental company sent me over a loaner today, by the way. Keys are in it, at the Marshall place."

"Thanks, Chet." She got up and walked over to Ty, who had been hoisted to his feet by Gage.

"I'm taking off for a bit," she said to both of them.

Ty frowned.

"It's personal."

"It's Ben," Gage said, meeting her eyes. Okay, so these guys knew her well.

"I'm leaving the chopper in your hands," she said, directing her attention to Ty.

"What do you think I'm going to do? Take it for a joyride?"

"It needs gas, if you do."

He gave her a look as he balanced on one leg.

"Can you keep an eye on Audrey too? I'll stop by the house, but I need to make this trip alone."

Ty nodded, his gaze going to Pete, then Garrett and the rest of the Marshalls, who now looked whipped and distraught. Ned was heading to one of the family trucks.

"We'll be here when you get back," Ty said.

Oh Ty. At least he wasn't mentioning any hunches. She called herself a traitor as she turned and ran to catch up with Ned.

But as she climbed into the passenger seat, she felt, for the first time in a year, whole.

14

ALL WAS EERILY QUIET as Geena, Nixon, and Brette pulled up to the Marshall family home. Overhead, the oncoming storm had blotted out most of the stars and the wind had started to stir the trees, but it was nothing to be alarmed about.

Save the red dollop of danger in the center of the Doppler radar screen. And the fact that Jonas hadn't answered his phone, not once.

Probably he wasn't picking up his voicemail messages either.

Which meant they were either still searching, or . . .

Jonas's Suburban, identified by the Vortex.com logo, and the winery truck along with another Suburban, sat in the driveway. The lights in the house were off, the main room dark.

It *was* after 10:00 p.m., but . . .

She got out, then went around to retrieve her duffel bag. "I'll call you," she said to Nixon and Geena. "Get home and warn your family. And keep trying to get ahold of the local weather station."

Please have found Creed. The thought thrummed through her as she stepped up to the door, hesitated, debated knocking, then eased the door open.

Jonas looked up from where he sat in semi-darkness at the kitchen table, the only light radiating from the microwave oven over the stove.

Oh no.

The lines on his face, the chaos of his short brown hair, put a fist into her chest.

"Jonas," she said, her voice broken. "Did you . . . did you find them?"

He closed his eyes, shook his head.

Oh. She set her satchel on the table and came over to him, pressed her hand on his arm. His hand curled over hers, squeezed.

"I shouldn't have left."

"There was nothing you could have done."

She wanted to wince at the ragged emotion in his blue eyes.

"We spent all day searching the school. We finally got into the locker room, where Ty thought they were, but . . ."

Oh Ty. She didn't want to ask where he might be, not right now, but he'd put so much hope . . .

How she hated hope.

"There was a cave-in while Ty was in there."

Her entire body froze. *What?*

She must have gasped, or something close to it, because he quickly added, "He's fine. Hurt his knee, but otherwise . . . although nobody's fine." He looked away then, his jaw tight. "Creed's probably dead. The Red Cross is still searching, I guess, but nobody knows where they could be." He took in a breath. "Ned took off somewhere—I think Shae went with him. My mom is upstairs with my dad. And . . . well, your friends are leaving."

"Leaving?" Ty was leaving?

"Well, not all of them. Kacey took off, left her daughter here with her grandfather, but I heard them talking. Ian and Gage are planning on leaving as soon as Kacey gets back."

She couldn't help it. "What about Ty?"

"I haven't seen him since we got back to the house. He left a while ago to check on the chopper, I think."

She didn't want to tell him, not right now, but . . . "Listen, I know you probably haven't been watching, but there's a storm front headed this way, and it's a big one. Lots of clutter, the kind that could organize into a funnel, or more."

He frowned at her, then reached for his phone. "Sorry. I left it in my truck for most of the day. I didn't see the calls. Six? Wow."

"And I left a voicemail. It basically says, 'Hey, Jonas, there's a storm coming.'"

"You came all the way back here to tell me that?"

And now, with his question, it did feel like overkill. But she didn't want to explore the other impulses, so she offered a shrug. "We were worried it would hit at night and no one would be prepared. Not with all the communications down in the area."

He opened the weather app and set the phone on the table, and she saw his meteorologist brain kicking in. "Yeah, you're right. See these two commas? Those could be funnels forming." He used his pinky to show her the blob that only he could truly read.

"I'll trust you for it," she said.

"We need to call the local weather service, get them to issue a watch."

"Nixon is on it. But you need to get your family—and everyone else—to safety. Do you have a root cellar?"

"It's a farmhouse in Minnesota. You bet." He got up, glanced out the window. "If I read the radar right, it'll be in here in less than an hour."

"I'm going to find Ty. Can I take the Suburban?"

"Keys are in it." He stood up even as she headed toward the door. But he caught her arm, swinging her around.

And in a second, she found herself in his arms, tight against a chest that belied the geek inside him. Apparently, Jonas was a geek with muscles.

"It'll be okay, Jonas." She found herself saying the words, not sure where they'd come from. Probably Ty rubbing off on her.

Jonas's arms curled tight around her. "Thank you for coming back, Brette."

She looked up at him, drawing away. "Of course—"

But she couldn't finish her sentence, which would have been "that's what friends are for," because suddenly, just like that, Jonas kissed her.

Just leaned down and pressed his mouth to hers, a hint of urgency in his touch, even . . . long-held desire.

Huh.

And for a second, she couldn't move, her heart caught in her throat.

Oh, Jonas.

She well knew the danger of raw emotions, how they could spill out and make a person cling to someone—even if it wasn't the right one.

Yet, in that moment she knew.

She'd found the right one to cling to. Not Jonas, but the man who'd kissed her back when she'd pulled him into her arms a year and a half ago. The man who had practically *begged* to suffer with her. To be there, all the way to the end, whatever that was.

She pressed her hands to Jonas's chest, just enough for him to break the kiss.

"Oh," he said. "Sorry. Apparently, I can't read radar at all."

She touched his cheek. "I'm not sure I could read my own radar until this moment. I . . . I need to find Ty."

Hurt flashed in Jonas's eyes, but she couldn't ease it.

He gave her a slow nod. "I'll get my family to safety. The storm cellar is near the windmill in the front yard. Make it back, okay?"

She nodded, and he let her go.

The wind had started to churn the old windmill, and she made a mental note of the doors, set at an angle, practically hidden next to an oversized hydrangea bush.

Climbing into the Suburban, she spotted a light flicker on upstairs.

The wind had kicked up during the ten minutes she'd been inside, and by the time she hit the street heading into town, the wind threw twigs and other debris onto the road.

No rain yet, however.

Her map app put the baseball field in the village park at the end of town, and she took a right at a Lutheran church, noting the darkness in the stained-glass windows. She hoped, wildly, that someone in the congregation might be praying.

She'd seen the size of that red amoeba, and even to her uneducated eye, the storm looked miles wide.

Zipping past sleeping, naive neighborhoods, she finally found the park on the right side of the road. She turned into the lot by the pool and flashed her lights into the baseball field.

There, in the distance, under an outfield light, sat the PEAK chopper.

She got out of the truck, and a sudden gust nearly grabbed her up and threw her into the chain-link fence. "Ty!" The wind caught her voice and flung it away, so she sprinted out into the field.

Except, even as she got halfway there, she realized she hadn't seen the vineyard truck.

Still, she stopped at second base and yelled again.

The chopper listed slightly in the wind, but she noticed the blades had been capped with what looked like socks, a line running from two rotors down to the skids of the chopper, another line attached to the tail and rotor section. A giant hood lay over the glass cockpit as if the bird had been blindfolded. And the entire machine was hooked with a line to the back chain-link fence.

Not that secure in a tornado, but it should withstand a storm.

Hopefully.

"Ty!" she yelled again, just in case, but after a second she turned and ran back to the Suburban.

She hadn't passed anyone on the road to town . . . which meant Ty might still be in Chester.

Unless he'd run.

Something *she* would do—not Ty.

She got into her truck, turned around, and sat in the gravel drive, watching the approaching storm bully the trees.

She needed to get to safety.

She pulled out and headed toward Central Avenue. Maybe he'd gone to get a bite to eat—

Or . . . no.

"There are days when I don't think about taking a drink—and others when the urge to find the nearest bar and dive into something easy and quick is nearly more than I can bear."

When he'd told her that story, she couldn't even imagine *that* Ty. But after today . . .

She took a left onto Central and noticed that trash cans had tipped over, one rolling into the street.

The only light in town pushed out from a tavern, a place called One-Eyed Jack's, with a stone exterior and a 1970s mansard roof. Enough Harleys were parked in front to suggest it might still be occupied.

She pulled up next to a truck and got out. Ran inside.

She'd entered a time warp, or maybe just an unfamiliar culture, but music, maybe something from a ZZ Top album, pulsed through the room, entertaining the handful of guys at the bar, many wearing leather. With small square tables and orange chairs, the place seemed more like a greasy spoon than a biker bar.

"There's a tornado coming! Take cover!"

The barkeep looked at her and set down the glass he was drying.

"Didn't you hear me?"

She scanned the room for Ty and didn't know how she felt when she didn't spot him.

No, she knew *exactly* how she felt—relief. She needed Ty to be bigger, stronger, the kind of guy who didn't let his demons take him down.

She needed him to have all the things she longed for—starting with the faith her mother had tried to give to her.

In fact, maybe that was why she had let herself lean in to Ty. Because he leaned in to faith, just like her mother had, and wow, she wanted that.

"There's no siren," one of the patrons said.

"It's coming—just take cover!"

Her voice shook her back into the moment. Maybe Ty had gotten past her, on his way to the Marshalls'. Where she should be. She ran out into the street, and in the distance, a familiar roar raised gooseflesh.

She should turn around and tell those idiots—

An explosion just a block away shot sparks into the night, and for a split second, she saw it.

A giant wedge, this one so wide it didn't seem like a tornado but a wall of storm and cloud and—

Then the lights flickered off, and everything went black. The streetlights, the bar lights, even the blinking stoplights.

Oh no.

She got into the Suburban and backed out.

Get to the Marshalls'.

She gunned it down Central Avenue. Lightning burst a few yards in front of her and she screamed, slammed her brakes a second before a giant elm cracked. It crashed in front of the Suburban.

She caught herself on the steering wheel, breathing hard.

The roar shook the vehicle, and for a second, she couldn't move. Couldn't breathe.

She was going to die, right here. Probably impaled by a tree as the storm picked her up and slammed her down on some side street. Or maybe pancaked her into one of the buildings.

And she'd be alone, of course. Because she'd pushed everyone away.

Pushed Ty away.

The storm stripped the leaves from the fallen tree, cast them across the windshield.

Get out of the car. She knew she shouldn't stay inside, except she found herself on the floorboard of the passenger side, her hands over her head.

Shaking.

Please, God, I don't want to die! I'm sorry I despised hope, despised all the other ways you've probably saved me. I want to believe you can save me. Please!

The door opened behind her, and the rain whooshed in. "What the—Brette! What are you doing here?"

She whirled around into the hands of . . . "Ty?"

"C'mon!" He yanked her out of the truck, and she fell into his arms.

He righted her, took her hand. "We can't make it back to the bar. We gotta find—there!"

The rain drove down in torrents now, drenching her through, blinding her, and she hadn't a clue what he'd pointed to.

Until he dragged her off the street and up the cement steps of what looked like a courthouse.

He clutched her to himself with one arm as he slammed his

elbow into the glass of the door. It shattered, but the sound died in the fury of the storm, and in a second he'd reached inside and unlocked the door. Pushed them into the foyer.

A split entry, and he chose the basement.

"We need a wall without windows!" Ty pulled up his phone, turned on the app, and flashed his light around the room.

A library. And an old one by the looks of the shelving—solid oak, with books piled tight into rows and rows of ancient collections. His light flicked off a long library table in the middle of the room.

"Over here!" He had her by the hand and dragged her—only now did she notice his rather pronounced limp—toward an inner room. His light flicked around what looked like a conference room, with inner windows and stacks of horizontal shelves, as if for maps. A rectangular table took up the middle.

He led her to the far corner of the room. "Sit." Then he went over to the table, and despite its size and his injury, he heaved it up on end. Shoved it toward her.

Then he came around and sat next to her, moving the table at an angle to protect them.

"C'mere." He reached for her then, and she realized she was trembling.

"Shh. We're going to be okay."

He pulled her to himself, rearranging so he could wrap his legs around her, his arms around her shoulders. She turned in his embrace, curled up against him, and he tightened his hold.

He shivered, so she pressed her hand against his chest. His heartbeat knocked against it.

Outside the monster raged, the wind frenzied, and the rain bulleted the building.

"What are you doing here?" His voice held an edge she had never heard, and she drew in her breath. Oh. Right. Last conversation they'd had, she'd told him to get out.

Of her life.

"I . . . I knew there was a tornado coming, so—"

"No, here. On this street. Why aren't you—I don't know, in Iowa, or Nebraska, or even at the Marshalls'? What are you doing *here*?"

She didn't know what to do with the anger in his voice, and she tried to push away, but he didn't let her go.

And she didn't really want to leave. "I was worried about you. The storm came up so fast, and . . . well, I knew you wouldn't be paying attention and—"

"I saw you run out of the bar and I couldn't believe my eyes. The last thing I need is for you to get killed searching for me."

She did push away then. "Why? Because only you can do the searching? Only you can be a hero? I was worried, okay? I didn't want you to be out here alone!"

He just blinked at her, his chest rising and falling, so much emotion in his eyes that she couldn't move.

And then he kissed her. Just wrapped his hand around her neck and pulled her to himself so abruptly, almost violently, as if she'd unleashed something inside him that he couldn't douse.

As the storm furied outside, she kissed him back just the same. Needing, oh, needing Ty's arms to tighten around her, to feel the outpouring of his emotion, all of it stirring deep inside her, awakening her to life, to hope, to a tomorrow she longed for.

Oh, she loved this man. Loved his courage and the fact that even when he was down, he reached up. Loved the fact that no matter how many times she pushed him away, he wouldn't budge, just waited for her to return.

And rescued her when she couldn't rescue herself.

He tasted of the rain and the darkness and the deep well of his emotions, and he kissed her with a thoroughness that spoke of desperation, his own fears, the wounds that still pained him.

Only then did she realize what she'd said.

"I didn't want you to be out here alone."

Oh, Ty.

She slowed her kiss, turned it tender and sweet, and he broke away, touching his forehead to hers, breathing a little hard. "Sorry—I . . ."

"Ty," she whispered, "I came back because I love you."

Yes, she'd really said that. She swallowed but managed not to pull away, not run screaming from the room, but to stay right there, meeting his eyes.

Reaching for all the hope, all the faith she could muster.

Outside, the behemoth roared.

But he smiled. "It's about time. I was starting to give up hope."

+

Ty hadn't a clue how he'd gone from nearly breaking a two-year sobriety oath to having Brette, here, in his arms, telling him she loved him.

Talk about timing. He still couldn't believe she'd shown up at the bar. Sure, he'd gone for something to eat, a desperate escape from the mourning and his failure at the Marshall family house, feeling pretty sure he'd never be able to face them again. But he also knew he shouldn't be around easy access to whiskey on a day like this.

He'd gotten up, walked to the bathroom, stared at himself in the mirror, about to make a decision he couldn't live with when he'd heard her.

"There's a tornado coming! Take cover!"

By the time he scrambled out of the room, he caught only Brette's departing figure.

And in that moment, he realized that somehow, God had reached out of the heavens and saved him yet again.

"Find cover! Get in the bathroom!" he'd shouted and ran from the room. Well, what he wanted to call running but more resembled a Quasimodo high-speed stagger into the streets.

Only to see her taillights disappear into the storm. Almost.

Except for the tree.

The providential tree that *hadn't* hit her but just stopped her so that he could sweep her up and rescue both of them.

"I love you."

Her words still skipped around his brain. Brette Arnold *loved* him?

He thought . . . well, he'd nearly given up.

Outside, the heavens had unleashed the apocalypse. Lightning crackled, thunder bombarded the tiny town of Chester, and behind it all, the ever-present rage of the wind, alive in the howling. Glass had shattered in the upper floors of the library, but the ancient building made of cement and stone and bricks just might withstand the storm.

Even if it didn't, nothing would move him from his hold on Brette. Or, even, her hold on him.

"What do you mean, it's about time?"

Oh, that. Outside, the warning siren finally started to mourn. Right.

"It's just . . . the fact is, I've been in love with you since last year. And I know it was only a couple days together—but being with you feels like . . . like I've stepped inside something bigger than I am, and I'm helpless to fight it. My heart has been yours for so long now . . . but yeah, when you told me to get out of your life, I . . ."

He looked away, but she touched his cheek, moved his face back to hers.

"I was scared," she said.

"I know."

"I'm afraid I have cancer again." Her breath tremored out, and he touched her cheek.

"I know."

She just blinked at him. "And doesn't that freak you out?"

"Only because I don't want to lose you. But if you think I'm freaked out by the opportunity to love you through all this, um, *no*. I meant it when I said I'd suffer with you. Just like you raced a tornado into town to find me. That's what love does—it goes into the storm to rescue, or protect, or just to stick around and share in the suffering."

Her eyes widened. "My mom used to say that suffering, and grief, is the price we pay for love. That the depth of our suffering is measured by the depth of our love."

She angled away from him, her expression bright in the light of his phone. "Oh my gosh—she always said she wanted to share in Christ's sufferings. What if she meant she wanted to love with the depth of his love?"

He'd never thought of that before. "Maybe that's why the Bible lists all these things that can't separate us from the love of Christ—tribulation, or distress, or persecution, or famine, or nakedness, or danger—because if death was the measure of Christ's love for us, then the rest is just debris."

He leaned his head back against the wall, feeling the building tremble around him. "I suppose I should add to that list cancer, or tornadoes, or a busted knee or . . . or failure." He sighed. "I failed, Brette. My hunch turned out to be just what you said—wishful thinking. I nearly got myself and the other rescuers killed, and we didn't find the kids." His voice hitched at the end.

"I know, Ty." She was still shivering, so he drew her against him, unable to look at her anyway.

"I've spent the past two years trying to hang on to the truth that despite my failures, God loves me. That even when life seems . . . undone, God is still on my side, that he'll show up, but—"

"Please, Ty, don't." She pushed away from him. "I need you

to believe for both of us." She pressed a hand to his soggy shirt, right over his heart, warming his skin. "Since my dad died, and Mom not long after, I've operated under the idea that I'm in this alone." He put his hand over hers, held it there. "But I'm desperate to believe that God loves me. To have that kind of faith."

He stared at her, her words like a hand grasping for something inside him.

And his spirit seemed to reach back, the words rising, filling his entire body with heat and truth. "If God is for us, who can be against us? He who did not spare his own Son but gave him up for us all, how will he not also with him graciously give us all things?" He looked down at her. "It's what your mom said about suffering. God let his only Son die. Imagine the grief. And now think about the love that equals it—that's the depth of his love for us. Amazing grace, how sweet the sound, that saved a wretch like me. His grace—his love—is equal, no, *greater*, than anything we could do to push him away. Our sins. Our anger. Our despair."

"'Amazing Grace.' My mom sang that song," Brette said.

"Mine too. When she was dying. She knew, despite the storm, that what waited for her was joy and peace."

She was watching him, a smile playing on her face.

"What?"

"You have no idea how you look when you talk about God. He's in you or something, because when you say it, I believe it."

"Really?"

"Mmmhmm. And it's completely . . . I don't know. Sexy. Or charming, or maybe just . . . breathtaking. The way you want to love God makes *me* want to love God. And believe that he loves me back."

And despite the torrent outside, the shredding of trees and perhaps even their shelter, heat suffused Ty right to his cells.

"Are you okay? You're trembling."

"I'm okay." He touched her cheek, met her eyes. Because God had shown up in a moment that wasn't pure desperation. Shown up and let Brette see his love for her.

"I'm not sure how, but this is probably the first time I've ever felt like I'm right where I'm supposed to be, doing what I'm supposed to do." Her words, but she spoke his heart.

Thunder shook the library.

She fisted her hand into his shirt.

"We're going to be okay," he said. "This is a stable building. The old ones were built well."

"It was probably a storm shelter, actually." She pointed to a sign on the wall near the door, and he shined his light on it. A symbol—a circle with three inverted triangles.

"A fallout shelter. Of course."

As he dragged his light around the room, however, he realized that the walls featured framed blueprints of the city buildings—the local library, the bank, a Germanic community center.

"Is that a school?" Brette asked and pushed away, as if making to get up.

"Stay here, I'll get it."

But when he tried to stand, he couldn't yank back his groan.

"Listen, the storm's dying. I'll get it." Brette was on her feet before he could stop her, stepping over the table and scooting to the blueprint on the wall.

The storm did seem to be dying. An eerie silence filled the room.

Oh no . . . "Brette—hurry up!"

The funnel hit.

Every window imploded.

Brette screamed, and he launched to his feet, lunging for her.

She dove into his arms; he pulled her to the enclave just as debris flew into the room, toppling bookcases, splintering wood, the room a wind tunnel of destruction. Books scattered, slamming against the walls.

He pushed her down, his body curling over her just as the inner glass window exploded.

She screamed again, and he wanted to join her. But he clamped down and hunkered over her, praying that his barricade held.

Neither death nor life . . . nor powers, nor height nor depth, nor anything else in all creation, will be able to separate us . . .

Brette pressed her hands over her ears and started to hum.

"It'll be okay. We'll be okay," he kept saying softly into Brette's hair, as much for her as himself.

And then he was back in the car, his mom's head on his lap, listening to her sing.

The earth shall soon dissolve like snow, the sun forbear to shine; but God, who called me here below, will be forever mine.

+

Kacey didn't do rash decisions. Rash decisions got people killed, or at least raised the risk for disaster.

But it could hardly be called rash to save their future.

The dark road ribboned out before her headlights, the night above starry, calling her east, to Wisconsin.

Please let Ben be glad to see me.

She took a sip of her coffee, sludge she'd purchased at a convenience store just before she crossed the border. Her third cup, actually, and her entire body buzzed.

Or maybe it was simply the anticipation of the look on his face.

Please let it be joy. Yes, Ben became insanely focused when he hit the road, although he usually called her every night.

Including tonight. Three times, actually, although he didn't leave his usual voicemail.

Maybe she should text him. The thought pulsed inside her as Kacey turned north, onto the two-lane highway to Colvill. The clock read nearly midnight, and he might be sleeping.

More likely, he'd be out with his band. He usually came offstage buzzing with the music, needing to unwind, often with a late dinner, sometimes by listening to the wannabes, searching for the next big act he might sign to Mountain Song Records.

Although he'd been known to hit the gym at his hotel, go for a swim, or even just channel surf while eating a soggy pizza.

Life on the road—she knew he loved the audiences, loved singing, but she knew too well the challenges of living out of a duffel bag.

"From the day Ben met you, he's been trying to impress you. Make something of himself so he could provide for you."

Oh, Ben, I'm sorry.

She should have joined him on the road, even if he'd stopped asking.

She checked her GPS and saw that the motel was only a couple miles ahead. *Thank you, Goldie.* She had rousted his manager away from some fancy dinner in Nashville to get Ben's hotel information, although she'd left out her mission objective: to elope with Ben. To steal him away, take him off the grid, and finally, *finally*, become his wife.

The first—and only—dream she'd ever harbored. Yes, she loved to fly, and had turned to the army out of necessity to provide for Audrey. But she would have stayed grounded if Ben had stuck around Mercy Falls.

"He loved music, sure, but he would have chucked it all and worked at the local lumberyard if he'd thought you wanted him."

Yes, she wanted him. Oh, how she wanted him.

She spotted the motel ahead, its lights shining out from an arched carport across the paved lot. The Village Motor Inn.

She parked and glanced in the rearview mirror. She'd pulled her thick hair back into a ponytail but had discarded her usual cap and had even run some mascara over her eyelashes.

She wore a pair of yoga pants, a T-shirt, and flip-flops, not the most attractive of attire, and maybe she should have thought of that. But her mission ops were to seek, hand over her heart, and find a preacher.

Kacey blew out a breath, then got out of the car and headed inside the lobby.

A couple deer heads framed the front desk at the end of a long cranberry carpet. Green overstuffed furniture flanked the walls, and a gold chandelier from the eighties dripped from the ceiling. An elderly man rose from behind the desk.

"Good evening," she said. "I'm looking for—"

It occurred to her that Ben never used his real name when he booked reservations. Probably Goldie wouldn't have either. She searched for and produced his moniker. "Bill Hickok."

An eyebrow raised. "Oh." His mouth tightened into a line of disapproval. "Second floor, room 212. But I've already told them to pipe down once, so . . ."

She frowned but nodded, then headed out the door, across the darkened pool area to the outside stairs. She took the stairs to the second floor.

Lights illuminated the balcony, and she found room 212 situated in the middle of the complex. She hesitated a moment and lifted her hand to knock.

Laughter spilled out from under the door. High and sweet, young.

Kacey stilled.

Then, the low tones of a male voice . . . singing? She pressed her hand to the door, listened to the familiar, sweet melody.

You've got a wild side
Something like mine
But when we're alone
Gonna take my time . . .

One of Ben's earlier songs, but it stirred up memories of football games, necking under the starry nights in the back of his pickup, even her singing along around a bonfire as Ben tried out one of his tunes to his eager crowd.

The voice was lower, deeper, contained a huskiness to it, not the polished version he used for his audience. For a second she imagined him sitting on a sofa, a couple of coeds at his feet hanging on every word.

She pressed her hand to her stomach.

Her eyes burned, but no more than her pride.

And not a little disbelief that he'd discarded her so quickly.

"You are a master of charm, Ben King. That's why you have so many fans who love you."

Maybe that was why Ben had done an about-face, why he'd stayed away from her—she noticed how he'd chosen to get into the car with the guys when Ty displaced him yesterday.

He'd been planning to escape to Wisconsin even before Pete called off the rescue search.

No. She refused to believe that this might be his regular behavior on the road. That the reason he had backed away from marriage so many times was out of guilt or the fear of truly being tied down.

She turned away as more laughing escaped through the door. She grabbed the railing and stared down into the dark pool area. The pool glistened silver under the moonlight.

At the least, whatever was happening in that room wasn't something she wanted any part of.

She blew out a breath, digging deep, and refused to run as she walked away from room 212 and the future she'd raced across the country to redeem.

Hitting the deck, she kept her head down and headed for the exit. The old guy at the desk had mistaken her for a floozy fan girl.

She put her hand on the gate—

"Kacey?"

She stilled. Shoot, how had he seen her? She debated a moment before she whirled around, the fury in her chest a live ember, and looked up at the balcony.

But he wasn't standing there.

"Kace, is that you?"

The voice came from the darkness on the other side of the pool, near the deck loungers.

"Ben?"

He walked out into the moonlight, a sheet wrapped around his shoulders, his hair sticking up as if he'd been sleeping. He stared at her, an expression on his face that suggested he might still be dreaming.

"What are you doing down here?" She glanced back at his room. "Were you sleeping on a lounger?"

He was still walking toward her—she noticed now his bare feet and the fact that he hadn't shaved after his concert. "We're the only room with a suite, so Moose and the guys are having a party in our room and . . . well, I'm not interested."

He came closer now, the sheet draped over his shoulders like a caped hero. "What are you doing here?" he asked again.

"You're not interested?"

He frowned, glanced at the room. "No. Of course not. I . . ." He swallowed, looked away. "In my head, we're married, Kacey, even if we haven't made it official. And maybe you don't want that, but I can't just let go of hoping . . ." He winced. "Sorry. I know that's probably not what you want to hear, but . . ." He sighed, looked back at her, such earnestness in his gaze that it could undo her. "I'm sorry I left. I shouldn't have put the music ahead of you—and the team. I just . . . I feared everything unraveling and—"

"Ben. I'm here because I want to marry you."

He stared at her. "What?"

"For a country music singer, you have a hard time recognizing a grand romantic gesture. I love you, Ben King. Catch up."

And then he smiled, and it swept away any lingering hurt, the faintest fear that he wouldn't close the gap between them and take her in his arms.

He dropped the sheet, and in two steps he had caught her up, his hand behind her neck to pull her close. And then he was kissing her. Something hard and possessive and whole, kissing her like he sang.

No, he kissed her like she might be his only fan.

And he might have thousands, but no one loved him like Kacey did.

The scents of summer and freedom and the mystery of the night rose from the husk of his skin, and she clung to his lean, toned body. His arms wrapped around her tightly, as if he feared her running away.

Not a chance.

She surrendered easily, letting him take over, control every nuance of their kiss, the tempo. Tasting the night, the music of his heart in his touch.

Ben finally came back to himself, slowed his kiss, lingering sweetly. He loosed his grip and brushed his lips down her neck.

Then he rested his head on her shoulder.

"I love you so much, Kacey." He leaned back, his blue eyes holding hers. "I want to come home. And I don't care if all I do is play at the open mic on a Friday night—I can't spend another night away from you, for the rest of my life."

She slid her arms around his neck, played with the hair at his nape. "Let's just start with getting married. As soon as we can. Tomorrow, even."

"Really?"

"Really. I need you, Ben. I need your passion, your strength, and yes, your music. I know you might not have noticed, but I'm a rabid, crazy fan, and it's time I got a permanent backstage pass."

He laughed then. How could she ever, *ever* have confused Ben's delicious rumble with whatever was happening in room 212?

"Babe, you're the *only* one who gets a backstage pass." He winked and kissed her again, capturing her inside the melody of summer—the tang of chlorine drifting from the pool, the cicadas buzzing in the surrounding fields, and the faintest country music tune lifting from a nearby room. She felt in his touch so many memories, and the sweetness of their future.

Ben.

Yeah, she was a fan.

She met his eyes. "Okay, really, let's get our daughter, your dad, and find a preacher."

He picked her up, twirled her around. "Yes, ma'am!"

15

GOD HAD ANSWERED HIS PRAYERS without him even asking. The miracle of that stole Ben's breath as he awoke to a golden dawn sliding over the pool area of the Village Motor Inn. He'd never seen anything so breathtaking.

Kacey, her eyes closed in sweet slumber, her face relaxed, a few remnant childhood freckles on her nose. Ben propped himself up on his arm, two fingers twining Kacey's copper red hair as the sun caught the highlights, turning them to gold. She slept on her side, tucked into his chest, her hands clasped in front of her, as if praying.

God had certainly heard the moaning of his heart to bring Kacey back to him. Now Ben had to figure out the rest.

She stirred in his arms, probably cramped from sleeping on the lounger by the pool all night, but he hadn't known what else to do.

Bringing her back to his room wasn't an option. Not with the way she kissed him, the very real memories of the summer nights now rekindling the fire inside him.

They'd waited this long to make things right, and he needed to be able to face himself in the morning. To be a true and real husband to her, not just the counterfeit he'd been before.

And traveling in the middle of the night seemed foolish.

But today . . . *"Let's get our daughter, your dad, and find a preacher."* He could barely think past that sentence still shooting fireworks in his head.

However, between the explosions of joy there was . . . the band. His other life—the one that he'd sweated over. He could take the music with him to Mercy Falls, but his band depended on him.

Ben blew out a breath even as she made a noise deep inside her body, her hand finding his chest and palming it. He caught it and brought it to his lips. She relaxed against him, and he closed his eyes, relishing the luxury of this moment, the kiss of the sunrise, the smells of summer, the sparrows greeting the morning.

Every day, just like this, *please.*

He must have sunk back into slumber because the nudge at his feet roused him, and he blinked awake to find Moose standing over him.

His drummer had bloodshot eyes and was bare chested and wearing sweatpants, as if he'd just risen. "Boss, get up."

Kacey raised her head to the words, and perhaps the tone.

"What's going on?" Ben said as Kacey sat up, blinking, looking just a little self-conscious at the tangle of their legs under the sheet he'd stolen from the hotel room.

Moose had probably left his own tangle, although less innocent than the one Ben shared with his fiancée. Yeah, he'd been right to escape Moose's party last night.

"Hey, Kacey," Moose said, even as he glanced up toward his room.

The blonde from last night stood at the rail, wearing one of Moose's oversized shirts.

Yeah, if he'd given in to Moose's shenanigans last night, this morning would have looked much different.

"Um . . . is Audrey here too?"

A weird question coming from Moose, and it had Ben sitting up.

Kacey grabbed the sheet, cocooning it around her as she climbed off the lounger.

"The TV was on and I woke to the morning news." He blew out a breath, glanced at Kacey. "A tornado hit Minnesota last night."

Ben stood up. "Where?"

"It looks like it was near Chester—"

"What?" Kacey stared at him. "Were there casualities?"

Oh, God, please—

"I don't know. But I thought Ben should—well, I guess both of you—should know."

Kacey had shucked off the sheet and was now catching her hair back and winding it up behind her head. "Thanks, Moose."

Moose offered a small smile with an apology in it as Ben grabbed his phone.

He couldn't fault Moose for a life Ben might have just as easily fallen into, had not the memory of Kacey told him he could have more.

And with God's help, he'd found it, had held it right there in his grasp until he let the music—no, the fear of his own ghosts—pull him away.

"Voicemail," Ben said. "Either my dad's phone is off, or the towers are down."

"I can't get ahold of Audrey, either." Kacey held the phone to her ear.

"It doesn't mean they're hurt," Ben said. He pocketed his phone. "Let me get my stuff and we're gone."

Moose glanced at him, a flash of panic in his eyes. Moose had been his backbone, best friend, the guy who understood his music, his cues, who riffed off Ben's rhythm like they'd been born to play together.

"I'm sorry, Moose—I gotta go."

"Of course," Moose said and stepped back, a hand cupped

around the back of his neck as if he were trying to figure out what to do with himself.

Ben headed to his room, Kacey on his tail. He reached for her and she filled his grip with hers.

They hit the second floor, and the blonde from last night stepped away, worry in her eyes.

He gave her a quick, polite smile and entered the room.

Oh my. An empty bottle of Jack sat on the table, crushed beer cans littered the floor. His guitar case was open, and the Gibson was propped against the wall.

He'd heard Joey's low tones last night, crooning out one of Ben's covers. He stalked back to the bedroom, where the television played. Kacey stood, arms folded across her chest, watching the news as he grabbed his duffel, shoved in the sweaty, dirty clothes from last night and a few toiletries he'd left in the bathroom.

He stopped beside her when the newscaster came back on and gave a report of the storm. He couldn't tell if it had reached the Marshall family farm, but the funnel had hit the southern edge of Chester.

No casualties reported yet, but the morning had just dawned.

"Let's go," Ben said.

Kacey just stood there, and only then did he see her face. "Kace, are you having a panic attack?"

She shifted her gaze to him, almost unseeing. Okay, *yes*.

He'd seen it a few times over the past two years, the residue of an attack in Afghanistan that had earned her a medal but left her ragged and unable to sleep.

PTSD.

He took her by the shoulders, centered her in front of him, and met her beautiful green eyes. "Listen to me. Kacey, eyes on *me.*"

It worked. She stared at him, blinking, her eyes glazing with tears.

"We're not going to panic. We're not going to assume the worst. We're going to hang on to what we know—that God is good. And he loves Audrey as much as we do. And whatever is going on, he is with her. And will be until we find her."

She nodded.

"And no matter what happens, we'll handle it together. I'm not leaving you, ever again."

Ever again. In the resoluteness of his tone, peace swelled into the core of his body.

Yes. Because if God had brought them back together, he would also provide. Ben didn't have to be the one who figured it out . . . he just had to trust the God who knew the deepest cry of his heart and loved him. Loved *them.*

Ben pulled Kacey tight against him, held her trembling body, and let his warmth calm her. "It's going to be okay, babe."

She wrapped her arms around him, and her breaths evened out.

"That's right. Just hold on."

She finally leaned away, met his eyes, and because he needed it too, he kissed her, hard and sure, pouring out all the truth he knew.

They could face anything if they stayed together.

"Let's go."

He slung the duffel bag over his shoulder and walked into the front room to pack up his guitar.

Moose stood there, wearing a shirt, his hair tied back, looking fierce and unmoving in his path. Behind him, Joey was still scrubbing sleep out of his eyes, and Buckley came into the room with Duke.

"You're not leaving—"

"Hey—"

"Without us."

Oh.

"We're family too, Ben." Moose raised an eyebrow as if in challenge.

Yes, yes, they were. Besides, the guy stood two inches taller than Ben and had played a defensive position on his college football team.

"Thanks, Moose," Ben said, his throat thickening. "Let's get out of here."

"Brette, wake up."

She'd like to wake up like this every day of her life. Ty's arms around her, the feel of his whiskers against her cheek, his fingers entwined with hers.

"We're alive."

And that brought her back to the reality that they'd spent the night trapped in a library. Her clothing was still soggy on her aching body. But all the same, she felt warm. She lay on her side, her head in the crook of Ty's arm, her arms wrapped over his chest.

She'd clung to him and never felt so safe in the middle of destruction and chaos.

The chaos had finally passed over them, dying out until only the hum of the rain remained against the distant shudder of thunder.

Sometime in the middle of the night, Ty had flashed his light around the room to survey the debris. A giant tree had shoved through the window, as if trying to escape the storm, and branches and brick and glass littered the room. The fallen bookshelves blocked the entrance. "We might be here for a while," he'd said and cocooned her against him in the dark.

Now she reluctantly pushed herself away and sat up. Her hair was probably sticking up on end, and she made a face and tried to tame it.

"It's cute," he said.

"Hardly."

"Trust me."

She made a face again, wanting to believe him. And then, why not? Because he looked at her with such sweetness in his eyes.

Except . . .

"We need to get out of here and find those kids, but then . . . we need to talk, Ty."

"About?"

"We were both pretty freaked out last night and said some things and . . ." She looked away.

"Wait a second here. You're taking it back? You said you loved me. No retractions, Ace."

She wanted to smile, but . . . "I am in love with you, Ty. And I want . . ." Her face heated. "I love waking up with you. I could probably do that for the rest of my life—"

"If we're going to wake up together, I'd prefer some different circumstances," he said, his mouth tweaking up on one side.

"Right. And it's about that. Because if you're thinking . . . well, of sticking around and—"

"I'm going to marry you someday, Brette. When you're ready. So yeah, that's totally on my agenda here."

Oh. She blinked at him, but her throat tightened and she looked away again.

"Brette?"

"I had a lot of chemo and radiation, Ty. I'm not sure I can ever have kids."

He was silent for so long that she looked up at him. His stricken expression made her heart drop.

"Do you think that's even *remotely* important to me after all you've gone through? So, we'll adopt, or whatever. Brette, I love you, period. You are enough for me."

"Even without . . . I had a double mastectomy, Ty." There, the words were out, and she couldn't even look at him.

"And you think that matters . . . how?"

She looked up, and his expression seemed . . . angry?

"Wow. You must really think I'm a shallow guy to imagine that I'd . . . well, sure, I guess if I'm honest, I loved all the parts about you, but I'm certainly a fan of you being alive versus you having all your . . . extras."

He met her gaze, not looking away. "This is never an issue for me. Ever. Okay?"

She closed her mouth. Nodded.

He touched her cheek, ran his thumb down it. Leaned close and kissed her tenderly. Then he broke away. "Now, let's get out of here."

She nodded, her heart so big in her chest she could barely breathe. "Right. Except, I . . . I have a hunch."

He raised an eyebrow.

"Help me pick up this table."

He managed to climb to his feet and helped her right the table. She walked over to a blueprint, its frame now shattered, picked it up, and put it on the table.

"I was thinking about this last night. Obviously, the kids weren't in the locker room, like you said, but maybe they'd found an old fallout shelter. Didn't Lottie say that the building was generations old and that Hattie knew every phase of it? Wouldn't she know where the fallout shelter was?"

He was reading the prints. "It seems like the elementary and theater wing comprise the old school. The theater sits where the gymnasium used to be."

"It has a basement—see, here are the utilities and the coatroom and even the kitchen and lunchroom were downstairs. I'll bet they ate in the gym, set up tables."

"I don't see a fallout shelter," he said. "Remember, they used to hide under their desks?"

Oh, right.

"Shoot. It was a good idea, though," she said. "Maybe the old journalist still lives inside me."

"Oh, I know she does."

"You think so?"

"Seriously? Brette, you are brave and smart and beautiful and have only gotten more so since your . . . over the past year."

"Since I beat cancer the first time?" She couldn't believe she'd dared to say that, but . . . yeah. She had beaten it, so far.

"You're going to beat it again." He wound his fingers through hers. "Except you have no idea if the cancer even came back since you haven't called the doctor back."

Right. That.

"I knew it," he said. "Today. Together."

"Fine." But she smiled. "You're like a dog with a bone."

His expression stiffened. A dog. He leaned over the blueprint. "Remember when we were in Lottie's house—Lottie had basketball trophies and a picture of her and her sister on the bookcase."

"She did?"

"Yeah. Which means that maybe they played basketball in this very gym. Which means—"

"She did go to a locker room." Brette leaned over the blueprint. "Except not the one in the new school, but her old school."

"Do you see one on the map?"

Her heart fell. "No, just a coatroom."

A beat. "What if that was the storm shelter Lottie was referring to?" Ty said.

"What is it now?"

"Empty space under the elementary school." Ty pointed to the room.

"The kind of space that might survive the crumbling of a building," Brette said.

He leaned down and kissed her. A kiss of triumph that stirred all the hope that lay dormant right back to life. "You're brilliant, Ace." Then he made a face. "Except no one is going to believe me."

"Then we'll just have to make them. If anyone can tell a compelling, inspirational story, well . . . that used to be me."

"It still is."

Wow, she loved him. She took his hands, squeezed. "We'll find them. You just need to have a little faith."

"Right. Let's get out of here." He tried his phone. "Still no signal."

"The team must be worried out of their minds," Brette said.

He gave a harrumph and tucked the phone back into his pocket.

"What's that for—that sound?"

He turned the picture of the blueprint over, released the back fasteners, took off the backing, and retrieved the blueprint. "We'll need this." He folded it up and shoved it into his back pocket then headed toward the door, picking his way past the broken glass, surveying the bookcases that blocked their path. "We should be able to dig our way out."

"Ty?"

He glanced at her. "The team has more important things to do than look for me. Sorry."

She lifted an eyebrow. "Are you serious right now?"

"It's just . . . well, I let everyone down pretty badly yesterday."

"Stop it. You're the heart of the team. The guy who—"

"Follows his hunches into trouble."

"I'd pick you to rescue me every day of the week." She grabbed his arm to steady herself as she climbed over the pile of bookcases in the doorway. "Besides, you're not the only one who thinks this is more than a hunch." She stood in front of the tree, put her hand on the stripped trunk. "We can't stop looking."

He wrestled his way over the blockade with just a few grunts, then came up behind her.

She glanced at him. "Right?"

He smiled then. Nodded.

The tree lay jammed in the stairwell leading up to the doors, but it was nothing they couldn't climb over, carefully. Ty steadied her as she worked her way across the trunk. Through the shattered front door window, she got her first glimpse of the destruction outside.

Downed power lines, trees uprooted and cast across the street—and down the road, Jonas's Suburban lay upside down, crushed.

Grunting sounded behind her, and she turned to see Ty gritting his teeth, fighting for purchase as his bum knee refused to work.

She grabbed his arm, braced him as he wrestled himself free. He was sweating a little, despite the chill in the soggy morning air.

"It's bad, isn't it?"

"It's fine. Let's get out of here."

He wrenched the door more open, and she wedged herself through, then pushed on it as Ty followed.

They stood on the front steps of the library, and slowly Ty reached out and took her hand.

Maybe to hold her up because the devastation could knock her flat.

Although, even as she surveyed it, she knew it could be worse. In fact, as she took in the downed lines, the trees, the shattered window fronts along Central Ave, the ripped awnings, and general debris that littered the road, she knew it could be much, *much* worse.

Oddly, the birds were singing, their songs light and clear. To the far horizon, past the upheaval, the dawn pressed back the darkness in breathtaking striations of periwinkle and gold.

"Maybe I only thought I saw a funnel," she said. "We'd see a clear debris path—"

"Brette!"

She spied Jonas climbing over a downed elm, moving like a man on fire.

He took off in a sprint toward them, and for a moment, the memory of being in his arms rushed through her.

She tightened her hold on Ty's hand even as Jonas ran up, his eyes wide and bloodshot.

"You scared us to death—where have you been?" Jonas didn't spare a glance at her handhold with Ty and pulled her into his arms.

Ty let her go, and she hugged Jonas back.

"I thought . . ." He blew out a breath as he released her. "Okay, I admit I thought you might be doing something stupid, like taking pictures."

Oh. "I left my camera at the house! I didn't get *anything*. Not one single shot."

"Are you kidding me?" Ty said. "We nearly died, Brette."

"Really? What happened?" Jonas said, and Brette made a face, pointed at his Suburban.

"Sorry. I kind of, well, got caught in the storm."

"She came looking for me and nearly got flattened by a tree," Ty said. "Although she probably saved my life. The sirens didn't come on until the tornado was nearly on us."

"Are you okay?" Jonas said, clamping his hand on Ty's shoulder. "Your team is nearly frantic looking for you too."

Ty's brow creased, but he nodded.

And then, as if to back up Jonas's words, Gage appeared, running down the street from the opposite direction. Jonas waved to him, and Gage stopped, bent over, and grabbed his knees, as if breathing hard.

"Did it hit the farm?" Brette said, watching as Gage turned and shouted behind him, maybe to the rest of the team.

"We're okay. We have some wind damage to the vines, one of our trees came down, and most of the apple orchard is stripped, but the house is unscathed."

"Ty!"

Pete's voice, and he came running down the street, almost full tilt.

"See," she said quietly. "Of course they'd look for you."

Ty gave her a half-grin, then limped over to them, and she watched as Gage pulled him into an embrace. Pete too, although he added a handshake between them.

"How many are hurt?" Brette asked.

"We don't know. The funnel actually hit on the outskirts of town, out of any residential areas, so . . ."

"It's not as bad as Duck Lake, then."

Jonas's countenance fell, and he shook his head.

The hunch just burned to life inside her. She couldn't help it—she grabbed Jonas's hands. "Listen, while we were in the library, we found the old blueprint plans to the school. The original plans, and we . . . we have a theory. I know it's a long shot, but—"

"Please," Jonas said, and for a second she thought he might stop her. No more hope.

Instead, his gaze latched on to her with desperation. No wonder the world needed people of faith to stand strong—they were looking to them for the smallest inkling of hope.

Amazingly, right now, she had it in spades.

Pete and Gage came over.

"You okay, Brette?" Gage said.

"Yeah and . . . I think we know where the missing kids might be."

Pete's mouth tightened in a grim line. "I don't think we can handle any more wild hunches."

"Actually, this is more than a hunch. It's . . . faith. And it's based on some pretty good information. And why not believe? It's all we have to go on. It's that or we let grief and despair take over. So either get on board with us or walk away, Pete. Because we are *never* giving up!" She looked at Ty and reached out for his hand.

He was staring at her as if he didn't recognize her.

But she recognized herself. The girl she'd been *before* the tragedies.

She would write again—but not about storms, not about the destruction, but about the heroes who faced the storms with faith and lived through them, not knowing what they'd see on the other side but holding on anyway.

Knowing that either way, beyond the veil, lay peace. Joy.

"Okay, so where are they?" Pete said as he looked at Ty.

"The kids are still in the school. But they're in a storage area in the old elementary building—the area that used to be the old coatroom, next to the gym where Hattie Foreman played basketball."

Pete looked at him, then at Brette. "Okay. Let's get going."

16

EVEN TY, THE CHIEF PROPONENT of long shots, could recognize the folly of believing his hunch—no, *their* hunch. The Marshalls had grabbed on to Brette's words with a contagious fervor.

But maybe he should have kept his mouth shut, because no amount of hope could clear the tons of remaining rubble from the demolished elementary and theater wing of the school. Ian's construction crew had cleared the cars, the twisted trusses, and some of the cement and brick debris that surrounded the building. Unfortunately, he'd sent the machinery back to Minneapolis last night. Whatever remained would take a small army weeks to dig away.

They didn't have that kind of time.

In truth, they were probably too late.

Recovery, not rescue. But Ty didn't know how to say that to the Marshall family. Or to Brette, who looked at him with a sort of triumph that he knew came hard-won.

Please, God, give us all a happy ending here. He let the prayer slip out as he got out of an unscathed winery truck. And with the prayer, he allowed the faintest rise of hope, because "why not?" as Brette had said.

Why not have faith in a God who could give them miracles?

And today, with the blue sky arching overhead, cloudless and bright, today was a day for miracles.

We can't give up now.

But he didn't say that. Because it sounded hollow. He needed to give them something more . . .

No, they needed more than him.

He drew in a breath, glanced at Brette, then Chet, and finally to Garrett. "A wise man once told me that we enter into salvation through the door of destitution. We can't get any more destitute than right now. But we can either give in to dread or we can trust in God's love for us. We don't know what we're going to find, or if we are even going to find them, if this is a wild-goose chase or divine inspiration. But it doesn't matter, because God is for us. He loves us, and nothing can separate us from that love. And that isn't just hope—it's truth." He looked upward, into the pale, storm-swept blue.

"We know the earth shall soon dissolve like snow, the sun forbear to shine, but you, God, who called us here, will be forever ours, no matter the outcome. Give us all of you today, Lord."

He let out a long breath, and his gaze landed on Chet, who nodded.

Brette took his hand and squeezed hard as the group grabbed gloves, shovels, and Garrett his chainsaw. Then she headed toward the pile of rubble.

His knee burned like the fires of Mordor, but he refused to give it quarter and grabbed the blueprint from his pocket.

"Where do we start?" Garrett said.

He was unfolding the blueprint when he heard gravel crunching behind him.

"Oh my—Ty, look!"

Brette's voice turned him around, and he stood wordless as Pete's Red Cross Hummer pulled up the drive of the school. Behind it drove the bus of volunteers, the Duck Lake fire department, and a line of cars.

A long line.

They filed in behind the Hummer, parking anywhere and everywhere as Pete got out. He strode over to Ty.

"What's going on?" Ty said.

"We're digging today," Pete said. "Where do we start?"

Ty unfolded the blueprint. "The coatroom and kitchen were against this far wall, so I'm thinking, along the edge?" He pointed to the wall of rubble, nearly a story high.

Pete turned to his assistant, Kate. "Let's make a bucket line."

So many volunteers. Forty, maybe more, got off the bus, and cars continued to pull up, emptying out crews of three, four, five. Half the town of Duck Lake, perhaps, and they moved like worker ants to the rubble.

A day for miracles.

Ty spotted a car passing the lineup of vehicles to park right beside the Marshalls' Suburban.

Kacey got out of the passenger door, searching the crowd. Poor Kacey—and apparently Ben, who had joined her. Ty could only imagine the news they'd heard.

They spotted Audrey hauling a bucket from the rubble, and yes, this day had at least one happy ending.

Just as Ty turned to watch the rescue activity, he spotted a news van pulling in behind a truck with a crew of workers in the back.

Oh, just super. Now the whole world got to watch.

Pete seemed mindless to it, barking orders even as he picked up bricks and dumped them into a bucket.

Ben came over to Ty, his bandmates behind him. Moose and Buckley, Joey and Duke—they'd all come off the road to help?

"What can we do?" Ben asked.

"I thought you were supposed to be on tour."

"The tour can wait. I'm still a part of this team."

"How did you find us?"

"We stopped by the Marshalls', and when there was no one there, we took a guess."

Ty frowned, but Ben's hand came down on his shoulder, squeezing. "We know you, pal. Since when have you ever let Pete stand in your way?"

He knew Ben was referring to Jess and their so-called dating relationship, but . . . oh well. He just offered a weak smile. "We think they're trapped in the old part of the elementary school. That's where we're digging."

"Okay, boys, let's do this," Ben said, as if he might be leading them on stage.

Ty followed them to the site, limping, just trying to stay out of the way of the activity. What looked like players from the football team worked together to lift a remnant beam. A group of women, Jenny included, piled bricks into buckets; others—Jonas, Ned, and a cluster of men—carried mangled desks, theater chairs, and twisted lighting to a nearby pile.

Others moved splintered plaster walls and joists, broken foam insulation, pieces of blackboard.

Ty found a rubber playground ball and kicked it away before realizing his folly. He nearly went down and hoped no one noticed.

He limped over and spotted the walls of the ancient basement. "Pete, over here!"

Pete scrambled over the mess. "'Sup?"

"I think we're over the storage room. These are the floor joists."

"Kate! I need a chainsaw!" Pete's voice lifted over the hum of work.

But Garrett appeared and without a word ripped the cord and started into the ancient wooden floor.

It parted under the teeth of the saw, and in a moment, he'd ripped open a gap big enough for a man to slide through.

Pete glanced at Ty, then his knee, a question on his face.

"You go," Ty said.

Pete didn't wait. He lowered himself into the hole, dangling for a moment before dropping inside.

Ty leaned over, staring into the darkness. Brette had come over to join him. Garrett crouched over the hole, Jonas and Ned behind him.

No one breathed.

God, please.

"They're not here."

Ty closed his eyes.

Barking. He heard it again, this time clearer, although it sounded as if it issued from the catacombs of the building.

He looked at Brette. "You hear that?"

She nodded.

"Pete, keep looking!"

From the darkness of the room, Pete said, "There's no . . . wait. There's an old door here, but the lock is jammed." Pete appeared below the hole. "Garrett, hand me that saw."

Garrett handed it down, then did exactly what Ty would have—lowered himself into the pit.

Ty was tired of his injury dictating his life. He got up, shoved the blueprint into Brette's hands, then climbed into the hole.

Brette said nothing, but her mouth tightened.

Pete had fired up the saw, was chewing through an ancient wooden door, his head lamp spotlighting the dust as it churned off the teeth. Chips of lead paint splintered off, landing on the damp cement floor. A few rusty desks, a row of wooden theater chairs, and a bank of wooden cubbies for shoes, perhaps, ran against the wall.

The former coatroom. They'd hit it dead-on.

The room reeked of old cement, rust, and mildew. Thick piping ran along the ceiling and dripped moisture.

Pete finished his cut, started another, and in a moment had drawn a rectangle through the door. He stepped back.

The barking turned raucous and echoed through the chamber.

"Stand back!" Pete shouted, his words directed at anyone behind the door, and Ty braced himself.

Please.

Pete's foot landed dead center, slammed through the cut, and exploded the panel inside.

For a long, desperate moment, no one moved. Then Pete dropped to his knees and flashed his head lamp into the space.

"Ty!"

Ty moved to the opening and looked inside.

Bodies, huddled together, arms and legs and . . .

A young man lifted his head and stared right into the light, his arms wrapped around a grimy, gray, curly-haired dog.

The boy released the animal, and the dog barreled for the opening. Pete shoved himself through and caught the animal, easing it down into his arms. "Hey, buddy, good job."

The young man sat next to a blonde girl. He started to rise, pulling her to her feet.

"Creed!" Garrett's voice boomed through the chamber.

They were all *alive*. Pete's light skimmed over the girl and Creed, who was now being crushed inside Garrett's desperate embrace. The other three students emerged from the shadows around the room. They looked grimy and tired, but in otherwise miraculous health.

"Are they alive?"

Gage, who'd followed them in, now stood at the opening.

"Yeah," Pete said. His light fell on a petite young woman, and Ty immediately thought of Spenser. He'd left their search group after yesterday's failure.

"April Maguire?"

Her eyes widened. "Yes. Have you seen my husband?"

"Yes. He's been looking for you." Probably still was.

Pete released the dog. It ran over to an elderly woman who was still seated on the floor. She hadn't moved, just leaned her head against the wall.

"Gage, we may need you over here," Ty said as he stood in front of her. "Hattie Foreman?"

She nodded, tears falling into the deep grooves on her face. "My sister, Lottie—do you know anything about her?"

"She's fine. She took a fall, but we found her. She's at the hospital in Waconia."

Her shoulders began to shake, and she pressed her hand to her mouth.

Gage came over and crouched before her. "You're going to be okay." Her breath shuddered in, back out.

Ty closed his eyes, fighting the swell of relief.

More voices. Jonas came into the room and wrapped Creed in a hug that looked like it could break bones. But Creed seemed sturdy enough. Ned came in next and grabbed Creed up. Ty turned back to Hattie and Gage, who was now taking her pulse.

"How do you feel?"

"I have to go to the bathroom," Hattie said. "And I'm very, very hungry."

"What happened?" said Pete. "How on earth did you end up here?"

Creed stepped back from Ned. "We were cooling off after our workout at the park—I'd just texted my mom, and then Hattie showed up with Walter. She was worried about the storm and said we needed to get to shelter. But Addie's junker—"

"It's not a junker—"

"It *is* a junker. And it had a flat so Hattie told us to get into her Jeep. I followed her in my Subaru. The sirens were going off, and by the time we got here, the wind was crazy, and we couldn't get to the front doors. Hattie knew about this cellar entrance to the old kitchen, so we ran around the building and somehow she got it open."

"We used to use this entrance when we wanted to sneak into the school to play in the gym," Hattie said. "It's the old kitchen area. It's right next to our old coatroom, where we'd go for storms, so I thought it would be safe." She pointed to the cellar door, undoubtedly blocked by the debris outside. "Thankfully, it still has a water pipe."

"We hunkered down in here," Creed continued. "And by the sound of it, we figured the school was hit pretty badly. My idea was to hide in the locker room, but we would have probably been killed."

No one commented.

"We heard machinery yesterday and tried to shout. What took you guys so long?"

Ty had nothing for that.

A local fireman came down on a ladder they had fitted through the hole in the floor, and with him came a bearded, dark-haired man who dove through the hole, then grabbed up Addie, weeping.

"Let's get these kids out of here," Pete said.

Gage and Pete took Hattie up first, then April, then the rest of the team.

Ty followed them up last. He stumbled away from the rubble to the mud of the lot and watched as parents found their children. Jenny wept with her arms around Creed's shoulders.

From the far side of the lot, he heard the voice. "April!"

Spenser sprinted around cars, across the muddy lot, through the crowd, and in a moment that should have been photographed, he caught up April, burying his face in her neck, weeping.

Really, this *should* be photographed. He spied Brette standing off to the side, just watching, a strange smile on her face.

He limped over to the winery Suburban then, and found her satchel with her camera on the floor from where she'd retrieved it from the house. He limped back to her.

She stared up at him, a frown on her face.

"This, you need to capture. The world needs to see miracles."

She took the camera. Smiled at him. "Ty to the rescue."

He managed a grin, then took a breath and hobbled away from the crowd, out into the field where the football players had dragged the girder. The sun had cleared the trees and was arcing toward the apex of the day, bright, unhindered, hot on his skin as he raised his face to the sky.

Then Ty let his knees buckle, let himself fall into the soft earth. He cupped his hand over his eyes, and in the joyous sunlight, he wept.

+

Brette sat outside under the pergola of the Marshall family home in an Adirondack chair, staring at the fire. It flickered in the pit, biting back the finest hint of chill in the air as the twilight descended. She pulled her legs up and wrapped her arms around her knees as she replayed in her mind the conversation with Ella on the phone earlier.

"Your storm season is over. Come back to Mercy Falls. Room with me. Let yourself breathe again, fall in love with Ty. Build a new life."

Probably she shouldn't have called Ella so soon after today's events.

Not with every part of her longing for the world Ella suggested.

Hope did that too—only seeded more hope. What was it her mother said—a longing fulfilled is a tree of life?

And her tree seemed to be leafing out, setting down roots.

Because Ella's words just might be true. *"Your storm season is over."*

What if?

The wind stirred the flames and they flickered; the scent of the smoke seasoned the night air. The celebration in the house spilled out in laughter.

"Let yourself breathe again, fall in love with Ty."

"Brette, you okay?"

And there he was, the man she couldn't escape.

Didn't want to escape.

Even if she tried, she knew he'd follow her, or at least stand in her shadow, waiting for her to turn around.

Ty had showered, and his hair was dark and shiny under the rising moonlight. He wore jeans, a black T-shirt with the PEAK logo on his chest, and bare feet. Between the nuance of fresh soap, the clean air, and his smile, she lost every thought but one.

She could love this man more every day.

Oh boy.

He didn't deserve what loving her might mean. But oh, she wanted to take him at his word. Needed him to carry her, give her a hand to hold on to.

Because he emanated the kind of hope she thirsted for.

And she wasn't a fool who didn't know the source of it, either. Because Ty reminded her so much of her mother, the way he radiated grace. The very essence of God's love.

No, she didn't deserve him. But maybe that was some kind of crazy point God was trying to make too. That he'd given her Ty eighteen months ago, and if she'd had just a smidgen of faith, of courage, she wouldn't have had to go through any of it alone.

God's grace had given her a second chance.

Ty came over, but instead of sitting down in the empty chair next to her, he stood in front of her and held out his hands.

She frowned but took them, and he tugged her out of her seat.

Then he moved into her space, sat down, and pulled her down onto his lap.

Oh. Well.

"You just looked a little undone."

Undone was one word. She curled against him.

"You okay?" His face was close, and she met his eyes, got lost in them for a long moment.

"I think so." No, she *knew* so. Her hand found its way to his chest, the heartbeat there. Strong, steady.

He wrapped his arms around her and pulled her close. And just like that, she was safe. Finally safe.

"Kind of an amazing day," he said.

"Kind of an amazing week."

"Thanks for . . . for pleading my case with Pete."

"I still can't believe we found them." She drew in a breath. "Wow."

"You got some great shots today, right?"

"Yeah. I totally forgot about taking pictures. I would have missed it if it weren't for you."

"Did you send them off to *Nat Geo*?"

"They loved them. And I accidentally sent them this amazing picture of a tornado with a rainbow—sort of a mistaken picture, but . . . they might use it for the cover."

"Brette—that's great!"

She leaned away to see his smile.

"Sort of like God saying he's there, in the middle of the storm." His fingers whispered across her cheek, a gleam in his eyes. "You're an amazing photographer. But I was talking to Jonas and your friends Geena and Nixon, and they mentioned that the storm season is probably over."

"It usually dies the last part of July, apparently. So . . ." She'd seen Geena and Nixon at the school. Nixon had finally gotten through to the weather station, as well as gotten home in time to warn his family. The warning siren probably accounted for the lack of casualities in Chester. Not one.

"So, how about coming home to Mercy Falls with me."

She examined his face for any hint that he'd had a conversation with Gage, and saw nothing but innocence. "Really?"

"I'm really not trying to take over your life, but I was talking with Chet about your blog, and I think you should brace yourself for a possible job offer from PEAK to run our blog and our social media, and who knows, maybe you'll end up on a rescue."

She didn't move.

His smile fell. "Did I interfere too much?"

Oh Ty. "No. It's very sweet. I mean . . . you just can't help it, can you?"

"What—wanting to spend every minute of every day with you, because I'm crazy about your smile? Uh, no."

She was so past undone, right into a sappy, soggy mess.

"Besides, I was thinking that maybe we need longer than a few days together before I can propose."

Her eyes widened.

"See? You're not ready yet."

She wouldn't exactly say that, but . . . "Are you sure you want to . . . I know I keep mentioning this, but . . ."

He touched her face. "Okay, let's get this over with. We're calling your doctor. You can't live like this—not knowing."

She closed her eyes. "What if—"

"No. Not what if. There's no what if. There's only when. When you find out, then we deal with whatever it is." His thumb caressed her cheek.

"Yes. Okay." She'd left her phone on the ground next to the chair and now scooped it up and pulled up the voicemail message. Not bothering to listen, she clicked on the phone icon and let it dial.

Put it on speaker.

She expected his service, so when Dr. Daniels answered, she paused. "Hello. It's Brette Arnold. You left a message a couple days ago, and . . . so, just give it to me straight, Doc. How bad is it?"

She met Ty's eyes, and he didn't even blink.

A pause, and in it her heart stopped beating.

"You're still in full remission, Brette. No signs of cancer."

A slow smile slid up Ty's face.

"I want to talk to you about reconstructive surgery. It's time to think about—"

She took him off speaker and pressed the phone to her ear, her face on fire.

"Your body has healed, and it's time to move forward. I can put you in touch with one of our best plastic surgeons—"

"You know I don't have"—and she cut her voice low on the slim chance that Ty couldn't hear her—"insurance for that."

"We have grants and . . . we'll figure it out, Brette. Just come in for a consultation, okay?"

"I'll think about it. Thanks, Doc."

She hung up. Looked away from Ty.

"You should think about it."

So much for him not hearing. "I . . . I can't afford it. And you can't pay for it. It's not happening."

"Whoa—take a breath. I know how you feel about me paying for things. Believe me, I'm not going to make that mistake again." But he winked, and it softened his words. "I just need to know—is that all that's holding you back?"

She made a face.

"It better not be me, because we talked about this. It's not an issue. Is there another reason you don't want to have the surgery?"

She drew in a breath, stared out at the darkening sky. The stars winked at her, as if daring her to reach for the truth.

"Reconstructive surgery feels too much like I might be . . . I might start believing I would be okay, and then if I wasn't . . ." Her eyes burned.

Ty's thumb caught a tear that streaked down her cheek. "Start believing."

She drew in a breath. "What do you think?"

His brow raised. "You want my opinion?"

"If I'm going to be your . . . well, someday, if you plan on making this . . . thing . . . between us permanent, then you might . . . sorta care."

"This *thing*?"

She lifted a shoulder.

"This accidental meeting we keep having?"

She nodded.

His face turned solemn. "I love you, Brette. And it's completely up to you. But if it's something you'd like to consider, I do have someone you could talk to."

"Oh, great, you know some bigwig doctor in New York."

He laughed. "No. But would you allow me to interfere just a little?"

"You can't stop yourself, so why would I even try?"

He leaned forward then, his lips nearly brushing hers, stopping just short, his breath sweet against her skin. "I'd like to interfere a little bit right now, if I could."

She closed the gap between them. He kissed her with tenderness, a sweet, slightly unbridled hunger that suggested he'd be interfering quite a lot in her life. She let herself sink into his arms, let the grace of his touch glue her tired, broken pieces back together.

He finally lifted his head. "Please tell me that's a yes to Mercy Falls."

"I'll need a ride."

"I'll ask Kacey if she can give you a lift."

"And the answer would be no."

Ty stiffened at the voice, and Brette looked up to see Kacey walking toward them. But she wore a smile.

Huh?

She sat on the chair next to them. "I guess it must be chilly out here. Huddling together for warmth?"

"We might need blankets," Ty said. "Throw another log on the fire, will ya?"

"Right," Kacey said. "So, here's the deal. I've got a little fire of my own to tend to." She rolled her eyes at her own words. "Ben and I are eloping."

"What?" Ty said. "Seriously?"

"It's a long story, but we're taking Chet and Audrey with us to Minneapolis, and then we're leaving for our honeymoon. Which means, Copilot, I need you to fly the team home."

Good thing Brette had her hand pressed to Ty's chest, because by his stillness, his catch of breath, she might have guessed that his heart had stopped beating.

"Me?"

"No, *Pete.* Yes, you. You're ready, Ty. Have been for some time. I happen to know you passed your biennial flight review with Chet. So I trust you to bring them all home safely. You just have to trust yourself."

"Of course he will," Brette said.

"Brette—"

"To quote someone I know . . . It's about time."

He gave her a look.

And the old Brette—no, a better, stronger, grace-filled Brette—said, "Don't be a pansy. It's time for us to go home, Ty."

"Now who's interfering?" Ty said quietly, but he smiled and nodded, so much delight in his eyes she couldn't help but grin back.

"Oh, for Pete's sake," Kacey said. But she dropped a log on the fire as she walked away.

Which, of course, was completely unnecessary to keep Brette warm.

17

"READY?" CHET WHISPERED the question in her ear as Kacey stood at the apex of the stairs leading down to the lookout over Minnehaha Falls, a park in the middle of Minneapolis.

A cheap and easy, impromptu venue that God had reserved for only them.

The sky arched blue and nearly cloudless above, and the scent of the linden and elm trees that shadowed the park conspired to create a breathtaking chapel.

Especially with her groom standing at the overlook railing, the mist of the falls rising behind him, the water quiet applause as it fell into the pool below. Ben was decked out in a freshly purchased black, tuxedo-edged suit and appeared as if he might be holding his heart in his hands, so much love in his eyes she nearly lost her words.

So, to Chet's question, Kacey just nodded.

In fact, it was all she could do not to sprint all the way into Ben's arms.

Except for Chet, his hand on hers, slowing her down to a reasonable walk. Her heart pinched, just a little, that she hadn't invited her own parents to this event.

But they barely tolerated Ben, even now. Besides, she'd called and promised a reception in the future, something her mother could plan and invite half the state of Montana to. Judge Fairing's daughter, finally hitched to her superstar fiancé.

It did feel awkward to have Moose stand up as her "maid of honor," even though he stood on Ben's side. But they needed a second adult witness.

And apparently, Ben's band meant it when they said they were family, because Buckley had pulled together the private dinner waiting for them after the ceremony, and Duke had tracked down a B & B in Chanhassen that had an available room.

Now, Joey played Ben's Gibson, his blue eyes twinkling as he sang the song Ben had penned for her so many years ago.

Hey there, pretty girl, let me sing you a song
In this mountain boy's arms is where you belong

"Let's do this," Kacey said and glanced at Audrey.

Her daughter wore a blue dress off the rack from some bridal shop—the same place Kacey had picked up her gown, a simple V-neck overlaid with lace. No train, but it hugged her curves, and frankly she had barely recognized herself after she walked out of the hair salon.

Moose had set that up. She didn't want to know how. But now she wore tiny flower buds in her hair, which was twisted up and curled in ways that could convince her she might be royalty.

Okay, so she *was* sort of marrying the King of country music, and that thought tipped her lips up as Chet urged her forward.

Chet had found a minister while she and Ben procured their marriage license, and by the looks of it, he'd done a decent job with a tall, nicely groomed man in his midfifties. Paul something.

"You look very pretty," Chet said.

She cupped her hand over his. "I guess I have you to blame for this. If I'd known you were conspiring to get Ben and me back together when you hired me to fly for PEAK . . ."

"Yes?"

"I would have come running. Or at least I would have wanted to."

"Ben said the same thing."

He did? When she caught Chet's eye, he winked.

Maybe it was true, because as she neared him, Ben reached up and wiped a hand across his cheek, as if he might be crying.

Joey, just behind them, kept singing.

Never forget our first kiss . . . we're gonna have more
Because you're the Montana girl I do adore

She stepped up to Ben and took his hand.

On the other side of her, Audrey beamed as she held a spray of wrapped white roses.

"Are you sure you're okay with—" Ben started.

"Shh. It's perfect. Let me marry you already."

He grinned then and nodded to the minister.

Around her, the sparrows sang, the water misted, arching a rainbow of tears into the sky, and somewhere in there, Kacey pledged her life to Ben King.

And his, to her.

He wove his fingers through hers, holding tight as if he might never let her go.

"You may kiss your bride."

Ben turned to her, so much desire in his gaze she almost reminded him that their daughter was standing there. But he kept it chaste.

In fact, he barely kissed her all night, as they celebrated at a local restaurant, a private dinner for just her, Audrey, and Ben.

Then, they dropped Audrey off at the hotel with Chet.

Kacey climbed back into the rental convertible Mustang, still dressed in her wedding attire. "To the B & B?"

"Not quite yet, darlin'," Ben said. He pushed the top-down button and the sky opened. Overhead, the stars scattered like diamonds, and Kacey leaned her head back, loosening her hair.

She worked it free, and Ben reached over, ran his fingers through it, helping her. "I love your hair," he said, a little rumble to his voice.

He drove them along the lakes of Minneapolis, then surprisingly, pulled up near a beach.

"What are we doing?"

"Joey didn't quite finish the song." He parked, got out, reached into the backseat, and pulled out his guitar.

Then he took her hand and walked her down the path, toward the creamy sand that had turned to silver in the moonlight. She stopped and slipped off her sandals, letting the sand squish between her toes. Ben picked a spot and sat, pulling her down beside him.

The skyline of the city arched high, sparkling, and a breeze rippled over the dark water.

She leaned against him. "Reminds me of old, sweet times."

"Times I've never forgotten, Kace. And times we never have to wait for again."

Then he reached out, cupped her face, and kissed her. It was the kiss he'd reserved for her, away from the crowds, their daughter, his band.

The kind of kiss that told her exactly where she belonged.

She finally pressed her hand to his chest, pushing away. "Ben . . ."

"Mmmhmm."

"Hurry up and sing me that song so we can go."

He laughed and reached for his guitar. "Anything for you, Mrs. King."

Let's get this marriage started
All night long, and when it's over, it's just begun
Because we're only just beginning our eternity
So, c'mon over here, girl, and please won't you kiss me . . .

+

Ty could see home from here. Mercy Falls was nestled just over the craggy jut of the Rocky Mountains. The peaks rose high against the fading blue afternoon, the sky streaked with runnels of golden light chasing the sun as it fell.

"It looks like clear skies the rest of the way." Chet walked up to the chopper, holding the printouts of the weather report he'd picked up from the FBO office in Helena. Ty had already downloaded his copies onto his iPad and planned the next leg of the journey.

Now, Ty looked up from where he was finishing his walk-around and final preflight visual check. Every five hours, since leaving Minnesota, he'd put down, ran another check, just because, well . . .

Too many scenarios waged war in his head as he'd climbed into the cockpit early this morning. Not a few included memories of his last flight, but with a cabin full of his PEAK cohorts, he tried not to let the what-ifs steal his nerve.

Especially with Brette watching. He'd been up way too late last night at the Marshalls', staring at the stars and having a little chitchat with the Almighty about today's flight home.

The fact that Brette had decided to go with them, packing her meager belongings and following him out to the chopper at the break of dawn, had sluiced through him a new kind of joy.

Peace.

"Don't be a pansy. It's time for us to go home."

Those words, more than any, had made him climb into the cockpit, place his feet on the pedals, his hand around the cyclic, his other on the throttle and collective.

Made him open the throttle, pull up on the collective, depress the left foot pedal to counteract the torque, made him ease the chopper into the air, the rhythm of working both the collective and his pedal like an old song stirring to life inside him.

It was a practiced dance, the way he moved the cyclic as the chopper lifted off its skids and nudged forward, transitioning from hover flight to full forward flight and ETL.

"You're ready, Ty. Have been for some time."

He had expected the shudder as the chopper escaped the rotor wash into clean air, and pushed the cyclic forward, increasing their airspeed.

"I trust you to bring them all home safely. You just have to trust yourself."

As they'd risen over the debris of Chester, he could see a few work crews out clearing the roads, collecting roofing tiles. He'd looked down at the library. Except for the tree destroying the basement windows, the building remained intact.

But that's how it was with storms—if you built your life on a stone foundation, maybe you survived—wounded, scared, but still standing.

And he supposed if you didn't, you rebuilt. Grew stronger.

Like Brette.

"You're doing a great job, Ty," Chet said, as if reading his mind. "I'm not going to say anything about how long it took you to get back in the cockpit but . . ." He winked and took a sip of his coffee in a Styrofoam cup.

"Choppers aren't meant to fly cross-country like this," Ty said. "We'll need to give her a thorough inspection when we get back to PEAK." He finished checking the cold air carburetor air duct, giving the hose a small confirming wiggle to check the clamp. Then he moved to the electrical terminals and finally to the fuel line.

He'd already checked the two oil lines, twice, as well as the oil level.

"The bird is in good shape," Chet said.

"We're not going to end up in pieces in the mountains on my watch," Ty said, maybe a little too sharply.

"Of course we aren't," Chet said and stepped back.

He stayed quiet as Ty finished checking the exhaust system, the v-belts, the clutch, the bearings, and the frame of the chopper. Finally, he checked the movement of the tail rotor.

He walked back to Chet. Ran a hand behind the strung muscle in his neck and stared at the sinking sun.

"We should get going."

"Take a breath." Chet glanced at him. "Take a breath and see how far you've come."

Ty frowned, but Chet nodded at the cluster of passengers. Ian and Gage, Audrey and Brette, laughing as they ate food from some vending machine.

Brette grinned, her eyes shiny, her laughter carrying across the tarmac, and when she turned, she caught Ty's gaze and lifted her hand in a wave.

His entire body warmed, buzzed.

"You did that," Chet said quietly.

"Come again?"

"You brought her from dark to light."

"You're giving me too much credit, Chet. That's God's job."

"But he uses us. We are the light of the world, right?"

Ty shoved his hands into his pockets, his gaze on the whisper of light still peeking through the mountains, shining down into the valleys, the last wink before darkness flooded the land.

"I've never told you this before, Ty, but you're my protégé. I love my son, but he has no interest in following in my footsteps."

"I thought Kacey was following in your footsteps."

"To take over PEAK? No. She's a talented pilot, but she doesn't have your heart for the lost." Chet turned to him. "And I'm not only talking about the physically lost, Ty. I'm talking about the lost in spirit."

He took a sip of his coffee. Considered it. "When I returned from Vietnam, I was an angry man. Hurting. I'd seen my best friends killed, tried to save a lot of them, and failed. I was bitter and wounded, and even though Ruthie was waiting for me, I couldn't go home. I ended up in Seattle, drunk most of the time, getting in fights . . . you know the story."

Ty drew in a breath. Nodded.

"Ruthie found me and dragged me home. Told me to sober up, but it wasn't until I hit bottom and found my way into a church that I realized God had more for me. Just like he has for you."

Ty frowned. "I don't—"

"Have you ever considered, son, that the burden you feel inside isn't just a calling to rescue the lost . . . but to rescue lost souls?"

The words swept through Ty, lighting his body on fire, tiny pinpricks of light and heat and . . .

Purpose.

He stared at Chet. "What are you saying?"

"I think you're called to be a pastor. Or a missionary. A member of the Lord's team of rescuers."

"I'm nobody special, Chet. Why would—"

"All you have to do is show up. God will do the rest." He smiled. "And you're very, very good at showing up, Ty."

He didn't know how to respond to that.

"I think that's why you've never found your place. Because God had one all planned for you—he just needed you to be ready."

Chet finished his coffee. Tossed out the grounds. Glanced at Ty. "Are you ready, son?"

Oh. Uh.

Chet laughed. "I meant, are you ready to go home?"

Ty smiled, but . . .

Yes. The thought found his bones, settled in, the heat no longer searing but a warmth that settled deep. Especially when Brette turned and headed back toward him, so much joy in her eyes he probably didn't need the chopper to be airborne.

Yes. Yes, he was ready.

Two months later

The only thing Brette could do to escape now was run.

"You okay, Ace?" Ty's hand curled over hers, tightened. "You're shivering." He stood and pulled the flimsy cotton blanket up over her barely there hospital gown, but it did nothing to stave off the trembling.

Not from the cold.

"I hate surgery."

Ty pressed a kiss to her forehead, her hand now clenched in his as he stood next to the bed. "Listen, this is a piece of cake. You already did the hard stuff, like licking this cancer thing."

She managed a tight smile. "For now."

"For good. That's what we're going to believe." He winked at her, those green eyes holding so much faith it cascaded right to her core.

But maybe that was what happened when you fell in love with a preacher man. It had made sudden, brilliant sense when Ty told her God was tugging at him to be a pastor.

A man with his kind of faith, his kind of hope, should be sharing it with others.

Helping them find the strength to look up, stop trying so hard, and just receive . . . a new life.

A new, amazing, hope-filled season that she couldn't believe she was living.

And today . . . a new body.

"Is she still—oh, good." Ella Blair had pushed her way into the room. She slung her satchel off her shoulder and onto a chair. "And I come fresh from the newsstand."

"It's out?" So maybe Brette could forget, just for a second, the chilly operating room awaiting her.

"Yep."

Gage had come in behind Ella, holding a cup of coffee and a magazine rolled up under his arm. Looked like a sports mag. Maybe something having to do with snowboarding.

"Here you go," Ella said and pulled out a copy of *National Geographic*. Held up the cover for her small audience, like she might be showcasing an item on *The Price Is Right*. "The cover of this month's issue, photo credit by Brette Arnold."

Brette tried to see it like everyone else might—the fibrous lightning reaching from the heavens against a storm-darkened sky, like bronchial veins, webbed and glowing. One strand jerked all the way to earth, a solitary trail of heat that touched down just beyond the tiny silo of an Iowa farm. "'Summer of Storms,'" Ella said, beaming at Brette. "By Brette Arnold." She handed her the magazine. "Eight pages, Brette. Eight."

Brette set the magazine on her lap, her hand only slightly pinching from the IV, and turned to the right page.

There she stood in a shot taken with the Vortex.com team. Jonas dressed in a pair of jeans and his Vortex.com shirt, arms akimbo and looking stern. Handsome Nixon stood behind him, holding up his handheld video camera. Geena stood on the other side of

Jonas, wearing camo and a sleeveless shirt to show off her tribal tats, her toughness tempered by her smile.

Brette stood in front of them all, her arms akimbo too, and yeah, she looked healthy and strong, her arms tanned, her hair short but cute in a headband.

Perhaps they'd done a little retouching, or maybe she glowed because Ty stood on the other side of the camera.

He'd even traveled to Boston to retrieve her personal belongings with her, then helped her settle in with Ella.

And yes, it might be too early to expect a proposal, but the answer would be a boy-howdy, high-five *yes*.

Yes, I'll hope in the future with you.

The article started with her story of the epic picture of the funnel she'd snapped in Colorado. When Gordon suggested she write a human interest story, she hadn't considered it might be her own. She even included a selfie she'd taken back in the days of her recuperation, her face gaunt, her head bald, her eyes hollow. Just to show the dark side of the storm, contrast it with the light.

The double tornadoes from Kansas made the next page, along with insets of the destroyed farmland she'd shot from the chopper. Duck Lake's bowling alley, a lone, dirty dog crouched next to a sodden doll in the street. She wrote about the life of a storm chaser, then chronicled the search for Chet. Her finger ran over the picture of Ty embracing his mentor.

"I love that shot," Ty said.

"Me too."

She turned the page to a long view of Chester's Central Avenue, including the broken windows at the library and the downed elm that had nearly flattened Jonas's Suburban. The story of the search, the blueprint find—with a shot she'd taken later of the folded blueprint, forgotten in Ty's pocket—and details on how they'd discovered the tiny room where Creed and the rest of the team had taken shelter.

Then the final page, with a wide-angle shot of so many families embracing, April and Spenser's desperate clutch in the middle. The searchers, especially the PEAK team, stood around, grimy and grinning. The only one missing had been Ty.

She'd put down her camera when she spied him, alone, away from the chaos, in the field, slowly falling to pieces.

How she loved a man who wasn't afraid to let his emotions have their moment.

"It's an amazing article," Ella said. "Congratulations, Brette. I think you need to ask PEAK for a raise."

She laughed. Oh, how she loved to laugh. Again. Finally.

"I'm happy with my meager part-time, hourly wage," Brette said. "It's just temporary until I figure out what I want to write next. I've already talked to my agent about some ideas." And had started a novel.

Because, why not?

"Um, you might want to talk to that agent about protecting your rights," Gage said. "This is the *Sports Illustrated* from a couple weeks ago. Look what I found . . ." He glanced at Ella, who frowned at him.

"This couldn't wait?"

"What couldn't wait?" Brette said.

"We didn't want to say anything—I thought we talked about this, Gage."

"What are you two talking about?"

Gage pulled the magazine from his arm, began to page through it. "Did Spenser ever mention what he did for a living?"

Brette shook her head, glancing at Ty. He shrugged.

"So, he never uttered a word about the fact that he was the

hot new relief pitcher for the Minnesota Twins?" He held up the magazine, folding the back away and handing it to her.

Spenser Maguire had a two-page, or more, spread, a picture of him in mid-throw taking up a full page. "'After the Storm, How Spenser Maguire Is Dusting Off and Showing Up.' What's this?"

"The Twins are in the pennant race. *Sports Illustrated* did a story about Spenser and how he searched for his wife after the tornado that hit Duck Lake. He gives all the credit to Ty and Pete and you. Turn it over."

She did and stared at a copy of her wide-angle picture of Spenser and April embracing. Although cropped, the picture still showed a few team members—Ian and his niece, Shae, along with Ben, his arms around Kacey.

"Oh shoot. I sent Spenser a copy of the picture on Facebook. He obviously didn't realize he needed to get photo credit." She handed the magazine back to Gage.

She was missing something, judging by the look on Gage's face.

"What—is it Ben King? You can't even really tell it's him—he's wearing a baseball cap and—"

"It's Ian and Shae." Gage showed her the picture again. "They're clearly standing next to each other. And Ian is named in the caption."

"Is this bad?" Brette asked

Ella glanced at Gage.

Ty slipped his hand onto her shoulder. "It's nothing, Ace. It's just . . . well, up until now, Shae's been a very missing Esme Shaw. But clearly, she's not missing anymore, at least to Ian."

"And Randy Blackburn," Ella said. "Unfortunately, Gage picked up this magazine at the gym."

Gage closed the magazine and flipped it over. "It's addressed to Blackburn. Either he left it there or maybe it's one of his donations."

She stilled. "Wait, are you saying that Blackburn—"

"He might have seen it. Might know that Shae is alive."

"That's a lot of mights, Gage," Ty said quietly.

"I'd say we were jumping to conclusions if it weren't for the fact that . . . well . . ." Ella made a face, glanced at Gage. "Blackburn's gone missing. Hasn't shown up for work for the past week."

Silence.

Then, "Did anyone call Shae?" Ty asked.

"I just found this," Gage said.

"I only know about Blackburn because he didn't show up in court yesterday to testify to a DUI. I asked around," Ella added.

"You need to call Ian, right now," Ty said.

Gage nodded and reached for his phone.

A knock, and the door eased open. A lean, tall woman dressed in scrubs, her brown hair pulled back, came into the room. "How are we doing in here?"

Silence. Brette didn't know what to say.

"We're good. Everything's going to be just fine," Ty said, reaching for Brette's hand and squeezing.

Yes. Come what may, she had to choose hope. Brette nodded, glancing up at Ty.

"Any final concerns?" the doctor asked. "Anything you want to talk about?"

She blew out a breath, glanced at Ty, and a smile tugged at her mouth. "Maybe I should upgrade to a size . . ."

"Stop." Ty was grinning, shaking his head. "Thanks again for doing this, Jan." He reached over Brette to shake Dr. Berkley's hand.

"I told you—anything for you, Ty." She winked, then directed her attention to Brette. "It's time to say goodbye to your fan club, Brette."

Oh.

Ty leaned down, his lips just a whisper away, his eyes holding hers. "I'll be waiting on the other side."

Then he kissed her, sweetly, promise and truth and the strength that was Ty in his touch. She wanted to hang on, but she didn't have to, to know he was with her.

"I'll meet you there."

Epilogue

EVERYONE WAS JUST OVERREACTING. Including herself.

No one was after Esme Shaw, aka Shae Johnson, not anymore.

Maybe Blackburn never had been, and she'd spent the past five years in hiding for nothing.

Shae Johnson—everyone called her that now, even Uncle Ian, although in his eyes, she still saw him hesitate just a second, the instinct to call her *Esme* front and center in his brain. She sat at the skirted round table watching the guests two-step in the middle of the PEAK barn dance floor and tried not to wish the last five years back.

Overhead, round paper chandeliers dappled light onto the wooden planks, and white tulle draped the rough-hewn beams. Over three hundred guests danced or sat at the round tables, so many headliner stars at the party that she'd stopped being surprised when Garth Brooks or Brad Paisley edged up behind her in the buffet line. The country music bash of the season. Plenty of selfies and snapshots were populating Instagram, she had no doubt.

Still, Shae had avoided any of the pictures. Even if Blackburn hadn't been seen for over a month, she didn't want to take any chances. But she couldn't help but think that Uncle Ian had been completely overreacting when he asked her to move home until Blackburn was found.

She missed her room at Ian's ranch, sold nearly a year ago to Ben King. For now, she'd agreed to the guest room at Ian and Sierra's new house, a cute bungalow in Mercy Falls, but she wanted the entire mess over. In fact, she'd met with Ella yesterday, and Ella had suggested she make a statement and file an affidavit about the events she saw, and agree to testify against Blackburn. In the event that he showed up to face his crimes.

She couldn't put her life on hold forever, thank you.

"Put the fork down and let's dance."

She looked up to see Ned Marshall grinning down at her. He indicated the way she was playing with the uneaten frosting on the piece of Ben and Kacey's massive white wedding cake.

If anyone could make her forget the limbo in which she lived, it was Ned Marshall. Tall, dark hair, amber brown eyes, with the kind of smile that stuck around inside a girl.

Ned made her feel safe in a you're-not-defenseless kind of way, as if he trusted her to take care of herself but stayed close enough in case she couldn't.

The fact that he'd driven twenty hours to show up for the reception . . . maybe she hadn't been dreaming the connection they shared this summer during the search for his brother and others.

A connection that continued, via phone calls and texts and Skype, since she returned to Minneapolis, then moved to Montana.

"I thought you'd never ask," she said and took his hand, found it warm and strong and everything she needed it to be as he led her to the floor.

Onstage, Ben's newest Mountain Song Records artist, Joey McGill, twanged out a cover of one of Ben's songs.

When you need a friend
A shoulder you can cry on
Someone who understands what you're going through
Just look over here, see me standing closer

Ned pulled her close, his hand on the small of her back. Despite his small-town Minnesota roots, his husky, cowboy fragrance enveloped her. He had worked for the past five summers fighting fires out west—although this summer he'd been sidelined by an injury—and had the body to prove it, with lean, strong legs and wide shoulders. She hung on as he two-stepped her around the floor.

Gage and Ella swayed together in the center of the room, and it looked like Ty was trying to teach Brette a few steps near the corner of the dance floor. Shae nearly didn't recognize Brette, with her hair now in a bob below her ears. Something else was different about her too, but Shae couldn't put her finger on it. Maybe it was just the joy that radiated out from her, the way she looked at Ty with such warmth that probably they didn't even notice the nip in the October air.

She'd spotted Pete earlier, dancing with some blonde, but she noticed the girl now sat alone at a table, watching the crowd. Shae remembered Pete from her time in Mercy Falls. Very hot, very reckless, the kind of heartbreaker Ian had told her to stay away from.

Apparently he hadn't changed his ways despite what went down with Jess in Miami over a year ago.

Shae grinned at Sierra, caught in Ian's arms, her short dark hair pulled back in a headband. She'd worked for two tireless months to pull together tonight's party, mostly without Kacey and Ben's help, thanks to Ben's summer festival schedule.

With Ty now helming the chopper at PEAK, Kacey had spent the better part of the rest of the summer in the front row of Ben's concerts, honeymooning between gigs. They'd even purchased their own RV and flown Audrey out to join them.

They'd all arrived home a month ago for Audrey to start school and to finally make Ian's old ranch house their own.

Yes, it was time everyone just calmed down and went on with their lives.

If only Shae hadn't overreacted, if she'd just trusted Ian and the law, hadn't panicked and taken her safety into her own hands, maybe she could have saved them all years of heartache.

Years gone by, my eyes are dry
But the echo of my heart won't tell a lie
I'm coming home to the one I love
Second chances, given from above

Second chances. Maybe, finally.

Sam and Willow danced by, a brilliant solitaire engagement ring on Willow's finger. She remembered Willow from her high school days. A hippie at heart, free-spirited Willow seemed exactly the right match for serious Sam Brooks, although Shae only really knew the deputy from her days with Dante and the few run-ins Dante had with the local law.

Sweet, misunderstood Dante James, her first real love.

Shae shook her head. Not now. She'd fought her regrets, her demons long enough. Lifting her face, she caught Ned's eye, and he smiled down at her, a mischievous glint in his eyes that made her laugh.

Yes, second chances.

The song ended, and he twirled her out, dipped her, and his lips brushed her neck.

She giggled as he righted her and he threaded his fingers between hers. "Want to take a walk?"

"Mmmhmm," she said, returning to her chair for her jean jacket.

They stepped outside, and the night turned magical, the stars so close she could pluck them free if she climbed the black, craggy horizon. The Milky Way ran a trail of diamonds to forever, and a pale moon had risen to light the way.

Ned pulled her close, his body heating her as he headed toward the chopper parked outside for the festivities.

"What do you have in mind, Ned Marshall?" she said, but let him pull her along.

They'd nearly reached the chopper, but whatever sweet mischief Ned had planned halted when she heard the voice, rising from nearby.

"I realize I owe you a conversation, but . . . what, are you dating her?"

Shae stilled, searched for the voice, and spied the source.

Jess Tagg was here? Shae remembered the EMT from a year ago, when they'd searched for Uncle Ian and Sierra, lost in the Caribbean. Jess stood outside the barn in a ring of light, her blonde hair shiny and her arms folded over a simple black dress over a white blouse with puffy sleeves. And across from her, Pete, in dress pants and a crisp white shirt rolled up to his elbows.

"No—she's just a friend—" Pete raised his hands as if frustrated.

"That you were kissing!"

"You're *engaged*, Jess. What was I supposed to do—wait forever? You made it pretty clear what you wanted."

Jess must have been crying because her hand went up to wipe her cheek. "I'm not engaged, Pete. You can't believe everything you hear or read on the internet."

"Yeah, well, I didn't just read about it. Ty told me. And frankly, he's a pretty reliable source when it comes to your secrets. And, by the way, I can hear *silence* pretty well. I haven't heard from you . . . in almost a year, isn't it? And you show up tonight, hoping that I'll just sweep you into my arms like nothing has happened?"

Jess's voice dropped, but it still carried in the wind. "You promised you would."

"Let's talk about promises, shall we, because the last thing you said to me was, I'm coming back, I *promise*."

"And?" she snapped. "I'm here. Right now. I'm here. And you're kissing someone else."

Ned veered them away from the spectacle. "That's not pretty."

"I think there's some history there," Shae said. But the romantic mood had shifted. Ned must have sensed it because they meandered away from the chopper, toward the parking lot. He led her to his truck. After putting down the tailgate, he lifted her onto it.

"That's better," he said, his face close to hers. "I really missed you."

"Me too," Shae said, and when he bent, she lifted her face to meet his kiss, decadent with the taste of summer and longing and new beginnings. She had settled in to let him deepen the kiss when she heard the hiccupped breath, a noise of surprise. Shae broke away from Ned to see Jess walking past, averting her eyes.

"Sorry," Jess mumbled.

"It's okay," Ned said.

But Shae slid off the tailgate. "Jess, you okay?"

To her surprise, Jess, the one who had held her together during those desperate days when they all thought Ian was dead, looked completely unraveled. Eyes reddened, her jaw tight, she shook her head.

"I'm an idiot. A complete fool." She pressed her hand over her mouth. "Sorry."

"Can we help?" Ned sounded genuine and not at all like he might be miffed at being interrupted.

Jess looked at them, as if considering their offer. Then, "No. I just need to see if Willow will let me take her car home. She met Sam here, and . . ."

"I'll drive you," Ned said. "C'mon."

See, Shae could seriously fall for a guy like Ned.

"Are you sure?" Jess said, relief in her eyes.

"Yes." Shae went around and opened the door to the passenger seat. After a moment, Jess acquiesced and climbed into the backseat.

Shae hopped in the front, and Ned fired up the truck, backed out.

"I know you heard the fight," Jess said.

Shae glanced at Ned, said nothing.

"It's not his fault—not really. Pete didn't know I was going to be here. And I wasn't sure he'd be here either. I . . . hoped so, but . . ." Jess took a breath. "Sorry. I'm just babbling."

Ned turned onto the highway toward Mercy Falls.

Silence, and apparently Jess surrendered to the need to fill it. "It wasn't fair, what I did to him. I just . . ." She sighed. "It's probably too much to think he'd forgive me."

Shae couldn't help it. "So, *are* you engaged?"

Silence, then, "Not right now."

Shae frowned but noticed Ned's movements, as if checking out the car behind him. "What's the matter?"

"I think that truck is following us."

Shae turned in her seat. Made out, through the darkness, an older truck, the lights round and barreling down on them. "Well, he is too close—oh." Her snarky reply vanished as the truck suddenly sped up. "It's going to—"

The truck rammed them. They jerked hard, her words turning into a scream.

"What the—" Ned shouted. He pushed the gas pedal down. "He's trying to run us off the road."

"Who is it?" Jess said.

Blackburn? But Shae's brain couldn't turn that fast. She was too busy sweeping up her phone.

The truck moved up beside them.

The speedometer hit ninety, and she turned cold.

C'mon, Uncle Ian. Maybe she should have called 911.

Ned's lights carved out the road, and Shae could see the Mercy River running alongside the pavement down in its canyon.

"Hang on!"

The truck came at them again.

Jess screamed. Metal crunched and Ned pounded the brakes, tires squealing. They hit the ditch, bouncing hard in the dirt. The truck sped out ahead.

Ned did a U-ey and floored it back along the highway, putting distance between them and the truck.

"Ian's not picking up!"

Jess had her own phone out. "Pick up, please."

"I don't know what he's driving, but he's got more under the hood than I have." Ned glanced in the rearview mirror.

Shae jerked around.

The truck's lights blinded her a second before he slammed into them. Ned fought as the truck took control, shoving them forward.

"Hang on to something!" Ned yelled as the truck bullied them sideways. He stood on the brakes, tried to turn the wheel.

The ditch launched them. Shae screamed, reached out for something—anything—found the dash, Ned's hand, maybe. They landed on the passenger side with a bone-crunching jerk. The momentum, however, shoved them over toward the river.

Heat exploded through Shae, her entire body on fire as they flipped.

Then the world turned dark as the truck rolled and rolled and rolled . . .

Acknowledgments

I'M KEENLY AWARE of the great host of people who help bring a book to life. People think it's the novelist sitting there alone every day, conjuring up words in her head, and yes, that is mostly true. But it is easy to get sucked into the weeds, caught into the mire of your own tangled brain, and emerge with something that is dark and snarled and unredeemable. Thankfully, the Lord has put into my life people who keep my head above the weeds and my eyes pointed in the right direction. People like Rachel Hauck, my faithful, creative, and brilliant writing partner who not only listens to all my crazy ideas and sorts them out to find those that are workable, but also keeps me on track between every scene. Everybody needs a writing partner who they can call in the wee hours of the night, or even during holidays, someone who says "no problem that I'm eating Christmas dinner, I'll just set that aside and go into my room and help you brainstorm your entire book over again. Yippee!"

I also need to thank the amazing people at Revell. What a joy to work with such a talented group, starting with Andrea Doering, my amazing editor, Kristin Kornoelje, my line editor, and then of course the awesome marketing team including Michele Misiak and Karen Steele. To work with this team of brilliant people who see the vision for the story and the rest in the series, to have them partner with you and help bring it to life, is like a gust of wind on a hot, humid day.

Obviously, I'm grateful to my husband for listening to my workings-out of the story during our morning walks. Of course I have to listen to his diagnosis of his current car restoration project, so it's sort of equal, but still, I'm grateful for his input on the male point of view. And, big appreciation goes to my son David, who is such a great storycrafter it blows me away. All the best twists are his.

And finally Jesus. Of course, Jesus, who really does show up to help me with every word. It's what I love most about writing a book. It stretches me and hopefully makes me into a better person because I get to spend time with the Savior in the desperate quest for words and story. And he is always faithful.

Thank you for reading *Storm Front*! Discover the exciting conclusion to the Montana Rescue series in *Wait for Me*, Jess and Pete's story!

Susie May

Susan May Warren is the *USA Today*, ECPA and CBA bestselling author of over fifty novels with more than one million books sold, including *Wild Montana Skies*, *Rescue Me*, *A Matter of Trust*, and *Troubled Waters*. Winner of a RITA Award and multiple Christy and Carol Awards, as well as the HOLT and numerous Readers' Choice Awards, Susan has written contemporary and historical romances, romantic suspense, thrillers, romantic comedy, and novellas. She can be found online at www.susanmaywarren.com, on Facebook at SusanMayWarrenFiction, and on Twitter @susanmaywarren.

IT'S THOSE WE LOVE WHO HAVE THE POWER TO HURT US MOST . . .

Gage and his team are called in for the rescue. But Gage isn't so sure he wants to help the woman who destroyed his life. More, when she insists on joining the search, he'll have to keep her safe while finding her reckless brother—a recipe for disaster when a snowstorm hits the mountain.

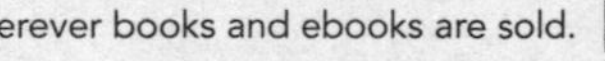

Connect with

Susan May Warren

Visit her website and sign up for her newsletter to get a free novella, hot news, contests, sales, and sneak peeks!

www.susanmaywarren.com

 @SusanMayWarrenFiction  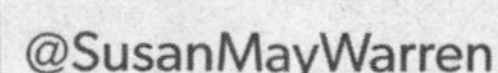 @SusanMayWarren